Nocturnity I:
An
Infinite
Beginning

I0676414

A Novel By
Theodore C. Jenkins

©2009 Theodore C. Jenkins

I

This book is for my wife, April.
Thank you for your support and encouragement.

About the story

This story is a companion to the next book and while intertwined, each is its own story.
They were written separately to bring facets of each story to light without tripping over each other. I give credit to the characters that stole this book from me and wrote it with my hands.

Table of Contents

Nocturnity I: An Infinite Beginning, Theodore C. Jenkins

Chapter 1

Clutter

The silence of the dark room was broken by the grating noise of an alarm clock. A thin-fingered hand crept shakily from under a thick blanket. The hand slapped clumsily around as it searched for the source of the noise. It found its mark, slammed hard against the clock, and silenced it. Todd Jennings threw off his cover and climbed sleepily to the edge of the bed. His hands roamed over his numb face absently as he grunted breath through his fingers. His waking mind struggled as he thought back to moments ago. The ability to reverse time by pushing the snooze button on his alarm clock had left him. Todd's lips curved into a crooked smile as he realized that it had all been a dream. He tapped the snooze button a few times with a smirk on his face.

He shuffled to the bathroom and tried to wring the ache out of his neck and shoulders. Hot water pummeled his back and neck, as he hunkered sleepily against the wall of his shower. Abstract thoughts of his distaste for early mornings ushered him into a meditative state. The furrow of his brow relaxed as a dreamless sleep overtook him. The water began to cool rapidly which shocked him awake and incited the end of his comfort.

"Piece of shit water heater," he mumbled as he exited the shower.

The aged and overused coffee maker came into view as he shuffled into the kitchen. The overhead cabinet door squeaked loudly as he opened it and rummaged around for coffee filters. He grunted and huffed in frustration as he labored to get a single coffee filter loose from the stack. This had to be perfect. If he rushed, he may bend a fold in the filter. The slightest imperfection would cause the integrity of

1

the filter to be compromised when moistened, inevitably flooding the coffee pot with loose grounds. A childish tantrum had begun to rise up in him as he became impatient. He managed to catch a fiber on the edge of a filter and lifted it gently. He placed it carefully in the bin and began to heap coffee grounds into it. Food encrusted plates clattered, as he clumsily rearranged dirty dishes, so that he had enough room in the sink to capture water. He lowered himself down to watch the pot fill and snapped the water off as it reached the desired mark. Having added the water he went meticulously through a mental checklist.

"Okay. Water? Check. Filter? Check. Grounds? Check," he said to himself as he turned the power button on.

The old coffee machine choked to life and bellowed steam from its backside. His pleading expression did not help to speed up the process as he watched the coffee drip lazily into the pot. He always waited for the last drop so that his perfect formula would not be tainted by the rigors of the morning.

"Mm," he thought adoringly of the flavor, as he flipped five heaping spoons of sugar into his only clean cup.

He then carefully poured the equivalent of four cups of coffee over the pile of sugar. He lovingly gathered up the large plastic cup he had titled 'The Chalice of Life' and shuffled toward the dining room table. He lowered himself slowly into his chair. Todd grimaced as he felt painful spasms shoot through his lower back.

"I have got to get a new mattress," he mumbled the words around a cigarette that he had placed between his lips.

He lit his cigarette and inhaled deeply after taking that first sip of coffee. A smile framed his mouth as the combination of sitting down, smoking, and having fresh coffee to drink came together. This is what Todd called 'Wake-up Utopia'.

A beautiful Golden Retriever entered the room. The animal carried a blue plastic bowl in his mouth. The dog's brown eyes stared mournfully up at Todd as it approached him. The animal dropped his food dish at Todd's feet as if offering it to him. The bowl wobbled around a few times and came to rest with an empty plop.

2

"Aw Max," he said, "I wish you had thumbs sometimes, buddy."

He bent down and poured a half of a cup of coffee into the bowl. Max watched the liquid splash into his bowl and licked his chops. He waited patiently for Todd to move away before he began to drink.

"I'll buy you some food this evening after I make a little cash," Todd said as he tried to mask the guilt in his voice.

"Why don't you eat your beans?" Todd asked and pointed at the dry, unappetizing red beans in a glass bowl on the floor.

Max finished his coffee and went outside through his doggy door without as much as a glance back at Todd.

By the time he had finished his first cigarette, Todd had decided to begin to get ready for work. He rubbed his chin, and felt the scratchy stubble on his face. His lip curled into a snarl as he realized that he would have to shave. His boss Lucy demanded that he do this. She even kept a small bag of those disposable plastic razors in her desk as an incentive to shave before work. Lucy often seemed to struggle to tolerate Todd's habits. He supposed it was because she was dating and intended to marry Todd's best friend, William Goldman, that she tolerated him at all. He lumbered to the bathroom to shave in order to be presentable for 'The Ho Show'. This was Todd's ritualistic way to refer to his job as a waiter. He hated his job and felt like he was a gigolo, forced to perform a service for money. Todd finished his shave and assessed himself in the mirror. He was a tall man at six feet, and he had to bend down slightly to see his face in the low mounted mirror.

"I need to remount this mirror," he said glumly as his lower back bemoaned strain as a result of his stooped posture.

His piercing green eyes stared back at him as he brushed at his hair. He flexed his biceps, sucked in his gut, and puffed out his chest.

"Let's hope the tips are good because sexy don't pay the bills," he thought as he appraised himself in the mirror before walking away.

3

He gathered up his cell phone and an extra pack of cigarettes and shoved them into his pockets.

He began to pat himself around the waist and muttered, "Keys, wallet, cigarettes, phone, and balls? Check..," as he walked out of his front door.

Todd slid into the driver's seat of his car and fumbled for the ignition key. The acrid smell of rotten soda mixed with cigarette ashes assailed his nose.

He looked into the rear view mirror at the backseat and thought, "Should've looked back there before I got in."

A friend had regaled him with a heavily embellished story that began with an unwanted passenger in the back seat, and ended with doom for the driver. Todd looked around inside of his car at the trash and empty cigarette packs that lined the passenger side floorboard and grimaced.

"I have got to clean that," he thought as he wondered if the discolored spot, left last week from spilled soda, would ever come out of his carpet.

Todd gripped the tattered steering wheel cover with his left hand; his right turned the ignition forward. The starter issued a metallic scream as it struggled to bring the old beaten car to life.

Todd winced and mumbled, "Gotta get that looked at," procrastination being one of his strongest suits.

The car cranked dutifully after several tries. It sputtered and wheezed as it choked on the old burnt motor oil that coursed through its vitals.

He drove slowly to work as he meandered through the country roads into the heart of town. He rolled his window down over half way and wind rushed in and mussed his hair. He groped at it in an attempt to keep it in place. The wind won the battle and he gave up, and then used the free hand to grab up his pack of cigarettes.

The rancid smell of a paper mill over thirty miles away carried to his nose. Todd wondered how the people that lived in the town with the mill coped with the horrid smell. The scent only seemed to drift this far on warm summer breezes.

Todd picked up his lighter and made to steer the car

with his elbows. He took a quick look at the road before he struck his lighter. He drew himself close to the dash and cupped his hand to guard the flame from the wind. The flame of his lighter danced brilliantly before his eyes. He drew deeply on the cigarette to make sure it was lit well. The car's old suspension creaked and thumped hard as the tires seemed to crush something in the road.

A sincere feeling of dread washed over him and he stomped the brakes hard. The car reacted slowly and the rear tires repeated the dull thumping noise. He thought momentarily of Max, who liked to wander into the roads early in the morning. Todd opened the car door, stepped out, and tried to see over the back of the car to no avail. He muttered to himself about getting the brakes looked at.

Todd was aware of his own fear to look around the rear of the car. He had paused and stood motionless as images of his flattened pet danced wickedly across his mind's eye. He forced himself forward tentatively and rounded the corner of the car's trunk. A sigh of relief was issued as the mangled remains of a trashcan came into view. The rubber trashcan had been left too far out into the road. Todd looked down the right side of his car at the broken passenger side mirror. A month ago it had fallen victim to this same trashcan.

Todd had been late for work and had passed a car on this very narrow piece of road. He had been forced to swipe the trashcan to avoid the oncoming vehicle. His passenger side mirror, having struck the immovable trashcan, exploded on impact. It sprayed glass all over the side of his car. The arm that held it, now hung broken and swayed when he drove. Todd looked down at the rubber trashcan at his feet and grimaced. The can, itself, was a dull shade of gray and impossible to see in the poor morning light. Todd hadn't taken into account that his headlights were filthy and only cast a faint yellow glow onto the road ahead.

"Why can't these assholes leave it in the edge of their driveway like normal people?" Todd exclaimed with his voice raised in hopes someone might hear him.

Todd pursed his lips, drew back his right foot, and kicked the can hard enough to send it flying twenty feet. It

5

would have flown that far too...had it not been filled with heavy wet trash. Todd's foot bounced off of it dully. He winced and it felt like the toes in his right foot were broken. The can slid a few inches toward the edge of its owner's driveway and stopped.

"Son of a..," Todd said loudly and steadied himself on the trunk of his car. He tried to massage his toes through his shoe. He turned, limped back to his car, and drove away as he angrily muttered to himself.

The car came to a stop a few feet further than he had intended and the front of Todd's car protruded onto the edge of the highway. The low gas indicator on his ash-covered instrument panel began to flash and it caught his eye.

"Damn. Forgot to get gas," he said in refusal to acknowledge that he had simply chosen to wait to buy some.

He struggled in his deliberation and was distracted by the pain in his toes. Finally, after a prolonged internal struggle, he veered away from his normal path to work and headed for a gas station.

He greedily drew on his cigarette and tried to '*get his money's worth*' before he turned off into the gas station. His lips began to burn as the filter of the cigarette buckled from the heat of the draw.

He flinched and pulled it sharply from his lips. With a masterful look upon his face, he aimed it out of the open window and flicked it into the wind. The cigarette butt tumbled away from the car. It flipped end over end at a rapid pace and exploded into a wash of orange embers. He returned his attention to the road to realize he was about to overshoot the turn into the station. He stomped the brake and cut the wheel in unison. The old car's poor brakes and time worn steering reacted accordingly. He narrowly made the turn safely, and clipped the curb with his tread-bare left front tire. His eyes were assaulted by the brilliant lights in the canopy of the gas station. He laid his head back on the seat for a moment and rubbed at them with his fingers.

Todd stepped out of the car and rose to his full height...slowly. He limped toward his gas tank and mumbled to himself inaudibly. The speakers overhead belted out a cheery version of a song that wished anyone who could hear a great morning. Todd snarled in disgust as he opened his tank and placed the nozzle into it. He squeezed the trigger and waited. Nothing happened. Todd looked over at the pump to try and figure out the problem. There, boldly written in crayon on a paper bag taped to the pump, was a sign that said:

'Plese pay bafor you pump'

Todd read it a few times before his 'Hillbilly to English' filter translated it in his mind. The attendant sat in a chair behind the bullet-proof glass, safely inside the building. He pretended not to notice that Todd was there. Todd became irritated as he thought of the inconvenience of having to prepay with cash. As if responding to the thought, his toes sent a painful jolt up his leg. Todd leaned into his car through the open window. He strained as he worked to pry open the compartment under the center armrest between the seats. It popped open under the pressure and his elbows struck the inside of the door painfully. His frustration had now reached a fevered peak just before his eyes fell upon the thick stack of cash in the compartment. His anger abated as he considered the money and wondered how it might have gotten there.

Todd vaguely remembered having put a few dollars in the armrest a few times but was amazed as he counted out the sixty dollars in mixed bills. This clump of money, like many others of Todd's possessions, had been absent-mindedly misplaced. He often found clumps of money, his keys, and his wrist watch in abstract places.

"I can use that tonight for drinks," Todd mentioned as the abstract thought occurred to him.

He looked at his watch.

"Fifteen minutes to 'Ho time'. Better get a move on," he said rhetorically.

He separated twenty-three dollars from the clump and limped toward the gas station's storefront. He looked with an unfavorable scowl at the attendant he recognized as Leonard. Todd reached out to open the door. He wrapped his fingers around the large pull plate of the door and prepared to snatch it open to show his displeasure with the inconvenience. Todd pulled hard and the fingers of his hand sang painfully as the door declined his force. He tried the other door to discover it too was locked. He looked over at Leonard who pretended to be interested in his newspaper.

"As if he can read," Todd thought to himself as he reflected on the misspelled sign attached to the pump.

Todd grabbed both plates and rattled the doors with an excessive amount of angry force. Leonard was startled and almost fell from his stool. He made to correct himself as he looked up at Todd, who watched him from the front door with a very amused expression.

Todd mouthed the words slowly, "Open the door, dumb-ass."

Leonard looked at him dispassionately for a moment. He then pointed to his own watch exaggeratedly and mouthed, "We open at six."

Todd tapped his own watch, very hard and said loudly, "It is six fifteen...dummy."

Leonard looked to his own watch now and stared at it in concentration. Todd tried not to laugh as he thought of what Leonard's thought process might be like.

"Okay the little hand is on the six and the big hand is on the..."

Leonard climbed off of his stool and lumbered toward the door. He held a huge blue piece of wood with a single key on a ring attached to it.

Todd seemed to smile warmly as Leonard unlocked the doors. He fought the urge to laugh at the big blue key holder Leonard held.

An involuntary giggle erupted from Todd as he walked past Leonard to wait at the counter.

"Nine minutes till the 'Ho'," Todd thought to himself as he glanced at his watch again.

"What can I do you for?" Leonard asked.

"Pack of smokes and a twenty in gas. When did you start the prepay thing?" Todd asked.

"People been stealing gas while we was busy," Leonard responded distractedly as he considered Todd's cash on the counter.

"Huh, imagine that, with a titan of awareness like

8

yourself at the helm? Imagine that," Todd quipped sarcastically.

Leonard took a moment from using his fingers to count back Todd's change and looked at him in confusion.

Todd headed outside toward his vehicle. He pumped the prepaid amount of gas, replaced the nozzle, and tightened his gas cap. After another glance at his watch, Todd turned and rushed hurriedly for the door of the car. He dove into the driver's seat clumsily and fumbled for his keys. The starter shrieked raggedly as it rolled over. The car, already warmed up, cranked easily this time and wheezed to life.

"Three minutes... I can do this," Todd said as he floored the gas pedal.

The car did not share Todd's sudden burst of enthusiasm. The vehicle lurched slowly forward from the pump at a labored pace.

Chapter 2

The Ho Show

The fluorescent lights inside the diner caused the interior windows to be reflective against the dim light of the newly risen sun.

Will Goldman stared at his reflection in the half mirrored front windows. He brushed a little at his buzz-cut blond hair. His lips drew into an exaggerated grin as he checked his teeth for scraps of breakfast. A large black piece of pepper near one of his front teeth caught his attention. He poked a finger into his mouth and buffed at the tooth.

"It's going to be busy today. People are already on the move out there," he said, referring to the unusually large number of cars that passed on the nearby road.

"Good. We could use the money," replied a woman's voice.

Lucy Donner, a petite red haired woman in her early thirties, walked into the kitchen with an angry expression. She held bowls of wilted salad, three across one arm, and one in her left hand.

She fixed her green eyes upon Will and said, "Ya know, I asked Todd to do one freaking thing before he left yesterday," she began and thrust the bowls toward Will.

Will caught the salads as she tossed them to him. Having no fingers left available he let the second two bowls thump against him and cradled them. He shifted and grimaced as he struggled to hold the unbalanced pile.

"'Please put up the salads before you unplug the mini-cooler.' How hard is that?!" she asked Will in frustration.

"He was a little out of it yesterday," replied Will as he poured the salads from the bowls into the trash.

"With all of his '*issues*'," Lucy said as she forked

10

quote signs into the air, "you would defend him to the death."

Will looked up at her from the cabinet, where he had knelt to select cookware, with an amused grin. He noted the severity of her anger and quickly became serious.

"C'mon Lucy, it's just a few salads. The guy needs people to look after him. He's a mess," Will said and looked at Lucy with mock plea in his eyes.

Lucy sighed deeply, "You're lucky that you're so damned cute. Normally, that would never work on me," she said as she shook her head in denial of her emotional weakness.

A slow smile parted her lips as she said, "You guys have been joined at the hip since grade school and you have been defending him just as long."

Will nodded his agreement in an attempt to avoid further lecture.

"Sometimes, I think you're only with me so that you can save his job," she said playfully.

"I'm with you for the free food and sex. The fact that you own the place is a perk," he replied.

She gasped, smiled at him, and threw a moist dish towel that landed squarely on his head. He grabbed the towel from his head, dropped into a bear like stance, and rushed at her as he bellowed a growl. He stopped short as he heard a rap on the glass of the front door.

"Speak of the Devil," Lucy quipped and then returned to the storage room to prep vegetables.

Opening the door, Will asked, "Are you ready for 'The Ho Show'?"

"Oh yeah. I can't wait," he replied and rolled his eyes in disgust.

"Lock that door, will ya?" Will asked as he headed back to the kitchen.

Todd followed Will behind the counter and tossed his keys to him.

"You forgot those damned salads last night," Will whispered to Todd as he looked around to make sure their conversation would not be overheard.

"Aw shit, I suck," Todd said loudly.

11

"Okay. Everything is done and we have two minutes till we open," Lucy warned from the other room.

Todd looked excited and forced a smile as he said sarcastically, "The slops ready, turn over the sign, and let the hogs in."

A burst of uncontrolled laughter forced its way from Will.

With extreme effort Will forced a look of concern onto his face as he asked, "Why do you keep working here?"

"I'm too tired to look for another job," Todd replied.

As the day winded toward a close, Todd held onto the idea that he and his friends would be going to the French Quarter that night. It was something to look forward to every weekend for Todd, who considered himself to otherwise lack a social life. He fantasized about closing early and being on his way already.

A customer raised his hand and stole Todd's attention.

Todd smiled and waved as he mouthed the words, "Be right there."

The customer smiled in reply and then returned his attention to the menu. Todd turned his back on the guy and rolled his eyes.

He approached the customer after having made him wait for a small amount of time and asked, "Can I get something else for you?"

The customer looked up and began to ask, "Do you have..."

He was interrupted by a young woman.

"Is Pastor Marvin okay, Brother Rolfe?" the woman asked with a concerned expression.

"He is fine and dandy. The heat just got to him. He has a repairman coming to look at the air conditioner in the church," Rolfe replied.

"I was really scared when Pastor Marvin collapsed. That was awesome of you to finish for him!" the woman added and dismissed herself.

"You're a preacher?" Todd asked conversationally.

"A *Deacon*," the man replied with a corrective, almost condescending tone that instantly aggravated Todd.

12

"Oh, I never really knew what the ranks were," Todd replied as he tried to irritate the man by feigning ignorance of his interests.

"Do you even *go* to church?" the customer asked Todd incredulously.

"Oh, me? No. I really don't believe in all that... *stuff*," Todd replied as he quavered both hands in an effort to convey skepticism.

The customer looked at Todd angrily. Todd was satisfied by this and returned the glare with a warm '*kiss my ass*' grin.

"Was there anything else... *sir*?" Todd spoke with heavy emphasis on the sir.

"We are very busy and...," Todd stopped speaking as the customer waved his hand dismissively, got up, dropped exact change on the table, and walked out.

Todd had fallen into a bad habit of '*clock watching*' as Lucy called it. He found himself unable to avoid a glance at the wall clock or his wrist watch. Being so aware of the time made the last few hours seem to drone on forever for him. The small bell over the entrance door caught his attention with its shrill ring.

He let out a disgusted sigh and began to work very hard to lighten his expression before he turned to face the new customer. Todd's counterfeit smile was reinforced by a real one as Andre strode in through the door passed the Deacon who held the door for him. Andre was clutching his hand and wearing a grimace. This particular customer's arrival was always a bright point to Todd. In addition to sparkling conversation, which dramatically helped to pass the time, Andre was in the practiced habit of leaving a fifteen dollar tip. Andre was new in town and worked as a security guard at the old Ronson estate on the edge of town.

* * *

Todd reflected on the first time he had met Andre. He had recoiled at Todd's reply of '*run while you still can*' to Andre's question '*what would you suggest*' as he looked at a menu. There had been a brief uncomfortable pause, which

13

had worried Todd, as he looked into the stolid face of this tall muscular man. The tension broke as Andre decided it was one of the funniest things he had ever heard and broke into explosive laughter.

Andre had gone on later to give him advice on how to sell daily specials and improve his tips. He had mentioned that he had been in marketing for some years before he got into his current line of work. Someone intentionally choosing to be a security guard over a marketing executive seemed very strange in Todd's opinion. Andre had said something to him during one of their conversations that struck him as exceptionally peculiar.

'If you can't dazzle them with brilliance, baffle them with bullshit'.

Even though he had nodded his understanding at the time, Todd found that he constantly mulled over the phrase. He had felt like there was some deeper meaning to it or that it could apply to facets of his own life. The phrase touted deceit, but at the same time success and it seemed like something he may have lacked in his own personality.

* * *

Andre bellowed, "Who do you have to know to get service around here?"

Todd returned to the present and almost tripped as he tried to hurry over to Andre's table. He paused, collected himself, and showed Andre *'the just one second finger'*. Andre nodded in recognition and returned his attention to the brightly colored menu he held. Todd prepared a tall frosty glass of soda and headed to greet Andre properly.

"Good evening, Mr. Andre," Todd said as he placed the glass within the man's reach.

Andre snapped it up and took a massive gulp which drained most of the amber liquid from it.

"Ahhhh," Andre hissed as he lowered the glass and appeared to be in pain.

Andre recoiled a little and covered his mouth with one hand. The eruption of a burp was muffled but sounded powerful to Todd as he watched Andre compose himself.

14

Andre's eyes were red and he appeared anguished as he punched himself in the chest and commented, "I love the fizz in the fountain soda here."

"What's up with you, my man?" Andre asked as he relaxed.

"Same old, same old," Todd said and then lit up. "However, we're going to the French Quarter tonight and that will be a blast."

"Make sure you're careful on the way home. There's a tropical depression that is supposed to be dumping its load between midnight and three a.m.," Andre warned.

Todd nodded his understanding as Andre began to speak again, "Tonight's my last shift at the old Ronson place. I'm headed back to Florida tomorrow around noon. I'm gonna try to stop by in the morning to grab a quick bite and to say goodbye, before I shove off."

"Aw. I'm gonna miss you around here, man," Todd said with genuine remorse.

Andre ordered his usual amount of assorted foods. Will, Lucy, and Todd watched him devour large quantities of food with astonishment.

"Where does he put it all? He is so muscular and sexy," Lucy said and covered her mouth with a little gasp of embarrassment.

Will snapped his attention to her and said, "Should I go get his number for you?" then, rolling his eyes, he returned his focus to Andre, "I would hate to have to buy his food."

"I bet free food and sex would be a big enough draw for him. Plus, I could probably get him to talk to me for more than five minutes at a time," Lucy quipped in an attempt to rib Will.

"Did somebody mention free food and sex?!" Todd asked with a crooked smile.

Lucy and Will snickered at Todd. They returned their attention to Andre who worked furiously to clean gravy from a plate with the last of his bread.

Andre was in the process of licking his fingers clean when Todd placed the check and a to-go bag on the table. Andre smiled up at him as he worked to dry his fingers with a napkin.

"Man. That was excellent," Andre commented as he drained the last contents of his soda cup.

"*They* aim to please," Todd said and motioned to Will and Lucy who quickly turned away and tried to look busy.

"I, however, am just the table jockey and want you to drag your big ass out of here. You need to leave before you're late for work. If you get fired, you won't be able to afford to pay my bills anymore," Todd quipped.

Todd fought a grimace that tried to play across his expression as he remembered that Andre would soon be returning to Florida.

Andre smiled, looked up at the clock and said, "Oh shit, your right. Thanks, man," and clapped Todd on the back so hard as to cause him to stumble forward.

Andre dropped enough money on the table to encompass the cost of the meal and an additional fifteen dollars. He sprinted out of the door promptly.

Todd finished composing himself, after nearly choking to death on the gum he had been chewing, and gathered the dishes Andre had left behind.

Andre reappeared in the doorway and said with a smile, "I do *not* have a big ass by the way," and ran out of the door laughing.

Todd guffawed with laughter in the wake of Andre's comment.
Andre's visit had distracted Todd from his clock-watching. It was nearly closing time already.

As the last customer left the restaurant, Todd smiled with approval and bid them a great evening. Lucy locked the door and turned the sign to the side that read: *closed.*

"Well that sucked nicely," Todd said sarcastically and looked down into the pouch of his apron at the meager tips.

"If you were to try to genuinely enjoy your job, people might notice and tip better," Lucy instructed as she passed.

"Baffle them with bullshit," Todd muttered to himself.

16

"Let's clean up and go," Will said in an attempt to change the subject between Todd and Lucy, "The faster we clean up, the more play time we'll have."

Todd enjoyed the quick cleanup process on the short days where they closed before dinner time.

Fueled by the desire to go out, Todd and Will completed the task in record time.

As Will locked the door and turned around, he saw Todd propped against Lucy's truck. Todd smoked a cigarette with a pained look upon his face.

"What's the matter, man?" Will said and placed his hand on Todd's shoulder.

Will lowered himself to Todd's eye level and looked at him with concern.

"I've forgotten something. I know that I have," Todd said disgustedly.

"I know what it is. I'm psychic," Will said and became serious as he placed the tips of his fingers against his temples.

"Okay, smart ass. What is it then?" Todd asked.

"Is it... the last time you got laid? It's been a while," Will said and laughed.

"No, I was at your Mom's house this morning," Todd replied with an evil grin.

"Oh well, it'll come to me," Todd said and shrugged his shoulders.

"So weak, still stuck on '*your momma*' jokes. You really need to get some new material," Will said and poked a finger into Todd's ribs.

Having been tickled Todd jerked and turned his back to Will defensively. Will reached down and pinched him on the butt.

Todd let out a gasp and jumped away from Will.

"I would swear, if you weren't with Lucy, that you had sugar in your tank. You're always touching my butt," Todd said to Will accusingly.

"I'm just checking you out. If you stop jumping, I'll know that you like it and my suspicions will be confirmed," Will said.

"Suspicions?" Todd asked curiously.

17

"Yeah, you've started to worry me. You haven't dated anybody since you went out with that teacher chick. She was pretty hot, dude. What happened with that anyway?" Will asked.

"We really had nothing in common. After a few months, I had to talk myself into seeing her. We would sit there and have dinner in silence. Then we would watch a movie in silence. I would go out of my way to make open ended conversation and she would usually respond with a one word answer, and then…back to silence," Todd responded.

"Some guys would call that the perfect relationship, as long as she was doing the stiff monkey lambada with you once in a while. Lucy likes to wait until the last few critical seconds of a game to ask about my feelings on important things like her weight, or something her mom said on the phone. She also has this weird habit of cornering me on the toilet and in the bathtub," Will said and laughed.

Lucy had rolled down the passenger side window of the truck and had been privy to their conversation.

"Well, mister busybody, if I could pin you down for five seconds any other time, I would talk to you then. It's always, 'I'm going to cut the grass,' or 'I'm going to work on my models in the garage,' or my favorite, 'Todd needs me; I'm going to head over there for a while.' I have to catch you when I can, or we would never talk," Lucy said and rolled her eyes.

"We talk all the time," Will said defensively.

"Yeah, keep thinking that. If I didn't pin you down, at key moments, we would never have a conversation. You should think about that before I run off and find a talker that likes 'free food and sex'," Lucy snapped.

"Hey, baby," Todd's voice took on a sugary tone, as he winked at Lucy.

Lucy and Will laughed at Todd, who displayed mock disappointment at being shot down.

"Get rid of that cancer stick and mount up, it's time to do this," Will said with ridiculous enthusiasm as he jumped into the front passenger seat.

Todd sat in the back seat of the vehicle and enjoyed

the way it listed between the sections of the bridge they drove over. He stared out over the water that stretched out as far as the eye could see, and waited for the city to come into view ahead of them across the expanse of choppy water.

"So, what do you think of the new additions to the menu that I'm planning?" Lucy asked Will.

"Dog food!" Todd said triumphantly and recoiled to see Lucy who stared angrily at him in the rear view mirror.

"*Oh no...* Sorry. I was trying to remember something earlier that I'd forgotten. Max needs a big bag of dog food," Todd said and relaxed as Lucy's infuriated expression melted back into a friendly glance.

"Hey, Todd?" Will asked.

"Hey, Will?" Todd asked in reply.

"Don't forget the dog food," Will said with a very self-amused expression.

"Ass," Todd said and rolled his eyes.

"Great ideas, but we need to go over ingredients to see if they will be cost-effective," Will said as he looked over at Lucy.

She seemed confused for a moment until she realized that it was a response to her earlier question. She opened her mouth to continue, but was cut short.

"So, when are you guys officially tying the noose, er, knot?" Todd asked correcting himself.

"The sooner the better, we think Lucy has a bun in the oven," Will said and reached over to pat Lucy's belly.

"What a sweet way of putting it," Lucy said and popped Will's hand aggressively.

"Oh wow! Congratulations, guys. I'm so happy for y'all," Todd said excitedly.

He was pleased to see Lucy's eyes as they smiled at him in the rear view mirror. Will, however, looked at him from the front seat sharply as to emote 'Don't get her started' in disappointment.

Lucy spent the rest of the trip telling Todd about the plans they were making. She covered dates and times and gave a long parental-like warning to rent his tuxedo early and to not procrastinate. She finished with a detailed list of things that would not be permitted at the bachelor party

19

Chapter 3

Dollars and Sense

Soon the trio walked down Bourbon Street in the French Quarter. Todd's eyes roved over the windows of the t-shirt shops greedily. His crooked grin would erupt each time he read some lascivious slogan on a t-shirt or sign in the windows. Todd always enjoyed these trips to the French Quarter. He could see past the neon signs of the strip clubs and the lights that flashed from the bars. The buildings and the architecture always held some deeper mysticism for him. The rich smells of Cajun cooking wafted in the air. Todd could hear the beautiful jazz, played by the street musicians, even though it was muffled by the thunderous drunken laughter of tourists. The trumpets had such a soothing effect on him.

"Always something here in the Vieux Carrè," he thought, "deeper than most can feel."

"I would sell my soul to the Devil for a beer. This humidity sucks," Will said and wiped the sweat from his forehead.

"Watch what you say. He might be listening," Lucy warned.

Todd looked at Will in deep concentration while he mulled over his comment.

Just then, a man bumped into Todd.

"Hey man. I bet I can tell you where you got those shoes for a dollar," the vagrant said as he turned to face Todd and looked him over.

Todd's eyes narrowed. He thought the man's tone and inflection were weird as though he forced himself to sound like a local.

20

Todd knew this was a scam. The con-artist bets you that they know where you got an item. They win based on a play of words. The correct answer is the location in which you are standing at the time, though it would seem to be correct to answer with where you purchased the item.

"Yup, I got 'em on Bourbon Street," Todd proclaimed.

The vagrant frowned and said, "I thought y'all were tourists, I didn't think you would catch that machination."

"There it was," Todd thought, "A drunk like him, using the word machination."

Something was off about this bum. Todd looked at him closely.

The homeless guy recoiled a little and said, "Looks like you want to kiss me or something."

"Would you sell your soul for a dollar?" Todd asked randomly.

The vagrant looked shocked by Todd's question. Then a condescending look washed over the vagrant's face.

He seemed to believe that Todd was an easy mark at this point, he began to snicker and said, "Sure, why not?"

Todd produced his waiter ticket book from his back pocket and began writing on the back of a page.

Lucy began to mutter something about paper cost but Todd ignored her, lost in his enjoyment of the situation.

It read as follows:

I_____, hereby give my soul to Todd Jennings for the sum of one dollar. Terms of this contract are payable upon death.

Signed: _____

Todd offered, "Print here, and sign here."

The vagrant looked suspiciously at the contract and then smiled.
He seemed to Todd to have suddenly thought of a way to dispel his own fear and superstition. Todd handed him the ticket contract with a mischievous look on his face. The man signed and gave Todd a disingenuous smile as he returned

the ticket.

Todd inspected the ticket and grimaced at the name.

"Well, *Mr. John Smith*, you know I get your soul regardless if this is your real name or not."

Todd gave the vagrant an evil smile as he handed him a crisp one dollar bill.

The vagrant backed away slowly and said, "God bless...," and under his breath, whispered, "...you freak."

Lucy then said, "Todd! That was sacrilegious!"

"It was just a joke. Did you see the look on his face? Anyway, he started it with the shoe scam," Todd fired back defensively.

Will chimed in, "I thought it was hilarious!"

"Let's go see if any of the other bums will go for it!" Todd said with a very self-amused expression.

Lucy looked disgusted, "I can't believe you guys can be so twisted!"

"Hey, at least they're getting some cash out of the deal. So in a way, I'm being a humanitarian," Todd said.

"And don't count me in there. It was *all* Todd," Will said defensively.

"What a wussy," Todd said and nudged Will's shoulder with his own.

"Yeah... Tell yourself that later tonight...when you're alone...with your hand," Will retorted slyly.

Todd continued to play this joke throughout the evening. On the way home, Lucy ceaselessly admonished him for having wasted his money and her waiter's tickets.

They dropped Todd off at his car and lingered to be sure it would start this time. Todd gave them a thumbs-up through his open driver's window. The wind and rain of the encroaching storm had begun to pelt his car as he arrived at home. He stepped in through his front door, shook his entire body like an animal, and flung rainwater everywhere. He removed the twenty-one slips of paper from his pocket, and laughed again. He drew a smiley face onto the contract that contained John Smith's name in remembrance of his first soul acquisition. He meticulously placed the wad of slips into a junk drawer for safe keeping. Todd removed his wet clothes and threw them into the collective pile of laundry in

22

the corner.

The fleeting thought, "I have to get those clothes done," passed through his mind.

He slid into his bed feeling his soft sheets suck him down into a deep sleep.

Chapter 4

Delusional?

A loud crashing noise ripped Todd from his sleep. He crept from his bed and walked slowly toward the door to the hallway. He held his breath, thinking that somehow it might help the door to open more quietly.

Just across the hallway there was a lamp that was always lit unless the bulb was burned out. Something was wrong, the hallway was black as pitch and it seemed eerie somehow. Todd remembered having changed the bulb recently. He flattened himself against the door frame as his heart pounded in his chest. It felt as though his head bobbed in time with the throb of his pulse in his jugular veins.

He slid his hand slowly across the wall toward the light switch then stopped with a jerk. "Just great, give away the element of surprise," he thought.

He crept back near his bed and picked up his cell phone. He pressed a button that caused the phone to emit a small blue light. It wasn't much, but it would allow him to see and he felt a lot more secure. He looked at the phone for a moment in deliberation of calling the police.

He envisioned what the call might sound like, "Yeah, this is Mr. Jennings. The raccoons have come in again through the doggy door. I need some heavily armed men to help get them out of my kitchen trash."

Todd smiled at the humor that somehow found its way out of him, even in his panic.

"Be a man," he muttered to himself.

Max was sprawled out right next to the bed. He did not stir as Todd held the light close to him. He spent a moment and wondered why Max had not been alerted. The fact that Max was aging passed momentarily though his mind. Todd went back to the door and edged out slowly and

24

held the phone out in front of him. He was forced to repeatedly press a button to maintain the faint light from the phone.

Todd moved cautiously through the hall with his breath held. He heard the noise downstairs again along with a new noise. It sounded like a group of people, who all whispered at the same time. It was quick and he was unable to make anything out. He stopped, cocked his head to the left and strained to hear.

"I could just... run to the end of the hall... slam on the light... and," this thought choked in Todd's mind as he began to integrate thoughts of potential danger.

"What's down there? A guy, maybe two...Or three... What if they have guns? New plan, I could just ease over to the stairwell and look down for signs of motion."

Todd's attention was stolen as he heard a noise occur directly behind him. It felt as though the bones in his neck broke as he swallowed dryly.

Tiny spikes of terror ran up his spine at the idea that something might be right behind him. His entire upper body twisted in a flash. He raised the cell phone up defensively. He saw nothing, breathed a sigh of relief, and returned his attention to the noises downstairs. Mid-turn back towards the stairs, the blue hue of the cell phone winked out. A deep foreboding horror rushed through him.

His body began to tremble in a spasm of panic and he was forced to disregard all logical thought. His fingers were frozen against the phone and lacked the dexterity to relight it.

The phone fell from his tremulous hand. He immediately dropped to the floor in panic, and felt around blindly for it. His mind struggled for a moment as the blue light came on directly above him.

Before he could look up to investigate the source of the light, something coiled its way around his throat. Effortlessly, and with feral malice, he was slammed like a rag doll against the wall.

The light of the cell phone, which recently had been a source of comfort and security, had changed.

It's even blue hue had been replaced by tendrils of

25

light.

Wave after wave of terror flooded through his veins like ice water coursing through him.

"Who... who are you?" he blurted out.

His throat threatened to fold under the claw's immense pressure. The figure stood motionless over him. His eyes fluttered as he labored to draw breath. Small beams of light floated in Todd's peripheral vision and danced in the absence of needed oxygen.

"Who are you?" Todd repeated heatedly as he expelled the last of the precious air from his lungs.

The sound of his own voice surprised him and had drawn on some inner strength that belied the hopelessness of his situation.

The grip around his throat loosened a tiny fraction. Todd greedily gulped ragged breaths to fill his lungs with air. The blue glow turned inward and illuminated the figure. Todd's eyes opened so wide that they hurt. He looked on as if a passenger within his own body and tried to make sense of the nightmare that faced him. Todd's mouth worked itself into a terrified gape. A tiny whisper of a breath escaped that may have been intended to be a scream. His muscles tightened and made him feel like he was covered in weighted stones. His hands found and clawed at the grip around his neck. Todd's eyes betrayed his desire to look away from the face of this terror.

He looked at what he thought to be a woman's face. But the vision constantly fluctuated. As he looked, the face seemed to flash for a split second and then morphed back into the feminine form. Her dark eyes seemed to look into him. The second ethereal image that continued to flash was beast-like. Its eyes burned with a yellow fire. The light seemed to shine with new intensity as though it became brighter as a measure of Todd's fear. The shadows were no longer able to mask the sheer horror of her. The flash of images seemed to morph into one face now. It seemed to be comprised mostly of the woman, but had amalgamated between the two.

Her jaw opened and the inhuman gape of her mouth gave full view to rows of fang-like, pointed teeth. Her voice seemed to come from far away as if she were inhaling her words.

"Is little Todd afraid?" she asked, her voice sounded feminine, but unnatural, and caused Todd's skin to crawl.

She continued, "You want answers, don't you, little man? You have blindly stumbled into a situation where you are powerless. Here, I have no equal," her voice was more of a roar as it trailed off.

She winked at him playfully. Her arm drew back in a flowing motion. She balled a fist and thrust it at his head.

Chapter 5

Carvings

Todd's eyes sprang open in panic as he looked around nervously. He found himself sprawled across his bed drenched in a cold sweat. He sat bolt upright and looked with wide terrified eyes around the room. He then patted himself down carefully and felt for injuries.

"That was a seriously shitty dream," he muttered and placed his open palm to his face to recover from the shock.

Todd slowly rose from the bed, and meandered towards the door.

As he walked into the hallway he noticed that the lamp was on again. He shook his head and realized it was never actually out.

The coffee pot was unmercifully slow this morning and his head pounded as though he had really been struck. Max sidled up to him and held his bowl in his mouth.

"Max!" he said breathlessly, "I forgot to get your food! Tell you what I'm gonna do," he said as he opened the refrigerator door.

"I was gonna save this for myself, but I guess you can have it," his voice became high and overly sugary.

Max stared at the dried bowl of chili and looked slowly up at Todd.

"It's still good," Todd said reassuringly.

Max lowered his face to the bowl, timidly to taste the chili.
The taste and smell seemed to assure him that the food would not cause him harm. He methodically began eating the bowl of food in small neat sections.

Todd washed out his cup and began to prepare his coffee.

He thought of the woman's face from his dream. It seemed to be burnt into his mind's eye.

He held the coffee pot over his cup and stared off, entranced by the memory of the dream.

Max let out a sharp bark as a reaction to a noise outside. Todd started and dropped the coffee pot. The pot smashed and sprayed hot coffee and shards of glass in every direction. He stared at the dark coffee marks on the legs of his khaki pants.

"Great...Just *great*," I have no clean pants!" Todd exclaimed in exasperation, and stomped his feet like a child throwing a tantrum.

After he sifted through the laundry pile in his bedroom, Todd donned a pair of nearly clean pants and stalked off to work bemoaning contempt for his situation.

When Todd arrived at work he threw himself into the normal rigors of his day. Everything seemed commonplace except for his tips. They were far below the normal amount for a busy morning like this. He supposed that his mood was able to override the pretense of concern he showed for the customers. Todd had settled into his habit of clock-watching and was morbidly bored.

"Todd?" Lucy asked, "Are you okay?"

"No," he said honestly, "I didn't sleep well last night, and things went south when I woke up this morning."

"I know you're having a tough time, but I can't allow you to take it out on my customers," she said with a mixture of concern and authority.

"I know," he replied, "and I'm very sorry."

"Well, I mean it in a nice way, but you look like Hell," she said, "Perhaps you should get some rest."

"Deal," said Todd.

Lucy gave a slight shudder, "I'm not making any deals with you after last night with your little display. I would let you leave early but I have to go out and pay bills this evening, so you're gonna have to stick it out."

Todd nodded his agreement and gathered dishes from a recently vacated table.

He watched with approval as Lucy's car left the parking lot. He decided to check in with the grumpy old man with the plaid hat that sat sipping his endless refill coffee.

"Can I get you anything?" he asked the old man as he worked to muster a smile.

The old man swallowed the last of the coffee and literally tossed him the cup.

With a scowl on his face the man bellowed the words, "free senior coffee," curtly.

Todd turned away and went to get the coffee as he rolled his eyes.

Will watched him pouring the coffee into the cup; Todd's agitated demeanor prompted him to ask, "What's the matter?"

"Plaid hat over there, I can't stand him. He is always so bitchy," Todd replied angrily.

"Yeah he is an ornery old dude for sure. And he drinks his weight in coffee every day for free. I keep telling Lucy that...Whoa!" Will said as he reached for Todd.

Todd winced as the cup's handle, greasy from the old man's breakfast, slipped slightly and poured searing hot coffee across his hand and forearm.

Will was able to catch the cup and correct it before the contents could do Todd more harm.

"Mother...," Todd's words were cut short by the bell over the door.

"Welcome. Be right with you," Todd called cheerily to the newly arrived customer.

Will laughed at Todd's ability to switch emotional gears so quickly.

The customer was a tall wide shouldered man wearing a hooded rain parka. The man had stumbled in the door and paused clutching at his chest as if searching the pockets of his parka for something he had forgotten. The large dark sunglasses he wore on his face masked it and he seemed to take no notice of Todd's words. He dropped his hands to his sides and lumbered to a nearby table.

Todd rubbed a handful of ice over his hand and arm as he tried to alleviate the painful sting of his burn.

"How about that senior coffee," Plaid hat bellowed from his table.

"I would like to shove that free senior coffee down

30

your angry old pie hole," Todd said, his voice barely a whisper.

Will laughed again and took the ice from Todd and tossed it into an empty sink.

"Be right there sir," Todd replied respectfully as he took a fresh cup of coffee and proceeded to go deliver it.

"I'll give you five dollars if you trip and throw it on him," Will offered.

Todd smiled at Will over his shoulder with a look that said 'very tempting Mr. Goldman'.

"Bout time. This ain't no way to run a bidness," the old man drawled as he snatched the cup from Todd.

"Sorry sir," Todd said as he made to go serve the new customer.

Todd paused and watched the new customer for a moment who sat at a table near the window. The customer, oblivious to his attention, slid his forearm toward the brilliant sunlight where it shone onto the table. As the arm was bathed in the light, the man winced and drew it back.

"Must be a sun burn," Todd thought to himself and inspected his own arm.

The customer had stood up and moved to a table away from the window and as Todd approached he realized this was Andre. He didn't look like himself. He looked ratty and disheveled and stared at a family to his left unabashed by his own obviousness.

Todd approached him and asked, "What can I get for you today Mr. Andre? I will bring you a soda when I place your order."

Todd was alarmed at the way Andre stared at the family and licked his lips. Todd glanced over at the family who had already noticed Andre's psychopathic glower. They sat uncomfortably and pretended to be very interested in the plates on the table before them.

"No drink, just a beef sandwich," Andre ordered gruffly as he continued to glare at the family.

"Sure thing. Be right back with it," Todd said professionally and wheeled around to place the order with Will.

Lucy returned and walked into the kitchen. She

huffed out air and stood in front of a fan. She noticed Todd and Will bent over as they intently watched something in the dining room.

"What is it?" Lucy asked.

"It's Andre. He's all *weird*," Todd replied.

She took Will's vantage point as he backed away to put Andre's sandwich together.

"You're back early," Will commented to Lucy.

"Yeah, I'll go after we close and drop night payments for the electric and gas. My damn air conditioner is out again," Lucy complained.

"I'll check it tonight after we close," Will groaned.

"Is he...licking his lips?" she asked Todd in disbelief.

"Yeah, it's creepy?" Todd replied with a shiver.

Will nudged Todd with the plate that contained Andre's sandwich.

"Go feed him before he eats one of the customers," Will advised, gesturing to Andre's meal.

Todd sat the plate down in front of Andre and took a step back.

Andre begrudgingly broke eye contact from his focus. He grunted or growled, Todd couldn't really discern which, as he turned to face the sandwich. He picked up the sandwich with no regard for its structural integrity. The bread broke and crushed between his fingers. The gravy rolled down the inside of his forearms which were planted on the table. Andre's mouth opened wide and Todd watched as Andre clamped down and took nearly half of the sandwich into his mouth. Todd looked to the family who were previously sheepish under Andre's piercing stare. They watched in disgust as Andre ravaged his sandwich.

"Do you need that drink?" Todd asked backing away.

"No," Andre's voice was barely discernible from a growl as crumbs and gravy dripped into his lap.

Todd strode quickly back to the vantage point where Will and Lucy watched Andre as he devoured his food.

"How 'bout a senior coffee," Plaid hat bellowed in a

32

loud rhetorical chant.

"Crap," Todd said angrily and left the comfort of his roost to go bring coffee.

As he handed the old man the cup, he was surprised to see him make an animated movement. He pointed away and was doing something strange with his eyebrows while he looked at Todd. He followed the old man's direction with his eyes. Andre was convulsing over his table. Todd arrived next to him as Andre vomited his sandwich and what looked like blood all over the plate and table.

Andre swooned forward and Todd made to steady him and put a hand on his shoulder. Andre angrily ripped his shoulder away and turned to look at Todd for the first time since he had entered the diner. Both men were shocked and amazed, as read in their expressions. Todd gawked at Andre whose lower jaw was awash in gravy and blood. Andre's head seemed to shutter as he looked at Todd. Andre reached up with his hand and slid his glasses down on to the bridge of his nose. Andre's blue eyes seemed to glow and radiated color hypnotically. Todd considered special effects contacts as he studied them.

Andre's eyes roved over Todd's head and upper body. He seemed to be amazed by whatever he saw in Todd. His expression melted into revulsion after a moment.

"What *are* you?" Andre screamed at him and began to back away toward the door. Andre produced his wallet and absently pawed a few bills from it and dropped them on the floor before he stumbled out of the door. Andre covered his head with his arms, shrieked in pain, and staggered out of view.

"Yep," Plaid hat said randomly.

"Yep what?" Todd asked still in shock.

"I knowed it...It's them drugs...I seen it on the tellemvision. Just like that," Plaid hat said with and accusatory point at the door.

Later that evening Lucy agreed to close thirty minutes early after she accessed the empty dining room.

Todd left and went immediately to the grocery store to purchase dog food. When he got home he filled Max's food bowl and went to watch television. He snorted in disgust as he flipped through two-hundred channels of infomercials. Todd's cell phone sprang to life and he wrestled it from his pocket.

"Hello?" he said and tried to not sound excited to hear from anybody.

"Hey, man. You okay?" Will asked and his voice was filled with concern.

"Yeah, I'm a little run down I guess," he replied.

"I plan to have a sleep-a-thon tonight though," Todd heard the microwave go off.

"Popcorn time," he said.

"Is that your dinner?" asked Will in disbelief.

"Yup," replied Todd.

"Gee, I wonder why you feel bad." Will retorted sarcastically,"Cigarettes and coffee for breakfast, no lunch, and popcorn for dinner."

Todd headed for the kitchen and held the phone on his shoulder. The rich smell of buttery popcorn filled his nostrils.

"Mm," Todd moaned, "This is gonna be smackin'."

"Well, at least try and get some sleep before you fall apart," Will said with a mixed tone of concern and skepticism.

"All right man. I'll see you tomorrow," Todd said through a yawn.

"Buh-bye," said Will.

Todd hung up the phone and drove his hand into the popcorn bowl. He walked back to the couch, plopped down, and began to shovel handfuls of popcorn into his mouth. Max came in through his doggy door, limped to a stop on the floor, and looked at Todd with baleful brown eyes. Todd went to Max with concern and placed his hands on the animal's sides inspecting him for injury.

"Are you okay?" Todd asked the dog superfluously.

Max responded with a small whimper and labored to climb onto the couch.

"I guess you are a bit older. Your puppy days are behind you. You're like five hundred in human years. You need to go to the vet for a checkup," Todd said as he helped the animal onto the couch.

Max ate directly out of the popcorn bowl as if it were his dog food bowl. Todd didn't seem to mind as he rummaged around Max's muzzle for his share. Todd's eyes began to get heavy.

Before he knew it, he had fallen asleep while watching infomercials on television. His body jerked, he felt as though he were being watched. He opened his eyes and struggled to focus them. He looked around the room nervously and saw no one.

"Okay, I'm going crazy!"

He put his hand on his forehead and slid it down the length of his face. He still felt disoriented from waking so suddenly. As he began to settle back onto the couch, his eyes glanced down toward his coffee table. Something was different. Something was wrong.

Todd sat up; he began to sift through the clutter upon the table, he noticed something odd. There were words deeply carved into his coffee table in a language that he didn't recognize. He swept the trash away and was surprised to see more.

"What is that?!" he said aloud.

Max looked at him and turned his head curiously to its side.

Todd decided that it was now time to call the police. The marred surface of his table proved evidence of an intruder.

"They could still be here," he thought as paranoia welled up in him.

He snatched up his cell phone as his heart raced with adrenaline. He ran outside to make the phone call. His hands shook as he pushed number four on the speed dial.

A voice came from the other end of the phone, "Nine-one-one emergency response. Do you have an emergency?"

Todd began to stutter, "I think someone is in my house. I've been hearing noises. I'm outside. I'm afraid to go back in."

"Sir. Calm down, sir. We are sending law enforcement officers to your home to check it out immediately. Just stay where you are. They will be there momentarily. I'll stay on the phone with you while you wait," the voice on the phone said soothingly.

Todd let out a sigh of relief.

"Unit six, what's your ten twenty?" Todd heard the operator ask someone in the background.

"We are at highway thirty-six and Saint Charles Street," said another voice in the background.

The operator spoke again, "I have a possible ten twenty-four, or ten eighty-nine for you at: 1 5 4 2 8 Sixth Street."

Todd listened to the blur of numbers. He did not understand what the codes meant, but his confidence rose as he listened to their professionalism.

"We're about one minute out," the other voice reported.

The operator then returned her attention back to Todd, "The police officers will be at your residence within a minute, sir."

Todd felt like everything was going to be okay. The thought that he had never given the dispatcher his address occurred to him. He was curious about this, but shrugged it off.

"They probably traced the call or something," Todd thought to himself.

The police car arrived very uneventfully. There were no sirens and no emergency lights. The officers emerged from the vehicle solemnly and approached him. Todd assessed the officer that he could see and showed him a look of approval mixed with gratitude. The first officer, a male in his early thirties, approached him. His shoulders were wide enough to obstruct Todd's view of the second officer.

"What can you tell us about what's happened?" the male officer asked.

"I think someone is in my house. I heard noises and there is something strange carved..."

Todd's words choked as he looked into the face of the second officer, a female in her early twenties.

"Let's have a look. You stay outside, Mr. Jennings," she said.

36

Todd looked at her closely; her hair was long and brown with a light reddish tint to it. Her dark brown eyes were fixed upon him. She had a 'thick-fine' frame, as Todd usually referred to a woman with her curvy shape. She smiled at him warmly.

"Now, where do I know her from?" Todd asked himself mentally.

He also remembered that he had not mentioned his name to anyone. Suspicion crept into his mind as he stared into the woman's beautiful face.

"Why didn't you use your sirens?" Todd asked the officers.

"We were only two roads over. There was no traffic...We wouldn't want to give away the element of surprise, now would we?" she said as she gave Todd a wink.

All the wheels of deductive thought turned quickly in his head. This was the woman's face from his dream, well one of the faces.

"Is this a dream?" he thought, as the two officers went into his house.

"Was it the same woman?" Todd thought.

She didn't look exactly the same as in the dream, but very similar. In turn, he could hear doors of his home as they were slammed open and the voices of the officers who yelled the word, "CLEAR!"

After a short period of time the male officer appeared at the front door.

"It's safe to come in, sir. The house is empty," the male officer motioned to Todd to beckon him inside.

"There's no sign of forced entry, but there is no doubt that someone was here, considering this terrible mess," the male officer gestured with a wave of his hand at all of the trash on the floor.

Todd felt his face flush with embarrassment over the condition of his home.

"Yeah, you have to be a real animal to do this to somebody's house," Todd replied in agreement.

Todd remembered about the coffee table and said, "Look at what they did to my coffee table!"

Todd brushed the clutter from the table with a

37

forceful swipe of his hand.

As the trash tumbled onto the floor Todd thought to himself, "Didn't I just clear this off before they showed up?"

"Where are the words?" Todd questioned loudly as he stared downward.

"Yeah, I know how you feel, having your place trashed like this," the male officer said in disgust.

Todd felt completely out of touch with reality and decided to go along with the male officer's misinterpretation rather than blather on about invisible carvings.

Just then, the female officer appeared on the stairs, "Well, everything seems to be in order, Mr. Jennings," she paused then added, "Although the bedroom is quite a mess."

She walked over to where Todd and the male officer stood. She looked down at the coffee table, as if there were something on it that only she could see. Her reaction was duly noted by Todd.

She bent over and ran her hand along the surface of the table evenly.

The female officer looked up at Todd and said, "I have one just like this at home."

"Lucky they didn't mess it up, considering the state of the rest of your furniture," she said and gave Todd an intimidatingly cold glare.

Todd felt as though his heart might burst. This woman was threatening him inches from her partner and he was unable to do anything about it. The male officer was oblivious to the piercing stare his partner gave Todd and continued to offer advice on home security. Todd was thankful when the officer finally stopped and prepared to leave, taking the weird female officer with him. The officers told Todd in parting, if he would like it, there would be a police report ready for him tomorrow at three P.M.

Todd nodded to the officers and was overly grateful for their departure. He went over to his couch and sat down wearily. His eyes drifted down upon the coffee table. He started in fright to see that the carvings had reappeared on its surface.

* * *

38

"Hello? Hello, Todd?"

The voice came from his cell phone which unexplainably was in his hand. He raised it numbly to his ear and asked, "hello?"

"Hey man, are you okay? I mean, you just told me that you were gonna have popcorn for dinner, a sleep-a-thon and then you just... got quiet," Will explained.

Todd, who was dumb-founded, asked Will, "Can you come over?"

"Is everything alright?" Will asked and sounded concerned.

"I can't explain right now. Can you just come over?" Todd asked with a quaver in his voice.

"Sure. I'll be right over. I just got done with the air in Lucy's truck," Will said as he tried to reassure Todd.

It wasn't very long before Will arrived. Todd walked out to greet him. As Todd turned to go back into the house, Will grabbed his butt. Todd jumped, gasped, and gave Will a smile over his shoulder.

"It's not gay until you stop jumping," Will said with a laugh as they entered Todd's house and closed the door.

Todd told Will the whole story. He was meticulous in the description of the events of his dream. He explained how the markings on the table had vanished at points. Then he went on to tell Will about the oddity of the police during their visit. He carefully recanted the details and pointed out the inconsistencies of their behavior that he had noted.

Will smirked, "So you had this crazy dream, all in the forty seconds that you were quiet while I tried to get your attention on the phone? It's funny, the lengthy dreams that you can have while only asleep for a short while," Will said.

"No, it was too real. It couldn't have been a dream! Besides, the markings are still here on my coffee table! The police told me that there would be a report ready for me by tomorrow at three P.M.! Look, I know full well if I were hearing this from anybody else that I would think they were a nut ball. I'm not crazy though...Well, I don't think I am anyway," Todd stammered.

Will looked down at the coffee table to see what all

the fuss was about.

"That's Italian," Will stated as he looked at the marred table top.

"How do you know that?" Todd asked impressed.

"Lucy has books all over the house, same language. She wants to go there on our honeymoon. She wants us both to learn the 'lingo' as she calls it," Will said with disdain.

"Great, what does it say?" Todd asked as he sat next to Will on the couch.

"Aw man. I can't even ask where the bathroom is in Italian, much less read *this*," Will said apologetically.

"Could Lucy read it?" Todd asked hopefully.

"Probably not, she's at her Mom's for the weekend anyway."

Todd stood up and looked excited. His expression went glum and then returned to excited again.

Will laughed and asked, "Did you just have some kind of mental argument with yourself?"

"Yeah, kind of," Todd answered as his face flushed red.

"I know I've told you before, but you're a *weird* dude," Will said with a smile.

"Your Mom loves it," Todd replied.

Will looked suddenly stricken with a profound sadness. His mournful expression was extreme and he looked as though he may cry. Todd had never seen this in their long years together and put his hand on Will's shoulder to comfort him.

"What's the matter man?" Todd asked Will with concern.

"It's my Mom, she isn't doing very well," Will turned his head away from Todd presumably to hide his tears.

"Oh, I'm very sorry," Todd said compassionately, suddenly very upset with himself.

"That's what she says. You're sorry because you can't come up with better comebacks," Will said with a look of glee on his face.

"You told me that to screw with me?" Todd asked incredulously.

"Yeah. I figured you needed it," Will said playfully.

"Ass," Todd said angrily and popped him on the shoulder.

"So, what was the argument you had with yourself about?" Will asked Todd.

"It wasn't an argument. I just had a few ideas and shot them down without saying anything out loud," Todd replied.

"See, that makes you seem a lot less weird. I do that too. I don't however have those crazy expressions like you. So did you end up with any usable ideas?" Will asked.

"Oh yeah!" Todd said as he remembered his idea. "We can use a translator page on the internet to find out what it means," Todd said.

Within a few moments the computer had loaded up a translator page. Will slid the coffee table over by Todd's computer chair. Will stared at it and began to type. He carefully entered in each character and then clicked on the translate button. The computer hummed and whirred but the screen remained unchanged.

The computer started to make a labored noise like a card that clicked in the spokes of a child's bicycle.

"Is it broken?" Will asked as he edged away from the dangerous sounds the computer had begun to make.

"It's doing some scan or something in the background, it does what it wants. The fans come on when it's struggling. Probably gonna be a minute," Todd said and shrugged his shoulders.

Will got up abruptly and followed Todd who walked away towards the kitchen.

"What do you think it's gonna say?" asked Todd.

"It says you forgot to pay your late fees at Ralph's video rental," Will said trying to force Todd to smile.

Todd grimaced, lost in his thoughts.

Will left him and went back to the computer. Todd walked into the room. The look of horror on Will's face almost made him go back into the kitchen. Todd turned and sat down weakly on the couch.

"What does it say?" Todd asked not really sure he honestly wanted to know.

41

Will looked slowly over to him.

"You didn't do all this to screw with me did you?" Will asked with a stunned expression.

There was a long silence. Will *always* had a joke for every occasion. This time, however, he looked so grave that Todd sank lower into the couch in preparation for the impact of the news.

Will spoke slowly without blinking or looking back at the computer, his tone was that of a father giving a eulogy for a lost child.

"It says, 'To obtain souls is to taste power and deny my torment'. Please tell me you're yanking my chain," Will said and felt gooseflesh forming on his forearms.

Todd looked at the writing on the coffee table again. He felt numb and disconnected from himself. The glass of soda slid slowly from Todd's hand. It seemed to fall for a long time. Todd watched it tumble down, end over end. The liquid never came out as it fell and then it shattered on the floor.

Chapter 6

Stupid Human Trick

Todd woke up as his alarm clock sang softly to him and asked, 'How do you mend a broken heart?' His new alarm clock, like most things in his life this past year, had a softer more soothing effect on him. Todd had changed his entire life, even moved away from his small home town of Abita Springs. He missed the town itself. He had disassociated himself socially from everyone except for Will and Lucy. But, the town, itself, would always be a fond memory. In the year that had passed, Todd had sold his home, and acting on the advice of his psychiatrist had changed his life completely. The new apartment had a host of modern conveniences that Todd had nearly forgotten existed. The toilet seat was high on his list of amenities. He had often remembered as he would sit in the morning, how he had procrastinated about fixing the one in his former home. Dr. Larry, the shrink, had impressed upon him the need to change his environment after the series of "episodes" he endured, which included having an assailant carve words into his coffee table, and had continued manifesting themselves in waking delusions.

"People have a funny way of making things sound nice," Todd had thought in reaction to the word episodes.

Like his cousin Rhonda. Rhonda slept with an entire bar full of men and then assaulted three police officers who attempted to arrest her. It was later passed off as a "drug problem". Nobody ever came right out and said that she was a crack-whore and a nymphomaniac. She simply had a "drug problem". It made things easier for people to deal with. He supposed he could be okay with his own psychotic delusions of being stalked and threatened by a woman, that only he could see, as having "episodes".

43

Dr. Larry had asked Todd to make a self-promise that he would avoid procrastination at all costs. Todd, true to his word, had kept his new apartment spotless. Everything from dishes to clothes were washed and neatly put away.

He walked sleepily into the kitchen of his four room apartment. He listened to the dripping noises the coffee made as it landed into the pot.

"Right on time," he thought to himself as he admired his new coffee pot that would begin working via a timer.

He poured coffee into a small porcelain cup and added several heaping scoops of sugar. Todd shuffled toward the table and sat down. He always missed Max at this time. Max had been given to Will and Lucy shortly after they had been married. The epiphany that he might have an e-mail from Will played across his expression. He opened his laptop computer and began to click the buttons with purpose.

"You have mail," the sexy computerized female voice said. Todd smiled and clicked open the message. It read:

"Lucy says hey. Here is a picture of Sebastian. Check out that expression. He either wants to eat the camera or he is making doo-doo."

Todd smiled at the picture of Will and Lucy's baby. While he had repeatedly told them how cute he was, he had always thought Sebastian looked like a mean old man.

Dr. Larry had said, "More than likely, this comes from a form of jealousy. You secretly long for the same stability that Will and Lucy have."

"No, he looks like some mean old dude," Todd would say with a condescending smile.

"*HOW 'BOUT THAT SENIOR COFFEE?!*" Todd screamed randomly at the picture of the baby.

Todd guffawed with self-amused laughter and then composed himself.

"I don't think I would even change my own godson's diaper."

He looked at the fat bottomed diaper in the picture of the infant.

"Don't worry kiddo, when you get passed that

diaper affliction, you and I can go fishing and play 'catch' all you want," Todd said to the picture of his godson.

Todd's watch beeped.

"Time to get dressed," he said and reset his alarm to ensure another beep that would alert him of the time to leave for work.

He entered his closet and surveyed the neatly hung shirts and pants. He picked out a pair of black slacks and a white dress shirt. A t-shirt that touted his cigarette brand caught his eye as he left the closet. He flinched a little and felt the pangs of his addiction to cigarettes.

He had been trying to quit for several months and was in the middle of an exceptionally long run of cold turkey. He grabbed the t-shirt from its hanger, bunched it tightly in his hands and tossed it in a wastebasket.

"Out of sight, out of mind," he muttered to himself.

*Beep...Beep...*Another alarm sounded and alerted him that it was time to leave for work.

He snatched up his keys, and headed out the door. As he stepped onto the street from the lobby of his apartment building he spied his car that sat two spaces from where he stood. The car, itself, was a pride point for him. The car was not sporty or flashy; it was a responsible car that did its job optimally. He had traded in his old car after much deliberation for this one. He had even bidden it a fond farewell as it was towed away from the front of his apartment by the company that had sold him this one. It had been one of the first few really large accomplishments that marked milestones in his new life. Todd climbed into the seat of his car and admired the fresh clean scent. He noticed a small piece of paper on the passenger side floor board. The paper was just outside of his reach and he strained to pick it up. He inspected it and then wadded it up and put it into the ashtray.

"Neat and tidy," he thought to himself as he drove away.

He arrived at work precisely fifteen minutes early. This had been a practiced ritual of the last several months. He enjoyed having the time to ease himself into his surroundings and get comfortable before the start of work.

45

"Good morning," said Tony, a fellow waiter in his early twenties.

Tony had been very supportive to Todd from the first day he had arrived. Tony had a talent for finding humor in any situation. His eyes held certain honesty, it seemed to Todd. When things got the most hectic, it was Tony who would provide the humor to get past the pressure.

"Hey, Tony," Todd said smiling.

"Came early to steal breakfast again?" Tony asked and pointed an accusatory finger at Todd.

"Don't point at me, Mr. Bacon munchin' bandit. Yeah I've seen you. Don't act all hoity toity with me," Todd responded playfully.

"Why ya gotta bring that up? It's because I'm black, right?" Tony asked with a forced stolid expression that threatened to collapse into a smile.

"Oh, whatever," Todd flourished his hand at Tony, "Go do something work oriented and stop distracting me while I plan the acquisition of my breakfast," Todd said, pretending to sneak into the kitchen.

"Hey, Don. How are you?" Todd asked as he grabbed a piece of sausage from under a heat lamp.

Don Reynolds, a short bald man in his late forties looked over at Todd and smiled. His slate blue eyes fell upon the sausage that Todd stuffed ravenously into his mouth.

"That's gonna come out of your check, ya turd. Between your sausage addiction and Tony with the bacon I'm gonna go broke," Don said playfully.

Todd nodded his agreement as he began to sample some of the bacon. Don had generously given Todd a job on his first day in town. Todd, who had been eating in the restaurant, approached Don, after having overheard his complaints about poorly performing waiters.

"So what's on the agenda for today?" asked Todd.

"Same as usual. Plan on making a million...Be happy with the three k that we'll actually make," Don replied.

"Today's gonna be great," Todd said optimistically.

"Tips been okay lately?" Don asked conversationally.

"Unbelievably good," Todd replied happily as he

finished a large crispy hash brown.

"That's good," Don said."Sales are up forty percent over last year. Which is going to come in handy for feeding the entire wait staff every morning," Don said as he threw a towel at Todd to thwart his attempt to get another handful of sausage links.

Todd prepared his waiter's station with neatly organized straws and napkins for easy access. It seemed like time was in fast forward today. He was surprised when Tony did his trademark whistle before unlocking the door for open. He took a deep breath as the doors were opened and people flooded in. The waiters all seemed to pause and give the guests time to seat themselves before they rushed among them to begin service.

"And how are you today?" Todd asked in a warm and friendly voice as the older gentlemen sat down at the table.

"I woke up alive…it's a good start," chided the old man.

"Are you ready to order now or would you like a few minutes?" Todd asked.

"I'm going to need a little while. I want to wait for my daughter," the old man replied.

"Can I get you something to drink while you wait?" asked Todd.

"I want a tall glass of scotch," the old man said with a genuine smile.

Todd's face worked into an amused smirk as he realized the man was picking on him.

"Just kidding I will take a glass of orange juice please."

"All we have is tomato," Todd said and looked at the customer apologetically.

"Really?" the old man sounded shocked.

"I was just pulling *your* leg," Todd said playfully as he jotted down the man's drink order.

Several minutes later the old man was joined by a young woman who wore a hat and large sunglasses.

"Good morning," Todd looked at her and smiled.
She looked up at him. He could see her give him a

47

head to toe appraisal. A slow warm smile passed over her face.

"Good morning to *you*," she replied.

"Can I uh...get you something to drink?" Todd stammered.

Todd looked at her and thought she seemed to be in her mid-twenties. Her shoulder-length blonde hair was pushed down close to her face on the sides. The sunglasses hung low on the bridge of her nose and she looked at Todd over them. She watched his eyes rove over her and enjoyed the expression of attraction she found there.

"Yes, may I have a glass of orange juice please?" she replied finally.

"Back in a flash," Todd said and hurried away toward the kitchen.

"She was using her x-ray vision on your butt," Tony said as he passed Todd.

"She wants it," Todd replied.

Todd returned to the couple with their drinks and watched as they read over the menus they held.

He sat the orange juice down in front of her and asked, "Are you both ready to order?"

"Yes. I *always* know what I want," she said with a playful grin.

Todd masked his amazement of her words.

"There was no way she could hear the conversation with Tony, was there?" he wondered to himself.

"I would like two lightly buttered slices of wheat toast and a half of a grapefruit," she said.

"And I would like a pork chop and two fried eggs over medium, no toast," the old man added.

"Very good," Todd said.

Todd turned and went to place the order with Don.

He could hear the woman as she chastised the old man about his cholesterol.

Todd hung onto the bar with an expectant look on his face as he waited to call his food order. Don looked up at him approvingly from the grill.

"I need an order of the icky wheat toast. I need two pigs and two chickens medium. I also need the *special*

48

grapefruit for table four," Todd said.

"All right, you can put away the puppy dog eyes. The sugar smiley face is a lame gimmick. You must be in a bad way. But you guys should at least try to get *me* a phone number once in a while," Don said playfully.

"I'll get you some booty as soon as I can Don. I'm almost to the point of having a flashing neon sign over my head that says 'desperate'," Todd told him with a concerned tone.

Don threw his head back and laughed. Todd marveled at the speed at which Don had finished the order. Don placed the order on the bar. Todd scooped up the plates and headed back to the table. Todd sat everything down on the table carefully and held the grapefruit till last. There was a smiley face drawn on top lightly with sugar.

"Oh how *cute*," the woman said.

Todd was pleased that she was amused; however, his confidence in himself failed and he struggled to retort.

"Can I get you… um either of you anything else?" he stammered.

"No, but have you noticed that neon sign?" she asked.

"What?" Todd asked and sounded like he had been punched in the stomach.

She pointed to the window at the neon sign that said "Don's".

"The sign is out," she said.

"Oh yeah, right, let me take care of that," Todd said as he climbed into the booth behind them and pulled the small rope to turn on the sign.

Todd was wondering if her statement was really just a random thought or if she could have overheard him somehow. Todd went back to the kitchen as he tried to shake his nervousness.

"How did it go?" Don asked and moved closer to listen intently.

"Well...it didn't go at all," Todd replied as he worked to hold back a forlorn look.

"Tough break, the grapefruit works every time, though. You must really suck," Don laughed at his own

49

cruelty.

"If it weren't for your words of encouragement and support, I would probably have a girlfriend at this point," Todd said sarcastically.

"I don't want to suffer alone," Don said and shrugged.

Todd made several passes to make sure the old man and his daughter had everything that they needed. He had to fight the urge to address the woman singly, every time.

"I been watching ya buzzin' that table ya horn-dog," Tony said to Todd playfully.

"Man, she is so good looking. I can't get over it," Todd replied.

The old man raised his head and looked at Todd from across the expanse of the restaurant.

"Check please," Todd thought and headed toward the table.

"Can we have the check, please?" the old man asked.

"Absolutely," Todd said and rummaged through his apron for his ticket book.

Todd quickly totaled the order and wrote the price on the bottom. He playfully drew a smiley face next to the total. He shuttered a tiny fraction as he thought about the last time he had drawn a smiley face onto a ticket.

"Don't dwell on the past," he could hear Dr. Larry say in his head.

The young woman doodled on a napkin. He plainly saw her write the name "John Smith" onto it.

The name on the napkin was the final straw. Todd could feel himself becoming disoriented.

"Have a nice day. Hope to see y'all again later," Todd drawled as he dismissed himself.

He felt ill and shaky, and considered a hasty retreat to the bathroom to be the best course of action. Todd washed his face with cold water and felt his equilibrium return.

Tony entered the bathroom and looked at him, "You okay?" he asked.

"Yeah, I'm cool," Todd replied.

"Well, you're pretty pale for a white guy," Tony

50

said.

Todd blew cold water through his fingers as a laugh erupted from him.

"I'll watch your tables for a few minutes. You get yourself together," Tony said and left the bathroom.

Todd emerged from the bathroom several minutes later and returned to his duties.

Todd had been right and lunch was exceedingly busy today.

All of the waiters worked furiously to accommodate the customers. Then, just as quickly as it had begun the work day was over for Todd. He enjoyed the short lunch shifts. Todd felt the fat front pocket of his apron. He rummaged his hands through the large amount of crumpled bills inside the pocket. Tony walked by and mused at him.

"Good tips, huh?" Tony asked.

"Yeah, it was a great day," Todd said with a grin.

"It's about to get better," Tony said and held out a small piece of paper.

Todd looked at it curiously, and then unfolded it. It simply read, "Brianna (Bree) 555-5012."

"Who?" Todd asked, curiously.

"Your first customers. The old guy and..," Tony looked at the paper and pointed to the name, "*Bree*."

Todd went back to the kitchen. He could feel the lightness in his step. Don finished the cleaning of a cutting board and looked up to see Todd, who stood there and smiled at him.

"The grapefruit worked!" exclaimed Todd as he showed the paper with the number to Don triumphantly.

"Good. Make it work. Then you can concentrate on fixing me up with her friend... or friends," Don laughed and gave Todd a wink.

"Do you really think yourself capable of handling more than one?" Todd chided.

"When you go without as long as I have, there is very little that you are not capable of," Don said with a smile.

Todd laughed and clapped him on the shoulder.

"Have a good evening," Todd said as he picked up

51

his keys from the desk and proceeded to leave.

"Thanks for this morning, Tony," Todd yelled across the restaurant.

The other waiters looked up and gave evil grins.

"Oh, I bet that sounded bad," Todd thought.

Tony finished his laugh and with a mock lisp said, "thure thing, thweetie."

Todd rolled his eyes as he pushed the door open and headed toward his car.

Todd was in a decidedly good mood. The phone number he had gotten made him feel attractive and alive. The excitement of the possibility for intimacy, or just a good time shared with another human being, was filling him with hope. It had been so long since he had even tried to date a woman.

Arriving home, he sat the phone number down on his dining table with his cell phone. He weighed the possibilities of how she might react to him having called so soon.

"Would her reaction be a positive or a negative one," he wondered.

He paced back and forth and added the pressure of time to the equation.

"If I wait too long to call, it'll piss her off," he thought.

He sat down and programmed the number into his phone. His thumb hovered over the call button as he read the word *Bree* repeatedly. He put the phone down again and began to pace.

"Okay, I'm definitely going to call her," he thought.

"What should I say?" he asked out loud, to no one in particular, as he paced back and forth for a while.

He spoke to himself as he paced, and tried different contrasts of greetings to compare.

"This is Todd. I was calling to give you a chance to be graced by my company," he said and smirked.

"This is Todd. I hope it doesn't seem desperate that I couldn't wait even a day to call you," he muttered and let the end trail off.

His head swam with the possibilities, the

pleasurable ache, of the unknown, twisted him back and forth between emotional poles. He sought relief from the torment and picked up his phone. He pressed the call button and fought the urge that he felt to hold his breath. He listened to the phone as it rang and began to feel a sense of relief.

"Worst case scenario: things don't work and I haven't lost anything," he thought to himself.

"Sorry to have missed your call," the smooth voice said on the line.

His shoulders slumped dejectedly.

Todd wasn't paying attention to the rest, he debated on whether he should leave a message or not.

"Hello?" said the voice on the phone.

Todd's eyes went dull as he struggled to think of something to say now. He opened his mouth to speak as his free hand rose up opened palmed as if he were trying to grasp words.

"Hello?" the voice repeated, it was more forceful and barely sounded polite now.

Todd's open palm closed and he went up on his toes nervously.

"Oh, I was about to leave a message," Todd stammered, his voice threatened to crack.

"Who is this?" asked Bree.

"It's Todd, Todd Jennings, you're uh...the waiter from this morning," he blurted out.

"Oh!" she sounded excited.

"I left my number so that I could ask you to stop flirting with me while I tried to have my breakfast," she continued.

Todd's face flushed red with embarrassment and his shoulders slumped again. There was a short silence.

"Just picking on you," she said her smile audible in her words.

"I thought you were an exceptionally nice guy and you seemed like you might know how to have fun," she admitted.

On the other end of the line, Bree rolled her eyes as she replayed her own words mentally.

She palmed her face thinking, "I should have waited to pick on him. Dumb Bree, very dumb. I should have..."

"My boyfriend and I go on picnics every weekend and I do crafts," Todd said and interrupted her thought.

A short, uncomfortable silence elapsed.

"Oh really?" she said and tried to maintain the enthusiasm in her voice.

"Of course he's gay, stupid," she thought to herself.

"I was just trying to get ya back," Todd said, a small high pitched giggle wrestled itself free from him.

Todd covered his mouth in embarrassment.

"Oh, a *funny guy,*" she said.

"So, would you like to go out sometime?" Todd tensed as he realized this random thought had been voiced.

"I would like that very much. You can bring your boyfriend along," she answered quickly.

Todd had prepared for a rejection. He replayed her answer a few times mentally. He felt the awkwardness of the silence tearing at his mind and he scrambled for something else to say.

"Okay, when do you want to set something up?" he asked.

"I could pick you up in about thirty minutes," she said.

"I was fixing my hair and makeup while you tried to decide whether or not to call me," she continued.

"How did you? Right now? A date tonight?" his voice cracked this time.

He flushed red and punched the air in victory and silently rejoiced in his good luck.

"This would be more like a date audition," Bree advised.

His mind began to quickly search for a witty or comical retort.

"I might need a little more time. I have to curl my hair and pick out a thong that will match my purse," he joked.

She laughed and said, "Good. I will see you in twenty eight minutes."

She hung up the phone abruptly.

Todd spun around on one heel and ran like a lunatic into his bedroom. He decided on a pair of jeans and polo shirt. He ran around and grabbed up his wallet and sprayed himself with cologne.

He stopped mid-stroke while brushing his hair.

"I didn't tell her where I lived," he thought.

He was already brushing his teeth.

"I can just call her from my cell phone and I can pick her up," he concluded.

He picked up his keys and headed out into the crisp night air. As he walked towards his vehicle along the sidewalk he heard his phone begin to ring in his pocket.

"Hello?" he asked curiously.

"Are ya gonna get in?" Bree asked, her voice brimmed with impatience.

"What?" he said and felt confused.

The passenger door of a car parked near his own opened behind him. He walked slowly over to the car and cautiously looked in. Bree sat there with a smile on her face.

"How did you know where I live?" he asked.

"I found it in the phone book, silly. Once you gave me your full name I looked it up to see where you lived," she explained.

"I wanted to see if you lived on the right side of the tracks. I started to drive while we talked earlier," she confessed.

"I guess I passed?" he asked, sat down, and closed the door behind him.

"Well... actually if you use north as a guide, you live on the west side of the tracks, but I was willing to overlook this if you would buy me a coffee," she said.

Todd was confused and tried to replay what she had just said. He had become lost in the beauty of her at some point. Todd considered her attractive when he had seen her earlier. She had fixed her hair and put on makeup now. 'Great looking' had become gorgeous. Her clothes were far less conservative than the ones she had worn at breakfast. The cleavage in the large V cut in her blouse acted like a tractor beam for his eyes. She had glanced over at him and looked for a response to her proposal of coffee. He averted his eyes as quickly as he could. A sort of knowing smile had crossed her lips. He struggled to recall what she had been saying.

"She looks so good. What was she saying? Coffee, yes. Coffee, that was it," Todd thought to himself.

"Since you've gone so far out on a limb to take a chance on me, I guess I could at least pay for a cup of coffee," he replied.

"What color did you decide on?" she asked.

"Color? What do you mean?" he asked.

"The thong," she answered.

"*Oh*. I decided to just let them roam free tonight," he said and made an effort not to blush.

"*Good.* I don't like guys who wear butt floss," she said with an evil grin on her face.

Upon arrival at the coffee shop, Bree sat in the car while Todd went inside to get the coffee. After a few minutes he appeared at the door and looked back at the cashier laughing.

She watched him and appreciated how he interacted with people. He approached the car and held the coffee awkwardly. He looked clumsy and off balance as he struggled to open the car door. She leaned over and pulled the latch on his door and pushed it open in an attempt to help. He wobbled a little as he tried to sit down without the use of his hands. He appeared to make a controlled fall into the passenger seat. He held both cups of coffee aloft and watched the white tops for any signs that they may have spilled. He seemed very pleased with himself for not having dumped coffee everywhere and offered her a cup. She took it and smiled warmly back at him.

"Perfect timing," he said, "I was hoping you would open the door. I was about to lose it."

"I know," she replied.

There was a pause, then Todd said, "Did you know I was gonna lose it or did you know I wanted the door opened?"

"Both," she replied.

"I have to tell you a secret," she said as she looked at him with a serious expression.

"You seemed to get a little freaked out this morning when I spoke. Did I say something you were thinking when you were near me?" she asked.

"As a matter of fact," Todd slid up in his seat and looked at her, "you did. So, where is this going? You said you had a secret? " Todd asked.

"That's my stupid human trick," she said. "It's my only real marketable skill. I get a flash... that's more like a feeling, and I translate it into a few words," she said as if it were the most normal thing in the world.

"It's nice to play with people sometimes," she said as she stared out of the windshield.

"So you're a psychic?" he ventured a guess.

"I wouldn't go that far. Really intuitive would be a better way of putting it," she answered.

"What other *feeling* did you get from me?" he asked.

"You mean like, 'she's really hot and she thinks I am sexy'?" She asked.

"Wow. That's amazing," he said with his eyebrows raised in disbelief.

"I didn't get that, but it's very flattering and you *are* pretty cute," she said as she smiled and started up the car.

She drove a short distance from the coffee shop then abruptly pulled over to the side of the street. She put the car into park and turned her attention towards Todd. Bree placed both of her hands on the armrest between them.

She looked at him and said, "Now, we get to know each other better."

Todd sipped his coffee and said, "This is good for me. I hate bars and singles scenes."

She pulled the rim of her coffee close to her lips. She flinched as a waft of steam threatened to burn her.

"That might be the reason I'm still single," he said and quelled the urge to giggle at himself.

"So tell me more about your talent," he said and turned to face her.

"My stupid human trick. It comes in really handy at my job," she said.

"Oh, what is it that you do?" he asked raising a

curious eyebrow.

"I am an insurance investigator, I try to disprove claims," she said factually.

"That sounds fun. You use your talent to help you *how*?" he asked.

"I have to question people when they file a claim. Then, if I get a feeling that they are lying, I change my questioning to trip them up," she said.

"That doesn't intimidate you, does it?" she asked.

"No," he replied, "I don't usually make a habit of telling lies."

Bree explained, "I only lie when I have to. You know, work, bill collectors, that kind of thing."

"I only lie about the size of my penis," he said and watched her for reaction.

She blew a little air into her cup as a shocked laugh erupted from her lips. She lifted the cup exaggeratedly from her and inspected her clothes for coffee spots.

Todd found himself drawn in by the tractor beam again but fought its pull this time.

"I like to say I have an unusually small penis. That eases the disappointment when I pull it out," he joked and smiled in satisfaction at her reaction to this.

She laughed loudly until tears rolled down her cheeks. After a moment, she regained her composure.

"At least I don't have to worry over whether or not you're conceited. Do you pull it out a lot?" she asked and looked serious.

"If it weren't for my high liquid intake, the poor little guy would sadly never see the light of day," he replied and tried to maintain a serious expression.

She seemed to be mulling over what he had said and then they burst into laughter together.

"That went really well," she said randomly.

"What did?" Todd asked as he tried to figure out what he had missed.

"I usually get brushed off if I mention the stupid human trick. You took it pretty well," she complemented.

Todd sat up in his seat stiffly and raised his nose high into the air.

"Like I always say; let he who is without psychological idiosyncrasy cast the first stone," he stated.

"So... What you're saying *is* that I'm a head case?" she asked.

Todd's rigid posture crumbled and a look of confusion came over his face.

"Oh nuh...*no* what I meant was....," he stammered.

"Just kidding, I know what you meant," she said and giggled.

"Good," he said, breathing a sigh of relief.

"So, how come you can't throw stones at me, if I may inquire?" she asked.

"I'm a head case too," he blurted.

They both laughed.

"No, I have been seeing a psychiatrist for the last year following a bit of emotional trauma that I suffered," he said slowly and watched her for a reaction.

"I started to have dreams and delusions about a woman stalking me," he continued.

"I even blamed this fictitious woman when I found my dog run over in the street in front of my house. The incident followed a dream where she had threatened his life," he said.

"Max," she said slowly.

Todd felt his whole body break out into chills upon hearing her mention his pet's name.

"That's cool!" he said.

"That's when I started seeing the psychiatrist and the dreams and delusions stopped," he finished.

"Dr. Larry," she muttered.

The nervousness and insecurity was audible in his voice as he said, "I could get used to you doing that."

"I'm sorry. I'm a little tired, it's hard to control," she said and looked at him with genuine sorrow in her eyes.

"No. No, I think it's really cool. So if you're not scared of me, I'm not scared of you, and we don't have to brush each other off," he said reassuringly.

"Would you tell me more? I am not repulsed, I'm intrigued," she inquired.

"What would you like to know?" he offered.

"I'm sorry about Max," she said sympathetically.

"Oh, he didn't die. I rushed him to the vet. They took him immediately into surgery and he managed to pull through," Todd explained quickly.

"So you still have him then?" she asked.

"No, I gave him to my friends before I moved to the city. They have a big yard for him and I didn't want to see him cooped up in my apartment all day and night," he said.

"So, he is alive and well and provides donkey rides for my godson now," he went on.

"Hah! That's cute. So tell me about the woman. I'm perversely curious, or tell me no if you need to," she said with empathy.

"It's okay. It's helpful to talk about it, and if our situations were reversed I would be morbidly curious too. I just kept having nightmares about her attacking me in my home and then a delusion of her being a police-woman," he said.

"Okay. I can tell when people are lying and as you relate this to me, you keep using the word 'delusions' but I'm getting a sense of realness when you talk about it," she said.

"Dr. Larry said, 'the mind believes these delusions to be real to compensate or protect from what's really bothering you.' At the time, I did believe it to be real," Todd explained.

"What happened in the dreams?" she asked.

"This woman...thing would wake me up by making noise in my house. I would search the house and find her. She would warn me about messing with her things and then begin to knock the crap out of me. I would wake up usually with a splitting headache," he said.

"I was creating her to abuse myself for procrastinating and being a slob. I subconsciously wanted neatness and order and that's how my mind lashed out," he said.

"So what about the waking delusion?" she asked.

"Are you sure you want to hear about this? You seem so cool and I don't want you to run away screaming. This part is overly creepy," he said.

"Todd, I wouldn't have given you my number if I

didn't have a good feeling about you. At this point the 'average guy' would be boring me to death, telling me about a college party. I'm very interested in you and would nearly beg to hear the rest of your story," she explained.

"Okay. We were at the college dorm and there was this *really* great party... just kidding," he chided.

"It started when I bought some homeless people's souls for a dollar each," he said.

He paused and inspected her face for any semblance of an incredulous look. What he saw in her face showed him that she anxiously waited for the rest of the story.

"Isn't that kind of cheap for a whole soul?" she asked.

"It's a buyer's market," he replied with a shrug.

"Well anyway, that's when the dreams started and then I found some Italian writing carved into my coffee table and I...," Todd broke off and made a quotation gesture with his fingers then said, "*Begin delusion,*" and continued.

"I called the police thinking that someone had broken into my house. When they arrived one of them looked kind of like the woman from my dream. She and her partner searched my house and concluded that I was currently alone. My shoddy housekeeping skills led them to believe that my house was broken into and ransacked. The Italian writing was not there in their presence. They told me I could get a copy of the police report and left," he paused.

"*End delusion sequence,*" he paused and made the quotation gesture again.

"My friend and I translated the writing that had magically reappeared on the table. Dr. Larry never came out and said it, but I believe he thinks I did it. When I went to get a copy of the report, I was informed that there was no record of a police visit to my home on that day. There were also no females on the police force," Todd took a deep breath as he remembered the embarrassment he had felt.

"So if it wasn't real, where did the writing on the coffee table come from? Do you know Italian?" she asked.

"No, I barely comprehend English, much less Italian," he replied.

"So, what did it say?" she asked persistently.

61

"To obtain souls, is to taste power, and deny my torment," he answered solemnly.

She huffed out air filling her cheeks before letting it go. Todd saw her brushing her arms and knew it was her turn to feel the chills of revelation.

"That is *so* freaky," she said.

"A few weeks later while I continued to suffer with the reoccurring nightmares, the thing happened with Max. I went to the shrink and a year later I'm all better," he said with an optimistic tone.

"But how could you have written that on the table if you don't know Italian?" she asked obviously still hung up on that piece of the story.

"I don't know. Dr. Larry said that I should not dwell on the how and the why, because it would cause me continue to validate the fantasy."

"Yeah, I guess," she said as she blinked rapidly and rubbed at her eyes.

"I have to go to work tomorrow at eight and it's nearly one A.M. I have to take you home now and drop you off so I can get some sleep. This will keep me from ripping the heads off of my co-workers and leaving them in a big bloody pile on my boss's desk," she warned.

Todd laughed out loud.

As they began to speed toward his house, he thought, "I guess a piece of booty is out of the question."

He jerked convulsively as he considered her ability to hear people's thoughts. He looked sheepishly at her; she had a huge smile on her face, but drove without looking at him.

"So, am I getting you breakfast tomorrow?" he asked her with an evil grin.

"What a seventies pickup line," she said.

"No. No, I meant at Don's," he replied incredulously.

"*Oh.* Maybe. Depends if my dad wants to eat there tomorrow, okay?" she replied sheepishly.

"All right then," he responded.

They arrived at his house. She looked at him and smiled.

"Thank you for this evening, I really had fun," he said.

"Me too. I know it's late but do you feel like having sex tonight?" she asked.

He was shocked. He looked at his feet, mustered his best suave expression and looked back up at her to speak.

"I would love to," he answered.

"Good, you go on and do it, and tell me how it was when I call you tomorrow night, *okay*?" she said and laughed at her joke.

"Okay," he guffawed.

"Talk to you tomorrow," she said pleased with herself.

He watched her drive away and felt the cool night air begin to strip away his warmth.

"It will be a miracle if she calls you again," he thought to himself.

He turned around and slipped his key into the lock, it turned with a metallic click and the door opened. Todd walked inside and hung his keys on the key rack just inside the door. He made his way into the kitchen and replenished the needed elements for his auto coffee pot. He entered the bathroom, took off his clothes, and deposited them into a hamper. He slid into his bed with thoughts of Bree playing through his mind. He hoped that she liked him and that he would hear from her again. Todd set the alarm on his cell phone and placed it neatly on the nightstand next to his bed. He hoped the combination of musical alarm, and annoying cell phone chirp would be enough to wake him for work. He smiled and sniffed his pillow and enjoyed the smell of the fabric softener as he fell deeply into sleep.

Chapter 7

A Penny For Your Thoughts

The alarm clock sang softly to Todd about laying him down on a bed of roses. He woke up slowly in stages. With one hand he rubbed at his eyes to alleviate his blurred vision. The other hand searched blindly for the clock radio's off switch. He sat up on the side of his bed and looked up out of the bedroom window. The sky was lightly orange; a few birds sat on the power lines and chirped mindlessly. He placed the backside of his hand against the window pane to test the outside temperature. The glass was extremely cold to the touch which caused him to recoil slightly.

"Feels like a jacket day. This will be a good day to wear that new leather coat," he said to himself.

The alarm on his cell phone began to screech. He reached toward it with his hand and swatted at it until the sound died away. The sweet smell of coffee drifted into his room. He tilted his head up and sniffed the air appreciatively.

Todd got up and began to shuffle toward the kitchen, nothing save the rich flavor of coffee could make him feel human again.

"Good morning," a random voice said.

Todd started, looked confused and then continued on.

"Good morning," the voice repeated.

Todd cowered instinctively and placed his hands out about himself defensively as he looked around the room.

"You're not gonna be able to see me. Pretty pointless trying," said the voice.

Todd dropped fully onto the floor. He looked under the bed, then scurried to the closet door and snatched it open. His neatly folded clothes offered no answers to the random questions that flowed through his mind. Todd had spent all of his bravery at this point. His heart pounded in his chest desperately.

He spun right, with his back flat to the wall in panic and looked into the bathroom. Again there was nobody there.

"I am in your head," the voice tried to sound soothing.

"Oh shit! *Oh shit!* I'm going crazy *again!*" Todd's thoughts assaulted him.

"No, you're not crazy now and have never been insane," said the voice.

"I died last night. There was a great bright light, then darkness. In the darkness I found your memories and began to read them like books. It was more akin to osmosis than a read-through of a book. Once I began, they poured into me. I have access to everything you have ever thought from here," said the voice.

Todd had large tears in his eyes and his lips trembled. His greatest fear of having gone insane was finally a reality.

"In life, my name was Bryce Hall. I want to convince you that you are not insane. Your reaction, while understandable, is unwarranted," Bryce said.

Todd slid down the wall and pulled himself into the fetal position.

"If you ran to Dr. Larry, 'The Quack', and tell him that you hear voices in your head, you are going to end up in a padded room. You will end up so medicated, that you won't know where you are. Then I am going to be imprisoned in your chemically befuddled thoughts. I would prefer to be able to interact with you," Bryce advised with a tone of clinical detachment.

"I guess," Todd's voice sounded very small and childlike.

"How did you end up inside my head?" Todd asked weakly.

"*I bet I can tell you where you got those shoes,*" Bryce said playfully.

Todd's mouth dropped open as he deeply inhaled a

gasp. His hands clawed into his scalp searching for sanity that seemed to be slipping away fast.

"The Contracts," Todd's voice escaped as a hoarse whisper.

He thought of that night in New Orleans. Todd could see the homeless man's face in his mind. The scene, of him buying the man's soul, played through his thoughts. Todd scrambled up and ran to his closet. He flung the doors open and spotted the box on the top shelf. Todd jumped up awkwardly and swiped at the box that was perched mostly out of reach. He tipped the box which spun and fell into his waiting grip.

The small box jostled around in his tremulous hands as he tried to hold onto it. He ran toward the bed and tripped as he went. Todd belly flopped onto the floor. The lid of the box popped off and the contents spilled out into a pile. He began to rifle through the contents with fumbling fingers until he found a wad of tickets bound together with a rubber band. The first ticket on top said:

I,_____Bryce Hall_____ hereby give my soul to Todd Jennings for the sum of one dollar. Terms of this contract are payable upon death.

Signed:_____*Bryce Hall*

Todd stared at the ticket wild eyed. His lips worked, soundlessly for a moment, to reread it in disbelief.

"That said John Smith...It said John Smith...I know it did," Todd's breath became heavier as he spoke.

Todd stared at the smiley face he had drawn onto the ticket. His chest heaved and his eyes watered as reality seemed to unravel.

"It said John Smith," Todd's voice weakened.

Bryce continued to speak but Todd was unable to pay attention.

As he became more self-aware, he realized that he was sweating profusely. His heart palpitated in his chest, and Todd could feel the cool currents of air that licked his skin.

66

His pulse began to rise and his balance began to fail. As Todd tried to lower himself to the floor, his vision faded into darkness. Todd fell to the floor limp and crumpled into a pile.

Todd started as he found himself slumped in a white lawn chair and began to look around.

"Where am I," he said aloud, unnerved by the reverberating tones his voice made in the darkness.

A brilliant light shown directly from overhead and cast its glow in a circle on the floor. Everything else was completely black. He looked around and saw a man who sat in a similar chair in front of him. The man had a sympathetic expression and his hands were in his lap pressed together in a prayer like fashion. The man wore small glasses low on the bridge of his nose.

He was neatly dressed in a white button up shirt with a bland paisley tie and khaki slacks. He reminded Todd of his math teacher from his sophomore year in high school. This man, like his teacher seemed, somehow out of place in a shirt and tie.

"I appear to you now the way I choose to be seen," Bryce explained.

"Where are we?" Todd asked the man seated in front of him.

A warm smile brushed over the man's face. He leaned forward extending his hand to Todd.

"I am Bryce Hall and I have taken up residence in your thoughts as a result of our '*Contract*'. You passed out, and in truth, it's probably for the best. This way we can have a face to face conversation...so to speak. I can feel your fear and doubt. I need you to try to listen and focus."

"This is a dream. I don't have to be afraid. I'm going to wake up in my bed and everything will be okay," Todd said and looked past Bryce skeptically.

"It's not really a dream, more like an altered consciousness," Bryce offered.

"Okay, so let's say this isn't a dream and that you're real. You just died and magically appeared in my head? A guy dies and mystically reappears in another guy's head, happens all the damn time. How the heck would you be so

67

calm?" Todd scoffed; his eyes fixed a cold stare upon the man opposite him.

"I am dead, Todd. What more can happen to me?" Bryce responded.

"Wow, this is pretty bland. I thought it would be a little more festive inside my head," Todd joked weakly and looked around at the environment again.

"It's on dual control at the moment. My plan was to promote simplicity so we could focus on each other. But, if you prefer we can be anywhere you have ever been or thought of," Bryce said as he made to stand and waved his arm in presentation.

The darkness around them began to slowly recede. Furniture and walls began to materialize out of thin air and took shape.

Todd was amazed as he took in the scene that formed in front of his eyes. Todd's disbelief and anger began to fracture to be replaced by nostalgia.

"... This is my old room at my foster home," Todd said and looked at posters on the wall of long haired rock bands.

Todd smiled as he looked down at an action figure. He picked it up, admired it, and placed it gently back in its familiar niche on the shelf. Todd waved his own hand and the scene melted into the two chairs and darkness again.

"Down to business then," Bryce said and sat back down in his seat.

"Let's say that this is possible. How would this happen?" Todd asked as he looked at Bryce.

"You made the rules, no matter what I signed, a deal is a deal," said Bryce.

"Is this for real?" Todd breathed the words heavily into his hands.

"It is as real as real can get. The concept of what is and is not real is no longer something that I can define. But, for the moment, it would appear we are fortunate captives of one another. Given what I have imagined the afterlife to be, this could be much less accommodating. Though I must admit, your run-in with that woman, demon, *thing* certainly would have more accurately fit what I had imagined," Bryce explained.

"How do you know that she is real?" Todd asked.

Bryce pointed sideways and a scene of an alleyway began to show itself like a reflection on darkened water. Todd marveled at the image that appeared and hovered in the void. He looked into it and saw an aged version of Bryce, as he was when Todd had met him in the French Quarter. The elderly Bryce slept in a pile of trash. Todd looked over at his companion in comparison.

"I was ripped from sleep when that thug dove onto me and stabbed me. I started to die and felt my body go cold and became tired. Just before everything went dark, that woman began to materialize behind him like a ghost. She whispered into his ear and he acted like a puppet with glazed eyes that followed her commands," Bryce explained.

Todd looked on in horror as the assailant lunged onto Bryce, stabbed him in the heart.

The attacker lowered himself and whispered, "*I am worthy,*" as he twisted the knife.

Todd saw the ghostly image of the woman attached to the killer's back like some sort of half ethereal parasite. Todd was terrified as he looked into her face and saw her from Bryce's point of view. It was the woman from his dreams. The look in her eyes was so purely evil and full of malice; it frightened Todd all the way to his core.

"It was not until I absorbed your memories that I recognized her. She seems to be limited to the form of a ghost-like puppeteer," Bryce said.

"Who is she?" squawked Todd.

"I never placed much stock in religion but she seemed to me to be as close to the Devil as I care to think about," Bryce said gravely.

Todd watched on as the man that leered over Bryce's body looked completely insane while he considered his kill. His attention then turned to a little girl that walked up behind him. She had witnessed Bryce's murder.

"Oh no. No!" Todd's eyes widened as the killer rounded on her.

The little girl tried to run as the insane killer dove on her. Her left leg broke and turned at an unnatural angle as the killer's superior weight landed on her. He hauled her head back and cut her throat cleanly. The killer tossed her body near a dumpster, and put a large piece of cardboard over her corpse. The image of Bryce's memory faded. Todd assumed this would have been the last vision the man's dying eyes had perceived.

"Either this ethereal woman is in no way tangible, or there are a set of rules somewhere we do not know about," said Bryce.

"So she's pissed about me buying souls. That would explain a lot," said Todd.

Todd rounded angrily on Bryce, "You're a freaking bum. How did you get so smart?"

"I was not born a bum. Earlier in my life I was a college professor with a PhD in Psychology. I had a wife, a big house, three cars, and all the money I could have ever wanted," Bryce answered solemnly.

"So what happened?" Todd asked feeling his distrust ebb away.

"I had an affair with a young student and it was made public. When my wife caught wind of this, she divorced me and took all of my money. I lost my job, began to drink, and ended up on the streets. I was quite insane by the time you happened upon me. For all intents and purposes, I am nothing but pure thought now. There are no chemicals or worldly concerns that affect my thoughts now. It was a little strange at first, but I feel very at home here in your thoughts. Do you feel a little better now? I know this is hard to accept but I think this could be a good circumstance for both of us. I can lend a different perspective to the way you think. I can also do a bit more, if a theory I have works. You can tune me out whenever you want," Bryce finished and smiled confidently at Todd.

"I guess it wouldn't be a problem. I feel sort of responsible for you. Can you feel what I feel?" Todd asked.

"No. Not in a conventional sense. I don't have a brain or a body. I am simply thought. I do not know at what level I am conscious, but I do share in your emotion. My only hope is that you will accept me. I have a deep fear of becoming nothing," Bryce said with a pleading tone.

"Then I accept you," Todd said.

Bryce gave a shark-like grin of approval. He leaned back in his chair and closed his hands together as if in prayer again and placed them to his lips.

"I am happy to exist at all. In life, I never knew this level of mental clarity. My thought is now unencumbered by outside stimulus. I can harness a thought and roll it, and look at it from thousands of sides at once. We now think with the power of two minds. So even while we converse, I am able to analyze thousands of thoughts at once. That assists me greatly in the theory I mentioned earlier," Bryce explained.

"Is there anything I can do to help?" Todd asked.

"Call out of work. Spend the day relaxing," Bryce advised.

"That won't pay the bills, and we will end up sleeping in an alley somewhere," Todd said.

"If I am correct, you will not have to worry about material concerns anymore," Bryce offered optimistically.

"You have an idea that will make enough money to support me in the manner to which I should become accustomed?" Todd asked, surprised by his own choice of words.

"Exactly that," Bryce began, "You will start to see that, with our minds shared, you will begin to be able to draw upon our collective knowledge. If I was nothing else in life, I was decidedly articulate. A silver tongued devil, if you will," Bryce finished.

Todd's eyes opened. He lay with the carpet sprawled out before him. His body ached as he stood up. He stretched and pulled himself up to his full height. His lower back and knees popped and sounded like twigs on a hot fire.

"I fainted like a woman," he thought.

"No, it was more like a little girl if you take into account the high pitched squeal you made as you lost consciousness," Bryce added.

Todd did call in sick and had Tony fill in for him at *Don's* for the day. Todd spent a long time immersed in activity on his laptop. A few times he stopped to take a sip of coffee and thought that it would be really nice to think he was not crazy after all. Todd let himself be consumed by a

71

game he played. He had all but forgotten about Bryce by that evening. When he heard the voice inside his head speak again, he jumped in his chair.

"I've got it! Todd, I've got it!" Bryce's excitement was obvious as he repeated himself.

"Good job," Todd congratulated, "what exactly have you got?"

"Let me offer you some background first," Bryce told Todd.

"All right. Shoot," Todd imparted his readiness to listen.

"I once wrote a paper about a patient that was diagnosed with dissociative identity disorder...," Bryce paused to allow Todd's question.

"Is that the multiple personality thing?" Todd asked.

"Exactly. Except this patient stood out in memory, most unanimously, I must admit. One personality was really timid and withdrawn, while the other was in sharp contrast, a homicidal genius. The unique attribute of the dark personality was that he could escape any kind of physical restraint placed on him. A staff member would come in to check on him. His absence from view through the monitor window in the door would cause them to enter. I'm sure you do not need the gory details as to what would happen next. It would suffice to say, he *belonged* in an institution. Anyway, I was allowed to interview him for a paper I did on focused mental projection. I had to have three muscular nurses aides accompany me. This patient could slip out of a locked straight jacket in an infinitesimal amount of time. During my interview, when I could get intelligible speech out of him, he told me that all he had to do was focus his thoughts on the restraints hard enough and he could just *will* them open," Bryce paused, having sensed Todd's curiosity.

"How did they keep him in there? Couldn't he open door locks and just walk out?" Todd asked.

"I asked him the same question. They kept him full of enough narcotics to tranquilize an elephant. According to him, the door locks were bigger, heavier, and more intricate, and that shut him down. The contents of this paper were largely based on interviews with a psychologically unstable

72

patient. I was dismayed that it was not taken more seriously. Throughout my professional career I followed, closely, all written material that was even remotely related to such subjects. Psycho kinesis is what I'm talking about," Bryce paused again.

"Didn't you say you could just project this into my mind earlier?" Todd asked.

"I had to reassess that idea. I think if I shoved this into your mind and you didn't fully comprehend it, or at least the basics, these alien concepts might do you mental harm. Like trying to breathe carbon dioxide," Bryce warned.

"So, you think together we can move stuff with our minds...?" Todd asked with a heavy tone of doubt.

Bryce ignored the question and returned to his explanation, "Psycho kinesis comes from the words psyche meaning life or soul. Kinesis is defined as movement or activity of a cell or organism in response to stimulus. Until now, I lacked the focus to actually move objects, but I believe I can augment or double your potential ability to do so."

"When can we try!?" asked Todd, excitedly.

"Right now, but you have to calm down a little. I can feel your excitement. I understand it but it will be counterproductive for you to be so riled up. You have to be able to be relaxed, focus on a singular object, and what you want it to do. There is something else I want you to understand before we try. This is not magic, there is no mysticism here. This is science and logic at work. For example, a penny is an inanimate object, meaning, it's destitute of life or spirit. There is no chance or probability that it will move unless acted upon by an animate force or energy. Thought is energy, the higher the focus or concentration, the more energy that is produced," Bryce explained.

"So by thinking about it hard enough, you affect or produce a probability that it will move?" Todd asked excitedly.

"Yes. Perfectly put. This is the first step. We'll practice on a penny; it is inanimate, small and light. Get a piece of paper and draw two small circles on it right next to each other," Bryce instructed.

Todd scrambled away from the chair and quickly returned with a pen and some paper. He drew the two small circles on the paper and produced a penny from his pocket.

"Okay, what now!?" Todd pressed.

"Put the penny in one of the drawn circles. Push the paper back away from you a little and place your hands at your sides. Now, the objective is to move the penny to the empty circle. You have to place it there with your mind. Think only of that, clear your mind of everything else," Bryce instructed, his words were almost hypnotic.

Todd placed the penny in the circle on the left then he placed his hands by his sides. Todd breathed in and out slowly. He had practiced relaxation with his therapist and found it easy to calm himself.

He stared at the penny and tried to will it to the other circle. Thirty-five minutes had passed and Todd's eyes had become itchy and red. He sat still and focused on the penny with every fiber of his being. His eyes strained in concentration as he looked on. The muscles in his jaw flexed as the hopelessness of this endeavor began to wash over him. He dropped both hands below the seat of the chair. He slapped at his own thigh angrily, cocked his head to the side, and exhaled hard from his nostrils.

"This isn't going to work," Todd said in an exhausted and angry tone.

"Just move the damn penny..., *waiter*," Bryce's tone was condescending.

Todd's face flushed red with anger and his hands clenched into fists. He pushed himself up in the chair. Todd raised his right hand and let his pointer finger flick up and reached for the penny. As the finger approached the penny, the coin slid to the right completely past the circle, at a blurred speed. The coin flew off the table and stuck into the wall. Todd stood up and gave chase as he followed the coin's path. Todd's jaw dropped in disbelief as he inspected the penny sized slot in the drywall.

"I... *We did it*!" Todd corrected himself quickly.

"Yes, we did. I am sorry about the '*waiter*' thing. I postulated that anger might give you a singular focus on the object," Bryce apologized.

"Don't worry about that. Look what we did! Bryce, can you see through my eyes?" Todd asked.

There was a short pause before he answered.

"Your eyes transfer images to your brain and so you see an image. I do not have eyes or a brain anymore, so what I do get are the thoughts that you have. That can be pretty vivid, not like actual sight, but the information is still there," Bryce explained.

"Oh," Todd sounded sad.

"Do not let it concern you. For a long time before last night, my mind was a jumble of diseased refuse. I had paranoid thoughts that people were after me for years. My days and nights were spent begging for money so I could purloin alcohol. Have you ever woken up from a nap on the ground at noon soaked in sweat, urine, and your own feces, with a hangover?" asked Bryce.

"No, and I never imagined that anybody else would either. That's a pretty rough picture," Todd confessed.

"Well, I held back the really grotesque details. This is a pleasurable release from my miserable life. Do not be doleful for my previous circumstances. Just know that I am grateful for this opportunity to share with you as long as it is possible," Bryce said appreciatively.

"Shall we try to do the penny thing again?" Todd asked.

"Yes, but with a little less passion this time. I bet you would like to get your security deposit back when you move from here. I am quite sure coins embedded into the drywall would be just cause for you to lose favor with your landlord," Bryce quipped.

Todd laughed and put another penny on the page. This time, he placed his hand about ten inches from the paper with his open palm to face the penny. The penny began to move back and forth. Its motion was slow at first but increased in velocity as it traveled. Todd raised his hand slowly up. The penny left the paper and remained ten inches from his hand and repeated the motion. Todd turned his hand over, the penny followed and floated above his open palm. The penny still swayed at a furious pace. Todd's brow lowered but his eyes remained fixed on the blur of motion that was the small copper coin.

The penny stopped and just floated in midair. Todd moved his hand away and stared at the penny just sitting there as if on an invisible pedestal. Todd held his open palm over the penny, and pressed it downward toward the coin. The penny began to lower at the same rate as his hand without coming into contact with it. He was unable to feel the intangible force that existed in the void between his hand and the object. The coin came to rest evenly on the table and Todd slowly pulled his hand back in amazement.

"Wow, isn't that *amazing*?" Todd asked.

"Very much so. Now, I have another concept to share with you," Bryce announced.

"Great!" Todd exclaimed with blind enthusiasm.

"We need to discuss the difference between animate and inanimate objects, in terms of weight. With an inanimate object there is no chance or probability that it will move unless acted upon by an animate force, or energy. Therefore, there is a definite possibility of an animate object moving on its own, either outright or at some level. So, as far as probabilities go, that 'dead' penny weighs more than, say, an elephant," Bryce paused and with a mischievous tone said, "...or a race horse."

Todd sat bolt upright in his chair. His expression was dramatic and dictated that he had reached some sort of epiphany.

"We could affect the probability of a horse race!?" Todd asked as piles of cash flashed through his mind.

"If the theory holds true, yes," Bryce agreed.

Todd's mind raced. He reached over, grabbed his laptop, and began to type furiously.

"I have nearly three thousand dollars in savings. Care to go to a horse race this evening, Bryce?" Todd asked.

"I think we should practice more and go tomorrow after you have had some rest," Bryce cautioned.

"You're right," Todd said as his shoulders dropped into a slump.

"By waiting and honing the ability we increase our chances for success. Rushing in half-cocked will successfully

76

increase our chance for failure," Bryce said with a warning tone.

"We don't have to mess with horse races. You could make millions writing fortune cookies," Todd said in a mocking tone.

Todd reached into his pocket and produced his cell phone. He dialed a number and then held the phone up to his head.

"Tony…Yeah, I feel a lot better. I wanted to ask you for another favor…Yeah, yeah, I want to take tomorrow off too. I'm gonna relax tomorrow and try to get myself right. Enjoy my tips, talk to you Monday…All right, Man. Bye," Todd said and hung up the phone.

Ten balled up pieces of paper spun like a cyclone above Todd's face as he lay still and watched them. He yawned and twitched his head slightly to one side. The paper balls flew into the waste basket next to his bed one at a time. He pulled the covers up to his chin, smiled and fell deeply asleep.

It had been a while since he woke up without an alarm. The red hue of the alarm clock offended his eyes but he braved the discomfort and read the time. It was eight thirty A.M. Todd rose slowly from the bed, stretched, and listened to his joints complain of wear. He patted his bed, thankful for the comfort it offered him when he rested. He started towards the kitchen and then he randomly thought of Bryce.

Panic gripped him and he asked, "Bryce, are you there?"

"Good morning, Todd," said Bryce.

"Great, I was afraid that yesterday was a dream," Todd said as relief washed over him.

"Perhaps a dream come true," Bryce commented.

Todd placed his hand out before him; open palmed, and cocked his head to one side. A porcelain coffee mug slid gingerly across the counter and came to rest next to the coffee pot.

"We still got it," Todd said and smiled happily.

"Actually Todd, I haven't helped since the first time you moved the penny yesterday," Bryce explained.

"So all the stuff I moved around last night was just me on my own?" Todd asked in a tone mixed with bewilderment and pride.

"Yes, I am astonished with not only, your skill, but, also the expedient progression of your capability. You and I together will be a force to be reckoned with. Look behind you," said Bryce.

Todd turned around and looked behind him slowly. The ten balls of papers he practiced with the night before spun ahead of him. He recoiled backward as one of the ten balls of paper broke ranks from a circular spinning pattern, and hit him in the head.

"We can work in tandem or individually if need be," Bryce explained.

"I need to tell you a couple of things. When we are out in public, concentrate on thinking thoughts to me and don't speak outright. You would look like one of those lunatics that talk to themselves. When you speak to young Miss Bree, we should maintain silence between us. Her talent will surely intercept parts of our conversation," Bryce warned.

"Oh man, she was supposed to call me last night," Todd's voice trailed away at the end. "I guess she thought I was a psycho," Todd said sadly.

"You give up way too easily, Todd. Where is your tenacity? In a manner of speaking, I have reviewed the tapes. I believe she will call you back," Bryce said.

"Well...I like her a lot... and she *is* very sexy," Todd remarked.

"Well, on to brighter subjects. Let us go win some money," Bryce said.

Todd practiced silent communication with Bryce. He withdrew all the money from his savings and drove straight to the race track.

Todd approached the bet counter, pulled a program from the rack and backed away to check out the choices.

"I have no experience here. I have never even been to a horse race, let alone bet on one," Todd said earnestly.

"We can learn together. Look for a horse that is not favored to win," Bryce instructed.

"Look for a column that shows the chances they have to win," said Bryce.

Todd's eyes found the favored to win column and traced to the bottom.

"*Bayjour's Hope* is ranked three to one on the list, but this program reads like Greek to me," Todd thought to Bryce.

"Let us try and make a bet on that one," Bryce suggested.

"How much do you think we should try to bet?" Todd questioned mentally.

"I guess twenty or thirty dollars, until we perfect our method," Bryce said.

Todd placed his bet at the counter. The attendant took his bet and looked at him like he was crazy. He had noticed Todd mouthing words soundlessly and making weird facial gestures. Todd found himself a good seat in the stands and settled into the uncomfortable molded plastic chair. The air was thick with the smell of horse manure and freshly cut grass. Todd surveyed the people around him and noted the excitement they exhibited.

"To some of these people the act of gambling holds as much sway as your enjoyment of cigarettes hold for you," Bryce offered.

Todd nodded, quickly caught himself, and tried to bob his head in time to overhead music.

He noticed a portly man who sat and stared at him over his shoulder. Todd waved to the man cheerily and enjoyed the way he snapped his attention forward.

The horses were led into their respective stalls. Todd edged up to the front of his chair as the start of the race drew near. His eyes narrowed as he tried to locate number eighteen. Todd spotted the horse that carried his thirty dollars on its back. There was a bugle call, and then what sounded like a gunshot. The gates opened and the horses bolted forward.

Todd's horse was dead last and it galloped along at half of the speed the other horses had achieved. Todd was dismayed as he watched it lag into the back of the pack.

"What should we do?" Todd asked Bryce mentally.

"Let's try to give him a little push," Bryce instructed.

Todd's eyes narrowed. The horse began to careen forward unevenly. Tragedy struck as it tripped and threw the jockey forward.

"This one is lost but we can use the rest of the horses to practice on. Let us try to hold back all but one horse," Bryce instructed.

"Yeah, I guess subtlety is required. We don't want to fill up the emergency room with horse jockeys," Todd said mournfully.

Todd excluded horse eleven but put reverse pressure on the rest of the pack. Number eleven began to pull forward. Several of the horses began to run in a serpentine fashion as though they tried to avoid unseen obstacles. Number eleven came in first with a narrow win. Todd stood up and walked hurriedly to place another bet.

This time he placed a bet of three hundred dollars on *Rerick's Prayer.* This horse, according to the program's odds column, did not actually have a prayer for a win. Todd visited the concession stand and returned to his chair. It was a considerable amount of time before the next race began. Todd sat in his chair and felt sweat form under his shirt as the sun beat down upon him. He tensed as the horses were led out onto the track. The bugle call was followed by another gunshot. The horses bolted from the line of stalls. Todd slid up to the front of his chair in a mix of concentration and excitement.

"Try to relax a little bit. Subtlety was never achieved through brutish impatience," Bryce warned.

"Right," Todd thought.

Todd regulated his breathing and concentrated. His head jerked once with a nervous tick as he applied reverse pressure on the horses. The other horses began to slow and lost ground as they made slight but erratic turns.

Todd's horse moved ahead slowly. The gap grew wider as the moments passed. Todd's horse won with a huge lead.

Todd punched his hand into the air, screamed "Yeah!" and then immediately looked around in embarrassment.

A few spectators seated near him grimaced at his display. Todd returned their scowls with a 'sucks to be you' smile. He took his ticket to the counter and patiently waited for the voucher for his winnings.

"There are two more races before noon. Bryce, shall we continue?" Todd questioned hopefully.

"I think it would be a good idea," Bryce replied.

By six P.M., Todd sat in his car and marveled at the huge clumps of cash in his lap.

"I can't even count this high!" Todd said excitedly.

Todd checked himself and looked around using his mirrors as paranoia stole over him.

"I am really sorry, Todd," Bryce said slowly.

"About what?" Todd asked with a sudden concerned tone.

"That we didn't have more money to bet today," Bryce's disembodied voice chided.

Todd laughed as he continued to shuffle through the money.

"Okay, let's go put a lot of this in the bank. The fact that I have had this kind of fortune, dictates that I need to be robbed for the universe to balance. We can keep the rest of the cash on us for when we come back to the track tomorrow," Todd thought with anticipation.

"That is not an intelligent plan. If you visit the same location frequently, you run the risk of being noticed. Being singled out or considered noteworthy is something that someone with your *talent* should be wary of. I have already felt your desire to tell someone about this. Let me take this moment to warn you of the negative side effects of overconfidence. On several occasions, during the course of my existence, my pride has gotten the better of me," Bryce cautioned.

"Yeah, good thinking," Todd replied mentally, a little disappointed.

Todd placed his money in a zippered bag that he kept in the car to hold his tip money. He stashed it under his seat and placed it meticulously so that his hand could find it every few minutes for reassurance. Todd backed slowly out

81

of the parking space and headed out of the lot. He stopped at an intersection for a red light. His window, over halfway down, made it easy for people close by, to hear him belt out pop music at the top of his lungs.

Todd's powerful high-pitched rendition, touting how he was saving all of his love for someone, had drawn the attention of people nearby. Todd looked over at the car that waited next to him. The man in the passenger seat convulsed with laughter and had lost the ability to make sound. The driver of the car also laughed hysterically and pointed at Todd like a baby that had seen something fascinating. Todd slumped down in his seat as he felt his cheeks flush.

He gave a quick look up at the light and tried to stave off the embarrassment. He looked over to the sidewalk to see if there was a larger audience. A woman sat with her back against the bricks of a building with an infant swaddled in her arms. Her eyes were full of tears but Todd seriously doubted if there was any humor involved.

He pulled his car over and got out, driven to interact with her. As he approached, he saw that her clothes were old, and tattered. The child in her arms coughed. Todd winced. The child's cough was full of a congested rattle.

The woman looked up from her child to him, her eyes still filled with tears. Todd removed his hand from his pocket and handed the woman a large clump of hundred dollar bills. The woman stared at him in disbelief. She reached up slowly and took the money timidly and never broke eye contact with Todd.

"Thank you," she said and looked at him distrustfully.

"You're very welcome. I hope it helps," Todd said with a genuine smile.

Todd turned on his heel and headed back to the car.

"Todd, that was a very illuminating display," Bryce said.

"Thank you. That just felt right. I just wanted to share the good fortune," Todd proudly thought to Bryce.

"It is very likely that you will never see her again. There is no chance of being repaid. No chance for greedy intentions to come to fruition. In that, it is one of the best

82

representations of kindness that I have ever witnessed...Disgusting," Bryce said curtly.

Todd mulled Bryce's statement over for a second before he decided that it must be humorous in its sarcasm. He belted out a quick laugh as he dropped into the seat of his car.

Todd went home after he had deposited nearly twenty-thousand dollars into his checking account.

He patted the ten thousand dollars in his pocket and thought, "This is for the track tomorrow. Oh wait, we need to hold off a few days."

Todd hung his keys on a rack just inside the door. He walked over to his chair a plopped down comfortably.

"Bryce, this is so *great*. I have all this money, more than I could have made in a year as a waiter. I am not even remotely tired or stressed out," Todd rambled on happily.

Chapter 8

Magic In Action

Todd was restless that evening as he continued to replay the events of the day. His mind was an abstract maelstrom of ideas that would garner money through use of his new found abilities.

"You made more money today than you did in all of last year, Todd. Your intentions to gather a large quantity of money would be considered to be greed by most standards. Would it not be enough to just live for a while on what you have?" Bryce asked in Todd's mind.

"I just want to get a really large amount together. I can relax when my financial holdings have reached a substantial quantity. I call it insurance, not greed. What if I, we, lose these abilities? I would have to go back to the waiter job...," the phone rang and interrupted Todd's train of thought.

"Hello?" Todd asked.

"How's your boyfriend?" Bree asked playfully.

"He has a butt ache and hasn't gotten out of bed all day," Todd retorted sharply.

Bree laughed explosively.

"I'm sorry I didn't call you back the other night. I was tired and near death from no sleep. Dad and I went to *Don's* this morning for breakfast. Tony told me that you were sick and had missed the last two days," Bree explained with a tone of concern.

"Herpes flair up," Todd's voice was emotionless and denounced sincerity.

There was a moment of silence then he heard Bree break into a fit of hysterical laughter. Her laugh was so explosive that as she tried to control it, she snorted loudly. This caused her to laugh harder and Todd joined in.

"Now you have earned a date," Bree said as she caught her breath.

"You're just sucking up because you forgot to call me," Todd said.

"Nuh uh, I don't do oral on the first date," Bree responded sharply.

"Damn! Then I can't demonstrate my cunning lingual skills to you," Todd remarked.

"I'm set to go whenever you are," Todd said.

"Well, come outside and get in the car, slow poke. I have a special place to show you," Bree explained.

"Wow. That's riddled with sexual innuendo. Your special place, huh? See you in a sec," Todd said, he thought he heard her call him an ass before the phone disconnected, but couldn't be sure.

"Okay, Todd. I am going to go blank until you call for me. I don't want to complicate your new relationship," Bryce said.

"Relationship. Yeah...Thanks, Bryce, for everything," Todd said thoughtfully.

He grabbed his keys and bolted outside. He immediately saw Bree's car and jumped in. She sat and smiled at him from the driver's seat of the car. She concentrated for a moment and looked into his eyes seriously.

"I saw a guy cut somebody off in traffic over there. I was calling him an ass. It wasn't directed at you at all," she said apologetically.

"What?" Todd asked bewildered.

"I wasn't calling you an ass on the phone. I picked that up from you...Sorry. Anyway, I wanted to tell you something, but I was afraid I would sound like a stalker," she said sheepishly.

"Just tell me and I will tell you if it sounds bad," he replied.

"I have thought of you constantly since the other night. I could hardly wait to talk to you today. I wanted to wait until this evening in case you were resting as a result of being sick," she confided cautiously.

Todd looked at her, lowered his eyebrows, then

85

turned and began to leave the car. He climbed halfway out of the car and looked back at her for reaction.

"Just kidding," he said, plopped down, and closed the car door again.

With a wide smile she said, "*Ass*," emphasizing that she was referring to him.

"I missed you too. I was scared that you had gotten freaked out by my little story and had decided not to talk to me anymore," he replied seriously.

"Sexy, witty, and riddled with feelings of inadequacy. Will you marry me?" she asked as she mocked a pleading expression.

"Not until we have had sex a few times. If you can get past my *short comings*, I will consider your offer," Todd joked.

"I'm sure the *little things* won't cause us a problem," she retorted.

Bree stopped at the coffee shop. Todd went in to get them some coffee. He returned quickly to the door of the coffee shop. Bree thought for a moment that she had witnessed him balancing the coffee cup holder on one finger. Todd climbed into the car and held the coffee perfectly upright. She watched as he adjusted for bounces and noted his unseemly grace. He sat down fully in the seat, obviously pleased with himself, and offered her a cup.

"Thank you," she said smiling at him.

"Guess what I did today?" he asked as he closed the door.

"A horse race?" she responded questioningly.

"Yup, and...,"Todd started to say.

"You won a crap load of money," she finished his sentence.

"How much?" she asked.

"I don't really know, but I don't have to work for a while," he said proudly.

They pulled up next to a large brick building. The fire escapes overhead were in disrepair. They looked rickety to Todd and added to the slum-like ambiance of the neighborhood. Pieces of tattered newspaper hung through the old rungs of the pull down ladders. Todd noted brightly colored, intricate graffiti on the adjacent buildings. Some of the paintings showed real talent if you didn't discount them for the use of explicit four letter words.

"Talk about the wrong side of the tracks," Todd thought to himself.

Bree giggled and said, "My dad owns this building."

Todd looked down toward his feet in embarrassment.

"It's okay. This whole neighborhood has gotten pretty run down over the years. How do you not know how much you won at the horse races?" she asked, randomly, as they both got out of the car.

"I hadn't counted it all before I gave some away," he answered.

"Homeless woman. Sick kid," she said as she absently placed her fingers to her temples and grimaced.

"Yes. She looked as though she needed some cash... Are you okay?" he asked with concern.

"I'm fine. It was just...a really long day at work. Did you get a contract?" she asked and flashed him a toothy grin.

Todd staggered a little as his eyes widened. He looked down as though he would find an answer in the litter strewn sidewalk.

Bree rummaged in her purse for her keys. As she unlocked the door she turned over her shoulder and asked, "Who is Bryce?"

Todd's silence drew her gaze upon him. Todd's face went ashen gray as he followed her through the opened door. It was obvious that he purposely avoided her gaze. He seemed to struggle mentally for a moment.

She turned from him and proceeded up the stairs.

"I want to tell you... And I will... But please, *please* understand that I can't right now," he implored her.

"That's okay," she said looking back at him and jutted out her bottom lip.

He followed her up, what seemed like endless stairs.

"Damn! She is sexy and that little pout lip thing gives me wood," he thought.

"Thanks," she said with an unseen smile audible in

87

her tone.

Todd's cheeks reddened with chagrin.

"Where are we going?" he asked as he looked down the stairwell and appraised the expanse of stairs already climbed.

"To the roof, it's not much farther now. You're probably weak 'cause of the loss of blood pressure," she said and playfully jutted out her bottom lip again.

"Stop that before you make me pole vault and fall," he replied as the red hue of his face deepened.

She laughed again as she turned the rusty knob on the large metal door. It creaked open and sounded as though it were rigged to squeak like a prop door in a horror movie. Cool wind washed over them as they emerged onto the roof of the building. She walked over and plopped down on top of a large metal air conditioner cover. She looked to him and patted the flat area next to her. He realized this to be an invitation and walked to join her where she sat. He found himself taken aback by her beauty. Her blonde hair flowed as the wind ran through it. She tried to hide the appreciative smile that spread across her lips as she reached up to brush her hair back. He sat down next to her and looked out at the view.

"Impressive," he said as he looked out over the vast expanse of lights in the distance.

"I like to come up here by myself sometimes to think. I have moments that drive me to solitude. I start to get this flood of mental crap and I can't turn it off. So, I come get some quiet time here until I can feel better," she said.

"What causes it to happen? You seem to have so much control," he asked.

"Usually when I'm tired it gets out of hand," she explained.

"That must be hard to deal with," Todd said sympathetically.

"It's not so bad. I just like to get away from it sometimes...To feel normal for a little while," Bree said.

"Well you could just always surround yourself with very abnormal people like *me*. Then you could be the most normal one in the bunch," Todd said.

Bree laughed at him and shook her head dismissively.

"Do you have to work tomorrow?" she asked.

"Nope. I have the next three days off in a row.

I don't know if I'm gonna go back to *Don's* at all. I need to think about it, it's a big decision. I have always been a waiter," he said thoughtfully.

"You're thinking of becoming a professional gambler because you had *one* good day at the track?" she asked with a concerned tone.

"Yeah. That does sound pretty bad, doesn't it?" he replied.

Todd placed his hand to his mouth, folded his other arm across his chest and looked down in concentration.

"Tell me what?" she asked.

Todd, who had been lost in deep thought, jerked his attention back to Bree.

"What?" he asked absently.

"You thought, 'I wonder if I should tell her.' Tell me what?" she asked as she snapped her fingers to entice him to focus on *her*.

Todd put his hands in his pockets and looked out over the view.

"I wonder if I should," he thought again.

Bree watched him with a very open expression.

"I would if I were you," Bryce's disembodied voice replied.

Bree stood up abruptly and looked around.

"Did you hear that?" she asked exasperatedly.

"Yes I did. You just read my thoughts. That's all," Todd explained sympathetically.

"No. I actually heard someone else speak," Bree retorted and looked around the rooftop.

"Say hello, Bryce," Todd called aloud to no one Bree could see.

Bree plopped down and opened her mouth but before her question could be uttered she heard the voice again.

"Hello, Bree. Pleased to make your acquaintance," Bryce said courteously.

89

Bree's hands quivered a few inches from her face. She fanned air into her face and tried to avoid an overspill of the water that rimmed the bottom of her eyes. Todd reached over to put his hand on her shoulder to comfort her. She recoiled violently as she tried to assimilate the alien concept that bombarded her.

"What's happening?" she asked as her voice cracked.

"I need to tell you what has happened to me. Or at least as much of it as I understand," Todd started to explain.

Bree looked at him again; her composure seemed to return slowly.

"This Bryce person is in your head?" she asked with an incredulous tone.

"Yes," he answered and waited for her next question.

"How? How is that possible?" she asked.

"When we were at *Don's* that morning and I was working on your bill, do you remember writing the name John Smith on that napkin?" he asked.

"Yes," Bree answered quickly.

"At the point when you got that, I was in the process of drawing a smiley face on the bottom of a ticket. The last time that I made a smiley face, was on the bottom of the first contract I wrote. This person signed 'John Smith' to the contract I made on the back of my waiter's ticket. That's why I had to excuse myself from your table so abruptly. I became violently ill from the recollection of the whole scenario. After our date the other night, when I woke up the next morning, there was a voice in my head. He introduced himself as 'Bryce Hall'. He used a phrase that this 'John Smith' used when I supposedly bought his soul."

Bree interrupted, "I bet I can tell you where you got those shoes," her expression was that of awe as she put the pieces together mentally.

"Yes...that's the one. I went to the ticket and the name had changed to 'Bryce Hall'. I still have no explanation for that. It was the only ticket with a smiley face on it. I should have thrown them away while I was in therapy, but I couldn't part with them. I felt a huge thrust to do just that at

90

times. I meant to destroy them at several points. My therapist advised that they simply represented a fond memory of time spent with close friends. It was his suggestion to keep them that insured that they survived. For the last two days I have been in mental communication with Bryce. He is part of me now," Todd paused.

"How is that possible? *Part* of you? How could you accept another person into your mind?" she asked questions as randomly as they came to her.

Todd was pleased as he heard strength return to her voice.

"I am as new to this as you are. I don't know how or why it worked, it just did. The yields of mutual discussions, between Bryce and I, have also allowed me to conclude that I was never out of my mind. I have always been afraid to lose myself or my individual thought. Even the concept terrifies me.

From the start, he has helped me. For that reason alone, I would be afraid to lose his voice. When you factor in how consistently I have been alone in my life, it makes sense for me to want to have someone to talk to. I was an orphan. Both of my foster parents are dead. I moved as far from my roots as my limited amount of money would allow. You are the first person in a very long time to even take any real notice of me. When you consider the other aspects of coexisting with this entity...Bryce," Todd corrected himself courteously, "in my head, it just reinforces how easy it is to accept him. I wanted to tell you all of this when I first saw you this evening. I figured, even if you ran away from me in fear, well...at least I was honest. There is more, but I don't want to waste time if this is fall..."

Bree interrupted, "Falling on deaf ears," she said.

"Yes," he responded.

"It's not by any means, I want to believe you, it's just so...," her voice trailed off.

"Crazy?" he offered.

"*No*. Not crazy. I have this need to hang onto reality. This power or talent you have, does not fit anywhere into a realm that could be called *normal*. I couldn't begin to come up with a way to explain it. The damnedest thing is,

91

you believe yourself to be truthful! And every sense I have tells me that you are."

"There is more that I want you to see," Todd said slowly.

His green eyes danced in the faint glow of the cities lights as she stared at him. He thrust his hand out in her direction. Her eyebrow's raised with curiosity. Her keys slid up and out of her purse as if they were on a string. The assortment of keys and miscellaneous key chains floated in front of her face.

"If you don't believe me, you could always...walk away," he said with a smile.

She raised her hands to her mouth in disbelief as she stared at the car keys that dangled before her.

"How are you doing that?" she asked as her hands, shaking, grasped the keys and stuffed them back into her purse.

"It's one of the perks if you own a soul. There is also a nice gift bag with soaps and lotions," Todd quipped. "Seriously though, if Bryce's theory is correct, we all have the potential ability to do it. When we both focus, it's effortless," he explained in earnest.

She reached out to him slowly as though he might turn into a wisp of smoke and disappear. He took her hand and placed it against his chest, moving in closer to her.

"It's fantastic and crazy...But it's happening and I am enjoying it," Todd spoke softly.

"What's going on in your head?" he asked and added, "I don't read minds."

"I have a million abstract questions in my head. I have to believe you. The power to move things, I wouldn't call that a talent, it's an ability. And isn't it an invasion of privacy to have another person inside your head?" she asked.

"You would think that I might feel that way. He is able to read my whole life through collected thoughts in my head. He knows every trivial or freaky thought that I have ever had. I could never have told another person all that he has gleaned. He knows more than I can consciously remember. I have no information left to hide from him. There is no reason for privacy in such an honest environment."

"If, for your entire life, the society that you lived in was devoid of prejudice, guilt, or any feelings of inadequacy, there would never be a need to hide anything. That is why it's so easy to share my mind. In fact, I believe I'm able to relay this to you based on articulated knowledge provided by him," Todd explained in length.

"That makes sense. I only got pieces of that prior to you saying it," she replied.

"Today we used that ability to affect the outcome of horse races. It's no more fantastic than the gift you have," Todd said in earnest.

"That's a matter of opinion. I can't control my surroundings. I just get tidbits and a built in lie detector. I am glad for you and I can accept what you're telling me. I don't consider myself to be a cynical person; it's really not possible with my talent. It makes things very easy. A person is either a malicious liar or they aren't. So I only surround myself with truthful people. I still have to say I would be on guard to some degree. Few good things in life come without a huge price tag," she warned.

"Mature advice," Bryce's voice commented between them.

A short silence passed between Todd and Bree. Todd reveled in the moment. He had been honest and it seemed to have paid off.

"What about the woman from your dreams?" she asked.

"I don't have answers to that yet. Bryce's murder was, in a way, her doing. He said that she was there and, somehow, controlled the guy that killed him. It seems as though she had to act through another person. Bryce recognized her from my memories and brought it to my attention," he explained.

"Oh that's *horrible*!" she said disgustedly.

"I have to accept that she is real on some level. What she did to Bryce is real, not some delusion. This woman...thing's involvement represents a problem on a scale that is way above my ability to deal with. If it weren't for her being after me and having Bryce killed, this could have been a really cool experience. With the exception of you looking at me like I was a monster shortly ago," Todd said as he looked at her dejectedly.

"I am sorry. It's just a lot to take in so quickly. When we came up here, I knew we would have a meaningful conversation but I didn't plan on anything like this. Is there anything else you can do with your mind?" she asked curiously.

"I am not aware of any additional abilities at this time. But if you came to me a week ago and told me I could move objects with my mind, I would tell you that you were crazy. This challenges what I considered impossible, prior to this whole thing," he answered.

"So, what about Bryce? I don't mean this in a negative way, but it's kind of farfetched that a homeless person could provide you with these abilities or the concept for them. How would you explain that?" she asked.

"I had the same questions. The facts are, he was a professor of Psychology in life. Psycho kinesis was a driving curiosity for him. A sad turn of events eventually led to him being a homeless man. In his own words, the state that he is in now allows him to complete thoughts without worldly limitations. It was because of the environment that we share, that he was able to complete the thought finally. We tried to apply it and it worked...somehow," Todd explained.

"Inside your head is to him like up here on this rooftop is to me?" she rationalized.

"Exactly that," he replied.

"When you talk to him, do you hear his voice in your head?" she asked as she poked herself comically in the temple with her finger.

"Yes, as if someone were to speak directly into my ear," he answered mocking her mannerism.

"Maybe that's why I can hear him when he talks to you. I'm sorry for the random questions; they seem to flow into my mind. In my tiny world I have always found a way to try and explain supernatural or surreal occurrences. But, I can't even explain my own talent. Because of the security it offers me, I just look past the weirdness of it. *This* whole thing that you're going through, just defies reality as *I* know

94

it," Bree explained.

She reached into her purse and removed a package of cigarettes. She opened the pack, removed one, and placed it between her lips.

She looked up at him abruptly and said, "Well, if you've quit, there's no reason to ask...unless you want one."

A cigarette flew out of the pack and into his hand. She stared at it as he placed it between his lips. The wind proof lighter floated up from the bag and struck. She recoiled from the flame. She edged forward and tentatively lit her cigarette. Todd watched her as she marveled at the lighter that defied gravity. The lighter drifted gracefully over to Todd. It hovered at the end of the cigarette Todd held between his lips. He cocked his head to the side and lit his cigarette. He was careful to avoid the flame as it danced in the wind. The metal lid of the lighter shut with a click and snuffed out the sizable flame. It floated down precisely into her purse, replaced in the exact spot it was procured from.

Todd recoiled after taking a deep puff of the cigarette. The ashy taste seemed to permeate his mouth. He coughed and dropped it. He stepped on it angrily and twisted his shoe to extinguish it.

"That tops the suave scale, I have to tell you," she said tossing him a small minty piece of candy from her purse.

"You have no idea how enjoyable it is to do it in front of you," Todd said.

"What? Choke on a cigarette and stomp on it?" she chided.

"To be able to demonstrate the ability to move things. I thought about it all day. I watched people scream for their horses and spit chunks of food all over themselves. They were so absorbed in themselves that they took no notice of me. What if they could see me do something special though? It's not as though I want to be a rock star or anything, but a polite smile or some small amount of recognition would be nice. I realize I have to keep it a secret unless it's someone I trust," Todd said as he crunched the mint candy between his teeth and swallowed it.

"Thank you, it's nice to be trusted. You are a special

person though. Perhaps you should find a way to be more open to people so they have a chance to see that. You said that I was the first person who noticed you in a while. I'm kind of aggressive and I have an inside track on people's thoughts. The average person might look at you as defensive or guarded. While they do notice you, you might not seem approachable to them," she said with a warm smile.

"Should I lie down on a couch before you go on?" Todd asked jokingly.

"It would be fun to be a psychologist. The insurance gig is kind of a bore," she said and laughed.

Todd joined her in her laughter and tried not to think of how beautiful she was.

She blushed and changed the subject, "Are you sure there isn't anything else you can do that I should be aware of? You can't find the socks I lose in the laundry all the time, can you?" she asked playfully.

"I slowed down a whole pack of horses today and I have moved all the furniture and major appliances in my house. I'm not at a level that would allow me to pick up cars and throw them just yet. And the mystery of lost socks is surely an advanced ability reserved for the privileged," he said.

"That's okay. I realize you have to have limits," she chided.

Todd looked over at her with a mischievous grin and began to levitate her. She was still in the sitting position but floated a few inches above the air conditioning cover. She could feel the invisible force as it cradled her. It seemed to adjust to every shift of her weight to maintain her balance. Todd lowered her slowly.

"That could save your back on the wedding night!" she said with an amazed look.

"Are you asking me to marry you again?" he asked.

"Not until we have had sex a few times. Just to be sure we don't have any *minor* problems," she smirked at him.

"Well, I'm sure we won't have the *tiniest* problem," he said.

"So, tell me more about you," he said as he tried to regain a normal conversation.

She laughed again.

"I'm surprised you didn't ask about the weather. What do you want to know?" she asked quickly.

"What do you look for in a man, so I can change?" he asked.

"I'm looking for a man who knows how to treat a lady in public and is equally skilled in the transverse. And I have always wanted a man that could surprise me," she said.

"'In the transverse, what a great way to escape the use of vulgarity," Todd said with a smirk.

"So, what are you looking for in a woman Mr. Smarty Pants? It's a rough question," she said and flourished her hand at him.

"I am looking for a woman that will make my heart melt every time I wake up and caress her soft skin. Did that sound good? I was trying to be cool like you," he asked sarcastically.

"At first I wanted to say, I wanted a woman like a dessert. Smooth, creamy and sweet to eat. But, I had to make it sound a little better 'in the transverse'," he said.

She grimaced at him and said, "Yeah-yeah, get it all out of your system."

"Actually, I want a woman that I can live in a perfect environment of trust and honesty with. I want to be able to share my experiences with her and get her input. I want to feel the closeness and warmth that we radiate together," he said honestly.

"You don't have to get all effeminate to impress me," she said.

Todd was stunned into silence.

"I'm just kidding. That was beautiful, the best answer I could have imagined actually," she said truthfully.

Todd exhaled a relieved breath. A high pitch giggle wrestled itself free from him. He covered his mouth and looked embarrassed.

"I also require that my man be a great kisser," she said playfully.

"When are you holding auditions? I have practiced on the inside of my elbow for a few years now. I think I might have gotten really good except for that whole drool issue," he said.

She reached out and grabbed a handful of his shirt and pulled him in closer. He might have gotten off another joke if not for the fact that their lips met, smoothly. Her tongue slid softly into his mouth and their kiss was deep and passionate. They kissed for a long time then slid slowly apart. Bree pulled her bottom lip into her mouth seductively with her teeth and looked at him. Todd tasted his lips and opened his eyes to meet her gaze.

"That was really, really good for a student of *The Elbow School Of Kissing*," she said playfully.

Todd smiled his approval as he enjoyed the left handed compliment.

"Wanna play a game?" she asked.

"Yeah a few great ideas come to mind, but what were you suggesting?" he asked.

She closed her jacket under her folded arms and closed her eyes.

"What color are my eyes?" she asked.

"Blue, a light shade, any slight loss of color and they would be gray," he answered.

"Good answer. What size are my breasts?" she asked.

"36 C, you wear bras that have no under wire and the straps don't cut into your shoulders. Your breasts don't sag at all so that means they are incredibly firm. You also get dressed in a hurry," he finished.

"Right. But how did you know I got dressed in a hurry?" she asked.

"You have a triple hook on the back, one was left undone," he answered and looked assured of himself.

"And what was the first word I ever said to you?" she asked.

"Good," he replied quickly.

"Good? Are you sure?" she asked.

"Yes, you said good morning just before I offered you a drink," Todd replied.

"Very nice. I like a guy who pays attention to me too," she said.

"Now let's play another game," she said, her voice

was now very seductive.

Todd became very aroused by the sheer sensuality she exuded.

"This is the pick-up line game, it's my favorite. Are you ready? A pause makes you lose points and this game is very important," she said, the words pouring from her soft lips like nectar to Todd.

"Yes, I am," he said confidently.

"I will start and you need to keep up. Quickly answer with a pickup line of equal or greater value," she said.

"Hey baby, you want to come to my house and work on your math skills? We add the bed, subtract the clothes, divide the legs and multiply!" she said.

"You look flustered, you should lay down on me," he responded without delay.

"Picture it: you, me, a twister board, malt liquor and baby oil," she said.

"A penny for your thoughts or fifty bucks to act them out," he responded.

"If you think you're gonna regret this in the morning, we can sleep till noon," her response was immediate.

"Do you know the essential difference between sex and conversation?" he asked her.

"No," she answered.

"Good, you wanna go back to my place and talk?" he asked.

"Yes...I do," she answered, her voice sounded more lustful now.

She pulled him to her and kissed him deeply.

"Let's go to my place. It's closer," she said breathlessly.

Todd awoke the next morning to the light that shone in through Bree's window. Bree inhaled deeply and rubbed her cheek against his chest.

"Good morning," she said softly to him.

"Good morning," he replied with a huge smile.

"Did you sleep well?"

"Oh yeah, I feel like a million bucks."

"Have you been awake long?"

"No, just a few minutes," she replied.

"I want to go to the track for a little while."

"Can I come with you?" she asked.

"Sure, I would like that."

"Cool, I can see your magic in action."

"You've already seen my magic in action," he replied and fought the urge to laugh at his own joke.

She laughed and left the bed headed for the bathroom.

Bryce waited until Bree had left the room before he reissued the warning that a return trip to the horse races would be inadvisable. Todd distractedly dismissed the warning as he stood watching Bree's shadow through the curtain. She gasped as he tore open the curtain and hopped into the shower with her.

Todd and Bree spent the day betting on and watching horse races. Bree had begun to make bets with her own money after Todd showed her how deft he had become at controlling the outcomes. They left the track at around five p.m. with a little under forty thousand dollars. They sat in the car together with hundred dollar bills spread all over their laps. Todd noticed sadness in Bree's face as he looked over at her.

"Everything okay? You just won a lot of money and you look like you lost a relative," he questioned her compassionately.

"I'm trying to shake that dishonest feeling. I just won this money on a rigged game of chance it feels like stealing. What are you going to do with all this money?" she asked to change the subject.

"I thought about going on a working vacation," he replied.

"You're marked at this track, huh?" she said.

"Yeah, they were watching us since about noon. I should have taken Bryce's advice," he replied.

"We need to figure out a way to make big money without being so noticeable," Bryce spoke for the first time since that morning.

"It looks like you won the lottery already," Bree

said as she rummaged through all the cash on her lap.

A big grin spread slowly across Todd's face.

"We could play the lottery," Bryce and Todd thought in unison.

Bree smiled and said, "I helped! I helped!" as she clapped her hands.

Todd looked at her approvingly and smiled.

"The lottery drawing is live on television tonight," Bree announced.

They stopped on the way to Todd's apartment and purchased a lottery ticket. After arriving at Todd's apartment they piled up on the couch and watched television until the lottery came on. Todd had moved to the edge of the couch and was fanning his hands to loosen up. Todd and Bryce focused all of their mental energy together to influence the outcome. Bree announced the numbers one by one. Each number was given randomly from small plastic balls that fell from fan forced air currents. To their dismay, none of them matched the ticket Bree held.

"We missed all five of the numbers," Todd reported as he stared over at the ticket glumly.

"I wonder what the difficulty is. I can only suppose we are inadequate to influence probabilities over great distances," Bryce offered.

"Or..." Bree piped in, "Maybe, even though it claims to be live, there might be a bit of delay."

"That could be it," Todd agreed.

"We should plan to attend the next live drawing," Bryce interjected.

Todd opened his mouth to speak and jerked violently. He appeared to be having a seizure. His body stretched out in length and bowed backward in an arc of pain. His hands clawed into the carpet and his muscles tightened. Bree rushed over to him.

Bree jerked as though she were being electrocuted as her hand made contact with Todd's arm. She staggered away from him and fell to the floor. He fought fiercely against a stress induced blackout that tried to pull him down into darkness.

Todd denied the atrophy of his muscles, as they

101

jerked and cramped, to turn his head in the direction that Bree had fallen. His vision had become so blurry that he could barely make her out.

Todd could see a fuzzy image that looked like two men approaching him. One wore a black jacket that may have said something like Devrote in large yellow letters across the chest. His vision alternated between slightly out of focus and complete abstraction. The other figure looked to be enshrouded in a hooded dark purple robe like a monk. The images seemed to flicker in and out of view before his eyes again.

Todd had somehow mentally detached himself from the pain that coursed through his body. His mind seemed to push away all other thoughts, and he questioned why these men would be here. His body had begun to convulse spasmodically. The pain reclaimed him and all thought was reduced to a mental blankness. The black shadows seemed to wrap themselves over his eyes. The tendrils of darkness widened and the light had become a fleeting commodity.

Todd shrieked. His body felt as though it were tearing itself apart. The sound of his own screams faded into nothingness.

Chapter 9

The Alibi

Todd slowly returned to consciousness and looked across the landscape of carpet in front of him. His eyes struggled to focus and thoughts of Bree's safety occurred to him. Just ahead of a chair, Bree lay crumpled on the floor, her nose underlined with dried blood.

Todd struggled to get his arms underneath himself. After an intense feat of self-motivation, he managed, through sheer force of will, to move toward her. He crawled weakly over to where she lay. He placed his hand upon Bree's shoulder, and softly shook her.

"Unnngh," she moaned unintelligibly.

She rolled over onto her back and stared at the light fixture on the ceiling.

"Are you okay?" he asked her, barely able to speak.

"What the Hell was that? You have dried blood under your nose, are *you* okay?" she asked and rubbed at the dried blood under her own nose.

"Bryce? Bryce, are you there?" Todd asked his voice was filled with panic.

There was no answer. Todd looked back to Bree. She had rolled up on her side and cradled her head with her arms.

"Are you okay?" she asked him again.

"I'm a little sore and it feels like a freight train ran over my head, but I'm feeling better," he said.

"Did you see two men?" he asked.

Bree shook her head and winced.

Todd shouted Bryce's name as if to call to him at a distance.

"I am here Todd," Bryce spoke softly.

"What happened? Who were those men?" Todd

103

asked in hopes that Bryce might somehow know.

Todd walked toward the bathroom as he waited for Bryce to respond.

"I have no idea what it is that you're talking about. Your thoughts, from those moments before you passed out, are thickly riddled with pain and concern for Bree. I can discern shapes that you viewed that looked like men. They seem like shadows that might have been a result of your hampered eyesight. The detail is distorted as a result of the trauma you suffered. I need a moment," Bryce requested.

Todd returned from the bathroom and handed Bree a cool, moist towel. He sat down weakly on the couch next to her.

"Twenty souls were injected into your consciousness at once," Bryce began, "People, whose souls you had purchased, were murdered. They felt hunger so strongly that the urge bordered on insanity. They were all led to a single point like lambs to the slaughter. The blast incinerated the entire building and its occupants within a second. You have receipts with their names on them. It would seem that I have the honor of being the voice, so to speak, of the collective which is your consciousness," Bryce paused.

Todd looked into Bree's eyes. He was aware that she fully understood the information Bryce had just related to him.

"I need you to do some things for me, Todd. I know you're ill and will be full of questions, but I need you to act quickly. Go into your room and get those tickets with the names on them," Bryce paused again.

Todd staggered to his room and got the tickets.

"I need you to put them into the waste basket and burn them. I don't know if it will end our union but it has to be done quickly," Bryce was silent again.

Todd's hand trembled as he paused for a moment and then lit one of the tickets. It flamed up quickly. He dropped it into the waste basket and began to drop several tickets in at a time. Within a minute all of the tickets had been reduced to ash.

"Dump the ash into the toilet and flush them,"

Bryce instructed.

Todd did as he was told. He breathed a sigh of relief as he heard Bryce speak to him. Bree labored to remove batteries from smoke alarms in the apartment that had begun to go off. Todd worked efficiently as he followed Bryce's instructions, unable to think for himself. He coughed a little, as the smoke made his lungs convulse.

"Now, I need you to wash the blood out of those rags you used to clean your faces," Bryce instructed.

Todd took the towels, rinsed them, and threw them into the dirty clothes hamper.

Both of you get your keys and leave quickly. Go outside now!" Bryce commanded.

They grabbed their keys and milled toward the door.

Todd began to regain more mental faculties.

"I can feel your questions Todd. There is no time. Please just listen to me, it's so very important," Bryce pleaded.

Bryce's voice exuded such concern and necessity that Todd and Bree walked with purpose and trusted their disembodied protector.

The two of them reached the edge of the street in front of Todd's apartment building.

"Get into your car and hit the rear end of Bree's car," Bryce thought to Todd.

"What?" Todd and Bree said in unison.

"Please. There is no time! No Time! No TIME!" the projection of Bryce's thought was forceful but maintained a hint of pleading.

"You can buy new ones tomorrow. Do it now!" Bryce thought.

Todd looked to Bree; she gave him a nod of approval. He jumped into his car and revved it up. Todd released the clutch and plowed into the rear end of her car.

"What now?" Todd asked as he surveyed the mangled cars.

"Bree, call the police and report the accident as quickly as you can," Bryce thought.

"What?" Bree asked as she dug in her purse for her

105

phone.

"Call the police and report the accident," Todd repeated.

The police arrived a few minutes later. The two officers completed the necessary reports while they tried to calm down a very convincing act of hostility between Bree and Todd.

They went back into the apartment afterwards and Bryce went silent. The apartment still smelled of burnt paper. Bree went to turn on the exhaust fan behind the stove. She turned the thermostat dial that caused the central air to start to circulate.

Todd plopped down in a chair, mentally and emotionally drained, "What was that about?" he asked.

Bree sat down in the chair across from Todd, lit them both a cigarette, and waited.

"That was about ass coverage, Todd," Bryce said.

"Okay. How?" Todd sounded agitated.

"The Salvation Café blew up four hours ago. Its location is a seven hour hard drive from here. I believe you will have police at your door with a search warrant in a few moments. They will no doubt be looking for that pile of tickets which contains the names of the victims. If they found you in possession of those tickets, there would be seriously negative ramifications. Now you have an alibi as well as no physical evidence in your possession," Bryce trailed off, lost in his own thoughts.

"Oh! I have an idea," Bree said excitedly.

Bree got up and went to the bathroom. She wadded up toilet paper and threw it into the waste basket. She then dropped her lit cigarette on top of it and waited for it to catch a little and smolder. She doused it out with water from the sink. She then returned to the living room and sat down.

"There we go. Coverage for the burnt paper smell. I used my cigarette to set some toilet paper off in the trash," Bree said to inform Todd of her actions.

Todd nodded in agreement and said, "I have done that a lot by accident. How long were we out and *why* were we out?" Todd returned his attention to Bryce.

"I believe about three hours. Unless you make a

mental note periodically of the time my perception of it is limited," answered Bryce.

"It was like a psychic triage in your mind. You received the souls of every person that remained on your ticket list, all at once. I tried to console them and explain, but they all had questions. The disembodied soul's last thoughts were of that demon...thing. She whispered in their ears and told them that they were starving. In the assimilation of information, I came to very certain conclusions. This was an attempt to frame or kill you.

As to why you were out, as a result of your newest arrivals, I have answers. You were out because of an instant massive infusion of psychic energy. Your blood pressure shot through the roof, caused your nose to bleed, and you passed out.

It was the same for Bree. She is receptive to psychic energy, so by the act of touch, she received a portion of the mental stress.

Now we have a police report of you being at a certain location at a specific time. It would be impossible for you to traverse the distance between the mass homicide and your traffic accident in the allotted time," a thick impatient rapping on Todd's door halted Bryce's recount.

A man's voice erupted from the hallway. The forced deepness of the voice and commanding tone caused Todd and Bree to freeze in place.

"This is the Police. Open up, we have a warrant!"

"I'm coming," Todd croaked as he bounded to the door.

Bree could see the concern and worry wash over his expression as he glanced back at her. Todd firmly grasped the doorknob and turned it slowly. The door was forced open abruptly. Four large men with pistols drawn rushed into the room. An officer's crushing descent upon Todd slammed his face down to the floor. Two more officers scrambled into the room, knees bent, and weapons pointed. They scanned the room and stopped with their weapons trained on Bree. Todd could barely hear what was going on. He felt his wrists jerked forcibly toward the small of his back by strong hands. The cold metal of the cuffs cinched painfully against his

107

wrists.

"Lie down on the floor!" the officer yelled at Bree.

Bree, in shock, slid numbly off the couch onto her knees with her hands up in surrender.

"*Lie down* and put your arms behind your back," the officer commanded impatiently.

Bree complied and her nose tickled as she went face down into the carpet. She felt strong hands as they worked to clamp cuffs onto her wrists.

"*We got these suckers...They were defenseless...Maybe they're not the right ones...They went down too easy,*" Bree heard random thoughts from the officers.

Todd watched the officers handcuff Bree. The sight seemed surreal. An officer knelt down and looked into Todd's face.

"Todd Jennings?" the officer asked him as he read from a small card held in his hand.

"Yes. That is me," he responded dully as he thought of how polite the conversation seemed in light of recent events.

"*Here comes the innocent act,*" Bree heard the officer's thoughts.

"What is this all about? I haven't done anything. Why are you doing this?" Todd questioned the very honest looking officer randomly.

The officer looked at him, smiled genuinely, and said, "Mr. Jennings we need you to come with us. It would be in everyone's best interest if you came quietly. You have the right to remain silent..."

Todd was listening to the other officer now speaking to Bree in the same calming tone. Two other officers were standing in sight just behind the couch. He marveled in the contrast of expressions between the men reading them their rights and those two other men.

The officer, who still droned next to him in his ear, could have been a long lost friend. His tone was light and friendly with a hint of forced clarity and pronunciation. The officer smiled as he spoke with that 'everything is gonna be okay' smile. The other two officers spoiled the illusion though with their deeply lined faces drawn into angry scowls. These same two men had written him a ticket shortly ago for hitting Bree's car. Todd had noted how calm and nice they had been under the previous circumstances.

Todd and Bree were taken to the local police precinct and booked under suspicion of murder. They were interrogated in separate rooms.

Bree's entire recount of the evening was very uneventful which included her departure from her job and going to visit friends. The friends had not been home and that 'Todd guy' had run into her car. They were originally hostile toward each other. Bree told them how, while exchanging insurance information, they had ended up apologizing to each other. The Todd guy had offered her a cup of coffee as a token of apology.

"We were just finishing those cups of coffee when you guys came busting in the door with the riot act," Bree said as she grimaced at them with angry impatience.

One more question the officer asked, "Was something burned in the apartment before we arrived?"

"Yeah," she replied sheepishly, "I accidentally dropped my cigarette on some tissue paper in his bathroom. It started to smolder and I poured water on it from the sink. He was just asking me about it when the police came to the door," Bree concluded.

Todd sat in an interrogation room and looked at his hands. He appraised the solidness of the hand cuffs. His right wrist ached as one of the cuffs rested against a bone. As he stared around the plain room, he looked into the reflective side of the one way glass. Almost imperceptibly, his left eyelid twitched. The very faint moan of bending metal could be heard. Todd lifted his right buttocks from the chair and grimaced.

"Did he just fart?" the female detective asked her partner as she stared at Todd through the one way glass.

Todd displayed an expression of relief as the pressure was alleviated from his right wrist.

"Disgusting," she said and shook her head in disbelief.

"He looks like a dumb kid," her partner, Andy

Jackman commented.

Detective Jackman was a burly cop in his late thirty's. Jackman had thick jowls that puffed out from the side of his head, which made him look like a blow fish. His short brown hair had begun to recede slightly from his forehead. The dandruff caps on the shoulders of his cheap sports coat looked like one of the many donuts he had eaten with his morning coffee. The corners of his mouth glistened with balls of white spit that seemed to rotate and vibrate when he talked. This drew attention from his brown eyes as he spoke. He breathed heavily; his chest wheezed a little as he exhaled. He looked at Todd in appraisal.

"He is either innocent or a great actor. Are you ready to conduct the interrogation, Angie?" Jackman asked impatiently.

Angie "Detective Fine Ass" Finer exhaled deeply and replied simply with the word, "Yeah".

She casually brushed her curly red hair over one ear and picked up a folder. She proceeded to the door with a look of determination on her face. Jackman watched as she pulled her small dress coat closed which hid her ample cleavage. They walked together toward the interrogation room, wordlessly. This was a practiced routine for them and took no preparation in its repetition.

Todd jumped as the door opened abruptly and broke his train of thought.

"Oh shit," he thought and looked at the bent cuff on his right wrist.

Todd slid his hands down onto his lap. Detectives Finer and Jackman entered the room solemnly. Todd appraised their very disingenuous smiles that flashed as they passed.

"What if they see this cuff?" he thought in panic.

Jackman noticed that Jennings looked suddenly very guilty. He moved around in his chair uncomfortably and burrowed his wrists into the crotch of his pants. Jackman's first instinct was to command him to place his hands on the table. He refused himself the pleasure, hoping to lull Jennings into a false sense of security. Jennings seemed preoccupied by his hands as they began to ask him standard

110

questions about where he had been this evening. Todd kept his answers short and simple trying to avoid a pause or break. He had, accidentally, hit the woman's car while parking in front of his apartment building.

"She was being a real bitch at first," Todd told the two police detectives.

Todd watched as they stared dispassionately and listened to his explanation. Their expressions poorly masked the distrust Todd could read in their eyes. This made him very nervous but he continued without falter.

"Then she turned all cool and we decided to have coffee. One thing led to another and... Does this have anything to do with old parking tickets?" he asked timidly and looked at them both with genuine sincerity.

The detectives looked at each other angrily and rolled their eyes.

Jackman turned back to Jennings and said very professionally, "You were booked under suspicion of subsequent murders that surrounded an arson based explosion at a homeless shelter. You might want to reel in that humor. It's apparent that you haven't opted to have council here with you. If you think that makes you look innocent you're very wrong."

Todd could detect more than a hint of anger in his tone. In fact, Todd could envision this man taking him out behind the building and shooting him. He felt like a criminal as Jackman glared at him.

"Why would you think that I had anything to do with this?" Todd asked as he reached deeply to remember that he had not done anything wrong.

Detective Jackman produced a white sheet of paper from the folder and showed it to Todd.

As he looked at it curiously, Todd quickly figured out that it was a copy of his social security card.

"My social security card?" Todd asked as he looked at Jackman curiously.

Jackman flipped the page over.

The back of the page showed what Todd realized to be a copy of the back of his card. 'I am the Antichrist' was written in bold black ink on the back view of the card.

111

"That was found inside of a freezer. It was protected from the blast. Any ideas as to how your social security card could've gotten there?" Jackman asked with a condescending tone.

Todd looked down at the mangled cuff on his wrist. He compared it to the other and concentrated on it.

The metallic bending noise sounded again. Detective Finer grimaced and Todd's face flushed red.

He compared the two cuffs again. Relief washed over him as he realized that he had perfectly corrected its shape.

"Excuse me. I get gassy when I'm nervous," Todd said and placed his cuffed wrists on the table between him and the detectives.

"I have no idea how that might have gotten there. But if I had committed this heinous crime, do you think I would leave my social security card behind with that cute note on it? Who would be that stupid?" Todd asked as his tone rose with subtle anger.

"Sometimes killers want to be caught. Did you burn something in your apartment before the police arrived, Mr. Jennings?" Jackman asked.

"No, but I did smell something just before the police got there. That Bree chick...," Todd stopped speaking as a curt knock erupted from the door of the room.

An officer walked in with a folder and offered it to Detective Finer. Todd looked directly at it and clearly saw the current date on it and the bold words *traffic violations*. His dismayed expression melted into an air of incredulous superiority. Detective Finer quickly flipped through the folder and showed the information to Jackman.

Finer followed the officer to the door and gave him instructions in hushed tones.

Todd let himself relax and watched them take in the contents of the folder.

"This should assuredly be the point where everything relaxes and they let me go," Todd thought hopefully to himself.

There was a polite rap on the door. One of the officers, who had attended the scene of Todd and Bree's accident, entered the room.

"Do you recognize him from this scene," Finer asked the officer as she handed him the folder.
The officer recognized the report he had filed earlier. He looked between the folder and Todd a few times.

"Yes. That is Mr. Jennings, same guy," the officer stated.

"Thanks," Finer said as she opened the door for the officer to leave.

He was startled to see that Jackman's expression remained angry. To make matters worse, Jackman had begun to flex his jaw muscles. Jackman looked at the floor and relaxed his expression. Todd waited a long time to make a decision on what Jackman may be thinking. Out of a necessity to feel security, Todd convinced himself that Jackman was through persecuting him. Almost involuntarily, Todd relaxed and exhaled a deep sigh of relief. A tiny hint of Todd's crooked smile twitched at the corner of his lips.

In that same second, Jackman jumped to his feet and lunged for Todd across the table. Detective Finer managed to wrap her arm around most of Jackman's waist as he dove. She reached forward and crumpled onto the desk, pulled by Jackman's weight. Her effort saved Todd from being mauled. Todd had stood up and flinched enough to evade Jackman's grasp.

The aluminum folding chair Todd sat in had been thrown backwards by his knees as he rose. The seat slammed against the white door behind Todd. It folded in upon itself and landed neatly in the corner.

Angie Finer had been looking into Todd's eyes as she struggled to pacify her struggling partner. Jennings had stood up and moved incredibly fast with fright in his eyes. He now watched Jackman thumping on the table with a sort of curiosity. Jennings' head tilted to one side slowly. The glare fixed upon Jackman was devoid of fear.

"Those people were burned to death! They died screaming in agony! Do you think that's funny? You son of a b..." Jackman's words choked in his throat.

Jackman looked down at his hands balled tightly into fists. Each fist was clenched and had taken on a thick purple color. They felt as though they were literally being crushed by some unseen force. Jackman stopped struggling against Finer, distracted by the intense pain in his hands. Detective Finer hauled him up with unseemly strength and thrust him back into a corner.

"That will be quite enough, Andy!" Finer thundered with a commanding tone that did as much to frighten Todd, as it did distract Jackman.

Jackman stared at her angrily for a moment. His expression relaxed and he massaged his hands. He then proceeded to straighten his tie never breaking eye contact with Todd.

"I'm sorry *Mr. Jennings,*" Jackman said, disingenuously as he glowered at Todd.

Todd regarded him in distrust and anger. His attention was stolen by Detective Finer's polite tone.

"Please accept my apology. My partner can become pretty passionate about his work. It *appears* that we have the wrong person. Can you think of anyone who would want to implicate you in something like this?" Finer asked patiently making sure her voice was as pleasant as possible.

"Not off of the top of my head. I don't have any enemies that I'm aware of," Todd responded.

Finer motioned for Jackman to follow her into the hallway, he did so begrudgingly leaving Todd alone.

As Jackman closed the door, Finer began to unload her frustration verbally.

"What was that? What *was* that? I would expect a stupid move like that from a newer detective, but *you* Andy? Come on! They have cameras in there. If he decided to file a complaint we would have internal affairs on our asses...again," Finer complained.

"I'm sorry Angie. There is something there. That little shit was smiling, actually *smiling*. I couldn't control myself," Jackman said apologetically.

"Alright, look. Let's send him home....," she began.

She raised her hand in a cautionary flourish to abate Jackman's attempt to protest urgently.

"I know what you're thinking. Let's just put him out there, and watch him for a few days. If anything comes up

114

we can just go collect him and lay down on him until he rolls. Right now, all we have is circumstantial. With you threatening to assault him, if we did get anything, this could all turn dirty," Finer warned.

Jackman grimaced and nodded his approval. Todd watched them nervously as they reentered the room.

"You're free to go. A squad car will return you to your home," Finer said as she gave Jackman a reproachful glance.

"You don't have any vacation plans do you? We may need to ask you a few more questions later," Jackman asked, the contempt still prevalent in his voice.

"Not at this time," Todd replied angrily as he waited to be released from the room.

"I am going to station a car outside of your apartment for a few days to be sure that you are safe," Finer said.

"Thanks, I appreciate that," Todd said as he doubted her motives.

Within twenty minutes Todd stood just inside the front door of his apartment.

He locked both of the locks and lay back against the door. He slid down the door into a crouch. He put his hands in his hair and exhaled deeply. Todd stayed like this for a few minutes and replayed the events that had recently unfolded. He thought of Bree and felt the necessity to call her.

"Bryce?" Todd thought to himself as he rummaged in his pocket for his phone.

"Yes, Todd," Bryce answered.

"What's going on Bryce? I didn't hear you one time in the police station. I'm already used to not being alone," Todd said distressed.

"Oh, *very sorry*. It's still absolute chaos in your head. I have endeavored to try to organize facts and sort out details. I will get back to you about it all, when I have more answers," Bryce stated.

"Great! My head is a boarding house now," Todd said aloud.

Bree was bent on getting back to Todd. She had

already mentally contemplated the complications that would arise from her being seen with him. They had feigned newness of each other to the police. If she strode into his apartment building, it might cause more suspicion. She parked several blocks from his apartment and walked inside of a large store. She moved swiftly, rounded a few corners, and watched to see if anyone from the building's exterior had made to follow her. She approached a saleswoman who worked furiously to restock a shelf.

"Excuse me; I think my ex-husband is following me. He is a bit of a nutcase. I slipped in here to hide from him. Is there a back way out of here?" Bree asked the lady.

Bree felt a rush of shame and her cheeks blushed with a soft red hue upon completing the lie. The woman misinterpreted this and thought that Bree was about to cry. Her expression, formerly a mix of curiosity and doubt, melted into one of compassion. The saleslady led Bree through the back storeroom toward a door with an exit sign prominently above it. Bree, assured that she was not being followed, walked with purpose toward Todd's apartment building. She halted at the last corner and peered around the edge of a building cautiously. A police cruiser sat across the street. She closed her eyes and focused on the officer who sat in the driver's seat. Her mind filled with a flood of abstract thoughts, as they occurred to the officer randomly.

She walked the length of the building toward the lobby door of Todd's apartment. The officer's thoughts remained an abstract scramble. Bree concentrated very hard on him.

"I'm hungry...This cruiser stinks. Rodriguez must have eaten beans.... It's bullshit that Dora can't take Ken to the dentist instead of me."

Bree listened as she walked. If he took any notice of her, she would keep walking. She grabbed the door knob and entered the lobby.

"Six more hours of this crap. I wonder what this guy did. Geez, my eyes are itchy."

The light knock on the door behind him made Todd jump forward and crawl away.

"Todd, it's me," Bree said from the hallway.

116

"What's the password?" Todd thought to himself.

Bree laughed and said, "The password is handcuffs," as she tapped gently on the door again.

Todd opened the door and took Bree by the hands. He led her inside. He nervously secured the locks on his door and turned back to her. Todd hugged Bree close to him; the sweet smell of her hair soothed him deeply.

"I think we need some sleep," he proposed to her.

"That sounds great," she walked away from him toward his bedroom.

Todd turned back and reached for the light switches. Each light switch clicked itself to the off position one after another until darkness blanketed the room. Todd looked at the palm of his hand. He thought of Jackman's purple fists and grimaced in sorrow.

Todd heard a voice in his head, "Dear Todd, please protect me from these horrible visions. I can't take this anymore. Will you accept me?" the voice asked.

"Yes. I'm sorry you got mixed up in all of this," Todd whispered absently.

"What do you mean?" Bryce's disembodied voice asked.

"Was that one of the new borders, Bryce?" Todd asked.

"What do you mean, Todd?" Bryce repeated curiously.

A faint light lit the hallway from the cracked bedroom door. Todd scratched his head distractedly and looked toward the bedroom.

"Nothing I guess. I'm pretty exhausted," Todd said dismissively.

Todd stood at the end of the bed and looked at Bree who appeared to be already deeply asleep. She was snuggled up to his pillow with a faint trace of a smile on her face.

He enjoyed the way the sheets clung to the gentle curve of Bree's breast. Todd removed his clothes and slid up next to her, and felt her warm skin against his. Todd drifted blissfully into a dreamless sleep.

Chapter 10

Cold Cash

(One year earlier)

Pastor Marvin Williams stood before his podium and surveyed the one hundred people, give or take a few which sat in the rows before him. His brilliant blue eyes were framed by his high cheekbones. His light brown hair was neatly combed back with a few streaks of gray that had formed at his temples. The hue of the light, which filtered down from stained glass, seemed to give him a golden aura. The crow's feet at the corners of his eyes were deep and added a careworn, yet, very mature character to his presence. He shifted his shoulders slightly to allow air currents to cool his white button up shirt under his jacket. He leaned forward on the podium and lifted his legs in turn. He stretched a little to prepare for his next faith empowered gallop across the stage. His white suit billowed slightly under the low currents of fan forced air. He had trained the fans on his podium intentionally.

The breeze was very slight but it kept him cool enough. This was part of his latest plan to fill the collection plate. He would implore his congregation to donate more money to have the air conditioning fixed. He had purposely removed a few necessary wires that he would easily replace later.

"Need a little more cash for my next investment," he thought.

Another two hundred and fifty thousand dollars and he would have exactly what he needed to retire comfortably.

Marvin had been the pastor of this particular church for only eight months and it had proven to be exceedingly

118

financially beneficial.

The church where Marvin had been a Pastor, prior to this one, had driven him out. He had not been careful enough in covering his misdeeds and was eventually discovered. It was his own fault, he realized. Avid churchgoers demanded to see the Church's financial records, after he had been sighted driving an upscale sports car. The church had fallen into disrepair, while his personal attire and jewelry had become more and more flamboyant.

Marvin was not an incredibly smart man but he did, however, learn from his mistakes. He purchased a beat up old lemon to drive and purposely wore out some of his clothes to complete his image change.

Upon introducing himself to the small patronage, his first sermon cautioned them that faith in God and their faith in him must be without question. These small-town people, he mentally referred to as hillbillies, ate up his sermons. These often began with the tale of the previous flock that he lost to the 'wiles of Satan'.

His mock sorrow, for having failed to save his previous churchgoers, gave them something to identify with. They took it as a matter of pride that they and not the previous church's townsfolk would be graced with a place in Heaven. These people embodied unquestioning loyalty and scoffed at any person who made mention of Marvin's character not being of holy demeanor.

Marvin had these people by their wallets and was not letting go. At the end of every sermon he would thank his new found flock of 'sheep' making sure to point out the church's improvements, never mentioning that they were free. Receipts of labor from fictitious companies crowded the Church's records. He knew now that if he maintained a poor appearance and the church looked as if it were flourishing, more and more money would be thrown his way.

A great many of the congregation volunteered time for bake sales, church expansions, and renovations. They were also in the habit of inviting new members by the truckloads. Each week the number of patrons increased steadily. Marvin was giving a sermon three days a week now, often twice on those days.

119

He loved the small church, local fire codes only allowed one hundred and twenty five people per service. More services meant more opportunities to pass the collection plate. He reveled, in the fact, that he could tell particular groups that they had donated the most, every week. This motivated them to drop even more untraceable cash into the plate. His retirement nest egg continued to grow and he was, on some level, appreciative of this. He took a trip every two weeks to deposit large clumps of untraceable cash. He had spread these caches among several storage units, each rented under a different alias. A large percentage of his actual earnings were used in high risk investments and had fortunately paid off time and time again.

"I'm worth it," he thought, looking out over them.

"I provide them with a sense of purpose in their otherwise meaningless lives. I provide them with answers that allow them to sleep at night. I give them explanations of all of the unfair things that occur all the time."

Marvin finished a paragraph of his sermon and bellowed, "Amen!"

The upturned faces of the congregation looked blissful. Their eyes had been closed in prayer but now they seemed to spring awake. They randomly repeated amen, that followed a line that Pastor Marvin had offered up. Each patron had the same rose pink hue in their cheeks, brought on by the blistery temperature in the church. Here and there, ladies dressed in their Sunday best fanned themselves with small fans made of paper. The men shifted uncomfortably as the heat permeated their suits. Marvin danced out from behind his podium with a look of wild excitement on his face.

"I can feel the power of faith in this room," his delivery was powerful and rich, "Oh; it's the power of the Lord shining brightly upon this, his most faithful congregation. The vile clutches of the dark one are being forced further away with every second and it's making me feel good! *Can you feel it*?" he asked rhetorically.

Men and women responded with whoops and hollers trying to outdo each other.

"I was sitting in my bed the other night reading my

120

bible and do you wanna know what I thought?" Marvin asked no one in particular.

He was delighted as over half of the congregation expressed pleas to hear his wonderful ideas.

He looked to his right at Deacon Rolfe. Doug Rolfe stared back at Pastor Marvin. Marvin could have laughed out loud at Doug's teary eyed expression of joy. Doug was so enamored of Marvin that he was considered to be a pet or slave in Marvin's mind. Doug longed to be a Pastor more than anything. He was, according to Marvin, on the longest road to being a pastor.

"When you have walked the path of the righteous long enough that you aren't affected by your dark past on the horizon behind you, you will be ready, brother," Marvin had told this to Doug uncountable times.

Marvin always used this to his advantage. He dangled the opportunity for Doug to do a complete sermon in front of him like a golden carrot.

Today, however, Doug was an obstacle to be overcome. Doug had been chosen to record the collection money today. Doug was always overly eager to do any trivial task the Church asked of him. This was the richest faction of the congregation. Marvin was accustomed to having access to the collections. Doug had been persistent about fulfilling the task against Marvin's wishes.

"I need to think of a way to get him off balance so that I can be alone with that money," Marvin thought.

Marvin appeared at this point in deep thought to the congregation. The audience still waited with rapt attention for Marvin's answer. He was prone to long pauses like this and had explained to the curious, that he was receiving the 'word of God'.

His expression told the flock that he had just had this wonderful epiphany.

"I thought that it would be great for me to share the delivery of the word of God," Marvin belted out and did a little jig for emphasis. "I know a man *bursting* with faith, so willing and eager to share with you, that it would be a *shame* to not......."

He dabbed a previously moistened towel against his

already cool forehead and pretended to succumb to the heat. Marvin motioned to Doug to join him and dropped to one knee. A gasp erupted from the flock. They compassionately watched their leader as he seemed to be sapped of strength by the heat.

Margaret Durning turned to her friend Donna who sat next to her and said, "Poor Pastor Marvin. He is probably near heat stroke with that suit on in this hot church."

Donna nodded and added, "He gives all he has to us. I'm going to put an extra twenty in the collection plate today. There is no reason for him to have to suffer in the heat like that," Donna said in length.

The sentiment of Donna's words undulated like ripples in a pond throughout the congregation in whispers. Doug rushed to aid Marvin, who now knelt with his head bowed. No one saw the cunning smile adorn Marvin's face as the last of the empathetic whispers drifted to his ears.

Marvin's thumb clicked the mute button on the microphone in his right hand. He looked up at Doug with a weak smile. Doug lowered himself and began to lift Marvin to his feet.

"Are you okay?" Doug asked with genuine concern.

"I'm fine, just needed to catch my breath, it's... so...hot," Marvin replied with a weakened tone.

"Please, finish this for me. I know you're the man to do it, before the plate goes out please ask for any extra donations to have the air fixed. I already have a man coming to look at it tonight. I'd be willing to pay for it up front out of my own pocket until the church can afford it," Marvin said as he breathed laboriously.

"Oh, you won't have to worry about that," Doug said with confidence.

Marvin stood up fully again. He dabbed the moist towel against his forehead and staggered a little. He clicked the mute off on the microphone and raised it to his mouth.

"Just as Brother Doug has lifted my weakened body up from this stage, please put your hands together and allow him to lift your souls toward heaven as he finishes my sermon for me," Marvin's voice shook a little and was very breathy in the microphone.

He handed Doug the microphone and was helped offstage by a large man that looked at Marvin with the deepest of concern.

Marvin smiled at him weakly and said, "Thank you, brother."

The man beamed with pride as he sat Marvin in a chair in his private ready chamber.

"Go on now. I'll be fine," he told the large man reassuringly.

The man smiled, left the room, and closed the door behind him. Marvin waited until he could no longer hear the man's heavy footfalls thundering away on the hardwood floor outside. He jumped out of the chair spryly. Marvin tossed his clothes off quickly and hopped into the shower. He smiled as he heard Deacon Rolfe's heartfelt plea for anything that could be spared to help get the air conditioning fixed. Marvin dried himself off and got dressed in his slacks and t-shirt. He was in the process of tying his shoelaces when a small polite tap could be heard at the door.

"Come in," he called out pleasantly.

The door opened and Doug entered. He looked to Marvin with a deep concerned expression and asked, "Are you okay?"

Doug looked like the victim of a heat stroke. His cheeks were flushed angry red and beads of sweat dripped from his neck and forehead.

"I'm fine. I just had a nice cool shower and I feel perfect," Marvin said as he took in Doug's overheated appearance.

Marvin smiled devilishly at Doug. His mind thought back to how he had turned off the fans trained on his podium. The burly man that had escorted him had thought Marvin simply tripped. Marvin had seemed to stagger and the man worked to steady him. Marvin used the distraction to turn off a switch with his toe as they passed. He thought of Doug up there and his struggle to walk and talk in the heat.

"Could you hear me out there?" Doug asked breathlessly and dropped heavily into an aluminum chair near Marvin's desk.

"Praise God, yes I could, brother. You are a

123

natural," Marvin told Doug and sounded very pleased.

"It just all came together. It was such an awesome feeling. I could feel the Lord holding my hand," Doug said and smiled.

There was another gentle tap on the door.

"Come in," Marvin bellowed.

A young woman entered the room. She held a large basket that was full of crumpled dollar bills. Doug began to slowly rise from his chair but Marvin zipped past him and relieved the woman of the burdensome basket.

"Thank you, sister," Marvin told her pleasantly.

She smiled at him and said, "You're quite welcome. You bounced back quickly."

"It's amazing what a cool shower can do for you," Marvin replied as he watched her leave the room.

He returned his attention to Doug who seemed to have turned a deeper shade of red.

"Well, Doug, fair is fair. You did my job and I will do yours. I'm gonna count this out and deposit it before the repairmen comes. I'm hoping to have cool air for tonight's sermon," Marvin finished.

Doug looked concerned and said, "Oh no, I..."

Marvin cut him off before he could finish.

"That was so great, I could hear your voice in here," Marvin said encouragingly.

Marvin was relieved to see Doug's expression change as he abandoned thoughts of counting in the collection money.

"Doug, I want you to get changed and get over to the diner and have yourself a meal on me. I insist," Marvin handed Doug ten dollars from his pocket that he had already stolen from the collection basket.

"What? Why?" Doug gestured curiously to the money placed in his hand.

"I really want you to go mix among the congregation as they eat their Sunday dinner. They all go to that diner to eat after church. You'll miss out on a big part of the Pastor experience if you don't get to hear the comments. I bet more than a few people walk up and congratulate you on your first delivery," Marvin said optimistically.

He delightedly watched the thoughts of glory dance across Doug's expression.

"I'll do it," Doug said happily

"I knew you would. That's a good puppet," Marvin thought to himself.

Doug lingered for a few moments with questions about his delivery, much to the annoyance of Marvin. Marvin pretended to busy himself with paperwork. He replied to Doug with words of encouragement as needed.

"It's hot as Hell in here and that idiot won't leave," Marvin thought to himself.

"All right, Doug, get along now. I want you over at that diner. You're missing your moment in the spotlight," Marvin told him politely as he exhausted the last shred of his patience.

Doug looked at his watch, smiled, and said, "Sure thing. I'll be back for the six o'clock service. Do you think I can speak again?"

Marvin's expression changed into more of a forlorn look. Doug's expression dropped a little surveying Marvin's face.

"Now look. I do not want to detract in any way from what you did here today," Marvin began, "I have no doubt that God has huge plans for you, in fact, I've had visions about it. But I'm here to prepare you for that greatness. If I thought you were ready to pick up the banner already, I would love to let you. I want to be sure in my heart of heart's that you're ready. That's my responsibility to you," Marvin finished and returned to his paper work.

Doug smiled warmly at him, "Thank you, brother, for looking after me," Doug said and bowed his head to Marvin in reverence.

"Can I hear about your visions later?" Doug asked excitedly.

"Of course, brother," Marvin looked up at him and smiled, "Get on now. I have work to do to prepare for tonight," Marvin said with a polite yet commanding tone.

Marvin watched Doug leave and thought to himself, "It should take me all of five seconds to dream up a vision for him to get me some more cash...that idiot."

125

Chapter 11

A Spurious Vision

Marvin sat in his comfortable desk chair and looked greedily at the basket of collected money. He no longer heard the energized clamor of the patrons or the laughter of their children. He loved this time after a sermon and felt it was the calm after a storm. He deprived himself the joy of the collection baskets perusal and left his office to secure the church.

He walked around quickly and locked doors. He tested each one carefully before moving on. Assured of his solitude, he relaxed. His facial expression, which usually reflected a look akin to glee, melted into a scowl. This expression was natural and through careful practice only surfaced at times when he was completely alone. He surveyed the parking lot through a side window. His beat up four door sedan, sat alone in the parking lot. The car, by every definition of reason, was on its last leg and looked the part. Bits of orange light cascaded through the trees of a nearby pine grove. The sun's light had begun to diminish but easily served to highlight dings in the passenger door and quarter panels.

"What a piece of shit," he thought disdainfully as he appraised the car.

Marvin thought fondly for a moment of his upscale sports car parked in storage. It waited for the day he could escape. His sour expression, morphed into the usual false glee that he wore for the public.

He skipped toward the back of the church like a child playfully yelling, "Thank ya Jeeee zussss," and chuckled to himself mirthlessly.

Marvin halted to a stop as he reached a small white utility door that covered the control unit for the central air. As he dug in his pocket, his tongue lolled to one side of his mouth and gave him a moronic look. He pulled his hand out of his pocket, opened it carefully, and sifted through loose change and lint. He found two small pieces of electrical wire with metal connectors on each end.

He held them up in front of his face and his eyes narrowed as he inspected them. Marvin labored for a few seconds and successfully replaced the wires on the control unit. He peered around the church, despite his own certainty of solitude, in paranoia. He walked to the thermostat and ran the dial down to sixty-eight degrees with a careless flick of his finger. The cool air flowed down almost immediately from overhead which inspired a much appreciated shiver in him.

Content with the completion of his 'repairs' he walked back to his ready chamber. As he entered his office he reached into his back pocket and produced his wallet. He hunted through the numerous pockets in it, for a moment, and pulled out a repair receipt for two hundred dollars. His air conditioning at home had gone out a week prior. Marvin, a creature of comfort, wasted no time before he contacted a repairman. When finished, the repairman traded a receipt to Marvin in exchange for two one-hundred dollar bills. Marvin looked at the undated receipt with the words 'paid cash' stamped onto it. It was at that moment that he had devised this clever deception. Here he stood triumphant again, another well thought out plan executed.

Unable to deny himself of the pleasure any longer, he forked his hands deeply into the basket. Marvin enjoyed the heavy amount of crumpled and folded cash that mixed like leafy green salad between his hands. He grimaced a little as his fingers struck half an inch of change at the bottom.

"I guess they had to break open their damn piggy banks this week," he said as an evil grin slid across his face.

A subtle shifting noise erupted from, what seemed like, the main chamber of the church. This caused Marvin to

127

drop into a defensive crouch.

"Oh shit," he thought, "I should have waited on the air...who the Hell *is* that?"

Marvin collected himself, walked out of his chambers, and tried to look calm. As he entered the main chamber he spied sheet music, from the organ, that had fallen and lay strewn across the floor.

"Hello? Is anybody there?" he called out across the empty room.

A gust of air from the air conditioning vent pushed more of the sheet music off onto the floor. He heard the noise again and trained his eyes on paper and watched it flap loosely. Marvin placed his hand on his chest as he relaxed and smiled.

"Oh, thank ya Jee zuss," he said out loud with a laugh in his voice.

Ching shhhh...

The sound of change sliding across the floor in his chamber grabbed his attention.

"Now what?" he asked as he turned angrily toward the sound.

This time, he jogged at a rapid pace to his chamber. The basket lay on the floor next to his desk with cash in clumps around it. A small border of change was in an arc around the mouth of the basket.

"I guess it fell. I am way to cool for all this panic," he thought to himself.

He dropped onto his knees and began to shovel the cash back into the basket. As Marvin put the change into the basket, he saw a blurred object run past the door in his peripheral vision.

"Was that a dog?" he thought, as he replayed the sight through his mind.

He stood up and set the basket firmly into the center of his desk and stalked back out into the church's main chambers.

Marvin looked around through the darkness of the shadowy main chamber. He began to hear a sound composed of, what he perceived as, a myriad of voices. It increased in volume and sounded as though hundreds of people gasped for air at the same time. He peered around suspiciously as his eyes had begun to widen with panic.

The sound then formed into the words.

"They are here for you sinner. It is your time."

The sheer unnatural quality of the voice overwhelmed him. No part of him wished to remain and try to figure out the specifics of it. Every fiber of Marvin's being cried out in terror. He let out a piercing shriek as he turned to run to his chambers. His body was on autopilot as he ran for his life. Marvin's brain failed to keep time with his actions and he staggered unevenly. He slowly picked up speed as he gained coordination through necessity. His feet slid as he ran. Panic wrestled to best all cognitive thought as he dashed forward. His heart thudded loudly in his chest and some part of his mind analyzed the noise in curiosity. His thoughts became focused, as terror took complete control, and his only intent was to lock himself inside of his chamber. He turned the corner of the hall that lead to his chambers. Even though his body turned, his momentum carried him into the wall. His shoulder left a slight indention in the drywall as he pressed forward to safety.

The velocity, at which he ran, carried him past the door of his chambers. He threw out his right hand, and grabbed the door frame. His grip clamped onto the door and he used it to drag his entire body weight into the chamber. His nails cracked, ripped, and embedded themselves into the door frame.

The motion, as he entered the room, was a spin. His outstretched right hand, with its bloody fingers, slammed the door shut. In a fluid motion, he leaned against the door to reinforce it with his weight. His left hand fumbled for the lock while his ragged breath blew saliva through his clinched teeth. His breath exhaled heavily and he was aware again of the sound of his heart, as it slammed into the inner wall of his chest. He tried to calm himself and his respiration refused to regulate. He braced against the door with his ear pressed to it and listened. He stared wide eyed at his left hand that sat flatly on the door next to his face. He became aware of the screaming nail beds of the fingers on his right hand. He winced, closed his eyes, and flexed the digits.

129

Marvin listened intently through the door as the gasping noises dissipated. Fear was replaced with anger as he began to analyze what was going on. He thought of the acoustics of the church and the sound system.

"Marvin, you dumb son of a bitch. This is probably some asshole trying to get to you," he thought to himself.

His anger grew in intensity and he glared at the door. He reached for the door knob and opened the door forcibly.

Marvin inhaled deeply and balled his fists as he prepared to rush out into the church.

A new noise came from directly behind him inside the room and froze him in place. His mind deciphered the noise to be fingernails, claws, or bone. They clacked unevenly against the tiled floor. Marvin's skin crawled in hackles and his shoulder's rose to either side of his head.

It seemed like a gallon of cold acid fell into the pit of his stomach. He turned in place and slowly forced his body to move through the fear. Before he could fully, mentally process the sight, his bowels released into the crotch of his pants. The thick liquid mass slid unevenly down the inside of the legs of his pants and into his loafers.

Filling the space between Marvin and his desk, three massive dog-shaped creatures stood and glared at him. All the skin and internal organs seemed to be missing from the creature's anatomy as they were comprised of nothing but visible muscle, bone, and sinew. Their thick legs ended in what looked akin to a human's hands and long exaggerated talons tipped each digit. The three snarling beasts swayed back and forth in predatory curiosity, balancing on the tips of their talons with a disturbing grace.

Long bat-like ears flicked to catch sounds unheard. Empty eye sockets spouted sickly yellow flames, but that didn't seem to stop them from remaining focused entirely on Marvin. Their wolf shaped maws gnashed rows of unevenly curved fangs together as thick steaming drool streamed from the beasts' mouths to puddle on the floor.

He was completely sure that if he turned away or broke eye contact with these things they would try to tear him apart. He took a cautious step backward. The creatures responded with a single step forward in perfect unison. They seemed to smile at him with their drool lined fangs. Marvin had never experienced this level of prolonged terror. An energized bolt of panic ran through him, which prompted him to turn and flee. He rounded the hall again, going back the way he had entered.

His loafers slapped the ground and made squishing noises as he plodded forward. He almost made it to the center aisle between the pews, when he heard three fast thumps against the wall. The sound of bone-talons clattered on the floor in closer proximity. He shrieked in terror as he realized the beasts were nearly upon him.

He poured on all the speed he could muster as he entered the center isle and headed for the exit. He must get to his car, this thought burned in him. The clacking bone noises were literally inches behind him now. They were joined by the noise of fangs as they nipped at his heels with sharp snaps. He had made it half way to the door when he heard the talons thump the ground and become silent. In his mind's eye, he perceived the muscular animals to have launched for the take down. The main doors of the church burst open. A woman stood there with one outstretched hand, her toes on the line of the threshold.

"Help me!" Marvin begged selfishly.

Her outstretched hand lit with golden fire. Marvin dropped, slid, and rolled over onto his back to see the dog like creatures as they finished the arc of their leap.

The closest animal's talons were about to sink into his face. The creatures exploded into dust that traveled past him toward the door. He looked up, dumbstruck at the woman who stood over him. She looked down upon him apathetically as the glow of her hand faded. He rolled over onto his knees; a look of insanity had seemed to overtake his expression.

Had he not been panicked, he would have considered her beautiful. The woman had long reddish brown hair that hung in ringlets below her collarbone. Her brown eyes were so dark, they were nearly black. Her curves stood out even in the loose white robes she wore.

He stammered, "wha what wuh was that?"

131

Her eyes fixed on him sharply.

"Those, *sinner*, were Takers," she said with a very stern tone, "and they were here to drag you to Hell expeditiously. So you could begin to endure torture for all eternity," she completed her sentence grimly.

"Are you an angel?" he asked as he began to sob uncontrollably.

She smiled at him.

"Why, yes I am," she said nonchalantly.

"You saved me," he sobbed.

"No. I have simply delayed what may have to be. The Takers only come for those who are meant for the deepest layers of Hell," she said as she looked down at him.

He began to stammer, "Deepest layers of...."

She cut him off, her voice very loud now.

"Yes. There are seven layers of Hell, increasing in severity to encompass punishment fit for the crimes committed by sinners such as you. I have only delayed your taking. If you fail to redeem yourself, they will return and quickly bring you to the seventh level as they were instructed to do," she finished and pointed a long slender finger at him.

Marvin's wide eyes stared at her as he took in what she had just said.

"I will redeem myself! Please, tell me how! I beg you. Please!" he cried even harder and rocked on his knees.

"Before I offer you the chance, I want you to see what Hell is. Then you can tell me that you truly do not wish to go there. Do you understand, Marvin, and agree to these terms?" she asked him.

"Oh yes! Yes, please help me! I agree!" he sobbed.

"We will start with level one and work our way down. I can only give you examples, as your own personal Hell will be much different and suited to the extreme profanity of your indiscretions in life," she said this and grinned wickedly.

Marvin didn't see her expression with his head bowed and eyes closed. Marvin felt disorientation brought on by a sudden weightlessness that he felt. The smell of salty water assaulted his nostrils. Water lapped at his face as he began to sink. He quickly paddled to remain afloat and fought the urge to panic. He searched for a bottom with his toes and lowered himself to the point where he accidentally aspirated water. He turned slowly and looked around, astonished by the changes to his environment.

"This feels so real," he thought to himself.

He coughed as he tried to clear the water from his lungs. Beautiful, crystal clear ocean stretched out around him for as far as he could see. There was no land in sight. As he turned jerkily, a thick clump of wet black hair plopped against his face. He grabbed at it to throw it off of him. He pulled at the hair and realized it was attached. He brushed it back out of his face. A small tremor of panic coursed through him as he saw his own hand.

It was effeminate looking and adorned with long fingernails. He touched his face. The high cheek bones and thin nose were not his own. He then realized an unnatural floating sensation in his chest. He reached down to inspect his chest and discovered large full breasts. His hands shot down to his crotch. His penis was gone, replaced by a small slit between his legs.

He spread his hands out treading water and thought to himself, "This is Hell... I'm a woman trapped swimming on an open sea?"

He threw his head back and laughed derisively. An overwhelming dull cramp from deep within him quelled his laughter. He began to feel deep stabbing pains in the lower part of his abdomen. He massaged at his lower abdomen as he tried to ease the pain. A thick, red cloud of blood appeared in the water between his legs. The cramps became minor but the blood continued to flow. He stared down at the large bloody cloud with wonder.

A shadow caught by his peripheral vision moved quickly into obscurity. The outline of another object passed into the cloud before he could affix a stare. He raised his head to look around, his mouth dropped open as he saw a gray fin pierce the top of the water.

A single word that escaped his lips named the terror aptly.

"Shark...," came out in a terrified whisper.

The cloud of blood had begun to dissipate slightly

133

and he was aware of multiple large shadows that moved below him. A rough surface brushed heavily against his ribs on his left side. He quickly turned himself to stare, as if it might stave off an attack. There was a quick powerful tug at his left foot. The pressure seemed to release and was immediately replaced with a white hot pain. He threw his head back and howled as the pain coursed up his ruined leg. As he screamed, a second shark tore off his left arm. His eyes were wide with pain and terror as he swam unevenly. Bloody stumps marked the ghosts of limbs that had been torn away. The wounds throbbed in agony, which seemed to only increase with every second. Panic was fully taking hold as the hopelessness of the situation dawned upon him. A fin appeared in front of him, and began to come directly at him. He tried to swim backward, the shredded nub of his left arm made small waving arcs that did nothing to help.

The fin was a few feet before him and the shark rose up out of the water, its bloody teeth a nightmare reflected in his eyes. His ears filled with the roar of breaking water and the beast seemed to float over him. He turned to one side defensively as the teeth clamped down across his ribs and spine. The deafening noise of bones being crushed inside of him, accompanied the symphony of pain that ripped at his mind. He opened his mouth again to scream, but there were no lungs left to push the sound.

Darkness engulfed him, but the intense pain lingered for a few more moments. The pain had become so intense, that is was replaced by a feeling of loss as it began to fade. He was relieved to find that he was able to release a deep sigh.

"Yes, you are whole again. Now, you will see the second level," the voice warned ominously.

"No...That won't be necessary. I'm ready to listen to you. I don't need to see more, please...no more," Marvin begged.

A sudden intense pain in his wrists and ankles crushed the rapt joy he had basked in all too briefly. He found himself to be stretched face down and bent over a large rock with rune like carvings all over it. Small insects crawled through the slimy green moss that grew on this ancient alter. He tried to free himself only to realize his limbs were immobilized where he lay, prone.

His eyes found his arm and traced it to his wrist. In horror, he spied the cause of the pain. The shackle that held him in place was a large fanged skull that had been crafted from some sort of metal and polished. The skulls had long razor sharp fangs the size of a pitch fork tine. They literally pierced through his wrist and any movement caused new waves of pain to course through him. He moved his leg the tiniest amount and felt that his ankles must be bound in a similar manner. He raised his head and looked around at the rocky walls. Ruined humanoid cadavers were chained to the wall and appeared to animate in the quavering light of ensconced torches.

"A cave?" he wondered to himself as he tried to ignore the bodies.

Thud... Thud... Thud...

The heavy footfalls came from the passage directly in front of him. He held his breath as the sound grew closer. His heart began to thump unevenly in his chest. In betrayal of his need to hear, he surrendered to his lungs demands for oxygen, and drew breath raggedly.

His view was partially obscured by shadows as the creature entered the room. As it lumbered forward, the undulating light from a torch partially illuminated its face. It looked like a cross between a man, bat, and lizard. Its large black leathery wings followed it into the chamber. Marvin began to thump wildly against the stone in panic. As he struggled to free himself, the fangs of the skulls clamped down harder. The pain was intense and Marvin threw back his head to scream. A long loud breath escaped him; there was no voice, no tongue. It had seemed to take no notice of him before, but the horrible face seemed to be drawn by the motion. He flailed madly as the thing approached him. It placed one foot on the stone and looked down at him and seemed to appraise his naked flesh.

Its oversized face was very human-like but covered in scales. A snake-like tongue darted out of the cleft in its upper lip and withdrew. The empty sockets of its eyes burnt

135

with that sickly yellow fire. It seemed to smile at him as he lay there. Marvin flailed helplessly as ragged, hoarse breaths escaped his gaped mouth. His eyes reddened and filled with tears as he lay there, vulnerably, and stared at the creature. Its pseudo smile widened as it seemed to drink in his hopelessness. The scales in its crotch, almost level with Marvin's face, began to part and a phallus slid out slowly.

The creature put his foot down and proceeded to walk behind Marvin. His eyes rolled up in his head as the creature began to defile him. The pain was at first exterior as it began, and then he could feel his insides being torn apart in a fast rhythmic sawing motion. He strained to tear his arms free of the bite of his bonds and as the pain increased, his strength weakened. The creature's claw-like hands tore at the flesh of his back. As he reached an acid etched crescendo of agony, he was again washed in darkness.

He felt his limbs being released. He drew himself into a ball and screamed as the pain slowly receded.

"It doesn't seem to me that you are enjoying this. Perhaps salvation is the correct path for you," the disembodied voice chided.

"It...It wasn't human. It killed me! I tried to...I tried to...I didn't have a tongue...It...It was s..so horrible," Marvin stammered.

"The dark powers of Hell delight in making you suffer. Each time that you are destroyed, your body is made whole. This ensures unending torture for all of eternity," the voice explained.

"I...*DO NOT want to see.....I do not ...I do not...No...No...*," Marvin pleaded.

"I am not inclined to believe you. You are, as a daily habit, a liar. You will endure the third level of Hell. Then, I will be able to tell whether or not you are truly bent on salvation," the voice said sternly.

Marvin realized himself to be crouched forward on his hands and knees. He slowly looked around in the dimly lit, cramped area he found himself in. He was inside of a square tube. The walls seemed to be coated in oily blood. He slid his finger through the coating and held it in front of his face, close enough to inspect it. The goop was heavily laden with pieces of ragged fingernails. Intent upon his own survival, he forced himself to smell it. The thick scent of decay and iron assaulted his sinuses.

He recoiled and fought the urge to vomit. The surface, on which he knelt, stretched off far into the distance and he traced the floor back to himself. He was now able to see scattered debris that lined the floor. He grabbed up something and raised it closer to his face to inspect it.

The object looked like a small bone that had rusty razors attached to it. He picked up something else and looked at it. This was a small piece of glass shaped like the head of an arrow. He selected a few more pieces of debris and looked at them. They were all sharpened objects designed to slice or stab.

"So I'm stuck here. If I move..." his thought was interrupted.

He stumbled forward and felt himself pulled backward as if on a conveyor belt. He lowered himself a little where he could see over his shoulder and panic struck him again. He saw two barrel-like wheels behind him, one on top of the other. Sharp spikes protruded from them and they began to turn together like the blades of a wood chipper.

"Please, hear me, oh God. If you get me out of this," he whispered to himself.

He tried to hold himself up using the walls, for fear of being pulled into the mechanism behind him. The slime-like coat on the walls made it impossible to find a handhold. In desperation he began to crawl forward.

The sharp pains began to pronounce themselves as the first of the sharp debris fulfilled the intention of its design. He whimpered like a child and mumbled inarticulately as he crawled forward and was forced to mutilate himself.

He looked over his shoulder, the blades were closer now. He could hear their keen whirring noises as the sharpened spikes sliced through the air, very close to each other. He winced as sharp objects tore at his forearms and shins. They made wet slicing noises as he crawled forward. He had pulled himself a long way and ruined his right forearm almost completely in the process.

He could see exposed, bloody sinews and bone just below his elbow. He looked over his shoulder to see if he had made any progress. The blades were right behind him, their shriek created a roar in his ears. He turned back and began to desperately crawl. His right arm, now ruined, flopped behind him. He repeatedly staggered as the tattered arm got caught under his right knee. The shredded remains of his left hand and the bloody stumps of his knees worked furiously to save him. The drums took on a different tone now, like a table saw that chewed into a sheet of plywood.

"Oh dear God, my legs," he thought through the pain.

He now felt himself drawn backward. The wheels greedily chopped and chipped at the bones in his legs. The two operational fingers that remained on his left hand clawed at the floor and tried to pull him free. He screamed loudly in a mix of pain and terror. The proliferated scream continued until it was garbled as he choked on blood. Everything faded to darkness again and the silence was deafening.

The pain vanished completely. He looked all around him and could see nothing in the darkness. Behind him a faint golden glow appeared. He turned to look at the light that was a flash of brilliance. The intense glow faded and the woman's face came into view as the flash blindness subsided. He looked down to make sure he had hands and then crawled over the church's threshold to where she stood, just outside and blubbered at her feet. She allowed him, what seemed like, a long time to collect his sanity before she spoke.

"So, dear sinner, do you need to visit the other four levels of Hell before you decide if redemption is the path you wish to take?" she asked him this, her voice was very stern and condescending.

"*NO! NO!* I'm ready to receive your instructions. I want to be redeemed," he shrieked and began to mumble again.

"It is very simple. You have a responsibility to guide one of your flock who is destined for greatness. For it is he who will stop the ascension of evil in this world," her voice was more soothing now.

"Rise up and accept this mantle then, Marvin Williams, and be absolved of your sins in a trade for doing the real work of the righteous," she said.

Marvin stood up and looked at her as large tears filled his eyes.

"One among your flock begs to ascend to greatness in service to the Lord. He faithfully does what is needed of him," she said.

"Doug...Douglas Rolfe?" he asked her.

"Yes. Tell him to go to the Seventy Squares and identify the dark soul that will end this world. Douglas will need to discover his identity so that he can be destroyed. He must identify him tonight," she finished.

Marvin repeated her words and committed them to memory like a sermon.

"Do you understand what I have told you, sinner?" she asked him.

"Yes...Yes, it will be done, I swear to you," he stammered.

She waved her hand close to his, and a small burn in the shape of a star appeared on the back of his hand.

"That star will serve as a reminder to you. I will appear to you again when there is more to be done," she said.

She smiled at him again and raised her hand. Marvin was struck in the chest by some unseen force that thrust him back into the church. He landed hard on his rear end and slid ten feet up the aisle, before slowing to a stop. He corrected himself and stood up, then bowed repeatedly to her. The doors of the church slammed shut abruptly. The woman stood there for a moment, an evil grin spread slowly across her beautiful face. The clack of bone-talons on the concrete next to her caught her attention. She knelt down and stroked the chin of the Taker, the yellow fire of its eyes reflected in her own. She slid her hand away and licked the slime-like drool from her fingers.

Marvin Williams locked himself in his chamber and took off all of his clothes. He knelt in the shower and prayed to God for forgiveness as he scrubbed his skin to the point of irritation. He dried himself off and got dressed in a fresh suit. He sat at his desk and continued to pray fanatically. There

139

was a light knock on the door of his ready chamber. He jumped in his chair as his hands flew to his desk to steady himself.

"Who is it?" he asked and tried to make his voice even.

"It's Doug," the voice came to him from behind the door.

"Good job on the air conditioning," Doug said as he walked into the room.

Doug looked at Marvin and said, "What's the matter?" as he recognized that Marvin was ash gray and sickly in appearance.

"I have had a tremendous vision Doug. I need you to hear me out and I pray that you believe me," he dropped on his knees before Doug with his fingers interlaced in prayer.

"Whoa," Doug said quickly as he reached down and lifted Marvin to an upright position.

"What is it, Pastor?" Doug's tone was filled with concern.

Marvin bit his fist and shook a little. Doug sat down in a chair in front of him and watched him with a mix of curiosity and sympathy.

Marvin looked him in the eyes and said, "An angel of the Lord appeared to me. She showed me things that made me believe beyond a shadow of a doubt that she was, in fact, an angel. She impressed upon me, with the utmost sincerity of importance, that I convey the message to you, from her," Marvin said and began to sob lightly.

"What did she tell you, brother?" Doug's eyes were wide with wonder.

Marvin looked up at him and spoke precisely, "'Go to the seventy squares and identify the dark soul that will end this world. Douglas will need to discover his identity so that he can be destroyed. He must identify him tonight.'"

Doug stared at him for a second in silence.

"Okay," Doug began and slowly wiped a tear from his own eye.

"That's the message and you're sure it's exact?" Doug asked.

"'I will appear to you again when there is more to be done,' she told me," Marvin added.

Doug sat back in the chair and covered his mouth and chin with his fingers in awe. There was a long silence between them.

Finally, Doug spoke up, "Well, seventy squares, is a reference to the French Quarter. I remember that from some class as a child," he said.

"Then you have to go there and look for this person," Marvin blurted the words as a command but recoiled after the delivery.

"The French Quarter is a big place," Doug said thoughtfully.

"Do what you're supposed to do, damn the details. It's obvious you will be led in some way," Marvin instructed.

"What am I supposed to do when I find him?" Doug asked.

"Identify him tonight. Just find him and be aware of him. That seems pretty straight forward to me," Marvin's tone was agitated.

"I would follow you to the gates of Hell," Doug told Marvin solemnly.

Doug reached in his pocket for his keys as he walked quickly out of the door.

Marvin slowly raised his head; his red tinged eyes stared at the door in the wake of Douglas' departure.

"Let's hope that you don't have to," he said as he covered his mouth with his hand and succumbed emotionally to the guilt that burdened him.

Chapter 12

A Taste of Bourbon

Doug started up his car and drove toward the long bridge that separated this rural area from the major city of New Orleans.

The radio announcer blandly stated that there was a tropical storm advisory for the area until three A.M. He cautioned motorists to stay off the roads later in the evening to avoid the potential danger.

"Just great," Doug said with a moan as he turned off the radio.

"The dark soul that would end the world... the Antichrist," he muttered as the thought occurred to him.

He looked thoughtfully out over the dark water that surrounded the bridge.

"Dear Lord, give me strength," Doug dried the tears from his eyes and sped up.

He arrived at his destination a lot quicker than he would have liked. He assumed the distraction of his thoughts had detracted from his perception of time. Doug parked his car, and carefully locked each door.

His father had engrained in him a distrust of the city and its inhabitants.

"They will steal you blind or kill you as sure as look at ya. Not many of them are much better than that," his father had said once in reference to anyone that lived here.

He put his wallet in the front pocket of his slacks to guard it from pickpockets and bums without a second thought.

He opened the trunk of the car and looked at the hunting knife which rested against his spare tire.

"Identify...But not eliminate," he thought to himself and closed the trunk.

As he began to walk down Bourbon Street, he had to work to exert his will over the panic that tried to control him. Marvin, in Doug's opinion, was a Godly man and had never been given to practical jokes. The fear and awe in his eyes dictated profoundly the importance and severity of failure. Doug steadied himself against the brick of a building.

The voice of his drill Sergeant thundered in his mind, "It would *behoove* you, Private Rolfe, to remember that you have a sack. It's always Charlie Mike, *continue* the *mission.*"

Doug's chest puffed up as his confidence returned and he walked more purposefully. As he walked along Bourbon Street, he would occasionally pivot on his heels in rapid succession and scan three hundred and sixty degrees. A large handwritten sign outside of a nearby bar caught his attention. It advertised, 'Bourbon Whiskey Soul Here' in large block letters.

Mistakes in handwritten signs were common but something about the word soul caused something in him to reflect to the point of action.

"Maybe I should hang out here," he thought to himself and looked for a good spot.

He sat against the wall with one foot behind him with his hands in his pockets, one of which held his wallet tightly. He listened with disgust as men tried to lure passing tourists into the bars and strip joints.

Just then, part of a spoken phrase caught his attention, "to the devil".

He looked over and saw a young blond haired man. The man worked to wipe sweat from his brow where he stood with two other people. Doug eased closer to the trio and made sure he wasn't noticed. He quickly assessed them. The blond guy stood with a short red headed woman and a taller guy with black hair. Doug stared at the thin black haired man who talked to a homeless person. He had to fight the urge to snap his fingers as he recognized Todd. This was the atheist waiter from the diner in town. He slid a little closer and tried to hear the conversation over the drunken laughter from the nearby bars. The waiter had leaned toward the homeless man, which made him recoil. Then, as clear as a bell, Doug heard the waiter ask the homeless man to sell him his soul for a dollar. There was a large burst of drunken laughter from a bar and Doug missed whatever else was said.

The waiter handed the homeless person a dollar that replied with, "God Bless," and walked in Doug's direction.

As he shuffled by the homeless man he looked directly at Doug. Doug noticed that the old man wore an ancient army jacket and loud plaid pants.

Then he heard the homeless guy mutter, "...you freak," as he pretended to smile and glanced back at the waiter.

Doug followed the trio for a while. Often times he was unable to hear their conversation over the other people that bustled through the streets. He picked up the word, sacrilegious, from the woman. The blond guy made off-colored comments about prostitutes that they passed on the street. He witnessed the waiter make deals with other homeless people. Doug watched as the waiter collected a signed receipt each time for their souls and handed them each a dollar bill, in turn.

"This has to be the guy," Doug thought.

He stared at the back of the waiter's head as he followed them.
He found himself beginning to hate him as he thought about the waiter buying people's souls.

"Taking advantage of them when they are most vulnerable... Only the sickest bastard would do that. A soulless bastard that could only be the Antichrist would do that."

A flurry of umbrellas popped up in front of Doug's face. He stopped, backed up a bit, and smiled distractedly at the large procession of Japanese tourists that walked past him. He tried to look over and around the umbrellas but it was pointless. The last tourist stopped, smiled at him, and took his picture. She giggled and trotted off behind the group. Doug looked down the street and was unable to locate the trio. He pulled up the collar of his jacket to avoid the slight mist of rain from wetting the back of his neck. Doug hunted the streets for them for over an hour. He stopped and looked into bars as he passed. He finally gave up the attempt

144

to find them and found solace in completion of the primary task. Doug drove to Marvin's house through a sudden torrential rainstorm to share with him the details of his evening.

Doug pulled up at Marvin's house sometime later and waited for the rain to subside. After nearly forty minutes, the heavy rain slowed to a light shower. He bolted onto Marvin's porch, slipped, slid, and corrected himself. He knocked on the door excitedly. The door opened until the chain caught and Marvin slowly looked out of the narrow gap. He peered at Doug and his red eyes quickly filled with tears. Marvin slowly undid the chain and walked outside. He wore a tattered old brown bath robe and looked to be in poor physical condition. Marvin lumbered over to the porch swing, sat down, and looked at his feet.

"Are you okay?" Doug asked Marvin as he slung rainwater from the sleeves of his light jacket.

Marvin looked significantly older and very mentally frail. Marvin raised his right hand and placed it over both of his eyes and convulsively sobbed. With his other hand he reached blindly into the pocket of the robe he wore. He wrestled a large white envelope free of the billowy pocket. The envelope, about three inches thick, was handed to Doug silently. Doug opened the envelope and his jaw dropped. A stack of thousand dollar bills sat neatly in a row.

Doug thumbed through them, amazed, and tried to return it to Marvin. Marvin held up his hand in denial.

"What is this? What is it for?" Doug asked.

Marvin's face was still a grimace of mental anguish and he began to choke back his sobs.

"It's for you to live on while you're in service to the Lord," Marvin croaked.

Doug looked to Marvin who refused to return his gaze as if ashamed.

"That homeless man, the first one, do you remember what he looked like?" Marvin asked.

"Yes, but how did you know...," Doug was interrupted by an angry wave of Marvin's hand.

"That's not important," Marvin began, "The angel told me that he has to die by your righteous hand."

145

Lightning flashed overhead and Marvin recoiled violently.

Doug tried to ask a question, but Marvin's angry eyes locked with his. Doug was silenced by Marvin's furious scowl.

"Be quiet and listen, for God's sake," he belted at Doug.

"The homeless man is now a soulless abomination and if you let him live, it will be the death of good Christians including myself."

"There is more," Marvin's eyes dropped again to the floor of his porch, "The angel told me that if you would look at me and commit to doing this with all of your righteous heart and soul, she would be able to speak to you directly. There is a large chance that you will perish in service to the Lord. But you have to commit for her to even speak to you. Your word is the bond. She has a lot of work for you to do and that money will help you along the way," Marvin said.

"Will you do as the angel instructed? My life depends on it," his voice took on a pleading tone.

Thunder shook the porch and both men recoiled in fear.

Doug composed himself and looked at Marvin with a stolid, serious expression on his face.

Another blinding flash of lightning occurred.

"Marvin there is no other way you could have known what I saw tonight. If the angel says this guy is a servant of Satan, I will kill him for God and for you....I swear it," Doug said with conviction.

Marvin's puffy red eyes looked at him gratefully and he said, "I saw four and five just now and I don't want to imagine myself..."

The thunder that belonged to the recent lightning flash, clapped loudly and Doug was unable to hear Marvin.

"Or seven...Thank you, Doug," Marvin said as he walked inside and slammed the door behind him.

Doug asked through the door, "Four and five...and seven of what?"

Marvin's only answer was to triple lock his door and walk away. Doug put his hand on the door and then turned away to go to his car. He stopped for a second as he heard a noise like animal nails ticking across the tin of Marvin's roof.

"Rain," he said, shrugged dismissively and went to his vehicle.

A flash of lightning shone brightly as Doug reached his car door. He recoiled from the flash blindness and rubbed at his eyes as he reached for his door handle. Several seconds later the thunder boomed heavily and shook his car. He sat for several hours waiting for the storm to subside enough to allow him a chance to drive home. Finally there was calm. The rain had ebbed to a stop and the woods around Marvin's home became illuminated by the recently exposed moon. Banks of fog traveled in tendrils around the woods. There was another flash of lightning. Doug counted slowly before being interrupted by the crash of thunder that rattled the loose quarter panels of his car.

"It's getting close again," he said to himself as he started the car.

As he drove home, he listened to a weather report that detailed the dangers of the oncoming tropical storm. Doug had become exceptionally sleepy and relaxed low in the seat. He contemplated Marvin's behavior as he drove home. The storm had begun to interfere with his preferred Christian station. Loud bursts of bass driven music with angry rap lyrics had begun to overtake the soothing sounds. Doug snarled in disgust as he reached over to change the station. He pressed the search button. More rhythmic bass blasted through the speakers.

He depressed the button again. Whatever it was that the rock music of his youth had turned into came through the speakers now. The vocalist, if you wanted to call him that, screamed the lyrics. His words were inaudible and drowned by thunderous distorted guitar riffs. The glove compartment was open. He craned a little and was able to see a cassette tape. Sure that it would have preferable music on it, he leaned over as far as he could and stretched his arm to reach it. He continued to watch the road, barely able to see over the dash. The cassette, just out of reach, would be easy to grab if he ducked below the dash for just a second. He took one last deliberate glance at the empty night road and lunged for the

147

tape. He grabbed it and sat bolt upright. He looked into the road ahead as the heavy metal music blared from his radio. The windshield was awash of rainwater. He saw the shape of man land in the road directly in front of him. The vehicle struck something hard and the hood flopped back and smashed the windshield. Doug braced himself on the steering wheel in shock and stood up on the brake. The car slid sixty feet on the wet pavement and came to a stop, sideways in the road.

"Oh...Oh no...Oh no," Doug said and sat in shock for a long moment.

He was unaware of how long it took him to actually get out of the car.

The rain had doubled in volume as he staggered down the center of the road. The cold accusing eyes of a dead soldier flashed in his mind's eye as he peered through the poor visibility at a dark lump in the road.

He stopped, stomped his feet, and screamed, "It was an accident...An accident...It could have been anyone....Why me?" his tortured upturned face asked the rain as it fell.

The dark lump undeniably called to his sense of morality. He trudged forward to face the horrible truth of what he may have done.

He was closer now and the rain began to slow. The dark shape seemed to be a four legged beast that lay on its back with its legs splayed in the air. He walked closer. The beast convulsed and jerked and he realized it to be the corpse of a large deer. He ventured closer and tripped over something. He bent and tried to see what it was. A distant flash of lightning ripped the sky and the deer's severed head came into view.

"Oh thank God," he said and grabbed at his chest as relief washed over him.

Chapter 13

Absent Guidance

As the tow truck pulled into Doug's yard, the thick foliage of the tall oak trees acted like a natural umbrella. His dilapidated mobile home was a sight for sore eyes and he smiled appreciatively as the flood lights of the tow truck illuminated its moldy siding. He paid the driver and thanked him. Doug looked at the wrecked car, which had been deposited next to his working car, by the tow truck driver.

"Damn shame, just got that thing running right," he said grumpily.

"At least I still have old blue," he said as he looked at the older model sedan.

He deposited his bible on his coffee table and went to take a shower. He tossed his wet clothes into a pile on the floor of his bathroom. His mind absently replayed the scene of the angry Sheriff's deputy that he had dealt with. The deputy, Aaron Welsh, had been a fixture throughout most of Doug's life. Doug recognized him as he approached and made to shake his hand. The deputy looked at the hand dispassionately, grimaced, and pulled a pen from his breast pocket. He turned protectively to guard the clipboard he held from small bursts of light rain. Doug watched Deputy Welsh dolefully as he prepared himself to conduct an interview. Doug was saddened that such a lifelong acquaintance could be so cold toward him. This had been a standard though. Everyone that had known him since childhood had turned their backs on him. The deputy had asked him if he had been drinking or speeding as they stood in the rain. He had been made to repeat the exact details of the accident at least five times. He had been worried and neglected to mention that he had looked away from the road. The deputy seemed to pick up on his nervousness and made the experience last much

149

longer than it needed to.

He enjoyed the hot water as it beat him on the back in undulating patterns made by his shower head. A loud clap of thunder reminded him that it was to be a quick shower and he exited and dried off. At the end of his evening he climbed wearily into bed.

He flashed back to the accidental death that he caused while in the military. It had been dreamlike, the way events had unfolded. His entire platoon had been punished for the deeds of a few. Doug had been forced to march all night through freezing rain. His squad had only slept for a few hours before the loud banging of a stick, on a metal trashcan, had ripped him from sleep. His legs ached as he had gotten quickly dressed and scrambled for the muster area. The Drill Sergeant had ordered him to retrieve two rifles from the armory. His dull wits propelled him to do as instructed. He walked awkwardly back toward his group and carried the weapons across his arms in an unsafe and improper fashion. Doug had been taught the precise and proper method to carry a rifle. For that matter, he could disassemble, clean, reassemble, and fire the rifle in record time with great accuracy. But his mind felt like mush this morning and he staggered as if drunk as he walked. The Drill Sergeant began to angrily yell at him for the manner in which he held the rifles. Doug raised his face to acknowledge the man's command with respect. He stumbled awkwardly and the rifles shifted and fell, stock first, toward the ground. He stooped quickly and tried to keep the guns even. One of the rifles fired as the stock of the weapon impacted the ground. There was a blinding flash. The barrel recoiled and struck him heavily across his chin and added to his shock. In his befuddled state of mind, he did not realize that the man, who crumpled and fell next to him, had been shot. He stared dully at the man, who had landed face down into the dirt. There was a large bleeding hole just above the man's ear. The body twitched spasmodically and jerked in the mud. The dead man's twitching hand held a helmet that would have possibly saved him had he been wearing it. The man's dead eyes seemed to stare at him accusingly.

"My dark past..," he whispered to himself as he

drifted off into sleep.

Doug found himself walking through the French Quarter again. This time, he wasn't on Bourbon Street. He glanced up at a sign as he passed it and read Rue Royal Street. The second side of the sign was bent but he could still read 'aint Anne Stre' written upon it. His mind translated the corner of Rue Royal and Saint Anne. He returned his attention forward and noticed a man who approached him. The man walked at a furious pace but he seemed to look past Doug. He tried to side step the man but knew they would collide. Doug narrowed his eyes and braced for impact. He gasped at the imminent collision but the man passed directly through him. Doug grasped at his own chest and felt it in disbelief. He looked over his shoulder at the man who walked onward unaffected by the encounter.

"This must be a dream," he thought in supposition as he watched a vendor smash his fingers with a metal window.

He walked aimlessly as he followed the impulse of his dream. Doug assessed the people that walked ahead of him. There was a man, a woman, and a small girl. He presumed they were a family. The man barked insults at the woman and the woman returned them heatedly. The little girl made exaggerated mocking gestures with her hands to mimic the woman as she insulted the man.

The little girl had pig tails on either side of her head that flopped lazily as she walked. She wore a pink calf length sun dress that Doug found tasteful in this day and age. Her white stockings sat sharply in contrast to the shiny black shoes she wore. Doug noted that she was wearing a small pink book sack with a golden cross on the lower right hand side. Her small arms were raised as she continued to mock the woman's mannerisms toward the man.

Doug smiled at this. A man walked between the couple and the little girl dodged him gracefully. Doug did not have time to react and braced himself for impact. This man passed through him, also. Doug looked back and watched as the man walked away. He never remembered this much clarity in a dream. Doug reached out to a nearby newspaper machine and tried to place his hand upon it.

151

His fingers passed through the newspaper dispenser, he withdrew the hand, and he looked at it curiously. Doug continued to walk in the direction he felt pulled. His attention returned to the couple who continued to bicker as they walked. The little girl no longer trailed in their wake. They continued to argue, oblivious to the absence of the little girl. Doug sped up and reached to tap the man on the shoulder.

He brought his hand down and began to say, "Excuse me".

His hand passed through the man's shoulder. Doug whooped and hollered in an attempt to be heard. The couple continued to walk and continued to fight.

"This is where it turns into a nightmare," Doug thought mournfully to himself.

Doug was compelled to find the little girl. He retraced his steps and peered around with delicate precision, for some small glimpse of her pink dress. He took a few steps and noticed a small alleyway to his left. He peered skeptically into the alleyway as he took stock of the dumpsters and trash littered ground.

Cautiously he entered the alley and watched for signs of movement. Reaching the largest open part of the alley, he saw an old homeless man.

"That is the man that sold his soul to the waiter," Doug thought as he looked at the man's tattered army jacket and loud plaid pants.

The vagrant was in the process of ransacking a small pink bag. Fear gripped Doug as he realized it to have belonged to the little girl, noting the small cross on the lower right hand side.

He stood close to the old man and waved his arm right through him. The old man made grunting noises as he dug around in the bag.

He dropped toys and plastic pretend makeup pieces as he fastidiously went through it piece by piece. Doug turned around and looked along the wall next to the dumpsters. His eyes fell upon a small leg, clad in a bloody white stocking. The leg jerked and kicked where it protruded from under a piece of cardboard.

Doug sat upright in bed and gasped for air. He ground the heels of his hands into his eyes, twisted them, and jerked them away as he tried to focus. He got out of bed, got onto his knees and began to pray. He muttered his prayer until the fear subsided and he returned to his bed. As he lay back he pulled the covers up to his nose like a frightened child. It was a long time before sleep claimed him but it was blissfully dreamless. Doug awoke the next morning and felt well rested but the dread of the dream had managed to linger. He decided that he needed some time in the church to feel better.

He got dressed and headed into town. As he approached the side road of the church, he saw Billy Morgan, the church's grounds keeper.

Billy was an older man with ash gray hair. He always wore blue bib overalls and green rubber boots while doing his grounds work. Doug enjoyed morning coffee with him on a frequent occasion. Billy had a common-sense way to interpret current events that endeared him to Doug. He pulled over and rolled down his window to bellow a greeting.

"Good morning, Billy," Doug said warmly.

Billy raised his pale green eyes to meet Doug's and responded in his thick Irish accent, "Ah, good morning to you, young Doug. Where's your newer car? I thought you were all proud of it?" Billy asked.

"I used it for deer hunting last night on the drive home, in the rain. I hit a deer...The deer won," Doug said sullenly.

"Those damned beasts are stupid. They just jump right out in front of a moving car and stand there. Seems we have a bit of a dark cloud hovering over us all, indeed we do," Billy agreed with himself.

"What seems to be the trouble?" Doug asked plainly.

"Somebody went to the parish council and told 'em about our sewer problem," Billy said mournfully.

"Until it's fixed, the old church is to be shut down. Pastor Marvin called me early this morning and gave the news to me. The right Pastor didn't seem to be himself

153

either," Billy explained.

Doug looked at his shoes in disgust.

Billy began to preach, "It's just a sign of the dark times we are living in, lad. We got natural disasters, taking God out of the schools, I mean the signs are there. And now some Atheist has closed down a church where people need to go to be given the very spiritual power to resist this kind of evil. It's a dark time lad, very dark," Billy finished and returned to his work.

Doug waved to Billy as he drove away. The words, 'Some kind of atheist,' still bounced around in his thoughts.

"Are you ready to do the work of the Lord?" a disembodied feminine voice asked Doug.

Doug's eyes began to tear up as he replied, "Yes I am, angel. Please guide me," Doug continued, "That church was the only place I have felt accepted since...since..."

Doug's mind re-lived the day he returned home after being discharged from the Army. He watched as people clamored to greet other passengers. Here and there people hugged, kissed, or shook hands. No one was there to meet him and the stark contrast of his solitude became daunting. Doug was a fourth generation soldier. His father had disowned him when he called home with the news.

"You're dead to me, Dougy. You killed an innocent man. I hope you rot in Hell. I have only contempt and shame in my heart for you."

"It was an accident...an accident...," he said to the air and slammed his hand against the steering wheel.

In his mind's eye, he could still see the dead man's eyes staring with their cold accusation. Doug shook his head in denial of the thought and drove on. He seemed to take random turns, but he was aware now of the whispering voice in his head as it directed him. He pulled up outside of a small white cottage in the middle of town.

"Do not be deceived by the normality of this dwelling. The man you identified as the Antichrist resides here. We are here to deliver a message to this abomination. You would do well to prepare yourself for a possible confrontation," the voice whispered in warning.

Doug fidgeted and considered the weight of the task

at hand.

"What am I supposed to do against the Antichrist? I'm just a man," Doug asked as he filled with doubt.

"Was it not you who prayed to God to give you a path to serve? Would you fold your faith and become so cowardly at the first hint of purpose?" the voice was incredulous.

Doug's face became red and heated with anger toward his temporary lapse in faith. He took in deep breaths and flexed his muscles.

"My faith is unerring and I will not recant," Doug said with conviction.

His words empowered the strength of his determination. He got out of the car and walked to the trunk and took in a three hundred and sixty degree view of his surroundings. He opened the trunk slowly and spotted the object of his search. Doug pulled the large hunting knife from its sheath. He regarded its thick deer-boned handle and razor sharp blade with reverence. He concealed the knife under his shirt. After he had surveyed the surroundings for his adversary, Doug cautiously approached the cottage.

He arrived at the cottage door and noted the animal door apprehensively. The door, itself, was disproportionately large and would accommodate a huge animal. Doug thought briefly of a large dog that would serve as a protector to this man. He made another scan of the environment and tried to look casual, in case someone watched him. Satisfied that he was unseen, he grasped the doorknob. The door opened easily and he found himself disconcerted by his ease of entry.

Doug raised the sleeve of his shirt to his nose. The inside of the house smelled of old rancid food left on unwashed dishes. He was aware of the faint whisper in his head again. Doug sat down carefully and removed trash from the coffee table. He was meticulous so that he could replace the trash exactly the way he had found it. He picked up a blue card and flipped it over. He smiled, as he realized it to be the waiter's social security card. He placed the card in his breast pocket and patted it thoughtfully. His eyes seemed to glaze over as he began to carve words into the coffee table with his hunting knife. He looked down and surveyed his work. The words he had etched into the table, with his knife, looked to be in some foreign language. He slid his fingers over them curiously.

"What does it mean?" he asked the air around him.

"It is a message designed to invoke fear in your dark adversary," the voice in Doug's head responded.

He brushed the wood chips and shavings into a pile and brushed them carefully into one hand. He stood up and looked over the writing and dropped the shavings into his pocket. He felt empowered that his actions might invoke fear or doubt in this thing. He covered the message with the trash making sure it was as unnoticeable as possible.

He placed the knife under his shirt again and made to leave. Behind him, a low guttural growl rose from another room. He could hear claws as they skittered across the linoleum in the kitchen. He swallowed dryly and pulled the knife from under his shirt. He lowered into a defensive stance to ready himself for an attack. The dog came into view; it clambered through the hallway, and picked up speed as it approached. The Golden Retriever launched itself at him.

He side stepped the animal easily and kicked it in the rear end as it dove past him. The added force he gave the dogs leap caused it to slam heavily into a wall. The dog gave a single whimper as it fell into a pile on the floor. He watched the dog's side where its fur rose and fell in labored attempts to draw breath. The animal made a wheezing noise and its side fell still. Doug lowered the knife that had been poised to strike. He let himself out and returned to his car.

He drove back to the center of the town distracted by subtle whispers in his head.

A loud siren pierced the air and caused him to recoil. His head darted around as the thought of an ambulance or fire truck came to mind. It was then that the flashing lights atop the patrol car behind him caught his attention. Paranoid thoughts ripped their way through his mind as he glanced over at the large knife on his passenger seat.

His hand grabbed for the knife as he tried not to move much, afraid to relay his guilt to the deputy behind him. His hand closed evenly over the handle and he slid it under his seat, out of sight. He took a deep even breath to steady himself and pulled over expressly. He groped for his registration and proof of insurance as he watched for the deputy to emerge from the car. Doug had collected all of his necessary information and sat patiently for nearly five minutes before the deputy exited his vehicle. Doug watched as the deputy walked confidently toward the driver's door of his car. The man stopped just outside of his open window and lowered himself as he took off his sunglasses.

Doug recognized him and smiled as he asked, "Good afternoon Aaron. What seems to be the problem?"

"That's Deputy Welsh to you Rolfe," he responded curtly.

Doug's lips pursed as he struggled to maintain a friendly demeanor.

"I needed to ask you a few questions," Welsh said as he read from a small notepad he held.

"Happy to help," Doug said as his voice cracked nervously.

Welsh gave him a distrustful glance before he asked, "You said last night that as you approached the deer you hit, its legs were jerking in the air, correct?"

"Yes it was," Doug answered and tried to keep it simple.

"And how long would you say it was between the time you hit it and when I arrived on the scene?" Welsh asked precisely.

"Maybe twenty minutes, maybe less," Doug answered.

"The Wild life and Fisheries people took the animals body and checked it over. The animals head was ripped off and not removed by the blunt impact of a car. It had a few more wounds on it that seemed to have been made a short while prior to its death. The really odd thing though," Welsh paused as he looked at Doug and placed his hands on his hips, "The animal didn't have one drop of blood anywhere in its body. Do you have any idea why that might have been?" he asked Doug.

"You saw my car...I hit it with my car. Its head was torn off. Maybe it bled out and the rain washed the blood away," Doug responded nervously.

"Yeah you would think so. I asked them about that. They said that there would have still been some blood in the animal's body trapped in organs and what have you. It kind of looks like the animal was tortured and killed before you ran it over," Welsh said as his eyes keenly watched Doug.

"No. I was driving home and I hit it in the road. It jumped out in front of me. It was alive when I hit it," Doug said heatedly.

As Welsh watched Doug speak angrily, his hand had slowly drifted to, and came to rest upon the butt of his pistol.

"Aw shit. You know I can't prove anything. I just pulled you over to rattle your cage," Welsh admitted.

Doug's angry expression deepened. Welsh saw this and indulged his urge to provoke him further.

"But, I bet you did something nasty to that animal and tried to make it look like an accident. That's what freaks like you do. I guess it's a damn sight better than you shooting another innocent man," Welsh spat the words out.

Doug was insane with anger over the accusation and had turned bright crimson as he faced Welsh.

"What is it, Rolfe? Do you wanna kill me too? How about I look away and you can pretend it was another accident," Welsh said angrily.

Doug breathed heavily and he had begun to click his jaws in anger. He pulled up one hand from the steering wheel and flexed it firmly into a fist. The knuckles of that hand gave audible pops as he looked at Welsh murderously.

"I wish you would do something. I would love to have a reason to nail your ass to the wall. Hell, for that matter, maybe a bullet between your eyes. Over half this town would call me a hero for that. Your poor old heartbroken daddy included, if he were still alive," Welsh chided.

The color of Doug's eyes seemed to become lighter and he relaxed. A deceptively polite smile slowly worked its way across his lips. To Welsh it seemed to morph into a

158

deranged grin that sat below murderous eyes. Welsh's finger flipped a small strap that held his weapon in its holster.

Doug turned and placed both hands on the door of the car as he faced Welsh squarely. His eyes looked to Welsh's weapon first and then roamed up to his face.

"You dare to stand there and threaten me?" Doug asked in an unnatural voice.

Welsh flinched and stepped back as Doug spoke. Doug's voice had split and he spoke as if he were two people at once. The added voice sounded almost feminine but contained a growl.

Doug's head slid slowly forward as he said, "You can pretend to be Mr. high and mighty to everyone else with your little badge and gun. You can pretend that you are better than me with your head held high, as you strut around and make accusations. But...I know you...Yesss. I know you quite well. Perhaps you would like to arrest me and take me in. The old Sheriff would *love* to hear the tales I have to tell. How about, how you stole video evidence of child molestation. You know the one you watch for...entertainment. Or perhaps he would like to know about the twenty two caliber pistol. The one you placed into the hands of that man you shot in cold blood. Or perhaps your wife would like to hear about the whore you sleep with while on duty. Don't worry, she wouldn't take it too badly. She spends lots of the same kind of quality time with your brother.
In fact they are together right now."

Welsh was visibly shaken and staggered where he stood.

"Wha…What are you?" he asked Doug in disbelief.

"Someone you should not bother again, if you want to continue to strut around in a pretense of innocence," Doug answered and sounded more inhuman than ever.

Doug shook his head unaware of the few moments that had preceded this one. Deputy Welsh stood before him and appeared to be mentally broken down. Doug cocked his head in curiosity at the man who broke and ran to his car.

"What happened to him?" Doug asked himself curiously, as the patrol car sped around his and drove away.

159

"I spoke to him and asked him to quell his harsh words against you and warned him to leave you alone. We need to go and watch the dark one," the disembodied voice said evenly.

Doug sat in his car dutifully and watched the diner. The spot, in which he had chosen to park, offered him a clear view of two sides of the building.

Doug's attention was drawn to the back of the building, where movement had caught his eye. The waiter walked out of the back door and struggled to carry a cumbersome bag of trash.

He could hear Billy's words in his head again, 'And now, some *atheist* has closed down a church'.

With some effort, the waiter tossed the bag of trash onto an overfull dumpster. The bag landed on the top of the pile, but immediately toppled down clumsily, and came to rest on the ground. The waiter stared at the bag of trash and took deep hurried puffs of his cigarette. He seemed awkward and clumsy to Doug. Doug began to imagine himself able to overpower and kill this person. The waiter seemed to look over his shoulder and smile at Doug. He recoiled and started to think of the waiter as a dark and powerful being.

Something his dad had told him as a child came to mind. "Underestimating your opponent is the first step in failure."

His father would impart these nuggets of wisdom each time he effortlessly bested Doug while they sparred.

Doug slouched low in his seat with his brow furrowed. The waiter finished his cigarette, flicked it to the wind, and returned inside. Doug passed the time with a read of selected passages in his bible, but looked up every few minutes nervously. The evening passed by slowly, and night had replaced day, as Doug sat and watched for his enemy to reemerge. The last of the customers had pulled away from the building. Doug made a mental note of the two vehicles that remained and watched for their owners to claim them. Eventually, the same trio he had trailed in the French Quarter left the building together and talked for a moment before they parted. The waiter climbed into the dilapidated car and Doug pushed himself to a more alert position.

Doug started his ignition and stared at the waiter's car as it bellowed out smoke and chugged out onto the road. He tried to maintain a good distance between them as he then followed the waiter. His eyes narrowed as the bland red glow from the waiter's brake lights appeared. The waiter slowed down in front of Doug's church. The brake lights dimmed and the car seemed to be on the move again. He passed through a smog-like cloud in the road. The thick smell of burnt motor oil caused him to recoil in disgust. He recognized this to be the side effect of a heavy acceleration from the old car. Doug slowed, thinking himself to be at the point where the waiter had paused in the road. The only thing he could see was the street sign from his church glowing faintly in the distance. Doug read the words 'Heaven help us to reopen our church'.

"That bastard was admiring his handy work," Doug muttered to himself angrily.

Doug sped up aggressively and tried to regain sight of the old car, which had vanished around a curve in the distance. He slowed as he sighted the car again. The waiter gave no warning and swept the car into a gas station that he almost passed completely. Doug pulled into a parking spot and faced away from the waiter's old car. He watched carefully in his rear view mirror. The waiter spent a small amount of time inside, emerged, and headed to his vehicle. Doug was able to make out the word *dog* on the large white bag, just before the waiter tossed it into his car. The waiter dropped heavily into to the driver's seat and started the car. Doug watched eagerly as the old car headed back out onto the road and he made to follow it.

"Got you some dog food, huh? Well, you won't need it," Doug said and envisioned the retriever, dead on the floor of this thing's house.

Doug parked near the cottage and watched intently as the waiter went inside. A few lights and the small blue glow of a television were apparent through the windows. A bush nearby fluttered and stole his attention. The bush and the small surrounding area were well lit by the streetlight.

The Golden Retriever limped slowly from the cover of the bush and headed toward the white cottage. Doug

161

wondered how the animal could have survived the impact with the wall. The dog staggered and limped as it traversed the width of the street. Doug felt a pang of sudden remorse as he watched. The old dog completed its trek, and then it lumbered in through the animal door.

The monotony of his surveillance was broken when the waiter ran outside frantically ten minutes later. He held his cell phone to his ear with two hands.

"He must have found our little note," Doug said with a smug smile.

The waiter turned toward the street and seemed to greet invisible visitors.

"He must be crazy," Doug thought to himself as he looked on.

"Your eyes cannot see the demons he speaks to," the angel's tone was very grave.

Doug noticed then, that the waiter's front door seemed to open by itself. The waiter proceeded inside as though he had been beckoned to, by some invisible invitation. The door opened again later and the waiter seemed to bellow a goodbye to unseen visitors. A short time later the large SUV truck, he recognized to belong to the evil thing's friend, pulled up and parked in front of the cottage. The blond haired man that Doug had marked as the waiter's companion looked around suspiciously as he emerged from the vehicle. The waiter came out to greet him and looked relieved by his presence. The blond man reached forward and touched the waiter's butt as he followed the waiter to the door. The waiter looked back at the blond man and smiled as they closed the door behind them. Doug's eyes narrowed as he watched this and grimaced in disgust.

"Demons and homosexuals," he muttered to himself angrily.

"It's far worse than that. The red haired woman also carries the seed of the Antichrist in her womb. Your faith will allow you to do everything that is needed. It will not be easy and blood will be shed," the smooth voice responded.

"I know that you're right," Doug whispered to the air in the car.

He continued to watch the waiter's house for several

weeks. He had tried to go inside of the house several times. The Golden Retriever had begun to watch him like a sentry. The dog would bark loud enough to draw unwanted attention and he would have to retreat each time, for fear of being noticed. It was a Thursday morning, approximately one month later. Doug watched as the waiter, who sat in his car, prepared to leave for work. Doug started his ignition and intended to follow him. The old Golden Retriever walked slowly out of the yard and toward the street.

"Destroy the animal!" the voice commanded.

Doug obeyed blindly and aimed his car for the animal as it entered the road.

Doug's skin crawled as the smooth voice in his head whispered, "yessss," as the dog dully thudded into the under carriage of the car.

Doug filled with conflict over his actions as he flung open his car door and ran to the back of the vehicle. He stood there and frowned at the dog's unmoving body. He felt genuine remorse for the animal. A little girl on the sidewalk shrieked and had her hands over her mouth as she stared at Doug in terror. He jumped back in his car and sped off.

He waited several weeks before he returned to the waiter's home. He had taken the precaution and purchased himself a newer model car and wore large sunglasses. He watched the house from a newly chosen vantage point. The house seemed empty and the car was gone. After much deliberation, he decided to try and have a look around. As he fiddled with the door knob, which was locked this time, he spied a meager sign that displayed the words 'for sale' posted on a wooden stick. He covered the sides of his head with his hands, to block the glare, as he peered in through a sidelight window next to the door. The house was empty inside, save for a few scraps of paper on the floor.

"What am I supposed to do now?" he asked the air for guidance.

But none came.

Chapter 14

Salvation In Flames

It may have been years or simply months since he had fallen from the angel's grace. Doug lived with no concept of, and placed no importance in, the current time or date. It seemed like an eternity to him since the angel's guidance had become silent.

He had tried to continue the pursuit of his mission for a time. He had stalked and researched the waiter's friends and had hoped for some lead to help him continue his task. During that time, he had seen the Goldmans get married and have a child. He presumed the child to be the dark seed the angel told him about. His mind had become a warped and angry jumble of thoughts. He contemplated the slaughter of the Goldman family as a possible way to display his dedication. He had not been proactive toward this idea, though he had planned it thoroughly.

Without the whispering of ideas and positive reinforcement of the voice, he felt abstract and lost. He tried to busy himself with strenuous exercise and study. He greedily read scripture, and even fiction, for ideas to defeat a foe that had become almost completely abstract to him now. Doug made no attempt to acquire employment and lived simply. He had abandoned attempts to visit Marvin. The Pastor had become insane and useless to him. During attempts to talk with him, Doug had pitied Marvin who often looked around for invisible attackers in paranoia. The few times that he tried to discuss the angel with Marvin had been disastrous. Marvin would look around and tell him to be quiet and dismiss himself. Doug had followed once, to find Marvin drawn into the fetal position in his bed.

Doug knelt in his own bedroom as he prayed for the

return of his guidance, on this particular day. The light from the candles, in their sconces, danced on the smooth surfaces of the crosses that adorned his wall. He produced a thick leather belt from next to his bed and flipped it over his shoulder as hard as he could. The belt made a rich smack as it stung his skin. The leather produced welts that rose on either side of the impact sight. His back was lined with deep long scars that crisscrossed each other. The scars were his regret, he thought as he brought the belt over his shoulder again and winced as the crack sounded sharply. Doug had the idea that each display could prove him worthy and the smooth voice of guidance would return.

He sobbed lightly as he continued to punish himself.

He began speaking to the air around him, "Please come back to me." S*mack*. "I need you." S*mack*. "I can't do this on my own." *Smack*.

The only answer he could see in the darkness behind his closed eyes was the accusatory stare of the soldier he had killed.

Blood ran down his back into the waistband of his jeans. The impacts became lighter. He lacked the strength to bring the belt against himself, hard enough to do damage. The jeans he wore were now red with blood. Small crimson pools formed under his shins where he knelt. He rocked and prayed mindlessly. He abandoned the belt eventually. His unsteady hand grasped the bottle of medical alcohol from his night stand. He labored to twist the cap off and dumped its contents down the back of his neck. The alcohol permeated the wounds. He bit his lip as the deep sting dug itself in like a burrowing insect. His eyes became cloudy and he collapsed forward onto the floor.

Doug was in the nightmare again. He had this same one every night. He would follow this little girl with the pink book bag until he became distracted. The little girl would vanish from where she followed the man and woman. The outcome, always the same, would lead to the little girl's horrific death. The homeless man would be discovered near the corpse of the child. This dream always had a surreal quality about it. This time, something was different, it was

165

more vibrant than usual and seemed completely real down to the subtle wind he could feel on his skin. He followed the couple now and realized that they approached the alley where the little girl would be abducted by the homeless man. They parted and a man passed between them. The man concentrated on his own shoes and Doug didn't flinch as he waited for the man to pass through him. Pain sang out in him as the man's forehead crashed into his lips. He fell back, and held his mouth and was amazed at the taste of blood.

"Watch where you're going," the man said angrily and rubbed at his forehead before turning to continue.

Doug pulled his hand down slowly and looked at the blood smeared across it. He looked up to where the couple trooped away.

The little girl was gone, as usual. He stood up and ran down the alley. His heart filled with hope as a result of the change to the nightmare. To his dismay, the rest of the events started to unfold in their usual manner. The man was there cooing and giggling as he dropped items from the bag and looked for something. The little girl's legs stuck out from behind a dumpster, one of them twitched.

The usual ebb and flow of this dream had been marred and he decided to continue to change the norm. With a tremulous hand, Doug grabbed and threw the piece of cardboard that hid her upper torso from view. Her blue, dead face was twisted into a mask of terror. A gasp escaped him as he looked at her and filled with dread. The dull ache from his lips broke his fixation on the girl's twisted visage. Shock and revulsion were replaced, with blind rage.

He turned and ran at the man's unguarded back. His angry charge was interrupted as the old man spun around to face him. He tried to stop, but slid forward, leaning back against his own momentum. It was not the face he expected to see at all, it was the face of a beast. Its mouth was distended and a loud roar bellowed past the rows of sharp curved fangs in its jaws. The empty sockets of its eyes burned and crackled with a sickly yellow fire. He thumped dully against the thing and drew his face back as they collided. He staggered back a few steps and felt a terrible burning sensation in his chest. It held in its claw, a still

166

beating heart. Doug groped at his chest and looked down to see a huge hole. He looked up at the demon, his body too weak to feel pain. His vision darkened as he slipped from awareness.

Doug started awake and gasped for air as he groped at his chest. His heart, thankfully there, thrummed violently inside his chest.

He rolled around on the floor and muttered, "please, please, please..."

"Are you ready to do then, that which is necessary?" the voice interrupted.

Doug flipped over, his teary eyes very wide, "Yes, yes..," he quickly responded as he moistened his chapped lips with his tongue.

"Seek out this abomination that would kill this little girl and end him," the disembodied voice commanded.

Doug readied himself in a practiced fashion and was in his car within minutes. Every fiber of his being was bent on following the angel's direction to the letter. He would not fail again and be abandoned. The trip seemed extremely long this time, as if fate tried to stand in his way. Upon arrival, Doug parked, rushed towards the corner where the dream had always begun. Doug's hand gripped the knife under his jacket tightly as he walked down the desolate street in the French Quarter. He gazed up at the familiar damaged street sign which read 'aint Anne Stre'. The sign was bent, presumably by a drunken reveler or some accident.

He walked as he had done, a countless number of times, in his dream. He noted all the familiar things. He was able to side-step obstacles and dodge people effortlessly, this walk having been repeated so many times. Questions played through his mind randomly.

"Am I really here? Even the people I've passed and the sounds are familiar, he thought."

He glanced over to see a concessions vendor who labored to open the metal windows that protected his goods from thieves.

"And he slams his finger and screams the word..." Doug's thought was interrupted.

"Shit," the vendor said angrily as he freed his hand

from where it had been smashed by the metal window.

"This is crazy. It's exactly like the dream," he said loudly, plainly amazed.

A woman that passed near him recoiled in fear as their eyes met.

"I'm talking to myself. She thinks I'm crazy," he thought as he watched her hurry away.

He rounded the corner and saw the familiar couple locked in their heated conversation. He increased his speed to get closer to the trio who normally took no notice of him. The little girl, however, turned and looked back at him for a second. This completely betrayed the normal sequence of events and filled him with hope.

"I'm going to save you this time," he thought to himself.

He smiled warmly at her. Her pretty young face drew into a smile and exposed her missing front teeth. The fateful alley approached and Doug spied the man that had bumped into him, inside of his dream. Doug's hand grasped for his mouth protectively as the man walked by and gave him no notice.

The couple walked past the alley with the child still in tow. Doug stopped at the point that he had been sure the little girl would break off and meander toward her doom. He looked down the familiar alley with wonder. He shot a speedy glance after the trio and veered off to take the practiced path. A sour stench clawed at his nose and he flinched as he exhaled and tried to shake his revulsion. Fear clawed at his mind as he saw the two legs, clad in plaid pants, where they protruded from behind a dumpster. The feet, adorned in mismatched house slippers, were splayed. The position of the upturned feet told Doug that his quarry was on his back. Doug felt a flutter of weakness rush through him. He stretched a hand out to the nearby dumpster to steady himself. The hand landed coldly in something slimy, and slipped. He staggered, took a step, and kicked a small aluminum can in the process. The can rolled and stopped, with a rude metallic clang, as it hit the side of the dumpster. Doug's eyes rose to the slipper clad feet in that instant, as adrenaline poured through him. One of the feet twitched in

168

reaction to the noise and an aggravated snore erupted from its owner. Doug crouched at the ready with the knife positioned to stab.

He drew in a short heavy breath of cold air and rushed around the side of the dumpster. He dove onto the supine form of the homeless man. The man's eyes sprung open in surprise as Doug's left hand wrestled to cover the mouth of his prey. The world moved in slow motion. Doug breathed in the horrid stench of his victim. The old man's eyes stared at him in terror as Doug brought the knife down heavily. The fearful eyes widened exaggeratedly as the blade pierced the heart. The victim's leathery hands were clenched on both of Doug's wrists. Doug's teeth were clinched and he had drawn his lips away from his teeth, in a bestial scowl. This man should be dead but he continued to struggle against Doug's attack. The victim's eyes were fixed on him and narrowed, as if they labored to memorize him for some unknown purpose. Doug could see himself reflected in the eyes now. He flinched as he looked upon his own expression, which seemed to him to be rapt with pleasure at this old man's destruction. Doug's strength began to fail as doubt washed through him.

"Now twist your knife in its heart and relish its death," the smooth voice whispered into his ear.

Doug did as he was instructed. He abandoned any fear of wrong doing. His teeth gritted together as he struggled to free the knife from the man's chest. He looked into the man's dying eyes and felt vindication wash over him.

"I am worthy," Doug told the dying man angrily.

"Be on your guard!" the smooth voice again whispered into Doug's ear.

Doug could hear the sound of bone on the concrete behind him. He rounded to see a dog-like creature, skinless and perched gracefully upon long sharp talons. A sickly yellow fire burned in its empty eye sockets.

There was no fear in his heart as he sprang at it. The thing seemed to try and get away as his knee landed on one of its hind legs. Fluidly, his hand grabbed the animal's taut-skinned scruff. The other hand expertly slit its throat cleanly. The creature fell and jerked violently. It sprayed blood across

169

the concrete in a wide arc from its neck. He continued to hold it down, with his body weight, until the last of the light from the fire in its eye sockets died away. He slid its corpse to the wall and covered it with a piece of cardboard. The knife in his hand dripped blood unevenly from its blade. He cleaned it with the remains of a paper cup. He hid the knife away under his jacket.

On the return to his vehicle, he noticed a sting coming from his left hand. He raised it and inspected it curiously, as he paused. A neat star shaped wound, stung where it sat between his pointer finger and thumb. He brushed at it absently and continued on. He seemed to be in a daze as he returned home. The thirty minute trip had elapsed in what seemed like a fraction of the time as he walked inside of his trailer.

For a couple of days, Doug did not leave his home. The time that had passed, since his trip to New Orleans, had been a nightmarish roller coaster of self-doubt and shame. A small shiver wound through him, as he reflected upon mental images of his actions two nights prior.

"Are you remorseful for doing the work of the Lord?" the voice asked incredulously.

"No, it was just so unreal. I killed that man and that...that *thing*," he responded distractedly.

"The four legged beast was one of Hell's own guardians, charged with the protection of that soulless abomination you stabbed through the heart. Each of the soulless, have similar protectors. These beasts feed on the innocence of the righteous. If you do not act quickly, the soulless one's protectors will extract their feasts. Perhaps even kill the little girl you saved," the voice warned.

Doug looked puzzled as he asked, "How am I supposed to track down and kill all of them?"

"I will lure them together into one place and you can burn them all. My influence, by design, is only a mere whisper of destiny. It is not my place to act on the strength of my conviction. These choices are in place for those who have been granted the privilege to do so," she advised.

"I understand. It's a test of faith. You are the guidance. I am the body of action," Doug responded.

170

Doug rose up dutifully with a determined expression and went to get dressed. Within forty minutes, he again walked the darkened streets of the French Quarter. The streets, themselves, were bathed in a thick fog given off by the nearby river. He smiled mirthlessly as he took in the scene of the foggy street, which seemed morbidly appropriate in relation to his mission. The smooth whispers in his head guided his steps.

"Burning hot one day...freezing cold another," Doug's mind distracted itself for a second.

He rounded a corner and was mentally directed to pause, mid-block. A beaten old neon sign hummed overhead. He looked up and read the sign, *The Salvation Cafe*. The sign seemed to be clinging to life in defiance of damage caused by countless hurricanes. He watched as hapless people, in worn and mismatched clothes, stood glumly in line to enter.

"This is the place? All of these people are damned?" he asked the air.

"Not all," the voice responded curtly.

"So they all have to die, in order to kill the damned that are mixed in with them?" Doug asked oblivious of the incredulity in his voice.

"You are questioning the will of your Lord, not my own," the voice warned.

"I'm asking if there is any other way," Doug responded as he tried to sound respectful.

"Those soulless creatures in there could kill thousands, maybe millions of people. Is it really your place to decide who should live or die? I thought you were a servant of the Lord. Have I been deceived?" the smooth voice asked.

Doug reminisced momentarily about the time he had spent unguided and lost. The importance of mental questions of fairness and righteousness dulled to the point of being unwarranted.

"No... I *will* do what is necessary," Doug said as his steamy breath floated away on the night air.

He rounded the block a few times and looked for entry points. He discovered a door that lead into the building from a dimly lit courtyard.

171

Doug used his knife to detach part of the ancient lock mechanism that held the door closed. He opened the door cautiously and peered in. The room he was in was dark but light shown around a door that led into another room. The scent of old wood and decaying magazines and pest droppings came to him. He detested the smell. He recoiled and breathed through the sleeve of his jacket to filter the stench as he looked around the unkempt storage room. He stepped forward and could hear, what he imagined to be, cockroaches being crushed under the weight of his feet. He crept furtively to the door and peeked through one of the small cracks.

Doug spied an overweight man with an apron on, who labored over a dirty stove. The crown of his head was bald and shined with a greasy reflectiveness. The hair that grew around the sides of his head tufted in unkempt puffs. His enormous girth protruded from the undersized t-shirt he wore. The waist of the jogging pants strained in elasticity to contain his ample gut, which spilled over defiantly.

Doug grimaced at him and mouthed the word, "glutton," soundlessly to himself.

A short cigarette with a lengthy ash hung in the corner of this man's mouth. The huge soup pot on the stove boiled furiously before him. He leaned forward to adjust the station on a small portable radio. The steam licked at the flesh of his exposed stomach which caused him to withdraw angrily. He watched the ash from his cigarette tumble down into the pot. The ash floated momentarily on top of the froth above the boil and then sank. He grimaced, shrugged, and stirred the pot carelessly.

Doug was reviled by this man and grimaced as he struggled to devise a plan to sneak by him. He became aware that something had begun to crawl up his left leg. He desperately wanted to bend and slap at the spot of his pants, but refused himself for fear of discovery.

The large cook walked to the right and out of view. He heard the heavy thud as another door slammed shut and felt wind rush through the crack in front of him.

"Another door off of that room," he thought as he shook his pants leg expeditiously.

He placed his fingers against the door and pushed with a slight, but augmentative, force. The door did not budge. He then slid his fingers into the crack for a hold, and pulled at it hopefully. It slid toward him and he recoiled as its worn hinges creaked mournfully.

Doug walked into the small kitchen and looked around. His head was lowered in concentration as he received informative whispers. He walked to the door that the man must have used to exit. He slid the bolt closed to lock the door. He pulled it to make sure it would secure him against an unwanted visitor. Doug picked up a black pen from a shelf nearby and produced a small blue card from his breast pocket. He wrote 'I am the Antichrist' onto it, opened the freezer door next to him, and tossed it in. A smile parted his lips as he stared thoughtfully at the rusty door of the freezer for a moment.

He was pulled back to attention as he received more directional whispers. He approached the stove top ovens near him and turned off the gas burner under the ash soup. He squatted as he opened the large ovens and peered into them. The pilot light eyes, which burned in the shadowy recesses of the ovens, flickered as currents of air passed. The half burnt remnants of large kitchen matches littered the bottom of the oven. Doug turned the pilot light controls on the oven to the off position. The blue flames died with a hushing noise. He then flipped the controls to high in short order. A loud, *shhhh* noise filled the room as gas fumes poured from the pilot burners. He paused and waited to see if they would light automatically and was pleased when they did not. The air was thick with the scent additive of natural gas and he tried to filter his air through the sleeve of his jacket again. A thud from the other side of the door caused him to jump. The sound of porcelain dishes being destroyed covered the noise made as the oven door was slammed shut. Doug envisioned the large cook slamming into the bolted door with arm loads of plates.

The whispers in his head sounded again. Doug went back through the door from which he had come, and closed it behind him. He could hear a gruff voice complain loudly about the kitchen door being locked and realized his time to

173

be short. He opened the back door. The faint purple hue shown in from a dim light in the courtyard and added an eerie ambiance to the old storeroom. The light, while meager, allowed his eyes to make out some detail in the room.

He saw a large cardboard box with bold letters stenciled on the side. The box read, Donations For: *The Salvation Café*. Doug produced a disposable lighter from his pocket and lit the box of clothes on fire. The orange glow from the fire caused teaming numbers of roaches to retreat for the safety of shadows. Doug turned, closed the door, and proceeded to walk away. He was nearly two blocks away when the thunderous roar of the explosion reached his ears. There was a subtle displacement of air from the distant explosion. The night was filled with screams and sirens as he walked thoughtfully away.

* * *

Marvin lay on the floor of his living room and tore at the flesh of his face with his fingernails. He writhed around and screamed as he did this. The dark woman stood above him and watched in amusement. A pair of Takers stood to either side of her and watched Marvin with curiosity.

"I hope you enjoyed the seventh level. That is your reward for your faithful service to me. In truth, I am far the opposite of an angel," she confessed.

Marvin howled in mental anguish, seemingly oblivious to her words.

"I don't want to hamper your enjoyment of my treat. I will return periodically to torment your pathetic soul, as it gives me immense pleasure," she said and vanished.

It was a long while before Marvin's delirium broke. He rolled over onto his hands and knees and cried helplessly. A noise, something akin to an animal's claws being struck on tile, spooked him. He ran to his desk and rummaged through the drawer. He stalked into the living room and pointed his gun abstractly.

He threw his head back and screamed, "Dear God,

please protect me from these horrible visions. I can't take this anymore. Please will you accept me?"

There was no response other than the clack of bone on tile in a nearby room. Marvin placed the barrel of the old forty-five caliber pistol into his mouth. Drool and tears ran down the barrel onto his hand and left gleaming lines as they dripped down his forearm. His breath was ragged and he pressed his eyelids shut trying to summon the will to pull the trigger. The clacking noise erupted and sounded closer this time. There was a loud bang and the back of his head was blown away. His eyelids sprang open and the lifeless eyes slid backwards into his empty skull.

Chapter 15

Anonymity's End

Todd awoke and felt panic through his weightless form.

As he looked down he found himself amazed to see Bree, where she slept alone, in the bed. His mind struggled to comprehend the vantage point from which he looked on.

He realized himself to be hovering near the ceiling and asked, "What the...?"

"I am quite sorry, Todd," Bryce interrupted, "I thought it to be necessary."

"What's going on?" Todd asked, bewildered as his feet sank softly down onto the carpet.

"I need to see you, Todd. Face to face, like when we first got to know each other. A lot has happened and I think you need to be made aware of it," Bryce requested.

"Okay, I understand," Todd said and sat down in a nearby chair.

Todd cleared his mind and allowed himself to fully relax. The darkness behind his closed eyelids was pierced by the brightening glow of a warm light.

Bryce's face first came into view and then the rest of his body began to slowly form. Bryce stared at him and waited patiently for him to reorient himself. Todd looked down at his own hands and slowly seemed to garner awareness.

"Okay. What's going on?" he asked Bryce with concern.

Bryce sat comfortably in a white chair. He stroked his bland paisley tie. His mouth was slightly opened and seemed to search for a point at which to start.

"During the night you began to receive souls at an

176

astounding rate. I feared it might have the same physical ramifications as last time. So, I raised us up and away from young Miss Bree," Bryce cautiously explained.

"Good thinking. But I feel fine," Todd said as he looked sharply at Bryce and asked, "An astounding rate? What do you mean by that?"

"I mean literally hundreds. Most of them left their mortal coil in accidents, some by natural death, and a… suicide. There is no rhyme or reason I could think of for them to come to you. As far as I can tell, you had never interacted with any of them, save one, before now. There seemed to be no trauma for you. Perhaps the introduction of souls has increased your mental defense against the bludgeoning you suffered last time. I simply feared that Bree would not have the same resilience. I have settled them all. There is one…," Bryce looked down at his feet, "that I thought you should be made aware of as soon as possible," Bryce finished and looked at Todd with concern.

Todd's expression tensed in worry as he nodded in consent of Bryce's suggestion.

A man formed from the darkened void and walked toward Todd, who marveled at his appearance.

Marvin fixed his blue eyes upon Todd. His exaggerated smile was a poor mask for the nervousness that coursed through him. He stopped inches from Todd's chair and made several jerky motions.

Todd watched as Marvin struggled to find a pose to stand in before he spoke.

"Hello Lord," the man spoke, his thick southern accent sounded very reverential.

Todd looked at the man for a few moments in silence.

"You're the big tipping preacher from Lucy's Diner," Todd said in recognition.

"Pastor," Marvin said and raised his hand in embarrassment for the correction.

"I am sorry I did not mean to…," Marvin said and looked panicked as he searched for words.

"You appeared to me as a waiter and I never knew you for who you were. I know I shouldn't have killed

177

myself...I was just so lost and scared...The things she showed me... Please forgive me," Marvin said and dropped to his knees before Todd.

"Stand up," Todd told him with a grimace, "I'm just a man. All this groveling and veneration is completely unnecessary."

Marvin looked at him and smiled very genuinely now.

Bryce spoke to Marvin softly and said, "Marvin, please tell Todd about the strange events that led up to your suicide."

"Todd," Marvin stated as he acknowledged the name and bowed to Todd.

Marvin looked up at Todd and began to tell him about his suicide and the events that led up to it. As he spoke, a glassy image appeared behind him that displayed a visual presentation of Marvin's narrative. Marvin began to talk of the false angel now. The woman's face formed and Todd shot a furtive look over at Bryce who nodded in recognition of the face. The Deacon's face appeared next as Marvin began to explain about him. Todd and Bryce both shifted as they realized him to be Bryce's murderer.

As he told his hard cold story, Todd and Bryce watched with rapt attention as Marvin filled gaps in for them.

Marvin finished his lengthy story by saying, "I called for you and you brought me here. Oh, thank you, Lord."

"I'm not a savior, Marvin, as I told you already. I am just a man. Also, I am afraid that I may just be a future victim to this dark woman, who accosted you with the nightmarish visions," Todd explained.

Marvin dropped low and rested his forehead onto Todd's arm, where he sat in the chair.

"Here I am, safe from the visions. We have a very different idea about who is and isn't a savior," he said as he looked up at Todd and smiled.

"Thank you Marvin," Bryce said dismissively and gestured toward the gloom.

Marvin stood up and bowed to them both and dematerialized into the darkness.

"Do you understand now, why I insisted upon this, Todd?" Bryce asked.

Todd nodded thoughtfully.

"So, this woman has the ability to influence others and has had Marvin set this Doug Rolfe upon you," Bryce said.

"That note on my social security card!" Todd said as he arrived at the thought deductively.

"Yes. This Doug person, left it like a calling card for the police to find you," Bryce agreed.

Todd leaned forward in his chair, ran his fingers through his hair, and exhaled. Thoughts of Bree's safety played through Todd's troubled mind.

"I have to be able to protect her from this guy. She is in danger while we're together, Bryce," Todd said and looked up sadly.

"I disagree, Todd. I think she will be safe in your care. Your thoughts are so powerful now. This recent infusion of souls has augmented your ability dramatically. I am afraid to think what you could do to someone who threatened you," Bryce stated.

Todd looked at him sharply.

"So, I continue to garner souls for some unknown reason now, and they are augmentative to my abilities. This woman...creature...is a very large threat to me. She seems to be able to beguile people and bend them to her will. She could be working to turn all kinds of people against me. I wonder if my abilities will be enough to protect us?" Todd asked and made no attempt to mask his concern.

"The images that she showed Marvin were very disturbing. They were enough to cause him to commit suicide. This Doug person may have been enthralled so completely, that he was unable to discern reality from fantasy. He may have seen me as some horrible twisted monster that he needed to destroy," Bryce said.

Todd added, "And that poor little girl," and shivered.

Bryce nodded his agreement and grimaced.

"You are going to have to be very aware, Todd, of all the things going on around you," Bryce warned.

179

"Well, at least I know what this Doug person looks like and will be able to recognize him," Todd added.

"Who is Doug?" Bree asked.

Todd's eyes opened and he looked up at her.

He sat closely to Bree at the breakfast table and told her about his conversation with Bryce. He repeated as much of the information verbatim as he could.

"So, with all of these new souls you can do more than you could before?" she asked.

Todd recognized her question as a pointed way to reassure her own safety from these threats. She seemed to smile apologetically in recognition of his thoughts.

He was aware for the first time of what Bryce had meant in regards to his abilities having been increased. The abilities had carried with them a subtle feeling before. He could not exactly locate it within himself, but he could feel it nonetheless. It felt different now, a strength, buried somewhere in the center of him. Todd raised his eyebrows and looked away from her at the cabinets. His brow lowered and all of the cabinet doors opened at once. The dishes, stored in the cabinets, floated out into the open air of the kitchen.

Bree sat up in her chair and looked at them in amazement. Drawers slid open. Cutlery and flatware flew up into the air to join the dishes. Todd's stare seemed to be unfocused as he looked on. A smile tugged at the corner of his lips. His head tilted slowly to one side as his eyes narrowed. Utensils and dishes whizzed by and made screeching noises as they tore through air currents. Bree raised her hands to her mouth and gasped in disbelief. His attention turned to her and the fear of upsetting her filled him. The objects stopped in that moment. They soundlessly flew back into their respective cabinets and drawers which closed silently.

"I'm not scared of you in the least," Bree said numbly as she stared at the cabinets.

Todd turned to her and smiled as he said, "That was effortless."

"Wow, that would be convenient for putting away groceries," she joked sharply as she tried to bring levity to the situation.

Todd threw his head back and laughed out loud. Bree looked at him and smiled. The tension crept from her shoulders and body. Todd opened his mouth to speak.

"Mmm yes, breakfast at Don's sounds like a *great* idea," she agreed.

"I just need to get dressed," she said over her shoulder.

"I need to go see Don. I need to let him know I'm leaving. It's just the right thing to do," he called after her.

"Okay," she called to him from the bathroom, where she labored to attach the third hook of her bra.

Todd stared out of the window of Bree's car, lost in contemplation, as she drove them to Don's. Shades of fear worked themselves through him as he thought about this Doug person. Bree slapped him in the side of the thigh and drew his attention to her.

"You have to stop being all doom and gloom over there. I'm trying to relax. You should too," she said.

At Todd's direction, Bree pulled into a parking spot half a block from Don's restaurant.

"This is the best spot to park. Traffic is gonna start to get really bad as people venture out from work to get lunch," Todd said as he looked at the time stamp on his phone.

The air was rich with the scent of freshly cooked foods that Todd associated with work. Todd momentarily remembered his first day at Don's. Don and Tony had made him feel welcome by picking on him at every possible opportunity. It was almost like having Will with him here in this self-imposed exile. Todd wondered if the solitude, that had been a desperate bid for sanity, had ever really been necessary.

"Well, at least you met me," Bree said as she rubbed at his shoulder reassuringly and pulled the door open.

"Yes, you're a definably bright point in my life," Todd said and took her hand as they entered together.

The small bell on the door chimed as Bree and Todd walked into Don's. Tony looked up at them and smiled from where he stood. Todd felt another pang of guilt over his decision to leave as he watched Tony walk toward them.

"I see you have a partner in crime today," Tony said and looked warmly at Bree.

"No, we're gonna pay for the food. No theft today," Bree said.

Bree worked furiously to hide a panicked expression as she looked into Tony's eyes. Tony's smile had faded for a second as he wondered how she might have put together the joke he was setting up for.

"Todd must have told her about me being after him for eating sausage in the mornings," Bree heard Tony's thoughts.

"He eats bacon every morning," Todd thought to himself, hoping to communicate the idea to Bree.

"I'm sure the bacon took a beating this morning," she chided.

Tony's expression relaxed and he said, "Well I'm gonna have to keep an eye on you anyway. You're guilty by association," Tony said and clapped Todd on the shoulder playfully.

Todd smiled at Tony warmly and made a quick hand gesture showing him two fingers.

"Oh, table for two. Right this way, sir," Tony said as he led them to a table.

"What can I get for you guys?" Tony asked as Bree slid into the booth.

"O.J. for the lady please, and I will have a coffee. I need to talk to Don," Todd said with a grim expression.

Tony looked obviously concerned and asked, "Is everything okay?"

"Things are excellent. I came into some really good money via...," Todd paused, "Some investments I made came through and I will be quite comfortable for a while. I just wanted to come in and be up front with Don, out of fairness," Todd finished and smiled at Tony.

Tony's usual happy expression returned and he smiled at Bree and said, "Well I'm glad for you. I won't have to compete with this goofball for tips anymore."

"Wow, it's nice to know how you *really* felt about me," Todd remarked and folded his arms in a pretense of

182

disappointment.

"Don't get all bitchy on me I was just kidding with you," Tony whispered.

Todd returned Tony's playful smile and dismissed himself. Todd disappeared through the door marked *Employees Only*.

"I will be right back with your orange juice," Tony said to Bree.

"Thank you," she said.

As Todd entered the kitchen he was surprised that Don was not at the grill, where he would toil in his usual frenzied fashion. Instead, three young men worked in unison to complete the task. They smiled up at him from where they stood.

"Where's Don?" Todd asked curiously.

The tallest of the three men pointed at the office door that adjoined the kitchen. Todd nodded to him thankfully, walked to the door, and knocked gently.

"Come in," Don's voice called through the door.

Todd surveyed Don where he sat and played a game on his computer.

Don desperately clicked keys. He seemed to try and steer the character he played with his head and neck motions.

"Just a sec," Don said without a diversion of attention.

His brow furrowed as his thick fingers pounded keys briskly. Todd surmised that something bad must have happened.

Don leaned back from the computer and hollered, "Damned rogues!" as he slammed his fist down on his desk and looked angry.

He looked slowly over and smiled as his eyes fell upon Todd.

"Hey, hey," he said to Todd and turned to face him fully.

Todd tried to smile as he sat down in the chair opposite Don's desk.

"What's going on in here?" he asked Don as he pointed over his shoulder at the kitchen.

"Oh, the guys? New hires. We're doing so well, I

183

hired em to run the kitchen while I hang out back here and do... paperwork," he said and pointed at his computer.

"Ha! That's great," Todd said.

"I hate to have to tell you this, Don," Todd winced as the smile faded from Don's face.

"I recently had a few investments pay off. Kinda like winning the lottery and I'm going to take a hiatus, as far as work goes," Todd said.

"Oh, cool. Good for you," Don said, the smile returned to his face.

Todd relaxed. Don seemed to take what he imagined to have been a crushing blow, exceedingly well.

"And you came all the way down here so you could tell me face to face. You're just that kind of guy, aren't you? Honest as the day is long. I still say you were hatched and not born," Don said and laughed at his own joke.

"How will I make it through my days without your sarcastic sense of humor?" Todd asked and rolled his eyes.

"I can't tell you that we won't miss you. I'm very glad for your fortune though, Todd. Perhaps you could give me a hand with stock acquisition at some point?" Don asked.

"Sure, no problem. Thanks for everything Don," Todd said as he reached to shake Don's hand.

"If you guys ever get in a pinch, you can call me at any time. I can be here ready to serve in fifteen minutes. I brought my girlfriend over for breakfast. I better get back to her before Tony puts the moves on her," Todd chided over their handshake.

Don nodded and smiled at this. A small silence passed between them.

"Okay. Gonna head back out there and have some breakfast. I'll let you get back to those...'damned rogues'," Todd said and pointed at Don's computer.

"Yep, as you can tell, my time is precious," Don said as he returned his attention to his game.

"*My time is precious,*" Todd winced as he muttered the words to himself with a mournful expression.

Todd paused and shook the thoughts from his head before he headed into the dining room. He returned to the table, pleased with the exchange between Don and himself.

Bree daintily spooned sections of grapefruit into her mouth. She pointed at the spread of eggs and meat on the other side of the table with a repulsed 'are you gonna eat all that shit' look on her face.

Todd smiled at the food happily and looked back to Tony and said, "*You know what I like.*"

"Oh Thop it and eat, you big thilly," Tony lisped and made an effeminate hand gesture to Todd.

The other waiters looked at them, grimaced, and then smiled. Todd looked through the window of the restaurant thoughtfully as he ate his breakfast.

"You think that Doug guy is here?" Bree asked with a tone of concern in her voice.

"I don't know where he is...and that worries me," he replied.

"He better stay away from you, or you can beat him up with the contents of your cabinets," she said as she brandished a spoon at him.

Todd belted out a little laugh and finished his coffee. Bree's attention was caught by a mother, several tables away, which made ridiculous faces at her infant son. Todd watched Bree smile infectiously, as the child giggled at his mother. His thoughts were quiet as he watched her. He had never met anyone that he enjoyed conversation with more in his life. Her every motion seemed like poetry to him and he wondered what she saw in him. Todd finished his breakfast and cleaned his lips with his napkin.

"*Oh, waiter,*" Todd said as he motioned to Tony, who rolled his eyes at Todd and headed toward them.

"Would you be so kind, my good sir, as to bring us our ticket?" he asked Tony and giggled at his own cleverness.

"I am afraid," Tony raised his nose into the air as he began, "Dear customer, that I will be unable to grant your request, as the proprietor of this establishment informs me that your money is worthless here," Tony finished and smiled.

"Cool. I will be here every day if it's free," Todd said and slapped the table.

"Thank you very much," Bree said as she popped

185

Todd's hand where it sat on the table.

"All right, Todd. I meant what I said about you stopping by for visits. If you don't, I know where you live. The last thing you want is an angry black man at your door," Tony bit his bottom lip and tried to look menacing.

"No problem, man. Plus, you know how much I like free food," Todd replied.

Bree popped him again.

"See you guys later. Keep this joker in line," Tony said to Bree and walked away.

"Bye," Bree said cheerily as she picked up her purse and stood up.

"So, what do you want to do now?" she asked Todd as he opened the door and caused the small bell to chime.

She quickly turned back at him with a shocked expression and slapped him in the chest. Todd grabbed at the spot where she hit him and feigned injury.

"Oh, come on. It would be fun," he said playfully.

"I agree, but I have to make you work for it. A woman has to have her mystery," she said.

She shook her head and poorly masked a smile that had forced itself onto her lips. Todd felt Bree's hand where it sat low against the small of his back as they walked together. He waited until an oncoming lady had looked up to them and recoiled as though she had grabbed his butt. Todd hurriedly pushed her arm away and said, "Fresh. Watch it Miss. I'm not cheap."

The lady in front of them looked at Bree and shook her head in disappointment, as she walked by.

Bree turned to face Todd and said, "I guess you thought that was funny."

"As a matter of fact, I did," he said as they collapsed together again and walked forward.

Todd put his arm across her shoulders and pulled her to him. The sweet smell of her hair drifted to his nose. He commented mentally on how wonderful it smelled and pulled her closer.

She smiled at the unspoken compliment and said, "It does smell good doesn't..."

Her sentence was cut short as their ears were

assaulted by the thunderous noise of vehicle tires, as they scraped unevenly across asphalt. They turned to witness the calamitous events as they unfolded. The careless driver of a car had sped through a red light and slid toward a truck. The truck was overlarge and unmovable and the car bounced off of it as they collided. The car flopped onto its side unevenly. The car's quarter panels produced sparks as it continued to skid over the ragged asphalt of the road. Todd could see the driver of the car, who hung sideways cradled, in the binding of the seat belt. The driver frantically turned the wheel of the car, pointlessly. The car continued forward, a spray of sparks and glass. Todd's eyes traced ahead of its path.

A man and a boy had entered the crosswalk and were frozen in panic as the car slid toward them. The man curled the child to him, crouched, and turned his back to the car.

Todd could hear Bree's scream through his fear-numbed senses. Todd's mind was barely able to fully process what happened next.

There was a bright rush of white light in his peripheral vision. The distance between him and where the man crouched, to shield the child from the car, seemed to close in upon him. He found himself crouched behind the man. He could hear the nightmare wreck of the car screeching toward them over his shoulder. He threw his arms around the man and the child strongly.

Todd meant to throw all of their weight to one side in and attempt to avoid the car crushing them. He looked to Bree's horrified face in that fleeting moment. Her eyes met his.

The white rushing light formed in the periphery of his vision again. Todd looked passed Bree to the safety of the sidewalk next to her. A tattered paper sign was taped to the brick wall where his eyes fell. The distance between him and the sign on the wall, began to collapse. The print of the sign, at first, too far away to focus on, became sharp and readable. Todd, the man, and the boy collided with the wall next to Bree and fell backward onto the sidewalk. Todd crawled around and waited for his equilibrium to return. His head jerked over his shoulder as the car slid onto the sidewalk and struck a nearby building. The vehicle wrapped itself around the corner of the building in a spray of chipped brick shards.

Bree barely had time to react and turned her back to the spray of brick. She looked down at Todd, who rose slowly to his feet.

"How did you do that?" she asked him.

"I...I don't know," he answered shakily.

A cell phone was thrust between them and she could hear the sound of a camera shutter. She stared at the device curiously before she traced the arm that held it back to its owner. The man recoiled at her angered expression. She pushed the large man away roughly, and he clumsily dropped his phone in surprise.

"Keep that thing outta my face," she demanded angrily.

Five more phones were thrust into her face and she could hear the camera shutter sounds again.

"Get out of here!" Bryce's voice filled Todd's head.

Todd shook his head to clear it. He took Bree's hand and led her away through the forming crowd. Todd pushed phones away from his face as they trudged through the mass of people. The short trek to her car had been exaggerated by the throngs of curious thrill seekers.

Bree pointed a remote and her car emitted a loud, shrill chirp. This took the people that followed them by surprise. The distraction provided a small lead. Bree blocked and pushed at the people who struggled to take pictures of Todd over her shoulder, as she let Todd into her car. She body checked a large man who fell sharply onto his backside. She slammed the passenger side door closed and locked the car with her remote. Todd sat in the safety of the car and watched her. It was pretty amazing to see this slight woman bludgeon her way through the crowd. She was livid and tossed people aside with reckless abandon on her way to the driver's side of the car. She singled out the car key and let herself in. She tried to crush several of the phones in the door as she pulled it closed.

Cell phones just outside the driver's window lined up as the people clambered to take pictures of her.

"They are getting pictures of you for the insurance

claims. More than a few of them are gonna need dental work slugger," Todd chided.

Bree laughed and started the car. She raced its engine loudly and the crowd retreated a few feet. She did it again and made the engine of the car roar. The army of cell phone wielding photographers quickly backed away and she pulled out onto the street and sped away.

"Let's go to my place, it's closer," she belted out as she leaned forward, fighting the powerful acceleration of the vehicle.

"Good idea, but loop around a few blocks. A lot of those people are behind us," he said as he watched people clamber into vehicles through the rear window of the car.

They rode in silence as Bree worked to elude the people who followed them. She was pretty sure that the late model passenger van would be the last one. She raced the engine and sped through a traffic light a split second before it turned red. The cumbersome van screeched to a halt at the intersection. Todd looked over at her confident smirk, with adoration.

She took no notice of Todd as she watched the van in her rear view mirror. With a sharp controlled jerk, she whipped the car into the garage of her apartment building. She selected a parking spot obstructed from view of the street. They hopped out and rushed hurriedly to meet each other at the rear of the car.

Bree looked up into his eyes and said, "You saved those people. You're a hero."

"I'm not...I don't even know how I did it," Todd said honestly.

"It's like splitting hairs with you, take the damn compliment," she said sternly.

"Those people took our picture, lots of them," he offered.

"Well, you can't get in trouble for saving people's lives," Bree explained.

"No, but if I don't want to be found by one particular person, having your face plastered everywhere is very counterproductive," Todd stated as thoughts of Doug passed through his mind.

Understanding dawned on Bree's face as she followed Todd toward her apartment.

"And how in the Hell would I explain the ability to do that flashy move thing, if asked?" Todd asked.

She was quiet and in deep thought as she followed him down the hallway toward her apartment door. He paused to let her lead.

"It just occurred to me that I don't remember which apartment is yours," he confessed.

"I was wondering, but you did pretty well. That's my door up there on the left," she responded and moved ahead of him.

She let them in and dropped her purse carelessly as she walked in. Todd closed the door and locked it. He watched as she tossed her personal belongings all over on her walk to the living room. He followed her and plopped down on her couch. She looked at him and forced a smile onto her face, in an attempt to comfort him. She winced at his thoughts, sat down next to him, and put her hand firmly on his leg.

"Maybe they won't tell anybody," she offered hopefully.

She could hear the jumble of his thoughts and concentrated to block them out.

"I have to keep Bree safe. How can I explain? What if Doug sees that? People will hunt me. What about the government doing experiments on me...I'm so thirsty."

Her perception of Todd's thoughts dulled and ebbed to a stop.

Todd looked up at her nervously and asked, "May I have a glass of water?" as he licked his lips dryly.

"I wish that water could wash this all away," Todd thought to himself as he watched her leave.

Bree jogged into the kitchen, opened the refrigerator, and grabbed a cold bottle of water. As she stood up, she noticed a large shadow, darken her window and she approached it to inspect the sky. The blue sky was now a torrent of angry dark storm clouds.

She winced as a burst of lightning flashed brilliantly. It began to rain in that moment. She grimaced as

190

she watched large drops of rainwater ravage the plants in her window box. She had often practiced the habit of placing the plants on the sill to catch rainwater. The drops were overlarge and heavy. The small plants drooped under the bludgeoning of water issued by the storm. She opened the window, grabbed up the plants, and brought them inside carefully. She closed the window, returned to Todd, and handed him the water. His mouth opened to impart a thank you.

"You're welcome," she said, unaware that his thanks had been unspoken.

Todd smiled at this as he contemplated her ability to hear his thoughts.

"Oops. Sorry. I'm a little stressed and didn't realize you hadn't spoken," she said in frustration.

He turned the bottle up and crushed it greedily expediting the water flow. A loud peel of thunder clapped outside.

"What are we going to do, Bryce?" he asked, as he hoped for advice.

"First, you have to calm down. We need to think of a way to explain your abilities. Those people displayed wonder and curiosity that you would associate with having been witness to such a spectacle. I would be inclined to doubt the possibility of them allowing this to pass without answers," Bryce warned.

"Right. It's the hot topic of the moment," Todd said as he waved his hand angrily in agreement.

"Yes. Shock, awe, and adoration are common in those types of situations. You have to consider that you saved people and that it was obvious that you had done so. However, the emotion that worries me is fear. Humans as a species are stupid, easily panicked animals. When faced with something they have no clue about, they are irrational and lash out by instinct. The propensity they have to feel fear of you needs to be squelched. Worst case scenario, the world knows your secret. If I were you, I would tout myself as an angel or some other mystical being in order to garner support and safety from those who believe in that sort of thing. It could work to your advantage if they believed you to be

191

something extraordinary," Bryce offered.

Todd nodded thoughtfully. He thought of droves of people being injured as they tried to shield him from harm.

"It's not a good idea. I don't want innocent people hurt over some lie. I am no angel. And I don't want to mislead people."

"I bet that man and that child think you're an angel," Bree said and nodded in agreement with herself.

"I don't know who would question you, Todd, but if you made yourself out to be this angel, and someone were to ask you questions like, how did you come to be here among men, or what have you. You could always play the 'I am unable to answer that question' card. I mean, an angel would have some larger agenda that people were not meant to understand," Bryce said as he tried to push his point.

"No. I don't want to go there. A lie is always more trouble than it's worth," Todd answered with finality.

"A very noble and heroic sentiment from someone who *accidentally* saved people," Bryce responded sardonically.

Todd ignored Bryce's irritated response.

"You could always give the beauty pageant answer," Bree offered.

"The what?" Todd asked.

"I want to promote world peace, love, understanding; blah, blah, blah, sexy bikinis," she said and laughed.

Todd smiled at her weakly, and was appreciative of her attempt to bring levity to the moment.

Bree's expression was suddenly pained and she muttered the word, "Dad."

Her phone sprang to life. Todd jumped as it rang and looked at her in wonder.

She forced a smile onto her face and tried to infuse it into her tone.

"Hello?" she asked.

"Briana? What's going on?" her father's questions were rushed and full of parental impatience.

"What do you mean?" Bree asked nervously as she curled the phone cord around her finger.

"You're all over the television. They keep showing this news story about that waiter from Don's. There are lots of pictures of you and him," her father's words were quick and excited.

"Oh, that," she said, as she worked to formulate an explanation.
"That is honestly, not what it looks like...There are some smoke and mirror tricks...That guy is...an actor...It's a promotion for a new movie," Bree's voice trailed off.

Her father laughed into the phone, "You always were a terrible liar. So, I guess you can't tell me about it right now, but you will call your poor old father and let him know what's going on as soon as possible, right?" the old man asked.

Bree smiled as she thought of the way her father always allowed her time to be honest with him. Through his patience, it had allowed her to be a more truthful person.

"Yes," she said with a genuine smile.

"You're safe?"

"Yes," she answered.

"You're happy?"

"Yes, Daddy. Very much so," she responded again and looked to Todd who watched her curiously.

"That's all I need to know. Call your poor old man and give him a clue when you can, Breezy," her father finished.

"I love you too, Dad. Bye-bye," she said into the phone with a genuine smile.

"Wow, we're in the news, already," Bree said to Todd.

"What?" Todd asked his voice barely a croak.

They piled up on Bree's couch. She pointed the remote at the television and as the screen lit up, Todd saw a picture of himself.

"Late breaking news," the announcer's voice said excitedly.

Todd and Bree's eyes widened as they watched the whole scene in perfect detail.

"This footage was taken from a security camera above *Don's Restaurant* in downtown Houston," the reporter said.

The first time it was shown, you could see the entire scene in a large panoramic shot. The car grazed off of a truck and flipped on its side. The car slid toward the shock-frozen pedestrians. There were three rapid bursts of white light. The car slid over the spot where the pedestrians had vanished in the second to last burst of light.

"Look at it again, in slow motion," the excited reporter commanded.

This view was enhanced and zoomed in on where Todd stood in shock with Bree. Todd became light, dispersed, and reappeared crouched behind the cars would be victims. In slow motion, Todd grasped the two people. All three of them became light and returned to the spot near, where Todd had started from. The car slammed into the building and people reacted in slow motion to avoid the spray of debris.

"This amazing scene unfolded just moments ago, and news six has the first look," the reporter proudly announced.

"People at the scene claim this, currently unknown, man miraculously saved thirty-seven year old Robert Gutenberg, and his nine year old son, Roland. At this time, we have no leads on the identity of this hero," the reporter added.

Pictures of Todd appeared on the screen from different angles. Todd was sure these were garnered from cell phones.

"The hero quickly left the scene without any thanks, in a car driven by this woman, according to eyewitnesses," the reporter said.

Pictures of Bree flashed across the screen. Todd was very close to the screen. He had hovered closer to it, all the while that they watched. Cell phone pictures continued to flash across the television. Todd spotted a picture of Bree's car as they drove away.

"Damn it," Todd yelled and tapped the screen.

"What?" Bree asked as she pressed the rewind button on her remote.

Todd watched for a second and then said, "There!"

as he pointed to the screen, "Your license plate number, big as day! Damn it," Todd said angrily.

Todd went to the window and looked intently down at the street. He was not surprised to see news vans parked in sporadic patterns along the length of the street.

People clambered from the vans in their brightly colored rain suits. They tromped through the ankle deep water toward the entrance of Bree's apartment building.

"We have to get out of here, *now!*" he exclaimed as he looked back at her.

Bree had already produced raincoats with hoods from her closet.

"We can dress up as a news team and sneak by them," she suggested.

"But we don't have any equipment or anything," Todd said as he clumsily climbed into the raincoat and grimaced at the shortness of the sleeves.

"Hooray for karaoke," Bree said excitedly as she handed Todd a large microphone from her entertainment center.

They were barely out of the apartment door, when the herd of reporters bustled up the hallway.

Bree quickly turned back to her door and began to pound on it as she screamed, "Open up, please, we just want to ask you a few questions."

The herd arrived and a woman among them with ridiculous collagen plumped lips said, "Stand aside. I'll get them out," as she pressed herself against the door and screamed, "Fire! Run for your lives."

Todd and Bree kept their faces low and milled slowly past the impatient reporters that flooded into the hallway.

"We just have a few questions," they could hear the fat lipped woman, pleading at Bree's door.

"Your car is no good to us. They know it and the street is blocked," Todd said over the loud plops of rain that struck the hood of his raincoat.

They walked for several blocks through the miserable conditions and finally were able to hail a cab. The cab driver looked at them in his rear view mirror apprehensively as they climbed into the backseat. Neither of them lowered their hood as they sat together. The male or he guessed he was a male, belted out an address across town. Todd added that a tip was involved if it were to be a short ride. Obviously driven to make a tip the cab driver sped quickly to Todd's apartment. Todd kept his hood low on his face as he stooped down to pay the cab driver. Todd noticed a police cruiser through the passenger side window of the cab. Todd straightened up and fixed his attention on the uniform-clad police officer. The officer was immersed in his perusal of a newspaper. The officer distractedly sipped at a cup of coffee. Todd's head ticked, almost imperceptibly. The cup in the officer's hand exploded, hot coffee flew all over him and the inside of the vehicle. All of the windows of the cruiser cracked. The officer was blind to the exterior environment. Todd took Bree's hand and they headed into the lobby of his apartment building together.

"Isn't that odd," Bree commented as she rushed behind him toward his apartment.

"Everything about today has been abnormal. What particular oddity were you referring to?" he asked over his shoulder.

"You pop all around, save people miraculously, and yet somehow, I'm the only one who gets identified," she said.

He turned to her with a mournful expression and said, "I am sorry that you're mixed up in this, but I'm very glad you're with me."

He smiled apologetically, turned back to the door, and opened it.

She smiled at him and he moved closer to her. Her smooth kiss warmed him and they backed together into his apartment.

Chapter 16

Malicious Intent

Doug packed the black powder into the small hole drilled into the hand grenade he held. The weather outside had become increasingly worse over the last few minutes. Large muddy puddles formed in the dirt outside, as he looked glumly out of his window.

"It is beginning," the smooth voice spoke from inside his head.

Doug sat quickly up in his chair and spilled black powder.

"What is it, angel? Is there more for me to do?" Doug asked the air around him.

"Yes. You will need to act swiftly. The dark forces mount as we speak. Your target has committed a false act of kindness. He intends to mislead the world and render them unable to see his dark purpose," the voice said ominously.

Doug licked his lips and swallowed as he tried to stave off the rush of excitement that washed through him.

"The storm outside is his doing. Note that it is as dark and violent as his purpose," the smooth voice taunted.

"What is this act of false kindness, Angel?" Doug asked.

"You can see it for yourself in your picture box. He is already sought after as a savior. His evil plan comes to fruition as we speak," she answered.

"Picture box?" he began to ask, thoughtfully.

Doug looked ahead of him at the darkened television. He picked up the remote and turned it on.

"Eyewitness accounts, along with this footage from a local diner's security camera, tell the tale of this miraculous guardian angel that saved these people," the announcer recited.

197

Doug's eyes narrowed in angry concentration as he watched open mouthed, as the story repeated itself. Pictures of the waiter and a blonde haired woman flashed in front of him.

"That is another of his whores," the voice returned to him.

"She can hear your thoughts if you don't protect them well, when you are near her. He will mislead the world and they will bow to him. He and his son will lead the world into the evil inferno of Hell."

Doug thought of the woman that owned the diner.

"Yes, exactly," the voice began, "If you destroy his seed and those that nurture it, he will be temporarily weakened," the disembodied voice finished.

"Can I destroy him then?" Doug asked.

"No, but it will weaken him. You have to remove all of his servants before he will become vulnerable enough for you to strike," the voice again spoke in an ominous tone.

Doug contemplated on this before he responded.

"So, I need to kill his evil child and those that care for him, first, and then his mind reader?" Doug asked the voice.

"Yes. When you attack his child, have them summon him, via telephone. He will arrive very quickly, so you must strike quickly and flee. His wrath would be swift and merciless if he were to discover you there with his murdered offspring. If you manage to accomplish this task and retreat to safety, the dread caused by the act, might be enough to tip the balance of power in our favor. Be warned, he will try to destroy you after you strike this close to his heart. You will have to move among the shadows and wait for the opportune moment to strike. He will turn people against you and make them think that you are the evil that you fight against," the voice warned.

"There are no depths of his deceptions. I will become hunted...but I must not let anyone stop me, or his evil will spread and drag the earth into Hell," Doug said through clenched teeth.

"You are very, very worthy," the voice in his head repeated.

Doug walked around his trailer, and carried a large duffel bag. He threw in clothes and books that struck him randomly as important. He lowered himself over a vent in the floor and used his fingernails to pry it up. He lay on the floor with his arm in the opened vent up to his shoulder. He stretched and strained until he found what he was after. He smiled, stood up, and held an envelope and his hunting knife. He looked into the envelope and flipped through the thousand dollar bills. He closed it carefully, shoved it and the knife into his bag. He went outside, placed the bag into the backseat of his car, and went back into the trailer. He made a sweep of the house for anything else that he may need.

He corrected his comforter and blanket on his bed, nervously distracted by his thoughts. He looked down upon the neatly made bed and thought, with remorse, of never seeing it again. Doug reached down next to him and opened the drawer of the table, on which his bible sat. He reached in and produced a large, thick piece of black charcoal chalk.

"This will piss it off," he said as he reached above his head and began to write on the ceiling.

Doug walked carefully though the ankle deep trash he had poured out onto his living room floor. Something caught his eye and he meticulously covered it with a half wadded sheet of paper. He stared at his home for a long time as he sat in the car. The ratty old trailer shrank from view in a series of glances as he drove away.

* * *

It had been a particularly rocky night for Will Goldman. His infant son, Sebastian, had woken him, what seemed like, every hour on the hour. Will had gone through the infant checklist each time.   First, he would check the baby's diaper for a 'land mine' as he called it. Sebastian seemed to make these when Lucy would feed him too many green leafy vegetables.

Then he would pick him up and rock him for a few minutes and hope for a burp. If all of this failed, it was time for a bottle of slightly warmed formula which would usually end up all over the front of Will's shirt. In any event, going through these steps would ensure that his son would go back to sleep, if even for a little while. Will smiled down at his son, who carelessly slept with a smile on his face. Crickets were performing a lullaby symphony just outside the window and he became aware of just how exhausted he had become. He threw an arm over his head and closed his red itchy eyes and settled back in his recliner. Will's eyes sprang open as he remembered that he would have to wake Lucy for work. She had warned him to be punctual, as she needed to write out checks to pay bills this morning. Lucy would never hear the alarm, and if he overslept, it would be disastrous. Will concentrated as he set his alarm for five A.M. Sure things were okay, he looked over at Sebastian. The infant nuzzled his pillow dreamily and replayed that smile, almost as if he knew Will watched him. Will settled back into his chair. It seemed he had just closed his eyes, however, the change of lighting in the window said differently.

"It should still be dark," he thought as he looked out into the bleak rainy weather outside.

"Lucy!" he bellowed as he clawed his way from the comfortable chair.

Sebastian woke up and began to stretch.

"Lucy wake up, we're late!" he hollered through the house again.

A heavy impatient knock rattled the front door.

"I'm coming!" He bellowed to the door as he wrestled a pair of khaki shorts up to his waist.

"Must be ole Sheriff Swayne doing a wake-up call," he muttered to himself.

Will lumbered across the carpet slowly, undid the lock, and opened the door. Without a look up, he stood aside to allow, whoever had braved the deluge of rain, entry into his home.

"Sorry, I was knocked out," Will said as he rubbed at his eyes sleepily.

Will never saw the heavy knife handle that came down on the top of his head. Will Goldman covered his head with both hands and staggered back a few steps. Will's eyes stared dully ahead as he lowered his hands to inspect the blood that covered them, with a child-like sort of curiosity.

His hands dropped to his sides and his eyes rolled straight up past his attacker. Will's large frame buckled, his knees crashed into the floor. He fell forward with a heavy thud, which shook the nearby walls. Lucy heard the noise, ran into the room, and saw Will crumpled on the floor.

"Will! Are you alr…" she began to ask.

"Psst," she heard behind her.

As she turned, the flesh colored blur of a fist struck her between the eyes. Lucy Goldman was unconscious before her head struck the leg of the baby's crib.

* * *

Todd stood and stared at Bree for a long moment, silently, as she browsed through his movie collection. He admired her beauty as her finger ran along the spines of movie cases. Her presence helped him to avoid thoughts of the nightmarish drama, which his life had become. She looked up at him from his copy of some romantic comedy.

"I love this movie," she said.

"Can we watch it later?" she asked.

He began, "Sure It's......,"

"Your favorite movie of all time," she said absently in completion of his sentence.

"Oh, dear Todd, save me," the random voice echoed through Todd's thoughts.

Todd winced as his hand shot to his temple.

"Bryce did you hear that?" Todd asked.

"Yes, I already knew this. You are also infatuated with a series of erotic movies that you saw as a young man," Bryce responded impatiently.

Bree giggled and covered her mouth.

"No, I meant the…never mind," Todd said dismissively.

A loud grumble came from Bree's stomach that sounded like a muffled bear roar.

"If that's gas, let me know, so I can run," he told her as he mocked fear.

"*No*," she said and swatted at him in a pretense of anger.

201

"That grapefruit isn't holding up as well as it needs to. I'm starved," she said and looked embarrassed.

"I have just the thing for you," he said with an excited expression.

She followed him into the kitchen, her eyebrow cocked up in curiosity. Todd turned back for a second, opened his mouth to speak, but Bree cut him off.

"Do I really want to know what a 'welfare burger' is?" she asked as she masked a smile.

Todd rolled his eyes and placed a large glass mixing bowl on the table.

"You're just gonna have to diversify your food preferences a bit. Just because you're beautiful and smart, doesn't mean you can besot the institution which is *the welfare burger*," he said playfully as he tossed a bloody hunk of ground sirloin into a bowl.

"This is *the* burger," he began, "Other burgers are plain and you have to add condiments to them to be able to choke them down. A 'welfare burger'," his tone was full of pride, "is mixed with seasoning and makes the mouth sing with every bite," he said excitedly.

Boxes of soup mix let themselves out of the cabinet and landed on the table, followed by eggs, and a box of bread crumbs.

Bree watched as he added spices to the bowl with wild abandon. He looked to her like the mad scientist in some old movie. She watched ingredients show themselves to the table next to him as he looked thoughtfully into the mix.

"He doesn't even know he is doing that," she thought as she watched a bottle of marinade drift down and land next to him.

"So, you don't measure the stuff you put in?" she asked, as she watched him crack eggs open.

Todd dumped the contents of the eggs and released the shells. The shells drifted as if on invisible strings and dropped into the trashcan behind him.

"You don't have to, really. All the ingredients are smackin. More or less of one or another, won't affect the taste that much," he said as if the information should be

202

common knowledge.

She approached the bowl and looked inside. It did, in fact, not look 'smackin', as he put it.

The bloody meat was mostly covered by brown powder and dried onions stuck out of it everywhere. One of the eggs slowly made its way down the side of a pile of breadcrumbs, coming to rest in a slimy pile against the side of the bowl.

"Can you mix that for me?" he asked her as he turned and grabbed the handle of a frying pan that seemed to defy gravity.

"I got it," he said and smiled as he noted her revulsion of the bowls contents.

"I don't know how to cook. I can burn water," she said and retreated slowly away from the bowl.

"*What*?" he asked incredulously.

He pretended to write a note in his palm and shot her a few analytical glances.

"That's going in your permanent file," he said and smiled as he drove his hands into the grotesque mixture.

The blob of meat answered his pressure with wet ragged burps. Bree smiled weakly and dismissed herself. She returned to her perusal of his movie collection. She found herself unable to resist the urge to place them in order of genre. This was actually quite easy, as over half of them would file under horror. The rich delicious smell of cooked burgers drifted into the room. She rose up and sniffed the air like an animal. Her walk to the kitchen was punctuated by another bear-like growl from her stomach.

"That smells *so* good!" she said as she entered the kitchen.

Todd sliced lettuce on a cutting board at the sink and pretended to look offended at her earlier reaction. As he turned back to say something, she went up on her toes, and covered her mouth with both hands. Her eyes were wide with anguish.

"What?" Todd asked with a look of concern.

She lowered one hand from her mouth and pointed to Todd's hand. A tear fell from one eye as her face flushed red. Todd looked back to where he had been cutting the lettuce. His own eyes flew open wide. The knife sat in his finger between two knuckles. He winced and waited to feel pain, as he slowly raised the knife. There was no blood. There was no cut. Todd flexed his finger in bewilderment in front of his face. His hand had become partially translucent. The hand solidified as they looked on. Her head was cocked on one side in sheer amazement and confusion. Todd turned to the cutting board again and slowly lowered the sharp knife toward his finger. Bree now joined him and placed her hand softly on his shoulder. They watched as the knife blade seemed to slice cleanly through his finger and came to rest on the cutting board. Todd pulled the hand back slowly, the finger passed through the knife blade. He turned the point of the knife toward his forearm and began to push it slowly. The blade passed right through his arm. He looked up at Bree curiously.

"Oh Shit is right!" she said, hearing his thoughts as she watched the blade pass through his bicep.

"Try to pass it through your finger after turning the flat edge of the blade down," Bryce instructed.

Todd licked his lips in concentration and lowered his face until it was level with his finger, where it sat on the cutting board. The flat dull backside of the knife just pressed into his finger and sat on top of it. Todd flipped the knife over and chopped at his hand slowly again with the sharp side of the blade. It simply would not cut him. He attacked his finger again with a barrage of short chops. He drew his finger back and made an agonized expression. He drew saliva through his clenched teeth as he inhaled.

Bree's hands flew to her mouth again and the look of panic returned. Todd erupted into laughter, and showed her his unscathed hand. She slapped at his shoulder as more tears fell from her eyes.

"You bastard," she said and popped him on his shoulder.

Bree's angry expression melted away, as she stared with wonder at the knife Todd still held.

"How is this possible?" Todd asked Bryce.

"I can only offer a theory. Perhaps your body knows when it's in danger. In some instinctual reaction it activates some sort of self-preservation ability. Maybe this ability vibrates your molecules at a different harmonic level. That would make any piece of you seem intangible, or untouchable, as harm would come in contact with it. Again, it's only a guess," Bryce explained.

The smile on Todd's face, as he prepared to speak, dictated that he had some sarcastic comment to retort with. Todd's cell phone had begun to ring in his pocket. Bree watched the phone that had risen to meet his expectant hand.

"Hello?" Todd asked as he dropped the knife on the cutting board.

"Tuh...Todd, I need you to come here, now," the voice was that of Will Goldman.

Todd, in the long years he had known William Goldman, had never heard him sound so scared and mournful. Dread filled him as he listened to Will, who tried to compose himself.

"Will? What's the matter?" Todd asked compassionately as he held the phone against his head with both hands in concentration.

"An old friend of yours is here. He says, if you don't come now...and come alone," Will's voiced trailed off.

Todd felt the blood leaving his face, and could hear the cries of a woman and a baby in the background.

"He is gonna kill us, Todd...If you call anyone," Will's voice cracked as he spoke.

The phone disconnected abruptly. Todd first felt terror course down his spine. His nose and upper lip numbed, as Will's words replayed through his mind. Todd looked slowly to Bree, exhaled, and tried to steady himself.

"Doug," Bree mouthed the words silently, as Todd's thoughts burst through her mind.

"I am going to kill him," Todd said as pure hatred worked its way through him like slow poison.

Todd pulled Bree to him and looked deeply into her eyes. She nodded her understanding of his thoughts. Her head lowered and her eyes were fixed on his. Her brow had furrowed in a mix of concern and anger.

Her tone was even and was filled with maliciousness as she began to speak, "I know you. In the

205

short time we have had together, I know you. You need to listen to me. If you intend to go there, it's for a specific reason. When the time comes don't pause, do it, and do it right. It won't be time for any concept of human compassion to surface. He killed Bryce, all those people and that little girl. He is dangerous, Todd...," she paused and her voice cracked as she said, "I don't want to lose you," she finished and pressed her forehead to his chest.

Todd nodded silently and pressed her to him. After a moment they pulled apart, he kissed her, and ran for the door.

"Please lock yourself in," he thought to her as he ran down the hallway.

The metallic click of the locks on his door, gave him solace as he stalked forward.

"He is gonna kill us, Todd," Will's words replayed through his mind.

He felt a horrible sense of desperation and he considered the distance he had to travel. His peripheral vision blurred again with the white light, he flashed, and he thumped off of the wall in front of him. He stood up and angrily proceeded toward the lobby. He pulled the lobby door inward forcefully and made to step out.

Several people stopped and looked at him as he exited the building.

"Hey you're that guy on the news," a woman said.

Todd looked at her dully as others stopped to gawk at him. He could hear the whispers of the group that formed around him.

"What is he? He looks like a normal guy...Maybe he is an alien...Is this where he lives?"

He looked past them for his car, parked close by. The flash effect happened again; he slammed into the driver's door of his car, and fell splayed onto the concrete. He tried to relax and avoid the white light flashes, as he opened the car door and sat down.

The group of onlookers had begun to clap at his display as they walked toward his car. Todd gritted his teeth angrily as he started the car and pulled out onto the road over-revving the engine. The car threatened to side slide as he drove off down the rainy street. Todd stared ahead as he mentally plotted his route.

"Try to calm down," Bryce warned from inside of Todd's head.

Todd slammed his fist into the steering wheel angrily.

"I have to hurry," he stammered, "Hurry to a location seven hours away, through all this damn rain," he said.

Veins began to pop out on his forehead, tendons stood out on the side of his neck as he grimaced in ire. He was near the Inter-territorial highway and followed dangerously close to a compact car ahead of him. The small car veered to the side of the road. He figured that the driver had decided to get off of the road due to the horrible rain. He was afraid that he might also have to succumb to the horrible visibility.

"I wish this damned rain would just quit," he screamed over his steering wheel.

The rain, which pelted the windshield, stopped abruptly. His wipers made a noise as they skittered unevenly over the windshield which had dried rapidly.

"Finally, a bit of luck," Todd spat the words sarcastically as he turned off his wipers.

Todd turned onto the Inter-territorial highway and accelerated as fast as he could. He reached over and pulled a time-worn package of cigarettes from the compartment under his arm rest. He fumbled for a moment for a lighter. He stuck the cigarette into his lips and stared through the flame into the road ahead. He drew deeply on the cigarette and held it for a long moment. He exhaled and felt a calming effect course through his veins.

He traveled at eighty miles per hour and snorted in disgust as eighteen wheelers passed him as though he sat still. He continued to puff on the cigarette. An ashy taste had begun to build up in his mouth and threatened to gag him. He grimaced, rolled down his window, and tossed it out. The road stretched out before him endlessly and he thought of Sebastian's face. He shook his head to clear it, let out a long sigh, and turned on the radio.

"Police officials have no leads in the stabbing death of a homeless man and a young girl. The bodies were found mutilated in an alleyway on..."

Todd's face twisted into a mask of anger as he thought about Doug's attack of the young girl. He gripped the steering wheel of the car and dropped the accelerator to the floor. The car's engine noise rose as it strained to perform. Todd's anger seemed to mirror the engine's noise. The news announcer's voice came from his speakers again.

"Police also have no leads in the arson based murders which occurred when a homeless shelter exploded..."

Todd looked far off into the distance at a sign. Another pang of desperation tore through him. He began to see the white lights in his vision again.

"Oh no. Not now," he thought in panic.

Todd's heart hammered in his chest as the peripheral lights flashed in intensity. His vice-like grip on the steering wheel slackened as his hands became intangible. Devoid of physical cohesion, he phased through the front of the car so fast that his mind was barely able to comprehend the process. The sign, formerly at an appreciable distance from him, enlarged as he approached it.

He took a few uneven steps as the ground seemed to solidify under his feet. He looked down at the street, disoriented, and tried to maintain his balance. He looked over his shoulder, alerted by a noise. His car flipped and twisted its way destructively toward him.

"It's gonna hit me!" he thought as he turned to run.

He had raised one leg and had begun to thrust a stride with the other. The white lights had begun to pop in the sides of his vision. He moved again and felt the force of his weight, as the distance ahead of him collapsed. He turned to look back again. The car was just a harmless puff of smoke on the distant horizon. He turned away from the wreck and walked away, still numb from the experience.

* * *

Will let the phone fall from the crook of his neck,

208

and stared up at the man in front of him. Will's hands had been bound behind him and he sat against the wall, as blood poured down across his face. Lucy continued to cry in unison with the baby.

"Alright, you said you would release us if, I did what you wanted" Will said expectantly.

Doug smiled wickedly as he looked into Will's frightened eyes.

"I did exactly what you wanted, said it word for word," Will added.

"I am going to release you," Doug said as he lunged at Will.

Doug's hand covered Will's mouth evenly, as the knife penetrated Will's heart. Will's large arms struggled helplessly against his bonds. Doug watched as Will's eyes widened with pain. After a few moments they relaxed and became dull. As Doug moved his hand away from Will's jaw, it dropped open lifelessly. Outside, a crack of thunder was joined by a brilliant flash of lightning. The rain pounded angrily against the tin roof, and muffled the baby's cries. Lucy was now quiet and stared at Doug with murderous rage in her eyes. She sat upright and was bound to the cabinet frame under the sink. A piece of silver duct tape was stretched tightly across her mouth. Her head was tilted forward and she stared at Doug under her furrowed brow. Doug ran the cold blade evenly across her neck and blood poured out over the wound. It ran down her chest in crimson tendrils and puddled between her splayed legs.

She never winced or sobbed as the blood left her body and her angry gaze only broke when her head finally flopped down on her chest. Doug turned, stood up, and looked down at the baby in the crib. The boy lay on his back; his blue eyes were filled with tears.

"Do it," the voice in his head commanded.

Doug's muscles were like slabs of concrete, too heavy to move.

The child looked very normal and this was very disconcerting to him. He thought momentarily that if the child were to be misshapen or displayed any sign of abnormality that this would be easier. The child had stopped

209

crying and looked at him with wonder. Doug's mind wrestled with abstract concepts of why he should *not* do this. These thoughts became murmurs of little importance when weighed against the whispering voice of direction. Had he been able to hear his own thoughts buried deep within the recesses of his mind, he would have realized this to be a betrayal of unconditional trust.

"Do not be deceived...This is not a human child," the voice warned.

Doug brought both of his hands together over his head and held the knife between them. Pain sang out as he was hit hard in the ribs. He puffed as the wind was knocked out of him. He staggered, fell over onto his side, and tried to draw breath. He screamed in agony as the Golden Retriever's jaws snapped down, like a razor filled vice, on his hand. Doug twisted himself and drove his injured hand at the dog. He landed a grip of fur, and pulled the animals gnashing jaws away from his face. He brought the knife over and into the animals gut. He spun around, leveraged his body weight, and threw the dog toward a far wall.

The dog's body slammed into the wall heavily and fell to the floor. A large pool of blood began to form under the animal's motionless body. Doug turned back toward the baby. He raised his arms again and held the knife over his head nervously. The smooth whispers drifted to his ears again.

Chapter 17

Southern Discomfort

Sheriff Roger Swayne sat at his desk and sorted through papers casually.

He flipped them carelessly, one by one, into the trash mumbling, "bullshit, bullshit, bullshit," as he let them drop.

His boots propped on the desk, tapped together in time with the slow, twanging, country music that belted from a small radio. The old sheriff started as his office door opened forcibly. He staggered forward unevenly and let his feet drop to the floor. He inhaled deeply as he readied himself to yell at the top of his lungs in anger. The young deputy took several small gulps of air before he spoke.

"Sheriff, you're gonna wanna see this," the young deputy said and disappeared behind the door hurriedly.

Roger stood up slowly and walked toward the door. He lumbered lazily and exhaled his disgust for the young deputy's enthusiasm. As he approached the group of deputies, that had made a small ring around a television, they parted to allow him a view. He paid no notice to the television at first. He inhaled again to unleash a dose of venomous anger toward the young deputy. The television caught his attention and his warning finger, pointed at the deputy, curled back slowly.

He watched as a man seemed to move as fast as light and save two people. His eyes narrowed as he watched it again in slow motion. A red banner flashed across the bottom of the screen. It said something about a car crash on Inter-territorial highway twelve, but he ignored it.

He watched the screen intently as pictures of Todd Jennings and a young blonde woman flashed by.

211

"Do you recognize him sheriff?" the young deputy asked Roger.

"I would recognize him faster than you could," Roger said as he looked at the young deputy angrily.

"I found him as a baby, out on Highway Fifty-Nine around thirty years ago," Roger belted out.

"I bet you couldn't even find your cock, if you had to pee," Roger said in a mocking tone.

All of the deputies turned away from the television to face Roger. Roger had a captivating way of telling old stories. Whenever the opportunity, or necessity, arose he would find a way to work one of these in. Something in his tone promised one of these stories. The men shifted to get comfortable and looked up at Roger expectantly. Roger paused as he collected his thoughts. He was pleased as he read eagerness and rapt attention play across the faces of his subordinates.

"I was still just a patrolman then. I was sitting out on Pearl Street over behind that big oak, watching for speeders," Roger began.

The officers' expressions were almost comical as they all nodded in unison.

"It was about three A.M. and there was a fierce rainstorm going on. We didn't have cell phones or the wireless internet back in those days, so I was really doin' my job," Roger paused and looked at them all accusingly for a moment.

They all seemed to cower and look guilty, as they shifted uncomfortably in their chairs.

"So, like I was sayin', I was real aware of my surroundings. I had looked out onto Highway Fifty-Nine just a minute or two before it happened. Had seen nothin', mind you. There was this heavy burst of light. I thought it was lightnin' and readied myself for the thunder boomer. But, no sound came. As my eyes readjusted, I caught sight of little Mr. Todd Jennings. There he was sprawled out in the middle of Fifty-Nine, naked as a jaybird. I suppose he was a newborn, but he may have been a few weeks old. I walked over there and looked at him for a second. Ya know, like 'where the Hell'd this baby come from?' I never found out. I scooped him up and took him to the hospital. Took em a few hours to make sure nothin' was wrong with him. I ended up droppin' him off at that orphanage later that night. He was adopted by a couple here in town," Roger paused to breathe.

"Remember when he came in last year and asked for a report, and swore we were out at his place?" the young deputy interrupted with his question.

Roger threatened the deputy with the back side of his hand. The deputy flinched and nearly fell off of the corner of the desk, where he sat. The other deputies grimaced at him for interrupting.

"That flash of light looked a lot like that," Roger said ominously as he tapped at the television screen, where Todd materialized in a flash.

All of the deputies nodded their approval of the story and rushed back to work.

"I'm gonna ride over to Lucy's Diner and get a cup of coffee. I suppose I'll ask William if he has any ideas about all this. Those two were thicker 'n thieves as far back as I can remember," Roger said with authority as he picked up his hat and swaggered out of the door.

Within several minutes, Roger pulled his cruiser into the parking lot of Lucy's Diner. He noticed a small group of old men embroiled in a heated discussion near the front doors.

As he approached, he asked no particular one of them, "What seems to be the problem here?" and placed his hands on his hips, to look authoritative.

The spokesman who wore a plaid hat inhaled deeply and began, "I came over here an hour ago for a cup of senior coffee. Been waitin' that long and there ain't not a soul here," the old man tapped the glass of the door accusingly to reinforce his point.

"I guess Mr. William overslept this morning, he is in for trouble with Lucy," Roger offered up in explanation.

The rest of the elderly men seemed to relax and nod.

Plaid hat drawled angrily, "It ain't no way to run a bidness."

"Well, he stays up at night with that new baby and has a spot of trouble waking up sometimes. I'll take a ride over there and give 'em a wakeup call. I wanted to talk to William anyhow," Roger said as he turned and walked to his car.

Roger haphazardly drove back out onto the road. A lady in a station wagon had to slam on the breaks to avoid a collision with his cruiser. Roger tipped his hat to the lady in apology as he drove away.

Chapter 18

Horseshoes And Hand Grenades

Todd's eyes narrowed as he looked ahead and tried to focus on the distant road sign. The Inter-territorial highway stretched before him endlessly as he walked.

"Please Todd, make this bastard suffer," Todd heard and paused as he placed his fingers to his temple.

"No. I didn't hear anything," Bryce responded before Todd fully prepared the question.

"That is happening with increasing frequency, though, is it not?" Bryce asked.

"Yes. That was a loud one, but I'm starting to hear the pleading whispers all the time. It sounded like Lucy's voice," Todd answered.

"You continue to gather souls, Todd. They are seemingly drawn to you after they die. I cannot fathom how you would have no perception of the arrivals," Bryce commented.

Todd could hear the hum of tires behind him and threw up a thumb. The blue sedan, filled with teenagers, seemed to slow as they neared him. They all threw him a 'thumbs up' sign and sped off. Todd grimaced in anger and walked onward dutifully.

"Think of a place near your destination. Try to focus on it, think of sights, sounds, and smells as though you were there," Bryce's voice offered evenly.

Todd closed his eyes and thought of the large white pavilion in the center of town.

"Think very hard of being there, Todd," Bryce added.

Todd could see the pavilion clearly in his head. He focused on a spot near it, a water fountain. He had stood

215

there so many times as a child. Todd pictured it and envisioned the smell of the nearby pine trees. His peripheral vision began to fill with the white light. He was aware of the movement. Trees turned into green and brown blurs as he passed through them. He staggered forward as his vision cleared and a child ran into his leg with a bicycle.

"Watch where you're going Mister," the child warned Todd and corrected his bicycle.

The child and his bicycle were confusing to Todd.

"How did he get on the Inter-territorial highway? Why would he be...," Todd thought to himself.

"Todd, you are no longer on the Inter-territorial highway. You have successfully transported yourself," Bryce explained before Todd could finish the thought.

Todd watched as the child rode away and gave him angry glances over his shoulder. He had moved himself a long way this time and felt lightly disoriented. He was stricken as he realized that he had gone from standing on the hot asphalt of the Inter-territorial highway, to this cool shaded place near the pavilion. He looked to a small bridge that crossed a creek nearby and thought of the fun he had there with Will as a child.

"Will," Todd said the word aloud as he flooded with dread for Will and Lucy's safety.

Aware of the mechanics of this talent, he thought deliberately of a spot behind Lucy's Diner where he often stood to smoke. The white lights, in the corners of his vision, prepared him for the move. He appeared behind the diner and stumbled past bags of trash. Todd tried the back door which he found locked firmly. He trotted to the front of the diner, in hopes of entry. As he rounded the building, he was greeted by an angry mob of elderly men grouped around the door.

Plaid hat spotted him and asked, "Where's your friends at?" as he pointed to his watch.

Todd hadn't seen this old codger in over a year, but immediately felt the usual level of disdain for him.

"They are up your ass and around the corner...you mean, angry, old bastard," Todd said angrily before he turned back the way he had come.

216

Todd ran to the back of the building and looked around. People were in view but no one paid any attention to him. He closed his eyes and thought of Will's front yard. Todd then stood in front of Will's home. A feeling of sincere dread washed over him. The door was open a few inches. Todd considered bellowing a greeting through the doorway. The image of Doug lying in wait for him flashed through his mind. Todd imagined Doug slashing at him with his freakishly large hunting knife. Todd looked at his hand and remembered how the vegetable knife had passed harmlessly through it. A mix of courage and anger coursed through him. He bowed his head forward and his lips drew away from his teeth in a snarl as he ran at the door. He jumped a little and drove his foot into the door. It flopped back on its hinges, as Todd landed firmly and peered around for any signs of movement.

He walked forward a few steps and the horror of the scene tore through him. Will's dead eyes stared up at the ceiling. His body sat on the floor in a pool of dried blood. A few inches away, he saw Lucy's body, where it sat, slumped against the kitchen cabinets. Her throat had been sliced in a wide arc under her chin. Todd's eyes roamed slowly to his left. He stared, but he couldn't make himself acknowledge what he was seeing. Sebastian lay motionless in his crib, the handle of a large hunting knife jutted out of his bruised and blood spattered chest. The strength began to leave Todd's legs and he lowered himself down onto the carpet. He raised his hands to his face and wept convulsively. Todd heard a noise several rooms away, down the hall. He raised his face and pricked his ears to listen intently. He saw writing scrawled onto the ceiling in black charcoal.

"Come get me, demon," Todd spoke the words aloud, as he read, and filled with renewed and intensified anger.

Todd crept slowly to his feet and stalked soundlessly down the hall. As he walked down the hall, his anger became a tangible force. Picture frames shattered as he passed them. The very walls undulated with every angry intake of his breath. A trail of blood rounded the corner into the room in front of him. He looked cautiously around the

217

corner. His eyes fell upon Max, who lay in front of a dryer, obviously wounded. Max licked his muzzle and stared up at Todd with his doleful brown eyes. The animal let forth a small whine to acknowledge his former master. His tail flopped and twitched as he tried to wag it. Tears poured down Todd's hot face as he rushed to Max and scooped him up into his arms.

"Max," Todd sobbed and pressed his face into the soft fur on the dog's head.

Todd's hand found the wetness on the dog's stomach. He turned him over to see the neat puncture wound there. Max's body shuddered. He let forth another weak whine and started to go limp in Todd's arms.

"No!" Todd thought and threw his head back with his eyes clenched in emotional agony.

Heat filled his body and flowed down his right arm. Todd looked down at his hand where it pressed against the wound. His hand glowed with the same white light that he would see in his peripheral vision, each time he traveled as light. The light became blinding for a moment. Max whimpered, some semblance of strength had returned to his tone. Todd looked down and removed his hand slowly. The wound was gone. Todd gathered Max to him and closed his eyes.

In the darkness, Todd screamed for Marvin. Marvin formed out of the darkness and moved toward Todd cautiously.

"Show me where Doug lives!" Todd commanded.

Marvin quickly began to describe its location. Todd stared angrily into the glassy rippling image behind Marvin that showed the shabby old trailer. There was a blinding flash of white light.

* * *

Roger was distracted from the murder scene for only a second. Perhaps his old eyes were playing a trick on him, but he thought he had seen a flash of white light. Roger looked down at the dead bodies of the Goldman family again. He edged soundlessly backward, out of the house to

218

call for backup.

* * *

Todd knelt in the grassy lot and held Max in his arms as he cried.

"Will....and Lucy...The baby...the baby," Todd continued to sob as Max watched him curiously.

The warm sun shone down on them. Todd was able to partially compose himself after a long while. The laughter of small children in the distance drifted to his ears. He raised his gaze above the tall grass curiously. Two young girls played on a swing set behind a nearby house. Their sun dresses swept back and forth like sails caught in the wind. Max looked toward the laughter and then back at Todd. Todd looked over his shoulder at the trailer behind him.

"I love you, Max," he said and wiped the tears from his eyes.

"I need you stay here for me. I have to take care of something. Can you do that, boy? Wait here for me."

Max whined and wagged his tail. Todd backed slowly away from Max toward the trailer. Max looked over his shoulder again toward the laughter. He plodded clumsily through the grass toward the children.

"You never quite got the whole stay thing down, did you ?" Todd said and smiled weakly as he turned.

Todd's expression melted into anger as he stalked through the field toward the old trailer. He took cover behind the shed that stood at the corner of a goat pen. Todd's eyes roved over the trailer windows, as he watched for signs of movement. The goats in the pen, having noticed Todd, began to crowd at the fence. They watched him curiously and bleated randomly.

"Todd, please...please move. I can't stand it," Bryce's tone was pleading.

"What is it?" Todd asked.

Bryce's voice quavered in his head and seemed to lose composure as he said, "I cannot stand goats. They disgust me," Bryce labored to respond.

Todd crept forward furtively to secure a new

position behind a large live oak tree. The front door of the trailer hung open and squeaked as it swayed on its hinges. Abstract thoughts crept through his head of Will, Lucy, and the baby. The tendons in his neck and jaws flexed in anger as a fresh wave of torment tore through him. Todd's hands were drawn into claws as he stalked out of hiding toward the door. Todd paced in an arc, able to see most of the first room and crept in slowly. His expression was a glower of anger. Todd's eyes peered purposefully as they swept the house for any sign of Doug. He surveyed the old cloth covered couch and the crosses on the wall. A worn, white, leather chair sat in the corner. Its arms were covered in, what looked to be, a mix of dirt and old motor oil.

The floor was littered with trash, ankle deep. Todd stepped high to avoid tripping and placed his feet deliberately with each step. He walked slowly down the length of the trailer and looked into each room. Doug was not here. The open and empty dresser drawers told Todd that he had already fled. He looked at a cross on the wall. The writing overhead caught his attention.

'*Your mind reading whore is next*', was scrawled across the ceiling of the bedroom. Todd turned and ran for the door. He slid a bit in the trash as he plodded through it to leave. Max met him as he passed between two couches and barked at his feet. Todd looked down to see pieces of fishing line draped around his shoes. At the ends of each line, small rings were tied neatly. The rings were attached to metal pins. Todd didn't have time to scream as the orange burst of fire carried him into the darkness.

* * *

Sheriff Roger Swayne hated these moments. It was time to review the evidence. A large manila envelope sat on his desk, and the thought of opening it filled him with dread. He had been able to stay outside of the Goldman's home while teams of investigators had swarmed in and out with equipment.

Carol Green, the coroner, was one sick bitch in his way of looking at things. She would walk onto crime scenes and her fat ass would wag behind her.

He had seen her flopping bodies around before. She showed, literally, no compassion for the person that they had been. He wondered if she had ever been in a good mood or cared for anyone.

There was an air of levity at most crime scenes. It was a self-protection mechanism in place, he believed. It helped anyone in law enforcement or first response teams to sleep at night. This had been one of those bad scenes that involved a child, moreover, a baby. People milled in and out of the house with the same melancholy expression splashed across their faces. There was nothing to save them from this type of atrocity. Roger was sure this would produce the nightmares he hated so much.

"And now, I have to look at these damned pictures," he thought remorsefully.

Carol was very much the artist. She put some of her personality into the job. Each crime scene was unique and she brought a visual style to each picture she took. In some other unbiased point of view, the shots would provide clarity and angles to help the onlooker to glean more of an understanding of the subject matter. But Roger believed that Carol was just a morbid shit and liked to bring out the true horror of the moment. He stared down at the glossy photos on his desk. The lifeless eyes of Sebastian Goldman stared back at him. Roger hated these photos. They represented so many things to him, most notably, his inability to protect innocent people from this type of horror. He remembered his wife, as she lay in a bed in a local hospital. The cancer, he couldn't remember its specific name, had nearly finished ravaging her body. She had become almost too weak to talk and coughed blood frequently. He thought of all the machines that were hooked to her. Each machine had a digital screen filled with numbers or lines that waved. He had looked into them for hours while she slept.

In some odd way, he felt if he could understand them, then he could truly know how she was.

"We remain hopeful that your wife will become stable," was the only response that the hospital staff would give him.

He was told that, right up to the point where she winced in pain, grabbed for him blindly, and died.

Roger was used to handing out that same kind of bullshit explanation. It was necessary to maintain an air of calm, during stressful moments. But his wife had slipped away from him. He had been powerless to do anything about it. He tried to think of himself as some great protector of the people. But, these things seemed to keep happening. The slaughter of the Goldman family had secretly put another chink, in a long line of chinks, in his emotional armor.

"What am I going to do? Welsh went nuts and killed his brother, wife, and then committed suicide last year. And now this...It's so senseless. The Goldman's never hurt anybody or made enemies of people. What kind of a monster would stab a defenseless baby in a crib? What do I have to do to stop this crazy shit? I don't protect and serve. I show up to figure out why people are dead. I'm like that clown that follows a parade and picks up horse shit with a scooper," he told himself angrily.

The, almost alien, feeling of moisture formed in the bottom of his eyes. His lower lip trembled as he stared down at the picture of the baby. There was a light, almost polite, knock on the glass of his office door. He drew in a deep cleansing breath, and placed his glasses on his face.

"Come in," he bellowed and noted the crack in his voice as he spoke.

The young deputy's head appeared from the small opening in the door.

"We have an I.D. back on the prints from the knife," he reported.

Roger grimaced at him and only held his open palm out toward the young deputy. The deputy entered the office, handed him the fax sheets, seemed to lower himself, and backed away slowly. Roger looked up at him from over his glasses.

"Good job, *Son*. Thank you," he said, his voice still faltered a little and waved his hand at the deputy in dismissal.

"You're welcome, Dad," the deputy said as he straightened up, smiled confidently, and walked out of the room.

Roger carefully placed the pictures of the Goldman's back into the envelope. He showed each picture the kindness that Carol had not when she examined the bodies. Roger began to read over the printed information. He stood up and placed his hat on his head and walked out of his office. He walked with more speed and motivation than he had displayed for anything in a long time.

"Listen up. We have a positive print I.D in the Goldman killing. One, Douglas Rolfe. Male age twenty seven, five foot nine inches tall, black hair, blue eyes. He is ex-military, dishonorably discharged after he blew a fellow soldiers head off. This guy has been active at the church, teaching Sunday School. Unemployed since the church was closed down last year. A Sunday School teacher!?" Roger said exasperatedly as he rolled his eyes in disgust.

A deputy approached Roger and said, "Got these to the state and federal boys already."

The deputy passed out large photos of Doug. They appeared to Roger, to have come from a military identification picture. Roger continued with a look of severity on his face.

"We have an address and we're about to go over there. I want you all to remember, we are professional law enforcement officers. Our job is to arrest him and let the courts decide what happens to his sorry ass. But, if you see a weapon or he tries to run away, by all means, do everything necessary to stop him. We gotta keep him from hurting himself or another baby," Roger finished and looked into each of the deputy's eyes over his glasses.

They responded silently, each man nodded with a knowing gleam in their eyes. Another deputy entered the room, a cordless mouth piece curved sharply in front of his lips.

"Sheriff, we have a fire reported over on Buford road."

Roger looked down at the paper in his hand.

"It's not 50126 Buford is it?" he asked.

"Yes sir, it is," the deputy responded as he raised his eyebrow in curiosity.

223

"Let's go, boys. Looks like Doug lit a bonfire," Roger said angrily.

Todd awoke and stared around the dimly lit area. The two chairs he and Bryce sat in during mental meetings sat empty before him. His hand groped around in the scarce light.

"You're okay," Bryce said and placed a hand on his shoulder.

"Your body is unharmed but you fell into unconsciousness. We need to move your body. It is currently located in tall grass near the smoldering remains of that killer's home. If it were not for the smoke, someone would have seen you already," Bryce warned.

"Why am I not awake?" Todd asked.

"Passing a knife through your finger was one thing Todd, but making your entire body invulnerable to shrapnel and flames, is another entirely. If it had not been for the constant infusion of souls, that gave you this much power..., I am afraid you would have been ripped apart," Bryce said.

"Max," Todd said heavily.

The goats in the nearby pen began to bleat, pleading for the crowd of firemen to feed them. Bryce's expression changed into a mix of horror and disgust.

"I can't stand those foul, foul disgusting animals," Bryce seemed to spit the words.

Todd could hear firemen who yelled to one another. He could hear the hiss as water extinguished embers.

"Move us now!" Bryce's voice was commanding and angry.

Todd thought of his bed, the smooth comfortable sheets and the smell of the fabric softener in his pillows. At some level, he was aware that his body traveled for a moment. Darkness overtook him again. Todd's naked body appeared in a flash and dropped softly onto his bed. The four large men that surrounded the bed, dressed in their neat black suits, stared in amazement at each other.

The men moved forward silently and wrapped Todd's naked body in his bed sheets. They worked together to gently lift, and carry him away.

* * *

Larry Phillips lay back in the driver's seat of his new rig. He thought that his truck was perfect, as he considered his new paint job. It was deep glossy black, covered in orange flames. His arms were placed lazily on the steering wheel of his eighteen wheeled freight truck. He admired himself in the small mirror attached to his sun visor. His blue eyes looked back at him approvingly.

"Just one more evening and I will have dropped off this shit," he said to himself.

He watched as cars merged onto the Inter-territorial highway, dangerously close to the front of his rig.

"Go on, ya stupid asshole. Those wheels won't forgive you if you get to close," he said as he brushed at his short black hair with his fingers.

* * *

Doug looked nervously down at the fuel gauge of the stolen car. The car had begun to lurch and buck in the last few miles. He patted the accelerator in hopes that the engine might even out. The fuel gauge had not moved in the last few hours of driving.

"Leave it to me to steal the only broken car," he thought.

The voice of the radio announcer droned as he looked ahead.

"Scientists have attributed global warming and sudden changes in oceanic temperature to the large number of disastrous weather based incidents around the world. African officials announced that rain water falling in some of the more arid regions was at first welcomed. But now, the rain has continued to drop torrential amounts of water, causing massive flooding and deaths. Seismic activity destroyed homes in the California territories this morning. No official numbers of deaths or injuries have been reported, as state and local authorities clamber to return power to the affected area amidst the chaos. Similar seismic activity occurred at exactly the same time half way across the

225

world," the reporter continued to list the disasters.

Doug turned the radio off to listen more closely to the engine. In addition to the lurching, the engine had begun to tick. He figured it was probably a lack of oil pressure. He slowed the car and pulled over to the side of the Inter-territorial highway. He popped the hood release on the car and looked over the wheel at the hood.

Small jets of steam started to waft up and he could smell antifreeze. He walked to the front of the car, raised the hood, and peered in.

An eighteen wheeler blasted its air horn as it passed and caused Doug to jump in surprise. His head slammed against the propped hood, which fell and struck his hands, where they rested.

His fists were balled tightly as he fought the urge to scream in frustration. The sound of air brakes being applied, stole his attention from the ache in his fingers.

He looked over his shoulder to see the freight truck. It drifted to the edge of the Inter-territorial highway, stopped, and emitted a hiss of air from the brakes. Doug went back to the car, picked up his duffel bag, and sprinted to the passenger side of the truck.

"I will give ya a ride if you have enough gas money," Larry called down to him over the ragged knock of the idling diesel engine.

Doug nodded in agreement as he climbed into the cab. Larry seemed preoccupied by his mirrors for a moment.

"Did you want to put your hood down? Somebody is gonna tear that thing into pieces and sell it," Larry asked.

"I don't care. Let's go," Doug responded.

"Hold up, swole up," Larry interjected.

"Let's see some cash. This truck don't roll an inch for free," Larry again belted over the engine noise.

Doug's eyes narrowed a bit as he assessed Larry.

Doug began, "When I saw you pull over I thought, 'Thank you Lord,' thinking he had sent you to me."

"Oh no sir, not at all. Benjamin Franklin and his buddies, Andrew Jackson and whoever is on a ten dollar bill sent me," Larry said.

"Do you ever just stop to help people?" Doug

226

asked.

"For free? Why in shits sake would I do that?" Larry asked incredulously.

"The Lord smiles favorably upon those who help others," Doug answered.

"Shit, screw that and you too, if you can't pay for a ride. Hell, since you're bein' an asshole and all, let's call it three hundred, I'm going as far as Houston," Larry offered.

Doug's hand tightened on the small razor knife in his pocket.

He released the weapon and grabbed a small wad of cash in the same pocket. Doug flipped out three hundred dollar bills and handed them to Larry. They listened in silence to a radio announcer who belted out news of freakish natural disasters that occurred globally.

"I'm hoping to get all this crap unloaded and get back home before the shit hits the fan here," Larry said conversationally.

"Shit? Fan?" Doug asked distractedly.

Larry seemed to crawl more upright in his seat as he said, "All the crap happening everywhere. The television and radio stations aren't giving out death tolls anymore. They're too high. I heard on a program last night that several countries have even blacked out."

"Blacked out? What does that mean?" Doug asked bewildered.

Larry seemed excited to relay the information and leaned toward Doug to be better heard, "No power, and no communications. They are having trouble with the satellites too. Something to do with solar flares or some such. The International Federation of Countries can't do anything about it. They are spread all over the world already. Not sure they really care. That whole one world government thing never set to well with me"

Larry enjoyed the alarmed expression on Doug's face.

"How long has this been going on?" Doug asked.

"Where have you been? Under a rock? It's been getting worse over the last few weeks or so. You can't turn on the television, pick up a paper, or listen to the radio

227

without hearing about it. If it keeps up, they said it will end up being a global disaster. One thing seems to be making another worse and so on. I wouldn't hang out in the south too long. The warm waters are brewin' hurricanes like crazy off the coast of Africa. The whole southern belt is bracing for the worst season ever," Larry explained.

"This is his doing. He is destroying the world," the whispers informed Doug.

"I wouldn't worry about it too much, Cuz. Since you're so tight with the man," Larry pointed up, "I wouldn't figure you had too much to be worried about either way," Larry finished and belted out a mocking laugh.

Doug watched Larry angrily as his hand stroked the cutter in his pocket.

"I don't believe in all that bullshit myself," Larry quipped.

Doug turned to face Larry and leaned in a bit.

"I was noticing the placards on the truck that were marked explosive," Doug mentioned.

"Don't shit your pants. I have some welding equipment in the back bound for Houston. Those placards are marked because of four acetylene bottles knee high or so. If they blew up you wouldn't feel a thing," Larry looked to Doug, in hopes to see fright in his expression.

"Oh, I'm not worried. I just wondered why the placards on this side of the truck were blank. I noticed the ones on the back as I walked up," Doug said as he looked at the road and smiled.

Larry worked furiously to see the placards in his side mirror.

"Damn kids must have turned them to blank. I can get in serious shit if they aren't marked," Larry said angrily.

Are there any checkpoints or weigh stations to worry about between here and Houston?" Doug asked shiftily.

"No, I'm solid. We can just breeze all the way there. Stuff is done digitally," Larry said as he put on his hazard lights before he pulled off the road.

Doug smiled out of the window as the truck slowed to a stop on the edge of the Inter-territorial highway. Larry hopped out of the door and slammed it shut behind him. Doug slowly pulled the razor knife from his pocket and watched Larry inspect the markers on the side of his truck. He was angry over the misinformation and stormed back to the driver's side door of the truck.

"It looks like your blind faith is just blindness, Cuz. Those placards are fine," Larry said angrily as he reached down low on his left side to release the air brakes.

As he sat up he felt a cold pain work its way across his neck. His hand shot to the wound to feel warm blood as it rushed past his fingers in a pulsing spray.

His fearful eyes looked to Doug who held a bloody razor knife in his hand.

Larry managed to croak the word, "Why?" before he slumped over onto the wheel of the truck.

"The Lord works in mysterious ways...*Cuz*," Doug said morbidly amused.

Chapter 19

A Safe Haven

Todd woke up slowly and looked around. He was aware of how sluggish his body felt. He stared into a white wall, visible through the safety rails on the side of this bed. Sharp pain assaulted the inside of his right elbow and he jerked his attention to it.

A young nurse, with dirty blonde hair, looked up at him from the hypodermic needle and smiled sympathetically. Todd struggled to ask what she was doing. A series of slurred words, that he himself could not even understand, rambled off of his tongue. She pushed the plunger down and withdrew the needle. The pain was minimal but Todd made to reach over and rub at it. His hand struggled to move, even basically, but did so slowly. His hand jerked to a stop at the end of a leather restraint that held his arm to his side. He looked over at it dreamily for a moment and returned his attention to the nurse. She labored to put a small cloth bandage on the puncture.

The nurse said, "You're going to be groggy for a few minutes, Mr. Jennings," and she turned and left the room.

Todd pulled his right arm up only to find another leather restraint holding it in place. He tugged weakly at the straps. He realized that he wouldn't have been able to physically free himself, even at full strength. He was becoming more aware and his vision cleared slowly. Todd noticed two small white chairs next to his bed. They were set up in a similar manner to what he would experience when he talked to Bryce in his head. The rest of the room was a white blur. The walls that were close enough to be focused upon, were slightly wavy and he realized them to be padded. Todd pulled at his ankles, which reacted as slowly as his arms had.

His legs rose slowly and bent at the knees. The motion was encumbered by something that held his feet. He assumed his ankles were in the same type of leather restraint. He looked for a long moment down toward his ankles, hidden under the thin blanket that covered him evenly. The effort to raise his head, to look down, was almost overwhelming. The muscles in his stomach were unable to hold him up and his head dropped back onto his pillow heavily.

He looked over to the cuff on his wrist and his eyes narrowed. He tried to will the leather restraint to undo itself. After a long moment, he gave up on the cuff. He tried to fight off the feeling of panic that rose in him. Todd stared up to the vaulted ceiling dreamily. He winced, as he looked directly into the florescent lights that illuminated the room. Todd noticed a cord and traced it down to a large light fixture that hung down over the chairs. His eyes darted around the room. He caught the fleeting images of heads and shoulders as people passed the large glass window on his door. He could now see tiny wires that ran through the inside of the glass to reinforce it. He began struggling to speak into the air, his words became clearer and clearer.

Finally able to form actual words, he whispered, "Bryce, Bryce where are you?" he asked helplessly.

A shadow at the door caught his attention. A large man, dressed in a thick white shirt, stood outside of his door and looked at him. Faint, almost like a whisper, he heard Bree's voice for a second before it faded away.

"Bree, can you hear me?" Todd asked the air around him, his voice was as loud as he could muster.

The door opened slowly and the man in white stood there, chewed his gum, and looked dispassionately at Todd. The man removed a key from the doorknob roughly and never lost eye contact with Todd. The cord attached to the man's keys retracted into the tiny metal box on his hip.

The man looked away from him and seemed to call a short distance down the hall, "Doctor, he is ready when you are," as he pointed into Todd's room.

Todd watched as the doctor came into view. He was

blurred at the distance he stood, and Todd could not make out his features. The doctor leaned against the far side of the hallway and stared down at something in his hand.

The doctor nodded to the larger man that had opened the door and walked toward Todd. The doctor became clearer as he walked closer and Todd recognized his psychologist, Dr. Larry Ashton. Dr. Larry paused inside the room and turned off the overhead light at the switch and then flipped on another switch which caused the bright light over the chairs to come on. The rest of the room grew dim. The light fell in a circle to cover the two chairs.

The large man approached Todd and lowered the rail on the side of the bed. He then quickly undid Todd's restraints and gave him a, 'if you do anything stupid I'm gonna pound you', look. The man's large hand was behind Todd's back and he pushed him into an upright position. The other hand gently lifted his legs and pulled them over the side of the bed. The man pulled him up from the bed, like a limp life-sized doll, and placed him carefully in a chair to face the doctor. Todd wobbled a bit in the chair and held onto the armrests to steady himself. Dr. Larry sat across from him and continued to concentrate on his notes.

"Thank you, Doug. Please leave a crack in that door for me when you leave," he said and smiled at the large man.

The man nodded to the doctor and gave Todd a 'you better behave yourself' look before leaving. Todd surveyed the environment and realized it to be a perfect replication of his meetings with Bryce.

"This must be a dream," he thought to himself as he heard Bree's voice faintly again for a moment.

Todd looked around the room for anything that might tell him where she might be.

"Hearing voices again?" Dr. Larry asked as he grimaced and made a note.

"I can hear Bree once in a while. Is she nearby?" Todd asked.

"Bree, who?" Dr Larry asked as he cocked his head to one side and looked at Todd curiously.

"Brianna Wilson, my girlfriend," Todd said impatiently.

232

"*Oh*, your girlfriend," Dr. Larry said and nodded his understanding as he jotted down a note.

"Yes, she is just outside. Would you like me to call her in?" Dr. Larry asked.

"Oh yes, please," Todd replied eagerly with a relieved tone.

"Brianna could you come in here for a second please?" Dr. Larry asked in a raised voice directed at the open door.

A woman walked in. Todd recognized her as the nurse who had just given him a shot.

"Brianna, how long have you been dating my patient?" Dr. Larry asked her as he chewed on his pen.

"I'm married, and I don't date patients," she said apologetically to Todd.

She held no resemblance to Bree and her voice, a high nasally tone, was different. Todd's eyes darted to her name tag which said *Brianna Wilson LPN*.

She turned and left the room. Dr. Larry watched Todd for a moment and wrote something else.

"Do you have any idea where you are today?" Dr. Larry asked with a sigh of boredom.

"In a hospital, I guess," Todd replied as he continued to look around.

"Do you know why you're here?" Dr. Larry asked.

"I was chasing after a guy that killed my friend and his family. I got blown up," Todd responded, bowed his head, and began to cry.

Dr. Larry uncrossed his legs, sat forward, and bowed down to look directly into Todd's eyes.

"Think about what you just told me. You say that you were blown up. How could you possibly survive being blown up?" Dr Larry asked and sat up to write.

"I'm not sure. A knife passed through me without being able to cut me and then I was unharmed but knocked out when I tripped an explosion in the guy's trailer. It was hand grenades," he said and looked up at Dr. Larry honestly with his red wet eyes.

"Come on Todd, think about what it is you're *saying*," Dr. Larry said as his voice rose and strained to hold

233

his frustration in check.

Todd looked away toward the wall in deliberation.

"Okay, and who is this guy you keep referring to?" Dr. Larry asked impatiently.

"Doug, Douglas Rolfe. He killed my friend, and his family, and blew me up," Todd said slowly.

Dr. Larry slammed himself backward into his chair, gripped at the armrests, and looked away in disgust. He purposefully looked around the room to avoid Todd's eyes for a moment before he relaxed.

"Doug, can I borrow you for a minute?" Dr. Larry said loudly to the gap in the door.

Todd sat up, gripped at the armrests of his own chair, and looked at the door, visibly frightened.

The large man, that had unrestrained and moved Todd, entered through the door and asked, "Yes, doctor?"

Dr. Larry tapped the man's name tag with his pen and looked at Todd.

Todd looked at the name tag which read: *Douglas Rolfe, Orderly.*

"Thank you, Doug," Dr. Larry called to the man as he left the room.

Todd's head was a stormy sea of confusion. He looked away from Dr. Larry weakly and cradled his head. The truth of it all crashed down upon him. Dr. Larry wrote swiftly and paused briefly once in a while to look at Todd.

"Todd, I am your psychiatrist. You are in a mental institution. You were brought here by the police after you murdered your friend and his family. You have been here for the last year and made zero progress. I have tried every type of drug available to try and get your mind to stay focused, long enough for us to have a chance to have sessions. Do you remember your assault on that patient last week?" Dr. Larry asked.

"I have no idea what you're talking about," Todd said, pulled his legs up in the chair, and wrapped his arms around them.

"Last week, you were caught beating Don Reynolds' head against the window during recreation. You were repeating the words, 'I quit' to him," Dr. Larry said and

234

looked into Todd's eyes for any sign of recognition.

"If what you say is true," Todd paused as his voice struggled to be heard, "It can't be true. I would never do that to my friends. I loved them," Todd stammered.

Dr. Larry flipped to the back of the file he held. He produced large pictures, held to a piece of paper by a paper clip. He winced as he looked at them and handed them to Todd. Todd looked at the first picture which was of his car. The driver side window of the car was smeared with bloody hand prints and was parked in front of the Goldman's home.

The second picture was of Lucy's lifeless body face down on the green carpet of her living room. A huge pool of blood surrounded her. Todd began to tremble as he had small flashes and saw himself stab her. The third picture was of Sebastian who floated in a bath tub full of water. The baby bobbed face down in the water, his body an unnatural shade of purple. Todd had a flash of himself as he held the baby underwater. The infant thrashed helplessly to survive. Todd began to cry fully and shook his head. Todd's face jerked as he flipped to the last picture. The image of Will Goldman, barely recognizable, came into view. In the photo, Will's corpse was sprawled across his living room chair which was stained with blood.

There were deep slashes across his face. The skin of his cheeks hung loosely down around his chin. Todd could see the large puncture wounds in his biceps and he had been eviscerated. Flashes of having done this to Will played across his mind. Todd tossed the pictures back to Dr. Larry and shook his head in denial.

"I need to talk to Bryce, he will know what's happened," Todd said as his voice cracked.

"Dr. Hall is no longer a member of this staff. He left for a better position at another hospital. He did feel, as I do, that you need more help than you are currently able to receive. I need you to accept what you have done and admit it to yourself. You create fantasy after fantasy to hide behind. In our last session you told me that you could move objects with your mind and travel as light," Dr. Larry paused and held up his pen.

"Can you move this?" he asked as he looked at

Todd.

Todd stared at the pen and tried very hard but the pen did not move. Todd did not answer and had become lost in incoherent sobs. He thought he heard Bree's voice again but fought the urge to search for it.

"You are delusional and paranoid. Even if you can't remember having done these things, the fact remains that you did them. I have done all I can to help you in my limited capacity. I fear that your condition will continue to deteriorate. Unless we do something extreme and soon, I think you will go irretrievably mad and never again be lucid. I am personally willing to do whatever it takes. I need to get you to sign this power of attorney, Todd. I can take the measures necessary to keep your fragile mind from being lost forever. Todd will you look at me? Will you please give me the opportunity to try and save you?" Dr. Larry pleaded as he flipped several pages over and handed them to Todd with a pen.

Todd looked into his eyes; there was no sign of deceit, as he looked at Todd sympathetically. Todd inhaled deeply, and corrected the pen in his hand and made to write his name on the line, indicated on the page.

"Dear Todd, please watch over...," The penetrative voice traveled through his mind and he winced and groped at his temples.

Todd looked down at the paper and flipped back a page.

Every line on the paper consisted of the repetitive phrase: *I give you my throne and serve you as my master.*

Todd continued to flip back through the pages and read the words in disbelief. He looked up at Dr. Larry who smiled at him with an unnatural grin. Todd made to speak but Dr. Larry had begun to convulse and struggle, as if something inside tried to tear its way out of him. His head had begun to toss from side to side and Todd could see it morph between dual images. He could see Dr. Larry and Bryce's face as they swapped places on the body of the man. Todd's eyes widened with fright as he looked on. The face of Bryce seemed to win as the body continued to shake violently. Bryce's face was still and strained as it looked at

236

him.

"Run Todd! Run to a safe place! I can't hold him for long!" Bryce said and closed his eyes under the strain.

Todd bolted out of the room. The hallway was dimly lit and dirty. The lights overhead flickered. Todd saw that bloody towels and body parts littered the floor. The walls were spotted with red hand prints of all sizes. He could hear pained shrieks of terror coming from distant rooms.

The orderly stood in the hallway with his back turned to Todd. Todd ran in the opposite direction. The gore covered floor caused him to slide unevenly. He worked to keep himself upright as he fled.

A gurney, on the side of the hallway ahead, held the body of what he perceived to be a woman wrapped tightly in a sheet.

The body thrashed violently against leather straps that held it down. Todd gave the thing a wide berth as he passed. A single claw-like hand groped for him from under the sheet as he ran by. He looked back over his shoulder and saw the orderly who had turned to face him. He looked forward and ran down the hallway, which seemed to lengthen ahead of him. This adversely affected his balance and he stumbled but caught himself. He spared a second and clung to the bloody wall to look back. The orderly ran toward him and looked as though he were melting into a dog-like creature. The metamorphosis was quick and as the last human pieces changed, the thing dropped to all fours and rushed even faster in his direction. Todd turned, ran, and felt fresh tendrils of fear work their way through him. He was aware of the sound that the animal's oversized talons made as they clacked against the tile floor. The sound caused his skin to crawl.

Ahead of him, two white doors were visible. The doors had large windows in them and Todd could see a brilliant white light through them. He summoned all the speed he could muster. His lungs strained painfully against his ribs as he drew breath. The sounds of the talons behind him were closer than ever and he lunged at the door with outstretched arms. As he burst through the doors into the warm white light he felt a falling sensation. The glare

237

subsided and Todd could see crystal blue water for an instant before he splashed through its surface.

His cheeks were puffed full of air and he quickly looked around. He expected the animal thing to land in the water with him. Todd was alone in what he realized to be a swimming pool. He looked up to see the rays of the sun, where they beckoned him to the surface. Todd broke the top of the water and wiped the cool chlorinated water from his eyes and took a deep breath.

Tall green bushes were visible and created a perimeter around the pool. Warm wind brushed through the leaves and they flourished under the pressure of the currents. He swam evenly in a circle until the back of a large white home came into view. Todd sniffed the air and smelled the rich scent of grilled meat.

"Come on Todd. The stuff on the grill is going to burn if you don't check it," Bree called to him as she approached with a baby in her arms.

Her long blonde hair flowed behind her as she maneuvered gracefully around pool furniture. She gave him a warm smile and raised her hand to brush her hair behind her ear. Her eyes seemed to be even more vibrantly blue in the sunlight.

Todd was bewildered by the realness of what he considered to be a dream. He walked bow-legged toward the grill as cold pool water continued to pour down his legs. He turned as he walked, looking at the vibrancy of everything. If this were a dream it was perfect right down to the feeling of the wet shorts that clung coldly against his thighs.

He approached the grill and raised its lid. Smoke and hot steam boiled from under the lid as he raised it. His arm was impervious to the heat. Todd looked back to Bree who labored to carefully set the baby girl down into a brightly colored playpen. She adjusted an umbrella attached to the playpen to cast a shadow over the baby, who smiled up at her. Todd turned back to the grill and noted a set of stainless steel grill implements. He chose a pair of tongs and began to turn over burgers and pieces of chicken that were being licked by the low flames of the gas grill. Todd inhaled the rich sweet smell of the barbecue as he completed the task. He looked curiously at his finger and slowly edged it toward the bottom of the hot grill. He felt no heat as his finger approached and it slid through the hot metal of the grill.

"Sera," Bree said, with a tone of authority.

Todd glanced over. The baby held her hands on either side of a small doll that floated, suspended in mid-air. The baby giggled and the doll dropped to the blanket on the bottom of the playpen. Todd smiled at the little girl and tears formed in his eyes. He looked at his own hand to see an unfamiliar band of gold on his ring finger. A similar band, along with a flashy diamond engagement ring, adorned Bree's finger. Todd closed the lid and walked over to where the child sat and played with her doll.

The baby girl looked up at him. Her chubby cheeks rose up and pressed upward at the bottoms of her eyes, as she smiled at him.

Her electric blue eyes returned to the doll she held in stasis. She caught it and offered it to him. Sera repeated a word that sounded something like dance as she shook the doll.

"See, I told you she would want you to keep doing that all the time," Bree laughed as she pulled the meat off of the grill and placed it on a large glass plate.

Todd placed an open palm toward the playpen and the doll rose up and began to bounce. The little doll's hair and clothes bounced up and down in time with the motion. He felt relief that he was able to manifest his talent in this facet of the dream. Sera clapped and repeated the word that sounded like dance to Todd.

"Can you bring her in for me?" Bree asked Todd as she walked into the house.

The doll dropped to the bottom of the play pen and Todd scooped the girl up and inspected her closely. Her small hands patted beads of water on his shoulder as he looked at her. While a different color, they were his own eyes, he realized. He walked toward the house and the baby wheeled to one side to see behind him. Her small hand pumped in a clutching motion toward the playpen. Todd paused and turned to look back to see what she could want.

The doll floated up and came to rest in the little girl's hand. Todd looked at her in amazement before he turned and headed into the back door. In the distance, as if carried by the wind, he could hear Bree's voice even though she stood before him in silence. She held her arms out toward him expectantly. He passed the baby to her as carefully as he could.

"Are you okay? You seem out of it today. I'm surprised you didn't float the baby to me like you normally do," Bree said and looked at him suspiciously.

"I am not who you think I am. You're just a wonderful dream," he thought and watched her closely for a reaction.

Bree offered no sign of recognition and turned to walk away. Todd slid the glass door closed behind him and followed them into the house. He tried to steal glances of the house as he followed them. He was afraid to look like a tourist to Bree.

"If this is a dream, I want to stay," he thought to himself as he appraised a vase on a marble table.

Todd had gotten left behind and he stood in the middle of a large living room. He turned on the spot and wondered which way Bree had gone. She appeared in a door way and tossed a pair of shorts to him. Todd dropped his wet shorts and made to replace them with the dry ones.

"You have got to stop that. There are little eyes in the house now," she corrected and pointed at a door to her left.

Todd nodded apologetically and placed the wet shorts in her expectant hand. She turned and went back the way she had come. Todd turned and walked the way she had pointed. As he entered the large dining room he spied Sera where she sat in her high-chair and prepared to toss a handful of mangled chicken.

"Whoa," he said as he mentally slowed, then stopped a large blob of meat that the baby intended to be a wall dressing.

The clump of meat returned gingerly to her plate and dropped wetly into the center.

The baby grasped the chicken in both hands, which

240

she raised in victory for Todd's approval. Todd smiled at her and laughed at her mouth surrounded in barbecue sauce. She looked like a predatory animal that had been interrupted while devouring its prey. Todd looked up at the expensive chandelier that hung from the vaulted ceiling. Extravagant crystal plates gleamed in the brilliant light of the chandelier. He walked closer to look at them through the window of the cabinet.

"No way we're gonna eat barbecue off of those. Oh damn! She got the chicken off of the table. I should have given her a piece to distract her. We were at the market earlier and I parked the buggy in the center of an aisle, where she couldn't reach anything. When I looked back she had filled the buggy with items from the shelves. She is getting stronger every day," Bree said as she wrestled a clump of chicken from the baby's hand.

Todd sat down next to Bree and picked up a burger and leaned over his plate. He fought the urge to laugh as he noted the large clumps of onions that protruded from the sides of the meat.

Todd ate two burgers and was deliberating on a third when Bree stole his plate and left the room. He could hear her say something about cholesterol and red meat.

"She is so in control of everything. This is how it would be if this were real," Todd thought to himself as he looked back to the baby.

The baby made pieces of chicken bounce around her and sang the dance word.

Todd tilted his chair back on its rear legs and peered into the kitchen after Bree. She labored to rinse dishes in the sink while she sashayed in time with music from a small radio. Todd smiled as he watched her and slipped silently from his chair. The baby watched him curiously as he stalked silently from the room. Bree continued to bop around the kitchen, unaware of his approach, as she mouthed lyrics with the radio. He tip-toed across the kitchen floor and grabbed her into his arms. She jumped in fright and dropped a small glass cup. The cup fell a few inches, stopped in midair, and drifted slowly over to lower itself into the sink. He pressed his stomach to her back and began to dance against her. She

241

covered his arms with her own and tilted her head back to lay it against him, while they swayed together. She turned to face him and he pulled her close as they danced. She sang softly with the song, and kissed him in the breaks between words. The song sang its way to the end and the volume lowered. The word dance erupted loudly from the baby in the adjoining room behind them. Todd and Bree turned toward the door in time to see a large mangled clump of chicken fly past the doorway. The food hit the wall and erupted into a spray of saliva and barbecue sauce. They both crumpled forward and held their stomachs in laughter. Todd worked to remove the chicken from the wall and floor with a handful of paper towels.

"Don't worry about that. You guys go ahead and I will join you out there after I start the dishwasher," Bree said as she wiped the baby's hands and face with a moist towel.

Todd scooped up the baby girl and headed back the way he had come in. He marveled at the expensive and expansive nature of the home.

"Where would we get all this money?" he asked himself.

He closed the sliding glass door behind him, and stepped down onto the deck. A breathtaking sunset had painted the sky with rich orange and pink hues. The sunset was coming to a close just above the bushy trees behind the pool. He turned his face to the sweet smelling baby. She grabbed at his cheeks and rubbed her nose against his.

"See the pretty light," he said and pointed to the horizon.

"I luh loo dah dee," she said as she smiled at him warmly.

"I love you too, princess," Todd said and hugged her as a tear rolled down his cheek.

He heard Bree's voice again which whispered from a place not so distant. He looked back into the sunset with a smile. The sights, sounds, and feeling of the child in his arms faded into obscurity as darkness became absolute.

* * *

Todd's eyes slowly opened. In his vision, the blurry outline of a woman came into view. She seemed to read to him from a book, but her voice was muffled and sounded as though it were far away. As his vision cleared, Bree's face came into view. He watched her in silence through the bars on the side of the bed. She finished, put her finger in the book, and looked up at him. He felt a smooth calming sensation flow through him as their eyes met. Tears filled her blue eyes and her lips trembled.

"I was so worried. You have been catatonic for nearly three weeks. I love you. I have been sitting here, afraid that I may never get the chance to tell you. The doctors said they didn't know if...if you would wake up," she spoke quickly.

"I love you too," he croaked as his dry throat strained to produce his voice.

Bree brushed his cheek softly with the back side of her hand as she reached to get him a glass of water. She grabbed up a large plastic box with a cord that disappeared under the bed and pressed at the buttons. The bed gave a mechanical whir as he was lifted forward. He could feel his neck muscles complain as they strained to hold up the weight of his head. She poured a little water over his lips. He coughed a bit as he worked furiously to swallow it. The muscles in his ribs were also weak. He struggled to raise his arm and took the glass of water from her.

"Bree, let me do it before you drown me," he said with a weak smile.

She dried the tears on her cheeks and looked at him with adoration.

"Could you hear me at all while you slept...or unconscious and unaware? The doctor told me that you might be able to hear me, and sometimes it was helpful to bring people around. I was so afraid. I couldn't hear your thoughts at all. There wasn't anything, like you were blanked out. I had nightmares about you being lost in a dark place and I couldn't find you," she finished and tried to avoid more tears as she fanned air into her face with her hand.

Todd concentrated before he spoke, his voice was very faint but it carried well enough for her to hear.

243

"I had a dream about us. We were married and had a baby," he began.

Todd winced and looked pained as a thought occurred to him. Large tears formed in his eyes, and he began to sob convulsively. Bree picked up the connection mentally, covered her own mouth, and her eyes closed hard. Todd covered his face with his hands, unable to calm himself. After a long while he began to make small gasps and seemed to recover his composure.

"I wasn't able to save them. It was over before I even arrived," his voice was very cold.

"He killed them all, there was blood everywhere. The baby...the baby," he tried to finish.

The monitor mounted on the wall beeped and the animated heart grew in size and pulsed faster.

"I know, I know," she said and placed her hand softly on his chest to comfort him.

Todd's face flushed and the muscles in his jaw flexed as he stared into the wall ahead of him.

"I went after him, to his place. He wasn't there. I wish he had been...He knows about us...you," Todd's eyes darted to Bree's lips.

"Your mind reading whore is next," her lips moved soundlessly.

Her hand gripped his. He could feel the fear in her. She sat down, looked at him, and tried to look stronger than she was feeling.

"When I tried to leave, I set off his farewell gift to me," he finished.

Bree looked at him and said, "Hand grenades."

Todd nodded to her.

"I *will* protect you," Todd said angrily as he looked at her, "if he gets anywhere near you I will...," Todd paused as he realized Bree could read the malicious murderous thoughts in his mind.

She looked horrified. He tried to change the subject quickly.

"What hospital is this?" Todd asked, "It's very nice."

"It's actually not a hospital at all," she said to him,

moved closer, and tried to relax.

"When you left, I continued to watch us on television for a while. I heard someone knock and thought it may be you. Your neighbor from apartment 7-a recognized you from the television and came to say hello. I told her that you had moved. A few more people came to the door. It was pretty much the same deal. I saw a reward offered for information on your whereabouts on the television and panicked. I figured, anyone of your neighbors would or could sell you out. There was another knock that scared me because it was so forceful. I asked who it was at a distance from the door. The man introduced himself as Andy Dickson, which was a lie and caused me to worry. He told me that he was there to help you that you needed to be guarded before the hounds came. I felt that he was telling the truth at that point so I let him in," Bree paused at Todd's curious expression.

"Hounds?" Todd asked.

"That's what he calls the media, the police, and the government. He told me that he had a car outside that would take us to his compound. He said we would be safe there. He believed this to be total truth. I didn't think we had too many options for help at the time. I told him that you had gone off on a personal errand and I didn't expect you back for several days. I went with him and he left men behind to escort you to me," she said and slammed back the large cup of coffee she held.

"How did he find out where we were?" Todd asked suspiciously.

"He seems to be a very, very smart man. The news stories showed a lot of pictures of Don's on TV. So, he canvased the area and asked business owners if they had seen us. He eventually ended up at Don's, and Tony asked if you were in trouble. Andy, or whatever his name is, seems to be very persuasive. He convinced Tony that he wanted to protect you. Tony told him where to find you and promised not to share the info with anyone else. His men brought you here a couple of days later. He brought doctors in and they set up this room for you. You were naked and unconscious. It was like you were dead asleep. I tried for a while to shake you awake. They left me to it for a while before they started the process of hooking you to monitors," Bree finished and looked at him.

"Why does he care what happens to me?" Todd asked.

"He just said he would explain it when the time was right," she said as she fixed herself another cup of coffee.

Todd seemed to be a little more at ease and he settled back into the bed. Bree turned up the cup of coffee and licked her lips.

"You should see the rest of this place. This room doesn't really give you a good idea of the scope of this building. I have only really seen the parking garage and this floor. When we arrived I noticed all of the men, who escorted us, were wearing guns under their jackets. I cannot hear the escort's thoughts at all, like they are all blocked somehow. This building has its own exclusive parking garage. I noticed as we drove up the garage ramps, that there were very few cars scattered out in the parking spots. As we parked, the black truck that had been following us, parked next to us. Two men in the other truck were also dressed in black suits and I could see the gun holders under their jackets as well. They swarmed around me like bees, as we approached the elevators. I noticed the men seemed to surround us at all times. If I paused, they paused. They were all looking in different directions all of the time too. You know how people look around when they walk? It wasn't like that at all. They seemed to be watching for something or someone. It was very strange to me but I admit I found it exhilarating. There were four elevators in the bay. We all stood in front of one that had a sign on it that said *out of order*. One of the escorts pulled out a key card, swiped it, and the elevator doors opened. We all loaded in. There were only two buttons in the elevator, neither of them had any markings. The elevator moved very fast and I noticed that there was a camera pointing at us from the corner of the ceiling. The elevator doors opened into a very plain white hallway," Bree paused, looking at him as she made herself more coffee, and then continued.

"All but two of the escorts left us and went through

246

one of the doors in the hallway. One of the escorts left us, trotted ahead, went to another elevator, and opened it with a card. This elevator had eight buttons, but the top floor button was the only one that was marked," she paused again, sipping at the coffee and inhaled deeply.

"When the elevator doors opened again, there was a short hallway ahead of us with a double door. One of the escorts opened the door and then joined the other one who had stood to one side of the door. Andy motioned for me to go in. He followed me in the room. All I could say was wow, this place looks like 'a luxury hotel on steroids'. We have our own chef and servant staff, they are always in the kitchen. But, I never see them come or go. They will engage in polite conversation but have no answers directly or indirectly about anything it seems.

It's the same with the doctors and nurse that have been coming in to check on you," she spoke quickly and drank more of her coffee.

Todd smiled at her, "You're so damned cute," he said.

She placed her hand on his and smiled back at him.

"Having a nice coffee buzz are we?" he asked.

Bree blushed a little, "It's not just coffee, it's really, really, good coffee. And it, like everything else, flows freely around here. I must have put on ten pounds, even though I have been waking up with an upset stomach every morning," Bree spoke rapidly again.

Todd was able to notice how jittery she was as he opened his mouth and began to speak, but Bree cut him off.

"Pregnant? Very possible. I am late, but don't get too worried, it's irregular more often than not," she finished.

"I wouldn't be worried or concerned," he said reassuringly.

"I just woke up from the longest dream I ever had. We had a child, you and I, and it was fantastic. If we can get through all of this stuff," he said and waved his hand over him in a circular motion, "I would like to get back to that dream in real life. Now slow down on the coffee. It isn't good for the baby," he chided.

She looked down at the cup that she was about to

press to her lips and moved it away as though something was suddenly very wrong with it. She sat the cup down on the table next to his bed.

"So, you wouldn't be freaked out by it at all? I have one of the kitchen staff working on getting me a couple of pregnancy tests so I can be sure," she said.

"Not at all," he responded as he took her hand and squeezed it gently.

"Todd, please help us," the sharp voice in his head demanded.

Todd rubbed at his temple with his fingertips. There was a short knock, and the door was pushed open. A woman with brilliant red hair, pulled back into a ponytail, entered the room. She wore a white skirt and blouse. She had a stethoscope draped around her long, thin neck.

"Hello Mr. Jennings. I am Anna, your doctor. Welcome back to the world of the living," she said.

She pulled a blood pressure cuff from a shelf near the bed and placed it on Todd's arm. She checked his blood pressure and then produced a small pen-like flashlight from her breast pocket. She shined it directly into the center of the bridge of Todd's nose. She then swayed it back and forth asking Todd to follow it with his eyes.

"Alright, you seem perfectly fine, I will have a nurse in here in a few minutes to get all these leads off of you," she said as she surveyed the monitors over the bed.

"What? Are you sure? I mean can you really tell I'm okay with a blood pressure check and a flashlight to the eyes? I have been in a coma for three weeks!" Todd said sharply.

The doctor looked shocked by his accusations and began to stammer, "You…really didn't have any physical…."

Todd's expression melted into a smile as he said, "I'm just messing with ya, Doc."

The doctor did not return his smile as she began to speak sharply, "You can get out of the bed and move around a little, once the catheter is out. I'm really sorry that nothing could be done about your testicles. We had to remove them," she paused as Todd's hand shot down between his legs.

248

"Just messing with you," she said with a stolid expression.

"The nurse will be here in a short while to get rid of that catheter though. You will need to stay relaxed and not do anything strenuous for a few days," she said as she chuckled to herself.

"Which reminds me," she said reaching into her pocket with a playful grin on her face. She pulled out three small pregnancy tests from her pocket and handed them to Bree.

"Good luck on whichever way you wanted that to go. I would suggest taking one first thing when you wake up. The third one was in case you were jumpy and wanted to just check it out," she said as she smiled at Bree.

Bree darted into the adjoining bathroom with one of the pregnancy tests in hand as Anna left the room. Todd raised the sheet and looked at the catheter that disappeared into the end of his penis.

"What did they do to you while I was out, little buddy?" he thought as he looked mournfully at his penis.

There was an audible burst of laughter from the bathroom.

"You big baby," Bree called out to him.

"Hey! Hey, there is no talking during a test," he responded as he forced a scornful look on his face.

It was a few minutes later when Bree walked slowly from the bathroom studying the pregnancy test in her hand.

Chapter 20

Slight of Hand

"Getting ready for muzzle loader season?" the clerk asked Doug as he placed the containers of gunpowder into a bag.

"Yes, indeed," Doug responded cheerily to the clerk.

The last six clerks had asked him the same question. Doug was relieved each time though, having not practiced an answer previously.

"Sign here, Mr. Phillips," the clerk said as he handed the driver's license to Doug.

He exited the shop, watched the men in the black SUV out of the corner of his eye, before he crossed the street. One of them seemed to be pointing at him through the darkly tinted windows. He got into his car. He pretended to look ahead as his eyes roved slowly up to his rear view mirror. He counted at least two men as he pretended to check his hair. Doug started the car, pulled out into traffic. He drove lazily back to the abandoned construction trailer that he temporarily called home.

* * *

"Why haven't we popped this scummy bastard yet?" Kevin asked his partner.

"I mean, we've been watching this guy for two weeks, buying welding shit and now..," he pointed to the almost transparent bag the guy was holding.

"Gun powder for shit's sake. I'm betting he isn't planning on baking a cake with that shit," Kevin finished.

Blake choked on his swallow of coffee and said, "Ha! Cake, that's pretty good. Look, Shepherd told us to tail this guy. I still want to know how he knew right where this guy would be at a precise time. You know how Shepherd is. At some point in the near future, he will give us the go ahead. Then we can...liquidate this baby killing jackass, but until then we just follow him. Does it matter that he is massing enough shit to blow up a city block? I mean, think about it. That's what people like him do. And people like us; we get to shoot him and shit. Hopefully we can give him the treatment," Blake said and laughed at himself.

"Oh, my God. I remember that poor bastard. Remember this? 'What are you gonna do with that hammer?' And Vincent was all like, 'we're gonna hammer out our differences'," Kevin threw his head back and they both laughed as they followed Doug.

Kevin and Blake parked behind a black eighteen wheeler with the flame designs that Blake seemed to like so much. They watched through binoculars as Doug unloaded his car and took the bags of gun powder into the trailer. Doug emerged one more time, stood just outside the door on the platform, and looked around. His eyes seemed to rove past them, where they sat slumped in their seats.

"Call Shepherd's voicemail and give him an update. Make sure it's low priority this time goofball!" Blake said smiling.

"You can't let stuff go, can you? That was like five months ago," Kevin said as he pushed on the face of his cell phone and placed it to his ear.

There had been no additional movement from Doug for hours. In his usual 'I'm in charge, cover down' fashion, Blake had wallowed into a ball in the rear of the truck and gone fast asleep.

The bright green numbers of the digital clock on the dash had just changed to one A.M. Kevin's swollen sleepy eyes darted over, having detected movement. He looked up again at the construction trailer. Blake had been snoring in the rear of the truck for a long while, but had become silent as Kevin continued to watch the trailer. Kevin shifted uncomfortably in the seat and looked at the time again.

A hand shot in through the open window covering his mouth. Kevin could feel cold steel pressing against his

251

temple. Kevin stared straight ahead, wide-eyed. He heard the sound of a hammer being pulled back on a gun. The hand over his mouth loosened and slid away. He slowly turned to see Blake pressing his gun into a man's temple. The guy just smiled and raised his hands, one of them holding a shiny lighter with a metal case.

"Damn it, Vincent. You're always screwing around," Kevin said.

"Gotta keep you old girls on your toes," Vincent replied.

"Where is Charles?" Blake asked.

A bright red beam flashed in Blake's eye. He followed the beam to its source. Charles crouched on top of the truck and was pointing a pistol with a laser sight at Blake's forehead.

"Boom, head shot," Charles whispered.

"Okay, you bastards got us this time," Blake said as his eyes rolled in disgust.

Vincent replaced Kevin in the driver's seat of the SUV, and Charles hopped into the passenger side and closed the door silently. "I'm gonna bring the shitty truck tonight. Before captain psycho recognizes this one," Blake said to them quietly, as they walked away into the night.

Vincent and Charles sat in the SUV all night and day watching the construction trailer. Aside from the wind blowing gently through tall tufts of grass near the truck, the entire area was motionless.

"Almost twelve-fifty. The old girls will be back soon," Vincent said, as he lowered the binoculars and checked the time.

"What do you think he is doing in there?" Charles asked.

"I bet he is making a bomb. He brought all that shit in there with him. What worries me isn't just what he is making, but what he plans to do with it. Remember the briefing, that family he killed. There are two types of killers," Vincent said thoughtfully.

"One is sane and kills for a purpose like greed, or revenge. The other is much worse, in the fact that you can't predict what they're doing it for. Our boy in there, he is a nut

252

ball for sure, he is after our guy and that shows focus, but just killing a family he knows, to screw with him...That's just evil shit. I think this guy is not just an abstract killer. According to Shepherd, he was after the Package," as they referred to Todd, "long before we were involved," Vincent finished.

Vincent cranked up the SUV, backed up, turned around, and drove a short distance.

"Damn, they brought the old truck," Charles said as he pointed to the late model, blue SUV with the darkly tinted windows.

"Let's give em the five second report and haul ass," Vincent said.

As they walked up to the driver's side door, Vincent back handed Charles' chest and pointed at two pairs of up turned shoes visible behind the back driver's side tire. They both crouched. Vincent pointed two fingers toward his own eyes, then pointed to Charles, and made a circular motion with his upturned pointer finger. Charles nodded silently, and slid his pistol from his shoulder holster. Vincent's eyes roved over every inch of the vehicle and his peripheral vision watched for movement.

Charles had backed away from him, swept away, and around the other side of the vehicle in a large arc. Vincent dropped down low and shined a flashlight under the vehicle. His eyes narrowed as he noted that it was only a pair of empty upturned shoes. Upon closer inspection, he could see that they were held in place by mounds of dirt. He rose slowly to a crouching position and began to open the doors of the blue truck. Vincent kept his pistol close to his body as he reached to open each door. Vincent flinched as he caught sight of his partner on top of the truck.

"How *does* he do that?" Vincent thought to himself as he grasped at his chest and rubbed it.

Vincent's eyes met Charles' eyes and Charles gave him a single nod, pointing his gun down at the roof of the truck. Vincent opened the rear doors of the vehicle and saw nothing. Charles hopped off of the truck and landed soundlessly and light next to Vincent.

"Think that whacko has been here?" Charles asked.

Vincent nodded as he pointed to the shuffle of shoe prints in the dirt near the driver's door of the truck. Vincent and Charles got back into the black SUV and closed the doors soundlessly. Vincent picked up his cell phone and began to dial. Charles made a breathy gasp and grabbed at the rope around his neck that pinned him to the back of his seat. Vincent's face snapped to the back seat where the muzzle of Blake's pistol waited to meet his gaze.

"A pair of observant bitches like you should be a little more aware," Blake said wickedly.

"Aw, come on!" Vincent said feeling anger rise in him.

"The Package is awake. I just got the word from Shepherd," Blake said, stepping out of the vehicle and heading for the older truck.

"Nothing to report," Vincent said as he shook his head and drove away.

"Owned like a pair of little girls," Kevin said as he closed the passenger side door.

Blake pulled up in the spot near the trailer and shut off the engine. He raised the binoculars to his eyes. The blinds that covered the window of the construction trailer flashed blue once in a while.

"I think the jackass is welding in there," Blake said as he handed the binoculars to Kevin.

Kevin looked for a long moment and then lowered the binoculars.

"I wonder if he is aware that welding in a small space with that amount of..." Kevin's comment was cut short.

The trailer exploded and jets of fire spewed forth in all directions from it. The force of the explosion shook the truck they sat in violently, causing both men to grab blindly to stabilize themselves.

"Holy shit!" Blake yelled, shielding his eyes from the intense light of the fire.

They hopped out and walked slowly toward the center of the fire. Pieces of debris fell here and there, and burned where they landed. Kevin stared straight ahead in disbelief as they walked closer.

A crunch was audible as Blake's foot crushed

something. They looked down and saw the smoking corpse at Blake's feet. Blake took a few steps back and brushed his shoe in a small patch of dead grass. The burning flesh still bubbled on the smoking chest of the cadaver. To their horror, it bucked once and belched smoke from the burnt flesh covered skull. Both men stared at the skull in amazement. All of its upper teeth and its entire lower jaw had been blown away.

"Is that our boy? Was he holding a bomb in his mouth?" Kevin asked, kneeling down to look closer.

Kevin winced and shielded his nose from the sick smell of cooked human flesh.

"Well, you can rule out dental record I.D." Blake chuckled.

"Ain't that a kick in the teeth," Kevin responded.

Both of the men roared with laughter.

Blake pulled a pen from inside his jacket and worked to remove the small chain that was disappearing into the bubbling flesh on the corpse's neck.

Kevin unintentionally held his own throat and grimaced while he watched this. After a moment, Blake rose up to his full height and held a set of charred dog tags. He produced a handkerchief from his rear pocket and dropped them into it. Kevin shined a flashlight at the handkerchief as Blake finished buffing the metal and opened his hand. The small rubber bands that surrounded the tag were intact and still smoked a little. Kevin waved his hand, displacing the smoke and read the tag.

"Douglas Rolfe, that's our guy," Kevin said and nudged the lifeless burnt skull with the toe of his shoe.

The sound of sirens began to pierce the air. Blake and Kevin turned wordlessly and sprinted toward their truck.

"Make the call," Blake said to Kevin as he started the vehicle and began to drive.

Neither of them noticed the rust colored sedan, which Doug drove, as he followed them.

Chapter 21

The Shepherd Summons

Bree smiled at Todd from where she stood with the pregnancy test display turned toward her. She playfully swayed a little as her head followed her body's motion.

I know something you don't know, Todd read in her expression. Todd let her enjoy the moment and finally broke down.

"Okay. You've had your fun. Dish it out," he said and motioned to the pregnancy test.

She walked toward him and smiled again.

"According to this...I'm pregnant," she mentioned cautiously as she sat down and watched his eyes for reaction.

"I love you," he said looking at her.

"I still need to take one in the morning, so don't be a weenie like me and get your hopes up until then. Then I can be the lone weenie," she said with a self-amused giggle.

"Do you think the baby will be normal?" he asked seriously.

She cocked her head back a little and looked at him.

Todd was afraid he may have offended her or brought a negative light on a previously joyous subject.

"No chance," she began, "Her mother can read people's thoughts, and her father can move things with his mind, flash around in a beam of light, and dodge explosions. So, normal isn't on the table at the moment," Bree said with a playful tone.

"Her? Does the pregnancy test tell you the gender of the child?" Todd asked bewildered.

"Nope. I just wanted to get my vote cast early," she said with a laugh.

The phone next to the bed rang sharply and shattered the moment. Bree reached for it as she looked away from Todd.

"Yes, hello?" Bree asked.

"Hello Bree. The good doctor informs me that Todd is conscious. I wanted to call and ask if he would be agreeable to meet with me later this evening, if he is up to it."

"Just a sec," Bree responded as she covered the mouthpiece of the phone.

"It's the guy that's been taking care of us. He wants to meet with you later this evening, if you feel like it?" she asked.

Todd inhaled deeply, looked at her, and nodded in agreement.

"What time?" Todd croaked as he looked around for his water cup.

Bree removed her hand from the mouth piece and asked, "What time would you like to meet?"

Bree looked at Todd and asked, "Is four-thirty P.M. okay?"

"Sure," Todd responded.

"That will be fine. Do we need to meet you somewhere?" Bree asked with a hopeful tone.

Todd thought of her being cooped up in this place for three weeks. Bree looked at Todd, nodded once, and smiled.

Her smile faded but she kept a light tone in her voice and said, "Okay, we will see you in your office then, good bye."

"Wow, there is a lot of crazy stuff going on," Todd said to Bree as he watched her replace the phone on its cradle.

"Yeah. I figure it pretty much has to be that way. While you were asleep, I thought about you, and the stuff you can do. Have you really taken the time to think about it?" Bree asked.

"Not really. Everything has been kind of pressed together for me. Since I got Bryce, it's been kind of like a surreal, supernatural roller coaster ride," Todd replied.

Bree watched the small plastic cup of water drift from the table to be grasped by Todd's expectant hand.

He drank the water greedily and released the cup, which floated back to its original spot on his nightstand.

"That...for instance," Bree began and pointed at the cup.

"I've noticed you do stuff like that all of the time. It's like your power is an extension of you and you don't have to concentrate to make it happen. That cup is very flimsy and soft. I noticed it didn't flex or bend until your hand closed on it. In addition to it being an unconscious reflex, there is a delicate control to it," Bree finished.

Todd looked over at the empty cup. It floated from the table and out over his bed. He looked at it and noted that it didn't bend or flex. The cup began to spin quickly end for end and stopped abruptly in an upright position. Todd's gaze was fixed upon it as it hovered there. The plastic began to fold in upon itself and then stretched out as it turned into liquid plastic. Bree watched it, thinking of beads of liquid floating in zero gravity from a science fiction movie. The floating plastic blob formed into the shape of a heart and solidified. The shape drifted over to Bree, where her hand opened to receive it. Bree looked at it in amazement and turned the flat piece of heart shaped plastic over in her hands. Her head was bowed and she looked up to him from it. Her blue eyes were filled with tears. Todd pushed himself up in the bed and looked concerned.

"I'm sorry. Have I scared you?" he asked worriedly.

"No, silly," she said and smiled through her tears.

"Aside from being amazing, think of the infinite possibilities of shapes you could have made. But, you chose a heart and gave it to me. It's what my dad calls 'an unspoken I love you'," she said as she placed the heart in the pocket of her jeans.

A nurse entered the room.

"Well, hey there sleepy head," she said to Todd as if they were long lost friends.

"Hi," Todd replied cheerily.

"You ready to get that catheter out so you can move around?" she asked.

Todd's smile melted into a scowl, he drew himself up in the bed, and glared at her.

258

The woman had stalled in the middle of a stride toward the bed, and seemed to bump into an invisible force. She stared curiously around for a second.

Bree slapped Todd on the shoulder and said, "Be nice!"

The woman was freed and continued toward Todd, still looking around curiously, oblivious to Todd's influence.

Chapter 22

An Internal Struggle

The early morning sun assaulted Doug's eyes. Through squinted eye slits, he intently watched the black truck ahead of him in traffic. The vehicle he pursued had almost eluded him several times.

In his attempt to remain unnoticed, he had allowed himself to be pinched off by changing traffic signals. He felt lucky that he had been able to reclaim sight of the vehicle. Doug was relieved when, half way through a block, the vehicle put on a turn signal. Doug parked and watched the black SUV, as it came to a halt at the security gate of the enclosed parking garage.

The sign over the parking garage's entrance read: *Haven Hotel Parking*.

The truck's driver flipped his wallet open and handed it to the guard. The guard inspected it, and then returned it to the driver. The gates opened, the black truck drove in, and the gates closed swiftly behind it.

Doug leaned out of the car to look up at the height of the building.

* * *

"Damn, I'm glad to be finished with that stake out," Blake told Kevin with a tone of excitement.

Kevin stared ahead with a grimace on his face and was unresponsive.

"You okay over there?" Blake asked Kevin.

Kevin looked at him and smiled weakly, as he produced a pill bottle from inside of his jacket. Kevin popped three of the pills into his mouth and chased them down with a huge bolt of coffee.

"Yeah, I'm all right," Kevin replied and continued to stare through the windshield as Blake parked.

Blake walked to the rear of the vehicle, stretched, yawned sleepily, and waited for Kevin.

Kevin seemed to be distracted and massaged at his temples as he lumbered into view.

"Level with me, Kev. What's going on with you? You know we have to depend on each other in this line of work. I've watched you taking those pills and having those episodes for a few days now," Blake said earnestly as he looked into Kevin's face.

Kevin looked him in the eyes, which had been a rare occurrence recently.

"These are anti-depressants," Kevin said as he produced the pill bottle and handed it to Blake.

"What are you depressed about?" Blake sounded very concerned as he passed the bottle back to Kevin.

"I'm just lost, I guess. All this death and destruction has caused me to ask myself some really hard questions," Kevin said as he turned his head to look out of a nearby portal in the parking garage.

"We haven't killed anyone in months, Kev. Did this guy blowing himself up mess with you *that* much? I mean, he's a baby killer for God's sake," Blake offered.

"It's not just him. I have done some really bad shit in my day. Do you ever wonder if all of this will ever catch up with us?" Kevin asked.

"What do you mean?" Blake asked.

"You can't turn on the television or radio without seeing a news story about things being torn apart by storms, volcanoes, floods, earthquakes, and shit. It's always happened, but just not so much as it has been recently. Kind of like the end of the world and all that. Do you believe in an afterlife, in God and stuff?" Kevin clarified.

Blake began, "I don't think about that kind of thing. I live in the here and now. Right here, right now all we have to worry about are hurricanes. We're so far inland, that by the time they could get here, we could be miles away, even with the Package in tow. We do what we do, 'cause we are good at it, and we can't afford a conscience. After I got out of the

261

service, I couldn't find a worthwhile job to save my ass. My recruiter told me that having signed up ensured success after my eight years. I could write my own ticket. Nobody told me that I wouldn't really be making a damn thing. That I would be charged out of the ass for everything I needed. I lived in that shit-bag place off base because I was sick of the constant, pointless inspections. Then, when it was all said and done, I was shit back into society, where I could barely fit in anywhere. I was almost thirty and my experience was in making things bleed. If it wasn't for people like Shepherd, I wouldn't have a damn thing. I don't see any God in all of that," Blake paused and issued a laugh as a thought occurred to him.

"As far as an afterlife, we're hooked up. We have sent so many people to Hell, we should get VIP tickets when we get there," Blake finished.

"Yeah," Kevin agreed as he nodded his head dreamily and tried to muster a smile.

"Try a beer with those, makes you feel way better. I took those for a while after the thing with the chick in Guatemala," Blake said and shook his head as he walked toward the elevators.

Kevin looked for moment at the star shaped burn on the back of his hand and followed Blake.

Blake held his card over the reader slot for a second and turned to Kevin.

"Look, whatever is bothering you, put it in its place. Shepherd is a smart man. He can smell trouble from a mile away. So, buck up and put on your game face for the debriefing," Blake told him with authority.

Kevin nodded in agreement and walked into the elevator.

"What do you think about the Package anyway, Blake?" Kevin asked as he tried to change the subject.

"I don't know what to think. Shepherd told us we were in for some really weird shit on this gig, but I had *no* idea. When he just popped into his bedroom from nowhere in a flash of light...I was actually afraid to get near him and wrap him up. I'm allergic to radioactive *anything*. I was wondering if he was an alien or something. I had to talk myself into helping wrap and carry him. I saw the stuff he did on the television later. I don't think he's the dangerous type," Blake stated.

"Really...? How did you come to that conclusion?" Kevin asked.

"His stuff speaks volumes about him," Blake began.

"Everything was all neat and tidy, even his fridge. Everything is in little plastic containers with foil on top, just so. He has no sports equipment anywhere in the whole place. No guns, no knives, no drugs, and not an ounce of porn to be found. I tried not to judge him for not having porn. But his lady friend does look like a proper sweet little treat," Blake finished.

"Yeah, she is pretty hot," Kevin winced and massaged his temples a bit.

The two men swapped to another set of elevators.

"I don't think he is an alien anymore though...," Blake paused in thought.

"If you notice his face, he was just as surprised as everybody else when he saved those people. I bet he is one of those people the government tried some kind of experimental shit on. Then they decided it would be fun to see how he would do, if he were sent back to a regular life. So, our boy up there is like a lab rat on the run. God knows we have seen a bunch of those government lab rats in the war business. It kinda goes with this whole lock down thing Shepherd has going on," Blake paused to let Kevin speak.

"Yeah, have you noticed the way things are set up? We can't take a shit without a partner. Like when we were having lunch and I went to the car to have a smoke. We were what, two hundred yards from each other and our phones rang? I'm not sure how Shepherd pulls that kind of knowing off," Kevin finished.

"That's easy, Kev," Blake began, showing Kevin his cell phone.

"Notice the upper left hand corner of your phone's display. When you and I get an appreciable distance between us, a little red symbol starts flashing in the top left corner, about here," Blake said as he tapped the phone display.

Kevin took his phone out of his pocket and looked

263

at it. The elevator doors opened and Blake held a hand up to him to say, 'stay there and watch'. Blake disappeared through a door and within a moment, the little red flashing icon Blake had described, popped up. Kevin went through the door and headed for the apartments. Blake stood outside of his door waiting for Kevin.

"So you see, if we're apart for too long we get the call," Blake said as he motioned Kevin into his room.

Kevin walked into Blake's apartment and plopped down on his couch. Blake walked back into the room and handed Kevin a glass of whiskey.

"No ice right?" Blake asked handing Kevin the glass.

"Perfect," Kevin responded.

Kevin took a gulp, held it in his cheeks for a second, and then swallowed it all at once.

Blake continued, "So, what I'm seeing is, all of us are making over a grand a day. We have this place to live in, clothes, and unlimited food and alcohol," Blake paused for Kevin.

"Yeah and exercise rooms, home theater systems, sweet rides," Kevin interjected.

"Right. Everything we can want or need. If you notice anybody asks for stuff and...Bam, we get it, like that," Blake snapped his fingers for emphasis.

"Why would you think that is, Kev?" Blake asked plainly.

"Because we're the best merc security force money can buy," Kevin offered hopefully.

"No, think about it. We stay here; we are given everything we need. Each of us has been handpicked as teams with a history of working well together. We don't have outings, except for the occasional 'chick hound' excursions and we nail them in the same motel. Never very far from each other or we get the calls. The big thing is the money. I mean, come on...Who gets this kind of money and digs for a security job? It's the Package, I bet you. Somebody somewhere would pay a lot of money for this guy. So, if we are paid good and kept on a leash, so to speak, it limits internal security breakdowns," Blake said and turned up his whiskey.

"You mean to keep us from being alone and possibly getting an offer we wouldn't want to refuse?" Kevin asked.

"I say it a lot but Shepherd is a smart dude. It seems he takes all this kind of stuff into account, long before he takes a job. I have been toying with the idea of asking for a lot more money. Like now, with crazy blowing himself up and the Package being awake. This job is worth a lot. I'm just trying to figure out an angle to approach Shepherd with. I need to not look like I'm considering other offers if you know what I mean? I don't want to look bad to Shepherd. I would bet all of the people on Shepherd's bad side, end up dead...or worse," Blake finished.

Kevin again nodded his agreement, as he headed toward the door.

"I'm going to change my clothes before we go to see Shepherd. I hope it's quick; I can get a nap in before the game. Be ready for it to be interrupted by the disaster coverage," Blake said as he watched Kevin leave.

* * *

Doug sat in the seat of his car and stared for a long moment at the map in his hand. He had marked his current position. He had begun to make random marks on the map.

"Now, if I get caught in this stolen car, they won't have any idea what I was up to," he thought as he folded the map neatly and placed it above the driver's side sun visor.

Doug looked into the driver's side mirror and checked for cars before he pulled away from his parking spot. He recoiled as the police cruiser drove slowly passed his car. He smiled to the officer in the passenger seat and nodded to him as they passed. Doug pushed the sunglasses a little further up on the bridge of his nose.

"The cops seem to be everywhere today. With all the natural disasters occurring everywhere, I guess they figure it's only a matter of time before things get bad here too," Doug thought to himself.

Doug pulled out behind the police cruiser and

maintained a healthy distance. A random pang of paranoia caused him to take an alternate route.

"The time is drawing near for you to strike at the heart of evil. You must be ready to strike when the opportunity presents itself," the smooth voice seemed to whisper in his ear, soothing him.

Doug backed his car in and made an effort to make sure every door was locked.

"Good afternoon, Mr. Phillips," Doug wheeled around to face the older man and clutched at the pocket of his pants.

Edward Durns, the motel manager smiled at him. Doug returned the smile and wiped his palm on the leg of his jeans to dry off the forming moisture.

"Good afternoon, I'm a little jumpy. The traffic here is horrible. Some girl, that looked like she was all of eleven years old, almost ran me off the road. I almost ran into parked cars to get away from her. She flipped me off and drove away like it was my fault," Doug lied as he extended his hand to Edward.

"Oh, yeah. I hate driving now, people drive like idiots. I would be a little jumpy myself, I suppose. Where have you been? I feel kinda bad charging ya for that room," Edward asked as he loosely shook Doug's hand.

"Oh, I got hung up at my job, and ended up staying in a room near my work," Doug replied.

"Got yourself another car, I see," Edward said as he gave him a suspicious glance.

"I...uh...yeah," Doug paused for a second.

"My car was damaged on a construction site," Doug was grasping for answers.

Edward looked over the car and noticed the bumper sticker that said pride, in rainbow colored letters. Doug watched Edward as his eyes narrowed suspiciously. Edward lowered himself to look unabashed at the Wisconsin license plate.

"I was really lucky I wasn't in it at the time. The foreman let me borrow this 'til I could get myself something," Doug offered.

Edward turned to him and smiled, "That was very

nice of him. This is your foreman on a construction site's car and he lent it to you?" Edward asked specifically.

"Yes. Very lucky for me," Doug responded as he unlocked the door to his room.

"Well, I think I'd better get on over to the office. I need to make a few phone calls and take care of some stuff," Edward said nervously.

"Were you able to fix the toilet?" Doug asked him.

"I don't know what you're talking about?" Edward responded curiously.

"I put a note on the office window before I left. The toilet was running water all over the floor and the wall behind it," Doug said.

Edward's expression changed and he looked over his shoulder at the office and then back into the open room.

"Best take a look at it real quick before everything gets water damaged," Edward said, hobbled into the room, and headed for the bathroom.

Doug gave the box cutter in his pocket a quick squeeze. He looked around the parking lot as he followed Edward inside and closed the door behind him.

Chapter 23

Need To Know

Todd sat on the side of his bed. His hands sat flatly on the mattress to help him to maintain his balance.

"Take your time," Bree warned as she watched him from the doorway of the room.

"I am. I feel a little off balance. I guess I should stop being such a puddin'. One little explosion and being in a coma for three weeks, and I turn into a little girl," Todd said sarcastically.

"Well, at least you have a pretty dress," Bree responded, pointing at the hospital gown with a floral print.

Todd looked down at it and smiled as he pinched up the cloth to look at it. He looked up at her with a smirk on his face, half amused.

"I took the liberty of painting your toenails pink while you were sleeping," Bree announced and looked mischievous.

Todd leaned over the edge of the bed to look and almost fell. He corrected himself and noticed that Bree had moved in to catch him.

"So, this is what a relationship is like," Todd thought to himself.

"It's not unfashionable to want to protect each other," Bree said to him with a smile.

"You know, when I was younger, I thought of relationships as being something far less important and shallow. Like you loved somebody and they loved you and you went to see movies and have dinner and sex all the time. Of course, that changed as I got older and thought of what I wanted from a relationship. But, I have to tell you, there are things I hadn't considered. Me being ill and being taken care

268

of, was one of those things. When I woke up and you were there reading to me, I realized just how it feels to have someone really care about me," Todd said to her.

"Well, I hope you haven't ruled out movies, and sex. I thought about raping you a few times, but that catheter was in the way," Bree said with an evil grin.

"Can't rape the..." Todd began to say.

"The willing!" Bree finished his sentence and erupted into laughter.

Todd laughed, leaned forward to stand up, and allowed his weight to evenly distribute between both feet. He swayed a little bit then released the bed and took a few tentative steps. He stared with rapt attention at his toes for a moment before looking up to her face.

"You clear coated my toenails?" he asked incredulously.

"Yeah, I was thinking the hot pink might be a bit too racy for you," Bree said as she pointed to her own toes.

Todd looked down at her bright pink toenails which undulated and appeared to be waving at him.

"Very nice. It might be a while before I'm secure enough to let you do *that*," he said with an exaggerated smile.

Bree jutted out her bottom lip in a pouting fashion.

Todd flashed her, his mischievous grin.

"A man in your condition should be in bed, on top of me," she said reading his thoughts.

"That's the kind of thinking that got you knocked up in the first place...," Todd chided.

She looked very seriously at him and asked, "Do you know why a woman is not like a light bulb?"

"Enlighten me," Todd said in a pretense of curiosity, sensing a joke unfolding.

"You can unscrew a light bulb...," she quipped.

They laughed together.

"I don't think that you can get pregnant twice...so, do you wanna?" Bree asked with a sultry tone.

"I would like that very much. I would suggest that we wait until later this evening. The doctor said that I should wait a few days for strenuous activity. This translates into a few hours. Did the people who brought me here think to bring clothes?" he asked.

"No, they did something even better. Come see this," she said, suddenly excited.

She raced over to him and took him by the hand. She led him to the door and looked at him as she opened it. Todd's jaw dropped as he stared in amazement around the apartment.

"This is our room?" he asked as he turned to look at her.

"This is just one of the rooms," she responded.

The sweet smell of fresh flowers drifted to his nostrils. Todd looked around at the expanse of space. Leather sectional sofas surrounded and faced the largest television he had ever seen. There were small mirrored tables all around the room. Each table held a vase filled with vibrantly colored flowers which helped to create a pleasant atmosphere. Todd could see himself reflected in the black marble floor, on which he stood. He looked out through the open double doors onto the balcony. The balcony seemed to him like someone had placed a water fountain with surrounding benches in the middle of a lush green rain forest.

"It's beautiful," he said earnestly, as he continued to look around the room.

"It gets better. Come see," Bree sounded like an excited child.

Todd felt stronger as he walked across the room, the muscles in his feet and legs were becoming more coordinated.

"Look at this bedroom," she exclaimed and plopped down on the huge bed.

"That's your closet," Bree motioned to a door to his right.

Todd walked over, opened it, and peered in. This closet was half the size of his apartment. Brilliant, overhead, florescent lights illuminated the neatly placed wire shelving where folded socks and underwear, in an assortment of colors and styles, sat. He inhaled deeply, enjoying the scent of leather. The entire bottom row held an assortment of male shoes. It looked like a shoe rack at a department store. He

270

bent down to look in them. The muscles in his legs cramped under the strain, and he placed a hand on the floor to steady himself. All of the shoes were size twelve. A long line of slacks and jeans hung neatly on the other side. Todd inspected the jeans, every pair his exact size.

"All of this....is *mine*?" he asked amazed.

"Yes. They took the measurements from your clothes. They figured out what kind of underwear, socks, and clothes you liked. All of it came in about a week ago. Some ladies came in and arranged it all," she answered.

Todd noticed a glossy black cabinet with a brass knob, under the tie rack. He opened it and stood there with a dumb, astonished expression. Jewelry, on velvet lined shelves, flashed up at him. Todd stared at it all, picking up a gold watch and a herringbone necklace.

"All of this....is mine *too*?" he asked again as he tried to mask his excitement.

Bree laughed from behind him.

"I have a closet that's bigger than yours. You should see *my* jewelry," she said.

"This isn't everything. There is a lot more. The kitchen is huge and there are always people in there, preparing our next meal. We also have our own toilets and shower stalls. There is a swimming pool sized bathtub as well. Anything you might ever imagine you could need is in the medicine cabinet. *And*, the closet in the bathroom has razors, shaving cream, lotions...It's like a damn shopping mall, Todd," she finished.

"There is something odd I found," Bree said as she led Todd back to the living room.

Bree stood to one side of the balcony door and placed her hand on a light switch. She worked for a second and the light switch turned clockwise revealing a button underneath.

"Wow, what does that do?" he asked curiously.

"I don't know. I was afraid to push it," she replied with a sheepish grin.

Todd walked up closer and looked in for a second.

"Stand back a second. Let a *man* do this...," he said rhetorically.

271

He rammed his finger onto the small button. He felt a click and pulled his finger back. The two of them stood there looking around.

"Did you see anything?" he asked her.

Before she could respond the overhead lights began to dim. Metal panels slid down to cover the balcony entrance and the windows of the room. Pots clanged and people could be heard scrambling around in the kitchen. Todd walked over and looked in the kitchen which had been vacated. A metal door slid down over the pantry door, which he assumed was some kind of passage, used by the kitchen help. Todd noticed that a metal panel covered the entrance door also. Bree and Todd stood together and looked around the room curiously. They heard a rap on the door. It reverberated with a metallic echo.

"Mr. Jennings, are you guys okay in there?" came the man's concerned voice from behind the door.

"Um, yes...we're fine, just looking around," Todd said looking at Bree and mouthed the words, "oh, shit."

Todd moved back to the switch again and pressed the button. The metal panels slid away from the windows, doors, and back into their concealed slots. The lights returned to full brightness. Four armed men filed hurriedly into the room. Todd moved in front of Bree.

* * *

The pistol in Blake's hand suddenly fell heavily toward the floor, he struggled to slow its decent, only to have his hand pinned painfully to the floor under the supernaturally increased weight of the weapon. Behind him, Kevin grunted having been immobilized much to Blake's surprise, in an identical fashion. Blake's focus suddenly returned as the pain of a now purpling hand grabbed his attention.

Let them go, they are on our side,"Bree said to Todd as she apologetically looked toward the men from behind Todd's shoulder.

Todd seemed to relax, and the men grunted as their hands were released. Vincent stood up and looked at his gun

272

in amazement.

"How did you do tha...ulf," Kevin's question was cut short by Blake's elbow, which hit him in the gut, sharply.

"Please accept our sincere apologies Mr. Jennings. The panic alarm went off," Blake said as he massaged his right hand and fingers.

"Call me Todd, and I'm sorry that I pushed it. I didn't know it was gonna cause all of this. I'm sorry about your hands. I don't really know how I do that," Todd said as he looked at Kevin.

Kevin didn't respond or acknowledge Todd. Kevin applied the safety on his pistol and holstered it under his jacket.

"Sorry again, Mr. Todd," Blake said, holding his hand up in front of him as he backed out of the room and closed the door.

"Did we just get owned or what?" Vincent asked, waiting for Blake by the elevator.

"What is wrong with you, asshole?" Blake asked as he slammed his fist into the wall and pressed his angry face close to Kevin's.

"What? What, I asked *one* question, c'mon, the thing with the guns, c'mon now," Kevin tried to turn his face to avoid Blake's angry scowl.

"We do NOT ask or answer questions," Blake blurted into the side of Kevin's face.

Kevin winced on every syllable as his ear drum rang from the abuse.

"Okay Blake, that's enough," Vincent said as he pulled at Blake's shoulders.

Blake refused to break the angry glare as the four men moved into the elevator together.

He rolled his eyes and said, "Look, I'm sorry Kev, Shepherd comes down on my ass, not you guys. I have to listen to it now."

Blake snorted in disgust. Kevin looked at the star shaped scar on the back of his hand.

"Yeah, I'm sorry too," Kevin responded staring ahead at his own reflection, "Very, very sorry," the murderous anger in his eyes stared back at him.

* * *

Todd walked over to a chair in the center of the room as he assessed the nature of its quality.

"I bet this chair cost at least five thousand dollars," he commented to Bree.

"Oh, I am sure, at least that," she responded as she watched him inspecting the rest of the room.

"So, these people just swoop in, save us out of nowhere, bring us here to the equivalent of a fortress, and provide us with food, clothes, and jewelry? I have to tell you, I am more than a little suspicious. Why would they have all of this stuff ready for us? How would they know that they would need to? Nobody does something for nothing...for anyone," he finished as he looked around the room skeptically.

"Didn't you give that woman on the street money? It was something for nothing when she needed it. Maybe it's cosmic payback?" she said optimistically.

"I believe in that. I do really, like karma. But, all of this seems especially suited for us. That money I gave her was abstract. What she chose to do with it, I will never know. But, all of this, it was planned. This isn't something you throw together over night. From the balcony, I can see we are at least ten stories up. This place is set up, literally like a fortress. It was built for this, not converted for it. So, that would mean, years of planning and execution for a need. A need that didn't even exist until several weeks ago when all of this stuff started to happen," he said as he looked at her curiously.

"Didn't you just melt a plastic cup with your mind a little while ago? This is much larger than you may be considering. I love you, and think of you as a man, and the father of my unborn child. But, from an unbiased standpoint, you're a commodity that others would want to exploit," she paused as she noted the curiosity in his face.

"What do you mean commodity?" he asked.

"You're a weapon, Todd. You would be the weapon of choice. You seem to be invulnerable to damage. You can move objects with your mind, travel in bursts of light, and there is no telling what else you will be able to do. In answer to your question, I guess these people are either protecting you from the world, or protecting the world from you," she finished.

Todd looked at his feet and nodded his head.

"Yeah, I guess I could be considered dangerous. I really hadn't looked at it that way," he said and looked ashamed.

"Don't beat yourself up like that. I know, and you know that you're a good person," she said reassuringly.

"Yes, but I want to kill Doug. I want to fold him inside of himself after breaking every bone in his body...slowly," Todd said angrily.

"Well, that's normal. You're still grieving over the loss of your friends. Vengeance is not a new concept, you didn't invent it. In fact, I see it as you protecting us from him," she said and patted her stomach.

Todd's eyes followed her hand and he smiled. He knelt down in front of her and placed his face close to her stomach.

"Hey in there, baby, it's Daddy. I love you," he spoke to her belly.

Bree laughed at him.

"Okay. I'm going to take a shower and get ready. We need to go talk to our benefactor soon. I am sure he will have all of the answers you need. You need to get dressed yourself, although the dress *is* quite stylish," she said as she pointed to his floral print hospital gown.

Within a few minutes, Todd was smartly dressed and sat down in the chair in the center of the living room. He placed the watch on his wrist and admired it.

"Bryce, are you there?" Todd asked.

There was no response from Bryce. Todd closed his eyes and regulated his breathing. In the darkness of his mind, he sat in the chair again as the lights dim glow began to illuminate the scene. Todd stood up and peered around into the darkness.

"Bryce... Bryce... Where are you?" he called into the darkness.

275

Again, there was no answer.

"Please Todd, save us," the whispering voices hit his mind like a hammer. He staggered and lowered himself into the chair as the voices faded.

"Hello, can you hear me?" he called after the voices.

There was no response.

"Marvin, anyone?" he called out, his voice was almost pleading.

Marvin lumbered toward him as he formed out of the darkness.

"Yes, Todd?" he stammered.

"Hello, Marvin. Where is Bryce?" Todd asked.

"I am not sure, Todd. He is separate from us," Marvin said.

"What do you mean, separate?" Todd asked.

"When I'm not here talking to you, I am bathed in warm cleansing light. I am formless and part of, what seems like, everything. Everyone is there with me, and even though we don't speak to each other, I can feel each one of them and the warmth they emit. Bryce does not join us. He is separate," Marvin finished.

"Okay...thank you Marvin," Todd said thoughtfully.

Marvin smiled warmly, turned, and walked toward the darkness. He stopped and looked back at Todd.

"There is one more thing," he said, his expression was grave as he continued to speak, "The man with the gun a little while ago, the one that asked you how you had done that? He had the mark on his hand," Marvin said, tilting his head forward to look ominous.

"What mark?" asked Todd.

"The same one I had, after that devil woman appeared to me. It's a burn in the shape of a star on the hand," Marvin said as he pointed to his hand just above the thumb.

"Thank you, Marvin. I will be careful," Todd responded.

"I don't think *you* have to be the careful one," Marvin said over his shoulder as he moved forward and dissipated into the darkness.

* * *

Blake paused in front of Shepherd's office door for a moment. He clenched and released his fists a few times and took deep breaths. Blake had to steady himself around Shepherd. He always felt as though Shepherd could see into him, somehow. It made him feel uneasy and he had to concentrate to guard himself. He slowly brought his right hand up chest height and rapped gently on the door.

"Come in," Shepherd's deep and muffled voice commanded through the door.

Blake drew himself up to his fullest height, sucked in his gut, and walked in.

"Hey there, Shepherd," Blake said in an attempt to sound friendly.

"Can you tell me what's going on with your men?" Shepherd said as he leaned over his desk with his fists planted in front of him.

Blake stared ahead at him as the thought that Shepherd looked like an angry gorilla, occurred to him. Shepherd's black, short hair was neatly combed back away from his chiseled face. The muscles in his jaw were flexing and the side of his face undulated all the way up to the gray hair in his temples. His white business-suit jacket seemed to be stretched to cover his enormous muscles. He reached into the pocket of his slacks and pulled out, what looked like, a cell phone. He reached down and touched its face. Blake listened to the device play back the conversation from when they had entered the Package's room.

Blake tried to look innocent as he heard himself say, "Look, I'm sorry, Kev. Shepherd comes down on my ass, not you guys. I have to listen to it now."

"You're damned right; you have to listen to it. I don't pay you to screw up or let the men who work for you screw up. I said to limit contact with the Package to yourself, yet your men seem to want to make a new buddy. It's fine that you addressed it, but it *does not* need to happen again. If they can't listen, I will have to find people who can," Shepherd finished and stared at him angrily.

277

"I think they were a little thrown off by the thing with the guns," Blake offered as he tried to remain calm.

"I have been taught to never let go of my gun. That covers, taking explosion impacts, diving from moving cars, and being stabbed. You always hold onto your gun, because if you don't have it, somebody else does. We walked in there and the guns pinned us to the floor. All four of us were as helpless as a baby for a second, and we realized, special doesn't begin to describe the man in that room. If he even *is* a man. I am perfectly willing to accept responsibility for the screw up. It has been addressed and further issues of that particular manner will not be a concern for you. If I may, sir," Blake paused to mask anger rising in him.

"I would ask that you make me more efficient at doing my job by giving me *need to know* information, at the very least. I, myself, felt more than a little shaky in there, and my nerves are like steel. I appreciate everything you have done for me, Shepherd, but tying my hands behind my back, kicking me off a dock, and then bitching at me for not being able to swim isn't acceptable," Blake said, folded his arms in a very brooding fashion, and stared back at Shepherd.

Shepherd considered him for a moment. Blake just stared at Shepherd.

"Perhaps you're right," Shepherd said, stood up, and seemed to assimilate the information.

"Regardless, I expect a lot from you, more than I should, but that's why I chose you," Shepherd continued.

Blake's arms dropped and his expression relaxed. This was very close to an apology, and would be a first from Shepherd.

Shepherd opened his laptop, typed furiously for a second, and spun it to face Blake. Blake lowered himself and read from the file.

Blake read soundlessly for the most part, but muttered, "to be acquired upon revealing himself by miraculous act on or about noon on.....subject will display qualities that will seem....interaction between protective staff and subject to be exclusively limited....."

Blake reached forward to scroll down, at which point, Shepherd snapped the laptop back and closed it.

278

"That will be all you need to know. I don't care what bullshit you have to feed your men. Those are the *handle with care* instructions I have been given, and that you will follow to the letter," Shepherd said with finality.

"Thank you Shepherd," Blake said and stood back up almost at attention.

"One more thing. I want you to keep a close eye on Kevin and report to me the moment you see anything suspicious. I have reports of him being, let's say, a little distracted. I would like you to escort the Package and his girlfriend here in about ten minutes," Shepherd finished.

"Understood," Blake replied, then turned, and let himself out of the room.

Chapter 24

The Prophecy

Shepherd gazed for a moment at the door after it closed. He sat down and exhaled deeply. He reached under his desktop and pressed a button. The door locks turned and clicked. He grabbed the laptop and turned it to face him more evenly. He typed for a moment and a small video popped up. He stared in amazement as he watched Todd liquefy a plastic cup as it floated in mid-air. The reflected image played across his glasses as he stared at it intently, before he pressed the email icon.

A pop-up message appeared on the screen that said :
This message has been encoded and sent. Purging files from hard drive.

Shepherd closed the laptop, removed his glasses, and massaged his sore eyes.

He swiveled in his chair, and then used the remote to turn on the panel of televisions behind his desk. There was a brief electrical hum and all of the screens lit at once. Each TV was tuned to a different station and the audio was a jumble of voices and music. His eyes roved over the screens until a radar image caught his attention. As he pointed the remote at that screen, the radar image spread over all of the monitors to create a larger image. The jumble of audio instantly snapped to the voice of a single meteorologist.

"Six fully formed storms have entered the Gulf of Mexico," the meteorologist said cheerfully.

"And this idiot seems overjoyed about it," Shepherd thought to himself as he watched circles being drawn around each storm.

"Six, count them, six fully formed hurricanes. At this time, there is still no possibility for communication with the Jamaican Territories. Our hearts and thoughts are with them," the meteorologist said as he looked forlorn for a moment.

His expression reformed into glee as he said, "At this time, we have no predicted path, as the weather conditions in the gulf are very erratic. But, we can be assured of contact with land in less than two days."

"He looks so very pleased to be bringing this wonderful news to us," Shepherd thought disgustedly as he turned off the monitors.

He looked at his watch and then quickly dialed a number on his cell phone. He placed the phone against his head and stared into the darkened monitors while he waited for it to connect. Shepherd leaned forward and pressed the bud into his ear with a single finger.   "Authorization code...Tango...Three...Delta...Delta...Yankee," his tone was very even and he enunciated each word perfectly.

A computerized response with a very flat tone said, "Voice authorization, Shepherd, confirmed. Please hold for a connection."

"October," answered the aged woman's voice after a brief time.

"Yes, good evening. The Package will be available via sat link four, in approximately twenty-two minutes. Confirm," Shepherd's voice was rich and even as he pronounced each word.

"Yes, thank you, Shepherd," croaked the old woman.

The phone disconnected immediately and Shepherd removed his ear bud and placed it inside of his jacket.

* * *

Todd sat in a leather chair and stared at the television screen in front of him. A knock on the door erupted. He looked to the door as he felt angst rise in the pit of his stomach.

Bree entered the room cheerily and bellowed, "Be right there!" her expression apparent in her tone.

Bree lowered herself as she turned to face Todd and

her expression darkened.

"Hold my hand the whole time. If anyone lies, I will squeeze your hand," she whispered to Todd.

"Wow, you look great," Todd replied loudly and nodded his understanding of what she had whispered.

"Us against the world my darling, I love you," he thought to himself.

She smiled and nodded to him as they held hands and walked together toward the door.

Blake smiled to them and waved his hand toward the elevators.

"Right this way," Blake said, very courteously.

Todd and Bree boarded the elevator, having watched Blake swipe his card to make the doors open. Todd examined Blake's face, as it was reflected in the elevator door. Blake met his gaze in the reflection and quickly looked away.

Todd cleared his throat and asked, "Where are we going?"

Blake regarded him for a moment as though he really wanted to answer the question, but responded, "Just follow me, Mr. Todd, we are almost there."

Blake looked at his watch and paused over the card reader. Todd and Bree stood expectantly at the wooden door and looked ahead.

Todd finally looked over to Blake, who seemed to be counting the seconds on his watch. Blake swiped the card and the door opened. Todd stood there for a moment after they entered a small chamber between the two sets of doors. He again looked to Blake who pointed at the next door in front of them.

"You're not coming with us, are you?" Todd asked.

"Nope, I will be right out here if you need anything though," Blake said and gave Todd and Bree a courteous smile through the gap just before the doors closed.

Todd approached the office door with his hand out, ready to grasp the knob, then paused, made a fist, and gently rapped on the center of the door.

"Come in," a man's voice boomed from inside.

"Are we ready?" Todd thought.

She smiled and nodded. He turned the knob and they walked in together. The man behind the desk gave a labored smile as he stood and shook Todd's outstretched hand.

"Andy Dickson," he said as his eyes shot to the bonded hands of Todd and Bree.

He noted that Bree squeezed Todd's hand abruptly.

"You can call me Shepherd. For all intents and purposes, it really doesn't matter what you call me, though. I have already been introduced to your companion," Shepherd finished and let his fake smile fade away.

"Todd, Todd Jennings, nice to meet you. First, I would like to say thank you for the kindness that you have shown us. I would also like to know what exactly is going on here." Todd announced as he looked into Shepherd's eyes.

The fake smile returned and Shepherd spoke, "In all fairness, your stay here is not my doing at all. I'm paid very handsomely to look after you. As to what is going on here, well, someone with more authority will answer those questions. I would like to be up front with you. It helps me to do my job. We are not friends or acquaintances. The less you know about me, the better I like it. As for the security personnel, I would appreciate it if you adopted the same mindset with them. The person you will meet pays us to protect you. That is the sum total of our relationship. I really shouldn't say anymore. If you will please excuse me, your hostess will address you shortly."

Todd and Bree watched him walk over to an alcohol cabinet and fix himself a drink.

"One more question, if I may?" Todd asked Shepherd.

"Sure, I will answer you if I can," Shepherd replied.

"There is a man after us," Todd began.

"Douglas Rolfe," Shepherd spoke over Todd.

Shepherd walked over to his desk, opened the top drawer, and reached in.

"He had a little accident with some gunpowder and a welding machine," Shepherd said and tossed him a small wadded piece of cloth.

Todd opened the cloth and found a set of charred

283

military dog tags. Todd read the name and noticed that the rubber guards around the tags were bubbled and melted.

"He is nothing more than a crispy little pile of bones now," Shepherd added.

Bree, who had been curiously looking at the tags, recoiled and covered her mouth in disgust.

Shepherd walked behind them and took a seat against the wall, then sipped at his drink. Todd and Bree exchanged bewildered glances as they turned forward in their seats.

A cloaked and masked figure appeared as one image on all of the screens. The effect made Todd and Bree jump in unison.

Todd's eyes went to an insignia on the chest of the mysterious figure's cloak. A circle formed by twelve faceted, colorful stones. The stones were linked together with golden threads. Todd noted that a small oxygen bottle sat behind the chair and a tube from it fed into the billowy dark sleeve of the cloak. Todd could make out the eyes through the white porcelain mask. The mask, itself, looked as though it were in the throes of laughter. The longer he looked at it the more unsettling it seemed to him. Finally, the figure spoke. The aged female voice seemed to be augmented by an amplifier.

"Good evening, Mr. Jennings," she said and turned toward Bree and lowered her head in greeting.

Todd noticed a small camera pointing at them from the bottom of the monitors. She inhaled between words in a much exaggerated manner. Todd understood the need for the oxygen bottle. The voice, however aged and labored, was very even and soothing. Todd adjusted his grip on Bree's hand. Shepherd grimaced slightly as he inspected their bonded hands again.

"I would like you to call me October," she said.

Bree's hand began to squeeze Todd's and then forcibly released, as though she were unsure of her opinion.

"Please let me apologize if anything hasn't been taken care of as far as your comfort. We went to great lengths to ensure that you would have everything you needed, but I know an oversight could have been made. I assure you, if we could have avoided all of the secrecy, we would have. It has thus far been for our mutual protection," she paused.

Her hand rose from her lap and motioned openly to Todd.

"Please, I am quite sure you have questions for me?" she asked Todd.

"Thank you. Everything has been great, really great. I do have questions for you. Why are you protecting me?"

Todd made a large circular motion with his hand and looked around saying, "I have come to realize this entire setup seems to have been in place long before I had need of it. Are there others like me?"

"Oh heavens no, this operation was made entirely *for* you. I should try to explain more and you can question me as you see fit," she said and raised her hand to her chest and cleared her throat.

"Let me tell you about myself and my life. We have to go back some years. My parents were very wealthy. I was shipped all over the world, almost every year to a different school. The most expensive, fashionable schools were the flavor of the year to my parents. I do not know if my parents realized the mental trauma I suffered as a result of it. For them, it was the ability to answer a single question with the most favorable answer. 'Where does your daughter attend school?' I rarely made friends, as I knew they would not be lasting bonds. The pain of losing friends is easily countered by not making them. However, I was in my last year of Werthner Finishing Academy when I met two girls that made it through my defenses. After graduation and for years following, we were inseparable. Eventually, one of them met a boy and after a whirlwind courtship, married, and moved away. Shortly thereafter, the other friend did the same. It was odd to me for the months while I was alone, how I craved friendships that I had previously shunned so forcibly.

"During that time, I met a shadowy man one night while I was in Paris. He seemed to appear from nowhere and to tell you quite honestly, even though we only spent a few hours talking, I fell deeply in love with him. His every word, though they were often spoken strangely, sung to my senses. He was dark and beautiful. I know that it is acceptable now but casual sexual trysts were frowned upon at that time," October paused and looked to Bree for a moment, the mask tilted as if its wearer were lost in deep thought and she began to speak again returning her attention to Todd.

"He disappeared in the night and I never even knew his name or why he had gone. My memory of him has faded over the years. Only the midnight purple cloak he wore still clings to my dreams. That was the closest I ever came to love and marriage in my long life. After having met him, I spent months in a depressive state, wondering where he had gone and if I would ever be graced by his company again. I was not to be so fortunate.

"Years later, I received an embossed letter from one of my friends, inviting me overseas to attend a social gathering. It was there, that I was reunited with both of my friends and an invitation was extended to join a society that they were forming. I threw myself into it, having no real regard for the society's foundations. I simply wanted to be among my friends," she paused.

"It's quite ironic that I am the last surviving member and your spokesperson on the society's behalf," her voice trailed away for a moment in thought.

"The society, in and of itself, was an abstract entity. All of the members were just wealthy, or well to do, and reaching out for the same social interaction. We funded relief efforts to impoverished countries for a while. We were active in socioeconomic politics. Each new crusade we partook of never really entranced us fully and would become faddish.

"It was a bit odd that an obscure endeavor was to be the catalyst that would bond us all. The younger brother of one of our members was an aspiring archaeologist. His name was Rueben. He had gone to some tiny, obscure country several times and had found the potential for some earth shaking discovery. As with everyone that had begged the society for help, he required funding. He had impressed upon us all, a rationalization for the pursuit of his endeavors, which would benefit our society. Most notably, it would ensure a huge financial gain and purloin notoriety for us through our financial support of him. Rueben, true to his word unearthed objects that *did* win notoriety and monetary success for us. There were plenty of major digs that yielded buried secrets and treasures.

"Finding the objects proved challenging. Getting them out of the country to become a national treasure, of whatever country we took up residence in, was even more challenging. It was fun and exciting. I remember well, having helped to plot the extraction of crated artifacts. The idea of personal danger never really occurred to me during that period of time. I sat comfortably in my offices and ordered people to move archaeological treasures around the world. Those contacts would have to deal with thieves, smugglers and all manner of undesirable characters to get tasks completed. We just threw money around and got what we wanted. I am grateful to have been a part of this whole experience. I can say though, had I known the costs in advance, I doubt that I would be talking to you now. There will always be consequences for any action. Ah...I have strayed too far from the point of my story," her voice trailed away again.

"Please excuse me a moment," October said as she motioned to someone in the room with her.

"Just take it off. I do not care anymore," she said against the faint pleas of the nurse who had come into view.

"I will die sooner if it stays on," her voice was commanding.

The nurse's shoulders slumped a little with disappointment; she pushed back the hood and removed the old woman's mask. The nurse produced a small moist towel and blotted away sweat from October's brow. Todd had moved to the front of his chair at some point and waited for the nurse to move, as he wondered what the woman's face would look like. Bree's hand pulsed a few times over his and he looked back at her. She gave him a very expressive 'sit back and sit up' look.

"Yes Mother," he thought.

The mental words were richly steeped in sarcasm. A smile tugged at the corner of Bree's lips in recognition. Submissively, he slid back in his chair and sat up straight. He looked over his shoulder at Shepherd who seemed to be upset by this turn of events. He shook his bowed head over his clenched hands. The nurse finally moved away and the old woman's face came into view. Todd looked at her deep-set, blue eyes and high cheek bones. He noticed the air tube below her nostrils, which flared as if she couldn't catch her breath.

"I do not care for your warnings, now be silent," she thundered to the nurse who had moved out of view.

With her head held high and a look of defiance in her eyes, she started to speak again.

"Ah, that is better. It is with some amount of pride that I now am able to show you my face. I have been hiding for so long. I am old and near my end. I will depart this world on my own terms," she said.

She looked thoughtful again and then continued.

"Now then, as I said there were many digs, but Rueben had been saving something extraordinary. We gathered to hear his pitch. He was electrified in his description of the potential for this particular dig. The cost was nearly quadruple of any previously requested amount. The bid was approved as a result of Rueben's past attainments. We felt it prudent that one of us should join him to ensure the safety of our rather substantial investment. Our most senior member Augustus Ronson joined his brother on the dig. August, as we would later refer to him, had sent a telegram and informed us that most of this extreme cost was a sort of hazard pay for the men. The amount of pay demanded, bordered on extortion, but was deemed necessary. His note expressed a sincere despair and fear that surrounded the exploration of these particular caves, among the expedition's members. The men were all locals and had some previous knowledge of the caves and claimed that they were haunted. I can tell you that I, like the others, did not read danger from these words. We felt the tantamount of excitement over the potential for greatness.

"If not for having found items deemed exceedingly rare and very ancient, the expedition would have been considered a failure. Seven men died in the pursuit of the prize, including one of Rueben's closest friends. Their lives were claimed by ancient traps set to protect the items. Relics of this magnitude usually were the hardest to get out of a country. But, when you have enough money, almost anything is possible. August had impressed upon all of us that these items were all very important to our own ends. I saw pictures of them, large necklaces with intricately cut gems faceted in them, and vases. They really did not seem that extraordinary to me. I, however, blindly followed the society's interest in them. We had to move them several times and had lost large security forces to attackers wherever we tried to store the pieces. We eventually built a storehouse for the objects. We used private contractors from around the world and bought the property through unassociated third parties. For all intents and purposes, the items disappeared for a few years. The story becomes darker now."

She inhaled the oxygen under her nose deeply and continued.

"All of the society's members began receiving social calls from less than reputable people. Offers to purchase the items were refused. We began to realize that we were in possession of items that put us in danger. Initially, most of us wanted to hand them over to the first thug that came knocking on our door. Just to be rid of them. They were kept under the rationale, that if people wanted them so badly, there must have been undiscovered value in them. We had become staunchly opposed to parting with the items by unanimous vote.

"As a safety measure, we all adopted the names of the months and moved to secure homes. We each employed large disciplined security forces which you can associate with the men that guard you now. We sent encoded messages to one another. It was very cloak and dagger, if you will. The whole affair introduced a hint of danger to our otherwise uneventful lifestyles. For the largest part, we all found it quite enjoyable," she paused and shook her head slowly as her smile faded.

"That ended when August was attacked and killed in his home. The police found evidence that he had been tortured, but were unable to find any evidence of forced entry. Shortly after August's death, there were attempts to steal the objects from the storehouse. We surmised that August had been killed to gain the whereabouts of the items.

289

We took extreme measures to protect ourselves from attackers. We created a new storehouse and ordered the objects moved.

"Before they arrived, the armored vehicles that carried them were attacked by a very organized force of mercenaries.

"The force was repelled, but the vases were destroyed in the skirmish. Rueben had taken his brother's place among us. He was dispatched to the storehouse to inspect the other pieces for damage and to see if there was anything salvageable from the collection of vases. It was then, what would later be known as the prophecy would be discovered. There were three small strips of paper riddled with writings of an ancient civilization, hidden inside the walls of the pottery. The security staff alerted us to the fact that Rueben, had attempted to steal the strips after discovering them. I remember being troubled by the fact that he had deceived us. It had taken eleven men to subdue him. Which was very odd, I thought at the time. He was a tall and very slight man. He did not seem capable of having strength of that magnitude. They locked him in an iron cage like an animal. The items were again moved to a new location to be hidden away and studied. Rueben was released, but never again trusted with the secret of the items whereabouts. For years the strips were studied by the best minds money could buy. All attempts to decipher the language failed. They could not find anything to use as a base for the language," October paused noticing Todd's look of curiosity.

"How could he fight eleven men at once?" Todd asked plainly.

"After he and August had returned from the dig, Rueben had seemed different. There was something dark and malevolent about him, but I could not discern what it was particularly. Whatever secret he brought back with him was unknown to me at that time. I will get back to that in a moment," October said politely and seemed unaffected that Todd had raised his hand like a child in class trying to get the teacher's attention.

"I didn't mean to interrupt, please go on," Todd said as his face flushed red.

"The answer was found some years later. One of the researchers noted that the cut of the gem, from one of the necklaces, would put out intricate designs when light was shone through it. The markings on the gem settings of the necklaces were realized as positional in relation to markings on the strips. The researchers began refracting light through the different gems onto the strips. It was then that they discovered and deciphered a language."

October paused and motioned for the nurse, who brought her a glass of water. October drank the water in several dainty sips, brushed at her throat absently, and waved the nurse away.

"There were three strips of paper and four necklaces. If I remember correctly, each strip said something different under the light shone through a necklace, and then more as the direction of each necklace was turned. There was a lot of information to be deciphered. Within four years, there were several books of knowledge produced. They had figured out a chronological order for the strips and then began to compile the writings. I was amazed as I read the first bits. The strips clearly outlined events that would unfold in the long years after they were buried.

"To all of our dismay, the writings told the story of Rueben and his misdeeds. They also told of him being cursed for having defiled the hiding places of the items. As penance, he had become a vile creature, cursed to prey upon people, much like the vampires of lore. It told of him killing his older brother, August, to find the whereabouts of the relics. The writings told us where to find him and how to bind and kill him."

Bree let out an involuntary gasp and covered her mouth in embarrassment.

"I am sorry if that information offends or frightens you, that we would so blindly follow these writings. We felt justified in our belief of them, as they chronicled personal events in our own lives that were known to be true by none, save ourselves. It was a horrible experience, rivaled by nothing else in its negativity, in my long life."

"What did you have to do with Rueben?" Todd asked curiously.

291

"Me? Nothing. I was simply a spectator. The writings instructed me to witness, as justice was exacted. I was accompanied by a well-paid elite security force," October paused to allow Todd to ask a question.

"What did they do to subdue and kill him?" Todd asked, thoroughly engrossed in the story.

"Bind him," she corrected.

"He had to be bound. He was discovered by us in his family's mansion. It appeared to us that he had drunk the blood of a person, and was in the process of ripping the body into pieces. Twelve strong men rushed forward, two were killed in the struggle. He allowed himself to be taken by the remaining ten. He was bound with large iron chains and drug out into the sunlight. He was greatly weakened by the sunlight, and his skin had begun to bubble and burn. The men then carried him to the family cemetery on the grounds. There was a large statue in the center of the graveyard. The men pushed it from its pedestal. Rueben was bound to the stone pedestal by the large iron chains, to burn in the sunlight until death," October paused and dabbed at the moisture that formed in the corner of her eyes.

"He admitted to killing his brother and relayed his reasons for doing so to me. I stayed close to him and spoke with him to ease his passing. I believe that he was truly remorseful for his actions. I felt sorry for him, but mercy was not mine to give. When the sun had finished ravaging him, his bones were left bound to the pedestal. We had a mausoleum erected around his corpse. A large fund was set up to protect the crypt and grounds, so that none would happen upon his remains," October finished.

Todd recoiled, covered his mouth, and contemplated what October had just relayed to them.

Bree, unintentionally, mouthed the word that had flashed across Todd's mind, in recognition, "Andre..."

"Wow, Rueben really was a vampire then?" Todd asked, intrigued.

"I am unsure as to what he was. I just simply know that he was no longer human. It was all very much a pity, prior to his trip to retrieve the relics, I found him an intelligent and interesting man. His evident infatuation with

292

me was complimentary, though unwarranted. This made it all the worse for me to endure his end. I have distracted myself from the point, back to the prophecy.

"The writings would also tell of major world events, such as war, famine, and natural disasters. Not all of them, mind you, but all of the major things. Thousands of years of events were chronicled in the writings. It even mentioned the formation of our society, its later purpose, and the deaths of its members. All except for mine," she looked into her lap for a moment with a troubled expression.

"More importantly, it detailed information and seemed to ultimately be about *you*," she smiled at Todd.

He removed his hand from Bree's, wiped their collective sweat from his palm and leaned forward with his elbows on his knees. He exhaled deeply and shifted in his chair. Todd felt his heart as it hammered in his chest. He sat there for a long moment, then straightened up and looked at October. She realized that he was answering a lot of his own questions.

Todd was doing just that.

"That's how they knew to set up all of this stuff," he thought.

A deeper question welled up in him. Todd sat up and looked into October's eyes. The room seemed to darken around his focus on her. Todd's lips poised to form the words and his voice rose from him.

"Why me?" he asked, shaken to his core.

She smiled at him sympathetically.

"You are the Peace Bringer. Your life is chronicled up to approximately the next ten minutes. Everything up till now is all here," she said and held up a leather-bound book.

"After that, it is said, in two days time, almost to the hour, you will bring peace to the world," October paused.

"How?" asked Todd, his voice cracked.

The spoken question encompassed so many meanings. Everyone else in the room felt the weight of the burden that sat squarely upon Todd's shoulders.

She leaned forward and said, "It does not say. It just says that you will. My people and I will not be able to guide you. Our purpose is to protect you until it is your time. There

293

will be an eclipse. During its cycle you will perform whatever act you are destined for."

Todd stared at October for a moment. He then looked to Bree. She smiled at him but seemed deeply in thought with her open palm placed to her stomach.

"And now," October tapped the book.

"It is time for my magic trick. Shepherd, if you would please?" October asked.

Shepherd rose slowly to his feet, walked to his desk, and reached into his pocket. He produced a key ring and had begun to pick through it. Having found the key he was looking for, he reached down and unlocked a drawer on his desk. Shepherd pulled a box from the drawer and placed it on top of his desk. He used a key to slice through the tape on the box and reached in. He rummaged through the protective packaging and produced a sealed envelope and a small cube of stainless steel. The envelope boldly said *Bree* in calligraphic lettering. Shepherd handed the letter to Bree and the cube to Todd. Shepherd then returned to his seat.

Todd and Bree looked up to October expectantly.

"So sad, this is the last answer I know for sure," October said as she looked to Todd.

"Place that cube in the center of your right palm," October explained to Todd.

Todd did as he was told.

"Now, cover it with your left hand," she instructed.

Todd followed the directions. One of his eyebrows rose above the other, giving him a look of curiosity.

"Now, I want you to think of a shape and turn that cube into it, keeping your hand closed. Please read the letter and pause before the last sentence," October said as she faced Bree.

"What's the point of this?" Todd asked.

"This will allow you to see the power of these words. They existed before you or I, were ever conceived. Hopefully, this will allow you to have the same faith in these words that I do," October explained.

Todd nodded, his hands tensed then relaxed, and he looked to Bree to do the old woman's bidding.

Bree read aloud from the page. The words were

294

verbatim as October had relayed them.

She finished with, "'What's the point of this?' the Peace Bringer asks."

Bree continued to read. The words on the page exactly matched all spoken conversation over the last few minutes.

"It matches exactly!" Todd said exasperatedly.

"Now, it is your turn, Peace Bringer," October announced as Bree read aloud the exact quote off of the paper that she was given.

Shepherd had risen to his feet and mouthed the words in disbelief as he read the page that Bree held.

Todd looked to his clenched hands and opened them. A perfectly sculpted, stainless steel ribbon sat there, twisted into the symbol for infinity.

Bree read the end:

"Behold the symbol for the measure of his love. *Infinity*," Bree said crying.

Shepherd stood above them, his hand covered his mouth. Large pools of water formed at the bottoms of his reddening eyes. He removed his glasses, wiped his eyes with a handkerchief, and walked behind his desk. Shepherd opened another drawer. He pulled out a very thick manila envelope and handed it to Todd.

"The prophecy does not say that I will, I choose to tell you this. It is mentioned several times that a dark force will try and manipulate you to its own ends. The writings are not specific, but I hope that advanced knowledge, arms you against it...in some way," October finished and smiled.

"That envelope that you hold, gives you more money than your children could spend in their lifetime. I have no idea what it is that you will do, but my hopes, dreams, and prayers go with you both," October said.

"Ms. Olivia, someone is on the grounds. Security is unable to stop him!" the nurse frantically screamed as she ran into the room.

Olivia, undaunted by the warning, turned back to the monitor and seemed about to speak again when her attention was stolen.

Todd and Bree watched as an arm protruded into

the line of vision. The arm was adorned by a long billowy sleeve of midnight purple cloth. A man's hand extended toward the old woman. She rose to her feet and drifted toward its unseen owner with her arms open in welcome. Tears framed the caring, timeworn eyes of the old woman.

"You came back for me. I hoped that you would," Olivia said adoringly as the hand wrapped around her back.

"My love for you, like my own existence, is unending. Without you, eternity would be unbearable," the Cloaked Figure stated.

"Alas, my love, a moment may be all we have. But take solace in the knowledge that a moment in your arms is the equivalent to an eternity of bliss," Olivia said breathlessly.

The old woman slumped in the embrace of the shadowy figure. Behind them, outside the door to the room, there was the sound of a heated scuffle. A moment later a single shot was fired. The Cloaked Figure turned toward the door. He took a step fully in front of the camera's view. He lifted the frail woman's body to him and turned her away from the door as if to shield her. The door of the room was pounded inward breaking in the middle but held. A second assault on the door caused it to burst into pieces showering the back of the Cloaked Figure with debris.

A tall muscular man entered the room holding a guard aloft by his neck with one arm raised high. The guard held firmly to the grip around his neck and kicked helplessly. The guard was tossed to one side like a rag doll showing the camera the face of the attacker.

"Andre," Todd whispered to himself.

Andre bent forward, his long finger nailed hands drew into claws as his eyes fell upon the Cloaked Figure. The nurse ran from the room covering her head with both arms and shrieking.

"You! What are you doing *here*?" Andre barked the question, his voice sounded unnatural and his eyes backlit bright blue.

The Cloaked Figure did not respond and only turned the woman's body away from Andre again as if to show possession. The Cloaked Figure lowered October to the floor gently, rose and turned to face Andre. Andre seemed to be trying to get a look at the face under the hood. He looked down at the woman on the floor. For a moment Andre's feral expression melted into concern as he looked at the almost lifeless form of the woman. He returned his glower to the hooded figure.

"What have you done to her? I will kill you," he declared, rolling forward into a leap with both of his hands open, reaching.

The Cloaked Figure stepped into his leap, and rammed his left thumb into Andre's mouth. The rest of the Figure's fingers curled around the back of Andre's neck. Andre was held aloft by the Figure, who displayed no strain in his stature. The Cloaked Figure's right hand went to the mouth of Andre and ripped one of his fangs from his head. The Figure's motion was almost too swift to perceive as he then threw Andre, who was roaring in anger, through a far wall. The Cloaked Figure dropped over the woman.

Todd, Bree and Shepherd gasped in unison as the Cloaked Figure stabbed Olivia in the chest, just over her heart with the fang. The Figure rose and stood over her. Olivia began to convulse, and she made gurgling noises, her face shielded from view of the camera.

The Cloaked Figure seemed to taste the blood from the fang to the horror of the onlookers. He moved aside to pick her up, and revealed Olivia's face. She had seemed to revert in age forty or fifty years and was touching her own face in amazement. Todd was on the edge of his chair and noticed his angst was shared by the others. A roar, something that could only be made by a huge angry beast, assaulted them distorting the sound from the speakers in its volume and intensity. Todd slammed himself back in his chair and watched wide eyed unable to look away from the screens. The Cloaked Figure drew her up into his arms. Inky black tendrils swirled next to them and formed a portal. The Figure stepped through dodging a second assaulting dive from Andre who slammed into the camera. The view spun into a blurred vision of the color of the walls and ceiling. Todd, Bree, and Shepherd watched the screens with their jaws hanging open in amazement. The connection broken, the screens went black.

"Well, I won't be sleeping tonight," Shepherd said.

Todd and Bree nodded their agreement.

"We can all agree that there are forces at work here that we cannot explain. This is why we have to stay on guard and be very mindful of everything going on. You know as much as I do at this point. We have to have open lines of communication. If either of you see, hear, or *feel* anything, you need to let me know ASAP...," Shepherd warned.

Todd and Bree nodded again still stunned.

Chapter 25

Under New Management

All three of them sat quietly in deep unresolvable deliberation.

"Well, I'm pretty disappointed," Todd's expression was unreadable as he broke the silence.

"What's the matter?" Bree asked.

"There wasn't any popcorn," Todd said sarcastically.

Bree popped Todd across his shoulder and dried a tear from under one of her eyes.

Shepherd made a weird wheezing noise, as he struggled to restrain a laugh. Shepherd picked up a remote and sat on the corner of his desk and pulled up a radar screen, showing the weather. Four of the storms seemed to have veered and were now heading toward their current location. Shepherd moved and sat down behind his desk.

"I got an envelope too. It details you as my current employer," Shepherd said to Todd.

Todd thought for a moment.

"Do you know anything about Andre Devrote or that thing in the purple cloak?" Todd asked.

Shepherd looked away from them for a moment. He turned back shaking his head in denial. Todd waited a moment before continuing, trying to abate his sudden feelings of distrust.

"Tell me about this building and its security," Todd said.

Without pause, and with a very confident tone, Shepherd said, "This is a ten story building. All of the windows and doors are blast reinforced. It would take a really strong bomb to blast through the walls. The building, itself, has its own radio communication, power, and drinking water supply. It has food supplies, enough to last several months. If we were left with no other choice, we could do worse in looking for a place to stay. My security force consists of thirteen men, eight of which are usually led by Blake. Four of Blake's men are on assignment at the moment," Shepherd paused to allow Todd to ask a question.

"What kind of assignment are they on?" Todd asked.

"They are separated into two teams and are securing two other facilities, like this one, that were built in other parts of the country. Just in time too. We may need to evacuate if this weather continues to press us," Shepherd finished.

Todd's fingers flicked up on one hand and he muttered to himself.

Shepherd began again, "The other five members consist of two communication officers who watch monitors all day in shifts. The other three are perimeter guards that take shifts, posing as parking garage attendants, twenty-four hours a day. We are quite secure and self-supporting. This whole setup, as you call it, has only a single flaw in my opinion," Shepherd finished.

"What flaw is that?" Bree asked.

"There is no flight-escape capability…" Shepherd paused as he noted the curious looks on Todd and Bree's faces.

"No chopper pad on the roof," Shepherd explained. "We do have a heavily armored transport truck that's made to look like a normal SUV, and it will get us to a hangar on a private airstrip, where a helicopter and a private jet are maintained for our travel needs. I'm sure you would agree that we have all taken in a lot of information this evening, and perhaps dinner and rest are in order?" Shepherd suggested.

"Would you like to join us for dinner, Shepherd?" Bree asked.

"No thank you," Shepherd paused, "Let me explain. I appreciate you both being so friendly. It is necessary for me and my security team to remain disassociated with you on a personal level. I have been doing this type of work for a very long time. Once we cross a professional line and forge any sort of relationship, it puts us both in danger. A soldier protecting a nameless person of unknown importance is able to make snap decisions that affect survival, without having to consider personal feelings," Shepherd finished.

"I can understand that," Bree said as she nodded her understanding.

Todd clapped his hands together and stood up.

"Well, I know I'm gonna sleep like a baby tonight," Todd commented to them sarcastically.

Todd and Bree left the room and proceeded down the hall to the door where they had left Blake. The wooden doors opened and Blake lead them silently back to the elevators. Bree entered the apartment first and Todd turned to face Blake. Blake looked at him, smiled, and turned his head to one side to look at Todd in curiosity.

"I just wanted to tell you, thank you," Todd said.

"You're very welcome, Mr. Todd," Blake responded as he turned and headed for the elevators.

Todd walked through the apartment on a search for Bree. He felt a need to discuss the information they had just received.

"In here," Bree called from the bedroom.

Todd followed her voice and looked at Bree. She had already changed into a t-shirt and jeans. Todd watched as she tied her tennis shoes, removed her earrings, and went to store them in the closet.

"If you can teach me how to do that, in a phone booth, I will be hooked up," Todd said to the closet door.

Bree emerged laughing and scooped his arm as she walked past him into the living room. Todd stumbled behind her and closed the bedroom door as they left.

"I felt it important to tell you that, when we actually eat in the dining room, we are served courses," Bree said to him over her shoulder as she walked into the dining room.

She paused and said, "When you asked Shepherd about the cloak. I heard him think a single word. It was *father*. I don't know if it means anything but I thought I should mention it."

Todd followed her and a familiar smell wafted to

his nose.

"Try and focus on doing everything manually. No floating food or cups. We wouldn't want to scare the staff," she said with a warning tone.

Todd smiled and held her chair as she sat down, and then seated himself next to her.

"What are we having?" Todd asked.

"A surprise," she replied.

A man walked in, from the kitchen, with two bowls and a small wire carrier filled with glass containers.

"This is Chon. He is our server," Bree said as she waved to the short Asian man, who approached the table.

Chon placed a bowl of salad in front of Bree, looked into Todd's face, and said, "Hi," and smiled.

"Hi there," Todd replied as he tried to sound as cheery as Chon had.

Chon placed the small carrier between them, bowed deeply, and disappeared back into the kitchen.

"What is..?" Todd tried to ask.

"Salad dressing and they make it from scratch," she answered.

"Oh, wow," he replied.

One of the bottles turned, the word Ranch came into view, printed on the side of the bottle. It floated slowly up from the carrier. Bree's hand closed over it and handed it to him.

"Oh, I'm sorry," Todd said absently as he took it from her.

"It's okay. It seems like; it's more natural for you to do things that way now. We're gonna have to work on you though. I can't very well take you out to a restaurant and have you doing all that...stuff. We would get smothered by cell phones again," she said.

Todd stopped chewing an overly large mouth full of lettuce and tried to smile. Chon appeared again, this time holding a large plate, covered by a reflective silver dome. Todd smiled to him approvingly as he sat the plate in the middle of the table.

"What are we having?" Todd asked Chon.

Chon's eyebrows dropped and he looked at Todd

302

fully with a confused expression.

"What are we having?" Todd asked Chon again as he pointed at the silver dome.

"Oh, oh," Chon began as he concentrated to pronounce the words.

"Woo fah boo gah," he stated proudly, his head bounced on every syllable.

"Enjoy," Chon said happily as he vanished into the kitchen again.

Todd repeated the term several times as he removed the lid to look for himself. Four hamburger patties sat on the plate surrounded by a leafy adornment of fresh lettuce. Todd noticed the slivers of onion protruding from them, still repeating the name Chon had used. A deep smile forced its way across his face.

"Ha! Welfare Burgers," he said, as a laugh erupted from him.

"You said it would be good regardless of how the ingredients went into it. I asked them to make it for you. Since we missed our chance to eat them together last time," Bree said, and seemed to recoil a little as she remembered the circumstances.

Todd's smile half faded for a second. He coated a bun with mayonnaise and lettuce, and seemed to struggle to decide on taking the largest patty. Bree prepared her own sandwich, but waited to eat. She watched Todd for a reaction as he took a huge bite and began to chew. She was already quietly cheering to herself as Todd's expression lit up.

"Wow, this is really good," he mumbled around a large second bite.

Chapter 26

The Foggy Future

Doug sat in the driver's side seat of the car slumped low. The banner that said: *Haven Hotel coming soon* swayed and grabbed his attention. Doug assumed that the banner was an attempt to camouflage the fact that the Haven Hotel would never actually open for business. He returned to watching the parking garage attendant intently. The attendant would periodically look down at a newspaper, but only for a second. He would then look up and down the street. A cab stopped in the street and a man, dressed similarly to the man in the booth, got out. The new arrival motioned to the cab driver to stay. The attendant exited his booth to greet him. The two men talked for a moment and then exchanged places. The original attendant sped away in the cab. The new attendant stood for a moment outside of the booth. He flipped through pages on the clip board as he smoked a cigarette.

Doug's eyes narrowed as he appraised the gun holster on the man's hip. He picked up a small pad of paper and looked at his watch.

"Guard change at seven P.M. Single nine millimeter sidearm," he muttered to himself.

"If that is a parking garage attendant, I'm a monkey's uncle," he said as he sat the pad down next to him.

The smooth voice penetrated his skull.

"Be ready. Forces of good are in motion to help you to achieve your goal," the voice said.

"Someone is helping me?" Doug asked.

"Of course. Another man, with all of your righteous conviction, waits to sacrifice himself. His sole purpose is to give you the opportunity to strike at the very heart of evil," the voice said reassuringly.

"How will I know when to use this?" Doug asked as he patted the cloth covered package on the seat next to him.

"I will let you know when your ally has completed his task," the disembodied voice responded.

"And this guy is gonna get killed?" Doug asked.

"Most assuredly. He will provide you with the time that you need to complete your task. His death will be slow and brutal, his agonizing torture absolute. Knowing this, he gladly answers the call to do his part. Within these walls, unspeakable acts of violence and malicious torture of the righteous occur. Your brother in light is forced to sit and watch this happen. He has had to master himself to endure this. He knows that his sacrifice will ensure the spiritual safety of the world. He places his faith in you to do your part," the voice trailed away.

"I will, I will," Doug said as large tears formed in the corners of his eyes.

"Is this going to work to kill him?" Doug asked, feeling the hilt of the large hunting knife under the cloth of his jeans.

"Yes, with his last defense removed, he will be mortal and able to perish under the stroke of your blade," the voice said.

"I will kill him," Doug repeated with angry conviction.

* * *

Kevin knocked on the door that said *security* and waited for a moment. A small camera on the wall panned to face him. Kevin made a vulgar gesture toward the monitor and heard a click. He pulled open the door and walked inside. The obese man, who sat at the desk surrounded by camera monitors, greeted him unenthusiastically. Kevin winced as the deep musky smell of methane attacked his nostrils. Kevin raised the sleeve of his jacket to his nose.

"Terry...you *stink*," Kevin said.

"Hey, it's not my fault. I have been crop dusting for fifteen minutes waiting for you to come. Good thing you're here. One of these air biscuits is gonna have a bone in it if I

305

don't get to the can," Terry said as he struggled to free his weight from the chair.

A flurry of crumbs and candy paper drifted down to the floor as he stood up and brushed at his chest. Kevin struggled to avoid gagging as the man stood up and seemed to renew the thick heavy stench in the room.

"Gonna need this," Terry said as he picked up a magazine and headed for the door.

"Same deal as usual. Monitors fourteen through twenty are off limits," Terry warned as he exited the room.

The door had barely closed. Kevin typed at the keyboard and looked expectantly at monitor fourteen.

The screen came on and Kevin grimaced as the cheesy bass line blasted in time with the naked bodies that slammed together.

"Always watching porn," Kevin muttered and turned off number fourteen.

He typed again and looked up as the forbidden five monitors came on. Kevin looked carefully through each one. Kevin spied what he was looking for and typed in a command to turn off the rest of the monitors. He then typed in the monitor-close command, and placed his finger on the enter key. He leaned forward and studied the image. The Todd-guy sat in a chair and watched television with his woman stretched sideways across his lap, asleep.

"Record numbers of simultaneous weather related disasters are occurring all over the world," belted the unseen news anchor.

Kevin reached forward to mute the sound. The Todd-guy who sat motionless, continued to stare at the screen, and was seemingly lost in thought. Kevin reached for the enter key to turn off the monitor, but sudden motion caught his attention. The Todd-guy placed his open palm over the woman. Her entire body lifted off of him, and floated neatly over to the couch. She drifted down and landed softly onto the couch, never waking. The Todd-guy never looked away from the television, and held his hand out expectantly. Kevin watched as a cup of coffee floated into that hand. The colors from the television started to flash in different hues across the Todd-guy's face.

"He is changing the channel," Kevin thought to himself and covered his mouth with his hand in disbelief.

"How am I supposed to stop that," he asked as he stared at the monitor.

A click erupted from the door, his finger dropped onto the enter key, and the monitor went black.

"Don't go near that bathroom till the haz-mat teams are finished," Terry warned.

Kevin stood up and moved away from the desk. Terry brushed past him uncomfortably, plopped into the chair, and breathed heavily. Terry opened a can of soda and ripped open a bag of chips. He rammed his hands into the chips and licked at the powdery flavoring on his fingers.

"Man, my schedule is total crap," Terry complained to Kevin as crumbs shot from his mouth.

"It's gonna be rough for all of us for the next few days, big man," Kevin agreed.

Terry was now furiously licking flavored powder from his fingers again. He rammed his hand back into the bag and paused before cramming an oversized clump of chips into his mouth.

"So why are we gonna wait till those hurricanes are right on us before we evacuate?" Terry asked and rammed the chips into his mouth.

"I follow orders like everybody else. It doesn't make an ounce of sense to me either. I have no clue," Kevin replied.

Several hours earlier, Kevin had posed the same question to Blake who simply responded, "For cover, Kev. There shouldn't be too many spying eyes out and about, in the wake of hurricanes. We're hoping to just drive to the airport, and fly out. Keep that to yourself."

"Well, one thing's for sure. No matter how bad things are, somebody always has it worse," Terry said and tapped at the screen of a monitor.

Kevin looked at the parking garage guard in the screen, who was desperately trying to stay dry as sideways rain pelted his tiny shack.

"True, and others have it way better than most," Kevin motioned to another monitor.

307

Terry looked up and watched Vincent and Charles as they sat behind a large wooden crate and played cards.

"Yeah, they look like they're having a rough time packing supplies for an evac," Kevin scoffed.

"Well, I for one wouldn't want to be down there. I know for sure, floor one has no central air," Terry said.

"Well they're used to outdoor conditions and they are just one tiny rung up on the evolutionary scale from a guard dog. That's not really fair to dogs for me to say that," Kevin said.

Terry laughed.

"Seriously though, all of the cameras down there stay fogged from mid-day till about five from the humidity. The goof brothers there were supposed to have put an anti-fogging agent on the lenses. But as you can see, they are *way* too busy," Terry finished and drank from his soda can.

Kevin looked away for a moment seemingly distracted in thought.

"I'm sure they will get to it," Kevin replied.

"Oh dude, what happened to your hand?" Terry asked and pointed at the star shaped burn on Kevin's hand.

Kevin looked at the infected burn for a moment.

"Somebody did that to wake me up," Kevin said absently.

"You guys go too far with all that kidding around," Terry said and shook his head.

"Yeah, I guess we do. Somebody *is* gonna get hurt," Kevin said and smiled.

Terry turned and used an alcohol wipe to clean monitor fourteen.

"Well, I gotta get back to work," Terry said as he buffed the monitor.

Kevin looked at the monitor and then to Terry as he labored to keep the revulsion from showing on his expression.

"Don't work *too* hard," Kevin said over his shoulder as he left the room.

Chapter 27

Tortured Dreams

Todd sat in the chair and watched the news in horror, as he flipped through the channels. Every station was littered with news of world disasters. He contemplated the information as he flipped channels and watched new footage.

"People were panicked and rushed to safety in the wake of hurricanes that were already destroying the southern tip of the Florida Territories," blurted the man holding the microphone as his electric blue parka flapped in the wind.

He looked into the camera intensely, as he belted out facts that had lead up to the current conditions. Todd watched as the newscaster guarded his face from the small pieces of debris and rain that pelted his face.

"Normally, when I cover these types of events, it's heartwarming to see people coming together to overcome adversity. It seems to me, that the worst brings out the best in humanity, usually. I watched a group of people trample an elderly woman as they clambered into the wrecked remains of a grocery store to procure food. There were pleas from local authorities, for motorists fleeing the low lying areas around the coast, to please try and offer as many people rides to safety as possible. However, as you can see from this footage earlier, that most of the motorists waiting to get onto the Inter-territorial highways are alone in their vehicles. This makes very little sense, as you can see people are still trapped here and are hiding under make shift shelters. The roughest conditions are yet to come. The two hurricanes that veered this way have effectively panicked evacuees. There was a total breakdown in social services and local authorities took flight shortly after they warned homeowners to leave the area. I'm sure there will be serious repercussions for that in the wake of these storms," said the reporter.

He opened his mouth to speak again but was silenced as a branch struck him in the back of the head. Todd watched as the reporter buckled and the screen went blue for a moment. The scene swapped back to the news room. The female reporter stared into the screen for a moment with a look of shock on her face. She cleared her throat and took a second to compose herself.

"We will be back in a few moments with storm coverage after these announcements from our sponsors," she croaked.

Cheery music erupted from the television and an image of an old man, who held a large glass of lemonade, walked toward the screen and began to speak. Todd winced and grabbed his temples as he heard the unknown voices again, with their pleas for help inside his mind. He turned off the television, closed his eyes, and regulated his breathing.

He sat in a white chair inside his mind. His eyes opened as the light began to shine down on him from above. Todd rose to his feet.

"Bryce, are you here?" Todd asked the darkness.

Todd paused as he strained to hear anything other than the faint constant pleas from the unknown voices.

"Bryce. Where are you?" Todd screamed again.

He received no answer. The scene around him began to change and he turned on the spot and marveled at it. Todd stood alone in the night on a country road. Fierce lightning struck repeatedly overhead and rain pelted the ground in large blobs which created an even plopping noise on the asphalt. Todd turned a few times and spotted a classic police patrol car. He ignored his mind's persistent questions of why this thirty year old cop car would be in use. He approached it slowly, guarding his eyes from the rain, and tried to see inside as he approached it. Todd realized that the rain was falling through his hand and, upon closer inspection, realized that he was completely dry.

He lowered his hand and walked up to the driver's side window. A young officer sat there sleeping against the window of the car.

His dreaming face, illuminated by the light of an old

310

CB radio, looked peaceful to Todd as he stared down into it. Todd leaned in closer. This man looked familiar to him.

"Could this be old Roger, the Sheriff?" he thought.

Lightning flashed overhead and brightened the man's face more fully for a moment. Todd stood upright and considered him.

"It looks like him. Maybe this is his son or a close relative. That guy couldn't be any older than me," Todd thought to himself.

The man seemed to stir for a moment and settled back into sleep. The CB radio on the dash lit up. The light from the radio was now on fully, and he watched as the man's head rolled across the seat for a moment. The man picked up the microphone and complained into it. Todd reached forward toward the glass. His hand slid through the glass smoothly and touched nothing. Todd leaned forward and put his head near the glass. He grimaced, narrowed his eyes defensively, and leaned forward even more, as he prepared for the potential impact. His head and neck slid evenly through the glass, as though either his body, or the window, were intangible.

Once his head was inside the car, he could hear the man angrily telling someone that he was not asleep and that the CB must be reacting to interference from the lightning. The man slammed the microphone back onto the small metal knob, which was its cradle, and looked around sleepily. He looked right through Todd and continued the path with his eyes.

A large, blinding streak of lightning erupted, but there was no sound. Todd reeled back from the car a few steps, rubbed at his eyes, and waited for his vision to return to normal. The rain seemed to slow considerably; he heard the door of the patrol car release, and squeak its way open. The patrolman stood up and shined a flashlight onto the road.

Todd looked over his shoulder, traced the beam of light, and was astounded to see a baby where it lay, naked on the asphalt. Its angry cries came to his ears at the same time he saw it. The patrolman shot past Todd and stood over the baby for a second. Todd knelt next to the patrolman and stared into the baby's face, illuminated by the flashlight. The

311

baby had stopped crying and looked with wonder into the brilliance of the light. Todd was in the process of pointlessly telling the patrolman, who seemed unable to hear or see him, to pick up the baby. The patrolman scooped the baby up and headed toward the car. Todd watched him in wonder. With a sudden rush of wind and an assault of noise, an eighteen wheeler passed inches behind Todd.

"Another moment and that baby would have been crushed," Todd thought to himself.

Todd watched the taillights of the rig as it passed into obscurity, disappearing into swirling mists of water vapors in the distance. He turned in time to see the patrolman as he drove away hurriedly. Todd made a few pointless steps of chase and then concentrated on the rear of the vehicle. The peripheral lights did not appear. He tried again to no effect. A dimly lit sign came into view. Todd's eyes strained to read it in the darkness. The sky seemed to answer his need for light, erupting in a flash of lightning. The sign read: *Welcome to Abita Springs Population: six hundred and two.*

Todd remembered the sign well, and turned on the spot now, as he recognized his location.

"That population number was always in quadruple digits," he thought to himself.

"Am I in the past somehow?" he asked himself.

The lightning flashed again, this time more brilliant than ever before. Todd gasped as he covered his eyes and rubbed at them. He lowered his hands and waited for the flash blindness to subside. Todd now turned around several times in awe, looking at his environment.

* * *

A brilliant newly risen sun hung low in the sky. He realized himself to be standing in the parking lot of a business. He walked toward the brick building and felt disoriented. He made to place his hand against the brick of the building to keep him steady. His hand pushed through the brick intangibly. He drew his hand back and looked at the brick curiously. He turned and looked at a sign that stood in the nearby landscaping. It read: *Saint Nicolas' Orphanage.*

Todd walked slowly toward the front door of the building, unable to feel the small gusts of wind that were obviously passing by. Small pieces of brightly colored paper, carried on the wind, passed directly through his hand. Todd watched in amazement as the wind carried the paper away down the side walk.

"This is so vivid...is it a dream? Is this going on in my head? Am I making all of this happen?" he asked himself.

The door near him opened slowly and Todd's foster parents emerged together. They passed directly through him. They looked younger than he had ever seen them. His mother carried a baby in her arms. They played with the baby that his mother carried, as they walked toward a car.

Todd followed and stood next to them as his father opened the door for his mother. He looked over his fathers shoulder into the baby's face. He had just seen this baby being carried away by the patrolman in the dark. Todd was looking into his own eyes, as he stared at the baby. His father closed the door of the car, the sun's reflection in the passenger side mirror hit him full in the eyes, and he instinctively closed them, and recoiled. Todd opened his eyes again.

* * *

Todd was disoriented as he looked around in wonder. He now stood on the second floor of the home of his foster parents, Rob and Tabitha Jennings.

"How did I get here?" Todd asked himself.

Todd could hear heavy metal music quietly playing from behind a nearby door. Todd smiled and walked up to the door and made a gesture as if he were about to knock. Todd stuck his fingers through the door and a smile brushed his lips, as he pressed himself through the wooden door into the room. His smile faded quickly as he took in the visage of his sixteen year old self. The younger version of him was lying on his bed with his eyes pressed shut crying. He seemed very small in contrast to the black suit he was wearing. Todd looked at himself sympathetically for a

313

moment, wiped at a tear in the corner of his eye, and proceeded back through the door. He looked fondly for a moment at a picture of himself and Robert Jennings, which hung on the wall, at the top of the stairs. They both looked into the camera with prideful expressions, holding up fish they had caught. Todd tried to brush the glass of the picture with the tips of his fingers, but his fingers only sank through the face of Robert. He turned and proceeded down the stairs inhaling deeply. As Todd reached the bottom of the stairs, he looked around at all the people that milled here and there in black dress clothes. Todd looked into the sad faces of aunts, uncles, cousins, and his father's coworkers, as they stood in separate groups, drinking coffee and having conversation. This was the day of his father's funeral. Following the service, everyone had come and spent the evening with his mother. He had tried to be strong for his mom, but overwhelmed; he had run to his room to cry.

He looked over to his mother. She sat comfortably on the sofa, speaking to a woman in a chair whose back was turned to him. Todd walked slowly through the groups of people toward his mother. Her face concentrated sharply on the woman she spoke to. Her warm and friendly smile stood against the sadness of the scene, in sharp contrast. Todd could see her pain through the mask, and his heart hurt, as he felt her deepening loneliness, even in this room full of familiar people.

He stood over her and looked into her eyes, taking her in. It seemed to have been so long since he had seen her. He remembered praying for the chance to talk with her for even a moment in the long years since her death. His thoughts were broken by the woman his mother was talking to, as a single word removed him from his trance. The woman's voice picked up at this point in his awareness.

"Prophecy is not set in stone and because of its ancient nature, there is no real way to tell if it's a factual thing at all. The police report of how your son was found, only recently came to my attention. With everything being computerized, the world suddenly becomes a smaller place. I will let you get back to your company. I am sorry that we arrived today, and I am sorry for your loss. My heart is

314

yours, my hopes and prayers are with you and your son. I will contact you at some later date and we can talk then," the lady said, dismissing herself as she stood up and walked toward Todd who stared into her pained face with sheer amazement.

A younger version of October paused momentarily. She pulled a handkerchief from her small purse and dabbed her eyes before heading out the open front door of the home. Todd turned to look at his mother. The room seemed to dull in his vision and he stepped toward his mother, but the scene was changing.

*   *   *

Todd stood next to a large fiberglass fishing boat. He stared wide eyed at it, as he stood next to his sixteen year old self, who furiously scrubbed at the hull of the boat with a soapy towel. He marveled at the younger version of himself who was unaware of Todd's presence. He tried to touch the younger version on the shoulder. His hand seemed to be intangible and passed through the boy who continued to labor away at his task.

Todd concentrated in an effort to change the scene. Nothing happened.

His eyes roved over the boat. He paused, looking at the name on the craft.

"Invictus," he mouthed the word silently, trying for a moment to reclaim the words to the poem that was a favorite of his father's.

He remembered his dad had struggled to come up with a name for his boat. He had hollered across the whole house when the epiphany had struck him.

He sat bolt upright and said the word, "Invictus," repeatedly to anyone who would pay him attention.

Tabitha, his mother, had wrinkled her nose, and said, "Boats are supposed to be named after women."

Robert ignored her. Todd remembered that he had thought that if his dad's skull were transparent, that he could have seen a picture of the hull of the boat with the word written on it.

315

Todd remembered having had so much fun with his father on this thing. Todd smiled and let his hand glide near the boat. The magic of the moment passed, as he was interrupted by his father's angry tone.

"And if you would have gotten your ass out here, we wouldn't be doing this now. Damn it son! I have to work like a dog all week and the little bit of time I get off, is precious. You have no responsibilities except for taking the trash out, bathing the dogs, and washing the boat. I have to beg you to do that. You have had all week to get this done, yet here we are, trying to get it done in the last few minutes before dark. I have half a mind to leave you home this weekend," Robert said as he approached the left side of the young version of Todd with his hands on his hips.

"What do you have to say for yourself?" he asked young Todd.

Todd covered his mouth now, with his hand. The color was washing from his face as he realized this moment for what it was. He noted the angry red color of his father's face. The arteries in his forehead stood out and pulsed exaggeratedly.

"No. Oh no," Todd said, dropped to his knees, and began to shake his head back and forth in denial.

"I don't even care about this stupid boat or you, and you can go without me for all I care. I had stuff to do. I would've gotten to this later," the younger version of Todd said loudly, and turned away from his father and folded his arms.

Robert made to turn young Todd's attention to him. His left hand reached for his son's shoulder. Suddenly his face twisted into an agonized expression as his right hand gripped weakly at the elbow of his left arm. Todd watched the blood vessels in Robert's widening eyes, bulge with pressurized redness.

"No," Todd whispered to himself, now unable to speak as the large tears rolled their way down his cheeks.

Robert dropped to his knees and fell forward into a pile on the grass.

Young Todd turned around and fell to the ground patting Robert's shoulder as he said, "Dad! Dad, are you

316

okay?"

Todd knelt in the grass sobbing uncontrollably for a long moment. He began to choke back the violent sobs. He squeezed his eyes together as he wished away the horrible things he was being forced to see.

* * *

Todd felt weightless in the darkness. His feet finally settled on something firm. He struggled to remain standing. From the darkness, a small country home appeared. Its green grass and white picket fence were surreal, as they emerged to take shape from the darkness. The light from the morning sun bathed the scene in its rich golden glow. Todd now realized himself to be standing in the front yard of the Goldman home. The front door was slightly ajar and Todd winced as he thought about what might wait for him on the other side. The house seemed to drift toward him where he stood unmoving. He was disoriented as the home positioned itself directly in front of him. Todd stood there and looked at the door helplessly.

He could hear a faint baby's laugh inside the door. He pushed away his fear and suddenly filled with hope, and pushed the door open. Todd hoped to see Sebastian's smiling face. But instead, he walked into the familiar scene of the family's slaughter. Todd knelt down in front of Will and stared into his lifeless eyes. Will's head bolted up and his angry stare fixated upon Todd.

"How could you let my family be slaughtered like pigs? I loved you like a brother!" Will asked him angrily.

Will's expression went slack and his head flopped back down. His eyes however remained fixated upon Todd and continued stare at him with an accusatory glare.

Todd turned away from him, only to see Lucy's body flopping uncontrollably, as she made wet gurgling sounds from the gaping hole in her neck. Todd looked at her with a mix of revulsion and sadness. The silver of the duct tape, covering her mouth, stood out against her pale white skin. Her body became still. Her head shot up from her bloody chest and her hand reached for Todd as he saw the

317

murderous anger in her eyes. Todd turned to run and now saw Doug standing over the baby's crib. Todd dove to tackle Doug but instead passed through him and came to rest on the edge of the baby's crib. He stared into Sebastian's eyes as the baby took the impact from Doug's blade. Todd gasped and threw himself backwards hard against the floor.

"NO MORE!" he screamed as he drew himself up onto his knees and closed his eyes.

* * *

He opened his eyes and raised his red, tear-stained face. He was kneeling on the floor of the apartment that he currently shared with Bree.

"Oh man," he said as he placed his hand behind his head and exhaled deeply.

A small piece of wood slammed into the window nearby. Todd stood up, walked to the window, and looked down to the street below. Rain, driven by harsh wind, buffeted the window. He could see debris flying around bouncing off the side of buildings. Bree entered the room carrying a small tan bag and a black backpack. The elation of seeing her healthy and unharmed pushed the illusory effects of his hallucinations further from his mind.

"Hey, have you noticed this weather?" he asked her as he felt a sense of safety and reality return to him.

Bree seemed to ignore him and walked over to the chair. Todd saw a copy of himself stand up and take the back pack and tan bag from her. He felt panic again. Todd reached out to the closest object. His hand passed through a table as he tried to steady himself. Shepherd burst in through the front door.

"It's horrible out there. I can't believe I'm asking, but can you...," Shepherd paused as he grasped for the proper term.

He looked up and continued, "*Poof* us away from here?" Shepherd asked.

"Of course," the copy of Todd said confidently.

"Hello?" Todd screamed and was dismayed as Bree, Shepherd, and his doppelganger ignored him.

Todd stood there and looked horrified, as he watched the copy of himself extend his hands to Shepherd and Bree.

"I have to rejoin myself," he thought to himself as he ran across the room.

He placed his hand inside the chest of the double of himself. He looked on as Shepherd and Bree each took one of his double's hands.

Todd's stare was fixed on his double, as the lights began in his peripheral vision.

There was a blinding flash of white light. Todd staggered as his searching feet found the soft grass beneath his shoes. Todd backed away and looked at his double, Shepherd, and Bree. Something was very, very wrong with Shepherd. Todd watched in horror as Shepherd began to convulse where he stood. He seemed to fight the overwhelming affliction and tried to speak, but thick globs of blood were all that passed from his lips. Bree covered her eyes with her hands and shrieked, as blood poured out of Shepherd's ears and nose. Shepherd toppled over backward and became still, his lifeless eyes stared up into the fading light of the day. His feet seemed to shudder a little and then he was motionless. Todd's double stared at his own hands for a moment in disbelief.

"Something must have gone wrong," Todd's double stammered.

Bree stared at him terrified and clutched her stomach. Both versions of Todd, rushed to steady her. Todd's double held her upright while Todd, himself, labored to become tangible. His hands passed through her arms. Bree was gasping in pain and held her stomach. Todd could see the wet shadow of blood forming in the crotch of her jeans. He stared in incredulity at it as he started to cry in desperation. Bree crumpled and Todd's double eased her to the ground as blood poured out of her mouth, down over her chin, and she began to convulse.

"What did you do to them?" he asked the top of his double's head, as he stared down.

"I didn't do this. It was all you, *waiter*," the double holding Bree said and looked up at him.

Todd felt faint as he stared into the face. Doug who had replaced his double now held Bree's dying body. Todd let forth a feral growl and dove headlong at Doug.

* * *

The world seemed to explode into tendrils of darkness and Todd felt weightless. Todd began to feel pressure against his stomach and ribs, as though he were being poked by something.

"I'm sorry Todd, but you have to wake up. Shepherd called and said we need to get ready to leave in a few hours," Bree said as she looked up at him with an expression of pleading.

Todd's eyes were still full of tears and he tried to figure out what was happening.

"Can you come down please? I need to talk to you?" Bree asked impatiently.

"Come down?" he asked as his vision cleared.

Todd now realized he was floating with his back against the ceiling. Todd lowered himself down onto the floor.

"I didn't want to bother you. I figured this had something to do with your prophecy thing tonight. But, the weather will be getting bad shortly and we have to be ready to go, when Shepherd calls for us," Bree said sympathetically.

"Wait, tonight? Not until tomorrow night, right?" Todd said as he rubbed at his eyes and clutched her to make sure she was there.

"You were up there for a day and a half," she said sadly.

"I missed you," she added.

Todd drew her into an embrace and looked into her eyes.

"I'm sorry, I had no idea. I think I was just asleep. I was having terrible nightmares about Doug," Todd explained.

"Well, he can't hurt anyone anymore," she said reassuringly.

"I packed us some stuff in bags and had them taken to the elevators. We just have to carry these two bags," she said motioning to a tan travel bag and a black back pack.

She felt Todd's body shudder as he looked at them.

"What's the matter?" she asked.

"I'm okay, just really bad dreams," Todd said.

Todd kissed her passionately.

"I'm gonna grab a shower. What time is it?" Todd asked her.

"Around one P.M.," she replied.

"Wow, I almost slept through the big game," Todd said.

"Would you mind if I joined you? I am starting to feel a little dirty myself," Bree asked with a mischievous glance.

"Mind, ha! I need you to scrub my back, *and* my front," Todd said and looked just as mischievous.

Bree walked away toward the bathroom and Todd looked back over his shoulder. He stared at the tan travel bag and the black back pack, and his brow furrowed in remembrance. Almost comically, his expressions portrayed an internal struggle, in which, some sort of optimism had won. Todd turned and went to join Bree in the shower.

Chapter 28

A Brother's Betrayal

Kevin sat on the toilet in his bathroom, with his knees drawn up to his chest, and rocked with a pained expression.

"I will do it, I will do it, please just leave me alone. I swear I will do it," Kevin muttered.

His head jerked around as he looked for something or someone, nervously. He opened his hand and stared at the pills for a moment. His hand jerked up, popped against his mouth, and catapulted the pills into the back of his throat. He swallowed dryly.

"Just stay away from me. I swear I will do it. I just need a few minutes," he said with a pleading tone.

He was sweating profusely and he bit the back of his clenched fist and cried.

* * *

Terry stared at monitor fourteen. Sweat was dripping down his brow as he groaned and gasped for a moment. He labored to zip up his pants with one hand while wiping his other hand under his seat. He produced an alcohol wipe and cleaned his hands. He opened a soda and tapped on monitor eleven.

"Man, those lazy bastards," he said as he watched the blurry outlines of Vincent and Charles load crates into an older blue SUV.

They were barely visible as the screen had begun to grow blurry with moisture forming from the humidity. He snorted in disgust. Terry opened a box of individually wrapped chocolate cakes and began working to open all six

322

of them. He placed the opened packages of cakes neatly in a row. He picked up the packages, one by one, removed the cakes, and crammed them into his mouth. Discarding the paper, he drew up his soda, took a swig, swished his mouth clean, and swallowed.

Terry clutched at his belly for a moment and mouthed the word, "oh."

He grimaced and tilted up on one side. The fart ripped to life, lasting for three full seconds. He plopped down flatly in the chair and inhaled deeply.

"Mm mm good," he said as he sniffed deeply, exhaled, and picked up the phone.

Terry held the phone to his head and watched as the occupant of monitor sixteen got naked to bathe with her boyfriend.

"That's some nice ta-ta's paw paw, I could sure..," Terry was cut short.

"What do you want?" Kevin asked angrily from the phone receiver.

"Hey, Kev, can you come relieve me for a few?" Terry asked.

"Yeah sure, give me a little while. I need to go get a status on Vincent and Charles for Blake," Kevin said as he breathed heavily into his phone.

"That's cool. This bun can bake a while. I just wanted to get myself onto your itinerary before it was too late," Terry replied.

"Oh, don't worry. You have a spot for sure," Kevin said and closed his phone.

Terry opened a can of pork sausages and drank the jelly from the top. He licked the grease from his lips, greedily. His large fingers zoomed in on the showering couple. Terry smiled approvingly, as he saw Kevin moving though the monitors toward the elevators.

* * *

Kevin stood outside the elevator for a moment. Large beads of sweat formed on his forehead and upper lip. He pulled a napkin from his pocket and wiped himself down.

He patted the pistol under his left arm, where it hung in its holster. He, in turn, then patted the other pockets of his coat and felt the preloaded clips.

"Locked, cocked, and ready to rock," he mumbled and patted around for the card for the elevator.

"Now, what the hell did I do with that damn card," he muttered to himself, as he suddenly felt panic.

His hand closed on the card, as he discovered it, in the left pocket of his slacks. A heavy hand fell upon Kevin's right shoulder. Kevin spun in place wielding the plastic card pointed like a gun at Blake, who held his own card pointed at Kevin in a similar fashion.

"Oh, *too* slow Kev-O," Blake said playfully.

Kevin slowly lowered the card and bowed his head in defeat.

"It's okay. Just remember that you're faster than Vincent and Charles," Blake said mockingly.

"Speaking of which, I'm on my way to go check on them right now. I was gonna give you a status after I checked up on them. Thought I would see how they were doing, under the guise that I needed a smoke. Would you like to come with me?" Kevin asked.

"As much as I would *love* to screw with them, I have to call and check to make sure we have a new home to fly to. I will meet you on three in about thirty minutes, if you want. We can compare notes and I can get a report into Shepherd before he calls for it," Blake said optimistically.

"That's cool with me," Kevin replied as he swiped his card and boarded the elevator.

"Good job, Kev. I appreciate you taking the initiative," Blake said genuinely.

Kevin nodded thoughtfully. He pressed the floor one button and moved over into a camera blind spot in the elevator. He undid the Velcro strap that held his gun in its holster. He placed the gun in his right pocket and slid his finger over the trigger. He paced slowly, watching the elevator doors until they opened. The expanse of the warehouse came into view and Kevin grimaced, as the moist warm air penetrated the elevator. He stepped out and looked around noting that this floors security cam was thickly

324

covered with condensation. Kevin lit a cigarette and walked past the walls of boxed wooden crates.

"Finally decided to do something, for a change?" Vincent grunted the question as he shoved a plastic case into the back of the older blue SUV.

"Nah, just came down to have a smoke and get some fresh air," Kevin replied as he puffed on his cigarette and inhaled deeply.

"That's like saying you're going underground to get some sun," Vincent replied mirthlessly.

Kevin walked close to Vincent, who stopped what he was doing and looked at Kevin. Kevin turned away from him for a moment. Kevin removed his right hand from his jacket pocket. Kevin pointed his right fist up at an angle toward the lip of the crates, piled overhead.

"How tall would you say Charles is approximately?" Kevin asked.

"About six even, I guess. Why do you ask?" Vincent asked, bewildered.

"Just wondering," Kevin replied as he shrugged, raised his fist a few inches, and closed one eye as he made a mental note of the angle and height of his hand's position for later use.

"What's your girlfriend up to, anyway?" Kevin asked as he turned back to face Vincent.

"He's in the bathroom with...your Mom," Vincent replied sharply as he motioned to the bathroom across the warehouse.

"Nice one. Want a smoke?" Kevin held the pack out to him.

"Don't mind if I do," Vincent said as he took the pack, pulled a cigarette out, and placed it to his lips.

Kevin now held a lighter in his open left palm.

"Thanks," Vincent said, took the lighter, and put the pack in Kevin's hand.

Vincent struck the lighter and seemed to go cross-eyed as he stared at the flame. He had barely pulled on the cigarette when he heard two metallic whispers. As the flame died, he could feel the burning in his heart. He could now see Kevin standing there, where he held his gun with his right hand at his hip. A small wisp of smoke lingered near the end of the silencer, attached to Kevin's pistol. The cigarette hung loosely in Vincent's mouth, as his right hand rose slowly to his chest. Vincent toppled face forward onto the concrete, dead. Kevin used the toe of his shoe to put out the cigarette laying a few inches from Vincent's dead face.

"Those things will kill ya," Kevin was saying as he heard the sound of grit between a shoe and a crate over his right shoulder.

Kevin threw himself to his right, crouching as he spun to take the impact of the floor, to his back. A single gunshot erupted. Kevin felt the searing pain of a bullet slicing through the outside of his right shoulder. Kevin fired two shots before hitting the floor. The first hit Charles in his heart.

Charles recoiled as the chest of his jacket exploded in a crimson spray. The second bullet struck him in the center of his neck, just below the chin. Charles flailed for a moment, and then fell forward, as though his last act would be that, of crushing Kevin with his dead weight. Kevin rolled to his left to avoid being hit by the top of the dead man's head. It made a dull cracking noise as it collided with the unforgiving concrete. Kevin stood up and brushed off his pants and holstered his pistol. As Kevin made to remove his jacket to dust it, his cell phone rang from the inner pocket. He pulled the cell phone from his jacket, as the small slice on his shoulder sang painfully. He looked at his cell phone, and then flipped it open.

"Kevin," he said into the phone as he gingerly kicked the corpse of Charles.

"Just calling to check. Something tripped the noise alarms down there, and of course, I'm still blind up here," Terry said with an aggravated tone.

"That noise was Charles dropping an aluminum ladder onto the concrete. They are actually working on getting those monitors cleaned up for you now. You will have to give them a little while. You know how slow witted they are. I'm on my way up to take care of *you* now," Kevin said as he stared into the dead eyes of Vincent.

"Roger that, Kev. See you in a few," Terry said

through a mouth full of chips.

Kevin closed his phone, returned to the elevator, put on his jacket, and then swiped his card. The doors of the elevator opened, and he entered, never looking over his shoulder as the doors closed behind him.

*   *   *

Terry was furiously trying to open a bag of chips with his greasy fingers, when he heard a knock on the door. He rose up on one side and a long staccato farting noise broke sharply from his bottom. Terry looked into the monitor to see Kevin making a rude hand gesture, from the hallway. He pushed the buzzer to allow Kevin entry, as he sniffed lightly at the air. He was pleased to see Kevin grimace as he entered the room.

"I gotta tell you, I hate walking into the scent of your ass every time," Kevin said as he closed the door and covered his nose with the left sleeve of his jacket.

Terry smiled and began to labor to push his chair away from the desk.

"Whoa there big man, you knocked over your soda," Kevin said as he motioned behind Terry.

Terry's chair gave a squeal as the man turned sharply, full bodied, to face his soda. The soda stood in its usual spot, upright. He stared at it for a second, wondering if he had opened two. Kevin fired two bullets into the back of his head. Terry flailed uncontrollably as he rolled forward off of the chair, into a pile. Kevin stepped over his fluttering corpse and turned off all of the cameras. He looked down into the bloated dead man's face.

"The perfect end to a shitty life," Kevin said as he shook his head and holstered his pistol.

*   *   *

Doug sat slumped very low in the driver's seat of the car and stared at the guard. The guard yawned lazily up from his newspaper and looked around the booth sharply for a moment, before looking down again to read.

327

"It is your time," said the disembodied female voice.

He shot up in the seat, pulled a long hunting knife from his boot, and laid it on the seat next to him. He then started the engine and checked his mirror for oncoming traffic. He placed a pair of large sunglasses on his face and pushed them high onto the bridge of his nose. He pulled out into the road and drove slowly passed the guard, holding a street map over the wheel. The guard looked up at him, smiled as he passed, and returned his attention to his paper. He rounded the block and picked up the hunting knife. He turned the knife up behind his arm to conceal the blade. The guard station was close now and Doug felt the adrenaline begin to course through him. He pulled into the driveway of the parking garage, then opened the door of the car while fighting with his map.

"How can I help ya?" the guard asked with a smile.

Doug's fist tightened on the handle of the knife beneath the map. The guard approached him reaching for the map. Doug had spent hours looking at the map. He thought of an obscure street on the other side of town.

"Trying to find Bullhide Avenue, but I will be darned if I can make sense out of this map. There is supposed to be a hurricane shelter set up over there," Doug said with an appreciative glance.

The guard was now fighting the map himself, and stepped around the car door walking over to the hood of Doug's car. Doug followed him, shielding the guard's view of his knife. He looked up and down the street for prying eyes. The guard's finger traced to the lower right hand corner and he tapped the map.

"The first thing you do is find the street name in the key," the guard said as he fought with the map, while aggressive gusts of wind buffeted the hood of the car.

"At least that nasty rain let up," Doug said as he sidled up to the guard.

Doug put his left arm behind him, to enable himself to get closer to the guard. The guard noticed that he had moved in, as if to see more clearly and returned his attention to the map. The guard began to speak again. His left hand

328

came around, clutched the guard's neck, and forced him down toward the car's hood. His right hand brought the knife up to meet the guard's chest. He stabbed the flailing guard several times.

The keenly sharpened knife continued to slide into the man, effortlessly. The dying guard vomited bile and blood as Doug quickly threw his convulsing body into the back seat of the car. He looked inside the guard's shack for a moment and saw a huge red button that was marked: *Gate Release*. He depressed the button and dove into the running car. He drove under the yellow arm into the parking garage.

Doug was sharper now, his attention, focused by adrenaline. He drove cautiously up the ramp, noting the signs *level one of six* and *elevators level six*. He drove up and up the ramp until he reached level five. He parked his car and placed the knife back in his boot, then reached over and picked up the bulky item next to him. The item was wrapped in a yellow cloth which completely hid it from view. He held it close to him as he walked up the ramp to level six.

As he cleared the top of the ramp he saw several SUV trucks parked close together. He paused between strides and listened to the whispering direction in his head.

He sidled up next to the largest truck, pulled a ratchet, a pair of pliers and screwdriver from the pocket of his pants.

* * *

Kevin staggered through the door of Blake's make-shift office on floor three. He gasped and held his shoulder, while grimacing in pain. Blake was finishing a phone call and turned to face him as he hung up the phone. Kevin seemed to be lumbering aimlessly; his right hand clutched his left side as he winced in pain.

"Oh man Kev, are you okay? You don't look well at all, man," Blake asked as he stood up and walked to meet Kevin.

Kevin grimaced and fell over onto a filing cabinet to support his weight. Blake's stride picked up as he moved to catch Kevin.

Blake leaned in to support Kevin. As their eyes met, Blake heard two clean metallic whispers. He staggered back away from Kevin and clutched at his chest. He looked down to see two blotches of crimson as they began to spread onto his white shirt. He looked across the room where his jacket and shoulder holster were hung over the back of a chair.

He made a motion, as if to take a step in that direction, and mouthed the word, "Why?" to Kevin.

He took a gasping breath as he staggered and fell back onto the floor. Kevin stood over him and pointed the gun into his face. Blake's sightless eyes lolled upwards. Kevin lowered his gun and then holstered it.

"I gotta tell you man, whacking the rest of these freaks didn't bother me at all. But you, you're like my brother. If I thought for a second that I could get your head out of Shepherd's ass, I would have tried. But not you man, no. It was part of what I loved about you. Ball busting Blake with his guns blazing till the job is done," Kevin paused and took a deep cleansing breath, "That counts for something in my book. I didn't spend any time talking to anybody else, I swear to ya. But, I wanted to tell you that I loved you, and I'm sorry for killing you. I couldn't give you the chance to defend yourself, you were always better than me. You taught me a lot, brother. Rest well, Blake," Kevin said and began to cry as he closed Blake's eyes with his fingers.

Kevin walked over to Blake's jacket and felt for the inside pocket. Finding it, he reached inside to get Blake's security card. He dropped the card into his own pants pocket. Kevin nodded to himself as he looked over Blake's unmoving form one last time.

He turned and headed through the door into the hallway, producing the security card from his pants pocket.

Kevin stood for nearly five minutes before the antechamber leading to Shepherd's office. In all of his carefully crafted planning he had not come up with a way to eliminate Shepherd.

His mind simply kept coming back to, "I will deal with it when it comes up."

The truth now stood before him as coldly as the wooden doors he faced. The man behind these doors was

330

more dangerous than any of them. He had proven himself smarter than them on repeated occasion, shooting down their best ideas with better ones, time after time. He was even physically better than any of them. Blake had pointed this out to him. Shepherd had mastered the art of the "no look" as Blake called it. Shepherd was able to survey a scene once and then fire on targets without looking again with deadly accuracy. Kevin winced as he thought about Blake. Kevin let out a deep mournful sigh and swiped Blake's card. The double doors swung open soundlessly. Kevin pointed his pistol at the door and made ready to knock.

"Drop the gun and turn slowly with your hands up, Kev. Don't mess this up, you know I can put you down easy peasy," Blake said with authority.

Kevin struggled under the pressure of the moment. Even as his mind raced for a strategic solution, part of him relished hearing the sound of Blake's voice.

"Come on, Kev. I don't know what happened to you, but I won't give up on you unless I have to," Blake's voice had lost its commanding tone.

Shepherd having heard Blake's shouts, was poised inside with his back against the wall to one side of the door. His pistol drawn, he held it in both hands, and regulated his breathing as he strained to hear the exchange.

"Come on Kev, last chance. Let's do this nice and clean. Drop the gun and give me the *no target* hands up. You know I don't want to kill you, brother-man," Blake said, his voice strained this time.

Kevin, having noted Blake's rapidly weakening condition, surmised that if he were able to keep Blake talking for a moment, he might still yet be able to get the drop on him.

"But there is still Shepherd to deal with," Kevin thought to himself.

"If I drop my gun, you're not gonna kill me?" Kevin asked, making his voice shake as he feigned fear.

"Nope. We're gonna talk this out. We might even go get a beer," Blake said, his voice, little better than a gruff whisper now.

"Okay, on the count of three I'm gonna drop my

331

gun, and turn. No sudden movements, okay?" Kevin said.

Blake did not respond this time. Kevin counted up to three very slowly and wheeled around with his gun. To his dismay, Blake was not as weak as he may have thought. Blake stood sideways, stiff arming his pistol at Kevin. One of Blake's eyes was closed; the other was staring at Kevin's forehead through the sight of his pistol.

They fired simultaneously, Kevin once and Blake twice. Blake saw the burst of crimson spray from his own chest. He felt the bullet burning inside of him as he fell and looked at the two neat holes in Kevin's forehead.

"You didn't learn anything from me, you piece of shit. First rule: two in the head, be sure they're dead," Blake's voice trailed away as he coughed and blood poured from the corner of his mouth.

Blake pushed himself up against the wall and labored to holler to Shepherd.

"He is down Shepherd, just outside the door. You gotta get out of here, A.S.A.P. It's going down now," Blake said weakly.

Chapter 29

From The Ashes

The door opened. Blake looked directly into Shepherd's office. His eyes roved around, but saw no one. His eyes fell upon Shepherd's gun, which was pointed at him from over the top of the desk. Blake labored to toss his pistol to the side and only managed to lob it a few feet.

Shepherd's face appeared over the top of the desk next to his gun. He looked first at Blake, and then watched Kevin's body for signs of movement.

Shepherd approached the spot where Kevin lay slumped against the wall, aiming at Blake's head unerringly. Shepherd looked over the bullet holes in Kevin's forehead, unsympathetically. His focus now turned to Blake and he walked toward him cautiously, with his gun still trained on Blake's head.

"What's happening here," Shepherd's voice was demanding.

"Kev went ape shit and shot me, the end," Blake said as he coughed blood, blinked, and tried to stay awake.

Shepherd holstered his pistol and moved to try to pick Blake up. Blake still, surprisingly, had the strength to push Shepherd away.

"Don't get your suit all bloody. I'm not going anywhere. You need to check all stations. I don't know if he left anybody alive when he made his rounds. Terry would have called you already, if he were alive. Flag one is gassed and ready. Get out while you can, and get those people to safety," Blake said weakly to Shepherd.

Shepherd held his phone to his head and simultaneously removed his weapon, realizing the need to have it at the ready. Shepherd pursed his lips, slammed the phone shut on his thigh, and pocketed it.

"Do you need anything? Are you in much pain?" Shepherd asked Blake.

"For starters, a cigarette would be nice. Yeah, it's the bad kind of pain," Blake responded and sounded weaker than ever.

Shepherd lit a cigarette, and stuck it in Blake's mouth. Blake struggled for a moment to raise his arms and let out a sigh. Blake took a long drag on the cigarette, inhaled, slowly exhaled and stifled a wet cough.

"I don't suppose you could spare a bullet?" Blake asked, barely able to finish the sentence.

Shepherd raised his gun with the lightning speed of a gunfighter and shot Blake in his forehead. He stood over him for a moment, as if he were going to say something, then turned and went back to his office. Removing a duffel bag from his closet he rummaged through it. He pulled a pair of sneakers from the closet and tossed them into the bag as he turned to his desk. Rifling through it he tossed bullets, wads of cash, and credit cards into the bag. He zipped it closed and walked to the door as he patted at the keys in his right pocket.

* * *

Todd sat in the leather chair in the middle of the room, which had been covered with a large sheet. Bree sat in his lap. They marveled at how fast the cleaning people had wrapped the place in white sheets and departed. She stroked his chin adoringly and looked at the length of his hair.

"You'd better clean up soon. You have a full beard and you're starting to look like a hippie. That's what my dad would call you," Bree said as she twirled the long hair on the base of his neck.

"Hey, where *is* your dad in all of this?" Todd asked her with a look of concern.

"He flew up north to stay with my aunt, after the thing happened in town, and my apartment got mobbed. Shepherd suggested it, saying that someone might be inventive enough to use him as a means to get to you," she replied in length.

"Yeah, that was good thinking on his part. I wish I had thought of that," Todd added and sounded forlorn.

"I know, huh? You were so busy being in a coma, you let details like that slip by you," she said and poked him in the ribs.

Todd wrestled her arms to her sides and when she finally became still and passive, kissed her deeply and withdrew, looking into her eyes.

"I love you very much. I'm so glad you stalked me 'til I caught you," Todd said seriously.

She tore an arm loose and popped him on the shoulder.

"No, no. It was you who used your weird powers to ensnare and keep me," she fired back at him.

Todd attempted to get off a retort, but she pulled him back into a kiss. They both started, as loud insistent rapping assaulted the front door of their room. They reacted as one. Bree sprang from his lap and Todd bounced to his feet.

"Who is it?" Todd asked.

"Open up quick, it's Shepherd," he demanded through the door.

Todd opened the door and noted the pistol Shepherd held, pointed at the ground.

"Is it really necessary for y'all to come in here with a gun *every* time?" Todd drawled angrily.

Shepherd looked disheveled. Todd noticed the spots of blood on his white suit, some of which had been smeared by the shifting, cross body strap of his bag.

"Grab only what you need. We have got to get out of here, now. All of the security is dead. I don't know if it was all done by the one that's dead near my office or if there are more. We need to move. Take only what you need," Shepherd said as he looked over his shoulder into the hallway.

Bree entered the room, holding her tan bag and the black back pack. Todd looked to the window at the driving rain as it pelted the window. Then, almost as if on cue Shepherd began to ask him if it was possible to do the white flash port, away to safety. Todd considered it for a moment

335

and denied the request. He worked hard not to show the panic that gripped him as he realized the close relation between these circumstances and his recent nightmare.

"I don't think it would be safe for the two of you at this time," Todd said and looked into Shepherd's face, gravely.

"Well shit, to the truck then. Just stay behind me. If I motion to you, stop. If I motion again, follow. Stay close and as quiet as possible," Shepherd said as he removed the bag from his shoulder.

He handed Todd his bag and walked ahead of them with his gun extended in both hands. Bree followed Todd with her left hand clasped in Todd's right hand. Shepherd was now working to get them to the elevator. After a few pauses, they found themselves at the elevator door. He motioned for them to wait as he swiped his card and leveled his pistol at the doors. As the doors opened, he swung his body and placed his back against the wall next to Todd and Bree. He looked at Todd and gave a wink. Todd looked at him quizzically.

"Little trick I picked up in the service. Two clumps of dirt, left rear corner on the floor. One dead beetle next to that. Two pieces of grape bubble gum wrappers next to the beetle. Two lights are out on the ceiling," Shepherd winked at Todd, proceeded into the elevator, and motioned for them to follow. Bree walked ahead of Todd into the elevator. Todd seemed to buckle and groped at his temples. Shepherd reached out, grabbed the crook of his arm, and dragged him with ease through the open doors. He pressed the button to close the doors before turning to face them.

"I need you there and you there," Shepherd pointed at Todd and Bree in turn as he assigned spots for them to stand.

Todd and Bree took up their directed positions on either side of the door.

"Stay in the corners so you're not in L.O.S.," Shepherd instructed.

"What is L.O.S.?" Todd asked.

"It means line of sight. In case there are a few of them waiting to open fire when the doors open," Shepherd said solemnly.

Todd and Bree looked at each other and swallowed dryly as they listened to the tiny dings that counted off the descending floors.

When the elevator stopped, Shepherd swung himself around, and placed his back against Bree. The elevator doors slid open and Shepherd pressed the *hold door* button. He swung across the open expanse of the doors and came to rest with his back against Todd.

"I thought I saw motion, better sweep again. I'm getting old after all," Shepherd said and went back through the motion and came to rest again, with his back to Bree.

"Okay, I am gonna go out and open the truck. It has a rear entry door with a center aisle, all the way to the front seats. When I say so, run. Jump into the rear of the truck and make your way into the front passenger seat," Shepherd said to Bree.

"Todd, listen for me to signal, and then head for the rear of the truck. Please, sit behind the driver's seat," Shepherd said as he pulled the vehicle remote from his pocket.

The trucks alarm emitted a high pitched chirp. Todd fought the urge to look out of the elevator.

"Come," Shepherd commanded.

Bree gave a frightened glance to Todd. He smiled and tried to will all of his courage to her. She smiled weakly and rounded the corner as she headed toward the sound of Shepherd's voice. Todd could hear the heels of her shoes as she clambered over the metal grated floor of the truck.

"Come!" Shepherd repeated.

Todd rounded the corner, burdened by the weight of the bags he carried. He hopped into the truck. Shepherd dove in behind him, and slammed the truck door closed.

"Leave the bags here in the rear of the truck," Shepherd said over his shoulder to Todd as he ducked through toward the driver's seat.

Todd let the baggage fall to the floor and chased Shepherd toward the front of the truck. Todd looked on, as the menacing winds tossed objects passed the windows of the concrete parking garage. Large pieces of cardboard stuffed into the orange dumpster, next to the window, were fluttering in the wind.

"Buckle up," Bree said as she tried to sound cheery.

Shepherd grimaced at her and raised a single finger to his mouth, as he placed his cell phone to his ear.

"This is Shepherd. Do we have clearance? Excellent. We have a twenty minute E.T.A. Fine. Fine. Goodbye," Shepherd said curtly.

He closed his phone, sat back in his chair, and exhaled a genuine sigh of relief. He thought for a moment then reached into the inside pocket of his white jacket and withdrew a thick envelope addressed to Brianna Dellor. He passed it to her and smiled weakly.

"That's for you, read it when you have time. You will realize there are very few coincidences in the world," he said looking at her with a saddened expression.

Bree nodded and slid the envelope into the pocket of her shirt and buttoned it.

Shepherd flipped through the key ring until he found the ignition key. He pulled himself forward, using the steering wheel for leverage. His right hand slid the key into the ignition. Bree was staring out of the window at the orange dumpster.

Suddenly she jounced in her seat and screamed, "WAIT!" as Shepherd made to turn the key.

She grabbed at his hand to stop him. Shepherd drove his shoulder into her, hard and knocked the breath out of her.

"Whatever you forgot can wait, damn it! We have to get out of here, now," Shepherd said as he rolled the key forward.

Bree clutched at her chest and was panting the word, "Dumpster..," as she struggled to try and catch her breath.

Todd's lips drew into a snarl as he reached for Shepherd's shoulder, in an attempt to reprimand him. But, his fingers slid through Shepherd's shoulder and down through the seat. Todd was drawing back his hand to look at it, as he heard the thunderous explosion, from beneath the truck. Faster than he could comprehend, the inside of the truck had become a white hot ball of flames. To his horror, Shepherd was visible only as black shadow through the flame, which seemed to melt away under the intense heat. A second explosion occurred now, as the gas tanks under the rear of the truck blew. The truck blew apart now, in every direction, in a hail of metal, burning plastic, and rubber. Todd crouched motionless for a moment and then rose from the center of the fire. The remaining small pieces of his burning clothing fell away from his body. He took a step and then another, turning back and forth as if lost.

His lips began to tremble as the shock passed.

"Bree...*Bree*..." scrambled thoughts played through his head as he looked around confused.

"Where are...?" he tried to ask as he choked on sobs.

Todd looked around trembling, at the burning pieces of the truck, littering the garage. Todd dropped to his knees and covered his face with both hands, crying. Todd drew breath until his lungs strained with the effort. Throwing his head back he screamed for her; defying the reality that Bree and his unborn child were gone. He knelt down, pressed his eyes closed and began to convulse as he sobbed uncontrollably. Hot tears flowed down his cheeks.

Chapter 30

The Peace Bringer

"Dumpster," whispered through his mind as he envisioned Bree clutching her chest and mouthing the word in his mind's eye.

Todd stood up and fixed his stare upon the orange dumpster. Under Todd's gaze, the steel of the dumpster groaned and strained as a physical manifestation of his rage. Todd's torso and upper thighs crackled with white electrical arcs for a moment as his head cocked to one side. The dumpster flew sideways past the window in the side of the garage. It was thrown, as if weightless, and smashed as it folded in upon itself. The force of the impact sprayed the surroundings with trash and concrete.

Doug stood up in horror from his crouching position.

The dumpster, that had formerly hidden him from view, had been ripped away. Doug moved now, walking slowly toward the window. Frozen in place by his gaze, Doug stopped and stared at Todd. The ensuing eclipse had begun to darken the sky; lightning flashed hindering Todd's view of Doug.

Todd's expression wasn't one of anger, but a deep mournful look of painful loss. Doug knew now that this was terribly wrong. He had followed the angel's instructions so blindly, but this poor man was not the vengeful demon she had portrayed. Suddenly the demonic woman appeared next to Doug. She gripped his shoulder and drew herself close to his ear.

Todd stood, staring in disbelief at Doug and the woman whispering in his ear. The white light formed in his peripheral vision and he now stood face to face with Doug, who had begun to cry.

"And now you will burn for all of eternity, for having been led astray," the woman finished whispering into Doug's ear and turned to face Todd.

Todd's eyes still glowed with an intense white light. Electrical arcs traveled over him in erratic patterns and his body hummed with power, as he stared into Doug's wide, frightened eyes. The woman took several steps away and folded her arms, giving Todd a satisfied smile. Doug stared deeply into Todd's eyes and began to tremble.

In the white void of Todd's eyes, he witnessed the birth and death of a thousand worlds, great wars, and upheavals. Doug saw visions of true angels, fighting each other in darkened skies. He watched on, in horror, as the angels locked in fierce and bloody combat.

His hair began to go white, starting at the roots and continuing to travel its entire length as he stared into Todd's eyes.

"Now that you know the truth, here is the payment for your faithful service to me," the woman said and laughed derisively.

Todd finally blinked and turned to look at the dark woman. Todd's attention was stolen, as he heard the sound of bone clattering against the concrete. He turned and watched, as dog-like creatures with no skin, half the size of a man, approached. The creatures broke into a run, bearing down upon the spot where Todd and Doug stood. The creatures pressed hard as they ran, picking up speed, and dove at them. They passed harmlessly through Todd; however, the creatures struck Doug in the chest. He was carried backward through the window and vanished into the shadow of the fading light, screaming. Todd rushed forward. There was no sign of Doug's body and Todd believed that he had been transported somewhere else.

"Where is he!?" Todd demanded as he rounded upon the evil woman.

"He has been taken to where he belongs," the woman chided.

She stared into Todd's eyes, which had returned to their normal green. His hands were bent into claws. He held them open behind him. The muscles and tendons, in his arms and legs, flexed out as he stood before her. She smiled into the murderous rage of his stare.

"Before I kill you, you will explain why you have done this to me!" Todd commanded.

She placed her hands on her hips, stared at him undauntedly, and began to laugh. Her mirthless laughter ended abruptly as she was thrust sideways into a concrete wall by some invisible force. She hit it forcefully and fell to the ground, with a whimper. Todd was already over her, having moved as light.

"I'm already dead...You can't hurt me," she said defiantly, but her voice was that of a woman now and some hint of fear had crept into her tone.

Todd plainly saw fear in her eyes and pressed his advantage. He could feel that she was not only hurt, but being forced to remain tangible by his power. She rose to her feet shakily.

"I want answers now!" he commanded angrily.

His gaze dropped to her arm. She shrieked as the bones in her right arm broke under the skin. The ruined arm fell as the other reached to clutch it.

Her eyes bulged and she staggered, as if to run from him. Her legs folded under her and twisted as the bones were pulverized. She fell on her side and pushed herself up to look at him.

"Help! Help me Master please!" she shrieked into the air around her.

Todd looked around mockingly for a moment and began to speak, "I don't think *The Master* can hear you," his voice seemed to readopt some of its chill and menace.

"I...He...Master, please? I have served you faithfully," she shrieked in obvious pain and disbelief.

The bones in the arm she supported herself on, crushed under the skin and she fell flatly onto her back, writhing in pain.

Todd appeared in a flash of light again, poised over her.

"You will speak to *me*! I will destroy you slowly, unless you tell me what I want to know!" he growled as spit

342

flew through his clenched teeth.

Her chest heaved heavily as she breathed and her eyes widened.

Audible snapping noises could be heard, as her ribs seemed to crack one by one. She was shaking her head and spitting blood all over herself as she begged incoherently.

"I always enjoyed your pain, my darling," Bryce said.

The sound of the voice comforted her. She began to calm herself and drew quick gasping breaths.

Todd stood up and backed away from her.

"It should be your *honor* to perish in my service, but no. There you lie, screaming for your master instead," Bryce chided.

The woman's eyes were now full of anguish and pain. The bones began to snap inside of her again. Todd stared at her in disbelief as her body was mauled by some unseen attacker.

"You have failed me, lover, and you will suffer forever for it. There are none as important as I. Did you think you would be at my side?" Bryce laughed.

The woman's heavy breaths stopped and her body eroded into dust before Todd's eyes.

"Did you kill her? Who was that? Why did you call her lover?" Todd asked aloud, searching the air for Bryce.

Todd closed his eyes and stood in the darkness of his mind.

The familiar meeting spot formed from the void. Todd angrily kicked the white chairs and they disappeared into the formless void, outside of the circle of light. Bryce walked into the light from the darkness.

"In this life, she was a student of mine. She was so young, so eager and easily manipulated into my service. She thanked me as I took her life and gave her the power to serve me," Bryce said as he smiled malevolently at Todd.

"Serve you? Why have you done this to me?" Todd asked.

"I have orchestrated the end of this ruse. I have removed all of your earthly ties, so that this existence can end and my accession to the throne can occur. I am tired of

343

living in the shadow of your light.

"You think that you are perfect. You think you can cast me aside time and time again. But I am always here, in the darkness. I have waited for my opportunity. And you, you created me to serve *you*. You made me the pinnacle of perfection in every way. And yet, you deny me my right to rule," Bryce's expression was now full of fury.

"What are you talking about? I didn't create you. I bought your soul. It wasn't supposed to be real," Todd stammered in confusion.

Bryce's expression relaxed.

"You did a *real* number on yourself this time," Bryce laughed.

"I just needed to find a way into you. It took a lot of work to get here. You have no idea the hard work and planning it took, to get you to openly accept me as part of you," Bryce said as he paced around Todd.

"Your word is law, and by speaking your acceptance of me, it grants me use of your power. Have you noticed the world is ripping itself apart? I admit, I am a little more methodical than some, at destroying a world. But why be impetuous and rush it? There is so much delicious agony and hatred out there right now," Bryce paused and inhaled air through his nose.

Todd was staring at Bryce, who continued to pace with his arms behind his back.

"Did you enjoy the visions I sent to you?" Bryce asked.

"That was you?" Todd asked.

"Everything is always me. I can do better, I promise you. I can treat you to the most horrific things you can imagine for all of eternity. A little display is in order, I suppose. You can be harmed here, I assure you. And you cannot leave without my permission," Bryce said with a smile.

Bryce moved incredibly fast and clawed the side of Todd's face with his elongated fingernails.

Todd staggered back away from him and clutched his cheek, feeling the warm blood trickle between his fingers. Bryce showed him the nails which receded back to their normal size. Bryce licked blood from one of his fingers.

"Your fears...your hopelessness, are a feast for the senses," Bryce said.

Todd staggered and clawed at his temples as the voices in his head cried out in agony for him to save them.

"Oh and there will also be that, lots and lots of that. The world you know is nearly destroyed. I have ensured the spot, in which your physical being resides, will be last. I want you to linger and listen to them beg, helpless to assist them," Bryce said as he sampled Todd's blood from another finger.

"I am not afraid of you," Todd said defiantly.

"Afraid of me? Don't worry. There will be a lot of physical pain, later. But for now, let's stick with a formula that you're receptive to," Bryce said as he backed into the darkness.

The light overhead dimmed until blackness blanketed the spot on which Todd stood. He crouched defensively and looked pointlessly around into the pitch black environment. He felt weightless and the fear of being forced through another set of nightmares ravaged his mind.

*   *   *

Todd now sat on the floor of the Goldman's home. Lucy's body began to convulse next to him unnaturally, as though it would tear itself apart. Todd pulled himself up from the floor and began crawling away. Bryce kicked him in the head and he sprawled forward into Will's lap.

"This was entirely your fault. You brought him here," Will said as he stared down at Todd angrily.

"I'm sorry, I'm so sorry. I don't know what's happening," Todd said as he choked back tears.

Todd rolled over and crawled away. He looked up to see a ruined version of Max, now facing him. The animal bared its teeth angrily. Todd whimpered. Half of Max's muzzle seemed to have been burned away. He raised his hand up to guard his face and Max grabbed it with his ruined half burnt muzzle. His teeth clamped onto the hand. The muzzle tore at the flesh of Todd's hand in a feral jerking side to side motion. Max forced him onto his back, released his hand, and continued to furiously snap at him. Todd's groping hand found a large hunting knife nearby. He grasped it firmly as he sprang at the dog pushing it over and straddled it, Max's eyes flashed white as he snapped at Todd. He raised the knife, and plunged it towards the flailing animal's chest. Mid stroke Max transformed into Sebastian Goldman, who lay helplessly crying before Todd. The baby's crying halted and his eyes widened as the knife sank into his chest.

Todd swiped madly at the air, as he fought an unseen torment. He struggled to distance himself from the infant's corpse. He fell and flailed on the floor, deep in the throes of mental anguish.

* * *

Another disorienting transition occurred. He was now lying in wet grass with a soapy towel in his hand. He felt anguish as he reached out to touch the grass in disbelief.

The sound of something crawling through the grass behind him caused him to flip over and crawl backward. The living corpse of Robert Jennings, with its deep empty eye sockets, crawled through the wet grass toward him. The awful cadaver had latched onto his shoes and worked to claw its way up his body.

"My time is precious, my time is precious," it repeated as it crawled up his body.

Todd wriggled himself around and pushed at the corpse as it approached his face. The cadaver, having reached its desired position, poised over him and stared at Todd with its empty sockets.

"My time is precious, my time is precious," it repeated, as dirt and bile dripped from its gaping mouth onto Todd's chest.

"No...No...No more!" Todd screeched into the air with his eyes closed as tightly as he could get them.

* * *

"No more indeed. We were just getting warmed

346

up," Bryce said as he paced around Todd's helpless screaming form on the floor.

Todd opened his eyes to see the room with its white light flowing down from overhead. He rolled over, pushed himself up, and sat back on his knees.

"Whu...What do you want from me?"

"Oh, just a tiny thing, really. You could end all of this suffering and everything could go back to the way it was. I want you to look at me and say: My throne is yours. I will serve you as my master. It's that simple," Bryce said and looked very amused by Todd's pain.

"You killed everyone I loved and tortured me for that?" Todd stammered.

"Yes, for that simple thing alone. But, I can rectify it all and take the pain away. I can make this stop and return everything to normal at any time. All you have to do is what I ask of you," Bryce said and bowed down to place his face close to Todd's.

Todd's eyes looked curiously into Bryce's face for a moment. Todd stopped trembling and a spark of anger rose up in him, so sharply that it became apparent in every facet of his expression. His lips drew into a snarl as he pushed himself up toward Bryce's face and spit. Bryce recoiled with his eyes fluttering and wiped the moisture from his face. The look of revulsion was replaced by that of contempt. Bryce answered by slashing the same cheek a second time with a clawed hand.

Bryce smiled at him and backed slowly toward the darkness.

"Let's see if you're brimming with confidence after a little more persuasion," Bryce chided as he vanished into the darkness.

Todd could hear labored wheezing breaths coming from the shadows outside of the circle. He turned on the spot, squinting, trying to catch sight of this unknown terror. The wound on his cheek burned, but he lowered his hands to defend against this new unseen danger.

A hand thrust in from the darkness onto the floor, just inside of the light. The flesh had been burned away from several of the finger tips. The boned fingers made the sound of chalk being dragged across a concrete floor and Todd's skin crawled. The ruined form dragged itself halfway into the light. Todd began to recoil as the burnt body crawled toward him. The body paused and moved in flickering unnatural jerks. It blindly clawed the ground, as it labored to reach him. It seemed drawn to him. The burnt corpse-thing, now made its way up to its hands and knees and lumbered there, staggering with its head bowed.

Todd's lips trembled, as he tried to form words. Tears welled up freshly in his reddened eyes and rolled down his cheeks. The thing's head began to rise and Todd felt as though his heart would explode inside of his chest. He began to shake uncontrollably. Some unseen force gripped him and refused to let him look away. Todd remained held in place, as the burnt head, with its partially exposed skull, raised up to look at him. Its face was now in full view, inches from his. The smell of burnt flesh assaulted his nostrils. The eyelids fluttered and opened. Todd fell spiraling into the abyss of despair as he looked into Bree's blue eyes.

Todd's body began to fail, blood poured from his nose and ears as he convulsed. His head dropped and the pressure that held him in place dissipated. He fell to the floor and was motionless.

Todd's body began to pop and sizzle as angry electrical arcs randomly traveled over it. His eyes sprang open, there was a flash and now he sat crouched in front of Bree's burnt form. He looked deeply into her blue eyes which had become the only recognizable feature left. Todd's eyes had been replaced by sharp white light that shone brightly from the sockets.

"I wouldn't even let an illusion of you suffer if I could prevent it. I love you," he said to her softly.

His breath exhaled as light, and drifted toward the spurious vision of the woman he loved. The light touched Bree and her body began to repair itself. Flesh covered bone and long blonde hair grew from the top of her head. Her blues eyes remained fixed on Todd, unaware of the transformation her body had undergone. She was lifted to a standing position by an invisible force. She floated in front of him, a visage of remarkable beauty, now bathed in a warm

348

golden light. She smiled approvingly, as the invisible force carried her up toward the light overhead. He watched, as she merged with the light. His face dropped and his lilting smile slowly melted into a mask of fury. He cast his gaze sharply into the darkness and raised a single hand. There was a scream in the darkness and Bryce flew toward him at a blurred speed.

Bryce was held in place by a white ethereal hand that mocked every movement of Todd's hand. The grip held Bryce like a doll, where he struggled helplessly against it. Todd fixed his gaze upon Bryce with his white-light stare. Bryce howled as the bones in his face began to change form. Bryce's arms flailed and his screams deepened as the metamorphosis continued. Bryce's face elongated and horns grew from above his ears, ripping their way through his skin. The ground beneath Bryce opened up and, at impossible depths; the orange glow of fire could be seen. Bryce's head was now goat-like. The screams which erupted from him, were as pained bleats. The glowing hand released him. Bryce fell into the shadow and flame below. The ground closed with a thunderous boom and Todd opened his eyes.

* * *

Todd stood in the debris strewn parking garage. He looked to one side, as his awareness alerted him to the presence of one who had witnessed these events, silently. His voice was cold and authoritative as he spoke.

"You have looked into the darkness. I hope, for your sake, what you saw there was not to your liking," Todd's voice thundered, shaking the walls and floor of the parking garage.

Todd flashed and now stood in the apartment on the tenth floor. He picked up a white dust cover and draped it around himself. He sat in the leather chair, in the center of the room. His mind had become as finely tuned as the power he exhibited.

Todd waved his hand and the ceiling and most of the walls eroded to expose the angry torrent of destruction outside. Strong, wind-driven rain pummeled the exposed room. The cool rain pelted him. The television nearby emitted static as its auto tuner searched for a signal from any station. The backup generators of the building struggled to continue to supply power to a ruined network of electrical wires. Electrical arcs snapped and popped from the remaining wall sockets. Hundreds of tornado funnels swirled in the distance, casting puffs of debris from them. He understood that life on earth, as he knew it, was a fleeting commodity, soon to be extinguished like the light of the sun.

"Please God, please," echoed in his head.

"God...God," he gasped the word in realization that he had never uttered it once in his life.

He rose to stand and staggered.

"God...Todd...God," he gasped.

The utterance of the word, God, had released something in him.

His awareness was growing exponentially. The voices in his head were no longer abstract whisperings. He was aware of each of the victims of this calamity. He could feel them, struggling to survive, asking him to protect them desperately. He felt omnipotent and powerless at the same time. He could not understand at what level he felt compassion. Sadness and the magnitude, of which he felt it, should render him insensible. But there was no release for him. His body surged with power.

As he looked around, he could see wind-driven fires eating away at the remaining buildings. He searched deep within himself to find the power to abate the disasters, to stop this senseless ending of the world. He was unable to stretch himself to do so feeling tethered somehow.

"I cannot endure the pain of their suffering," he screamed, throwing back his hands, his chest heaving.

"Tsunami's have begun to strike the eastern seaboard," the voice of the television reporter said as the television randomly struck a still airing channel.

"The death toll in South America is already at..."

Todd winced and focused on the television. The large television compressed, melted, and blew away as dust in the strong wind.

"They are suffering and I have the power to end it,"

he thought.

"I can be the merciful God that they need. *The Peace Bringer*."

"Help us..," the multitude of voices sang out in a desperate choir of anguish.

"I must soothe them."

The voices called to him now. There were millions more, all at once. Todd concentrated to remove this shackle, this hindrance, with all of his might. The physical manifestation of this would have killed a normal man. His muscles bunched and flexed. His hands drew into fists, fingernails digging into clenched palms. Blood began to trickle from the wounds. The painful throb of the wounds undulated up his arms as he wept in gratitude for the ability to feel anything. His hands opened, the blood flowing from his palms began to trickle from his wrists. He was aware of blood pouring from his nose. His mouth was full of the salty tang of blood. Something fell from him, an encumbrance of some sort. He felt a sense of loss at some level, looking down upon a lifeless body, only to realize it as his own.

Todd was now a being formed of pure white light. He could no longer feel the wind or rain that now passed through him. Millions of eyes where cast into the nightmare that had become the sky. Trumpets sounded as titanic waves washed over every continent. The voices, the teaming millions of desperate voices, pleading for salvation, were abruptly silenced.

He mourned the loss of so many beautiful lives. A symphony of rushing water, crackling wood, colliding stones and those soothing trumpets filled the air. He cast his eyes to the eclipse as the suns light faded from view. Absolute darkness washed over the earth.

The Earth, now a shadow of its former incarnation, had been diminished by the forces of darkness which had sought to destroy it. The being suddenly became aware of the circumstances that had led him here. He had forgotten himself by design, allowing him to walk in the warmth and light of mankind. In the darkened expanse, cosmic forces demanded balance.

In compliance with this demand the being readied a

response. In a commanding voice which encompassed infinite power he spoke the words, "Let there be light."

Epilogue

The Watcher's Decent

Crouched behind the large concrete pillar in the parking garage, Andre pulled the worn blanket around him tightly. The light of the sun outside, even hidden behind thick tufts of storm clouds, had the ability to make his skin feel as though it were being abraded. The wet concrete under his bare feet was uncomfortable. He had not mastered the ability to control himself while he sprinted and it had cost him another pair of running shoes. The wet cloth of his slacks had frayed and hung in tattered disarray around his calves. To reassure himself, he took a moment to tap on his titanium case. He repositioned the case, which was still safely stuffed in the waistband of his slacks.

Ahead of where he crouched, a man worked furiously to attach something under the largest of the black trucks. The sound of ratchet sockets and the small clinks of tools against metal, had assured him that he had been unheard upon approach.

The Mechanic, as Andre had come to think of him, remained unaware of his audience. Andre's eyesight, inhumanly keen, was hindered by the subtle daylight that shone in through a nearby window. He pulled at the blanket absently, to cover himself more evenly. The cloth strained and made a ripping noise as his fingernails pierced the material. He slackened his grip and prepared to move if need be. The Mechanic crawled out from under the truck and began to peer around the parking garage.

Assured of the security of his furtive position, Andre observed the Mechanic curiously. It was easy to recall two instances where he had seen this man before, neither of which provided information of his identity. The Mechanic

353

was sticking tools into the pockets of his cargo pants. He tugged aggressively at the snap of a pocket on his right leg. The hilt of a large hunting knife was visible for only a moment as the Mechanic shifted the pants leg. An involuntary flex of muscles rippled through Andre. The simple threat of the concealed weapon invoked a readiness in his blood.

The nearby elevator had begun to emit a series of dings. The Mechanic shot a few panicked glances toward the elevator, as he worked furiously to find a spot to hide.

Andre pulled his blanket around him tightly and rolled from the view of the elevator doors in an even turning sweep. He was aware of the man in the elevator that had looked right at him as he rolled out of sight. He smiled as he thought of his own grace and speed. He may have appeared as a blur or a play of light, to the old man's eyes. He had lost sight of the Mechanic and flexed his awareness. He shut out the sound of the heavy wind buffeting the garage, the grating noise of a civil service klaxon, and the heavy breath of three passengers in the elevator. The Mechanic had a slight wheeze which provided enough of a signature for Andre to track him. His eyes narrowed as he followed the sounds to a large orange dumpster, some fifty yards away. Andre pivoted and arched where he crouched in an attempt to remain unseen. The older man brandished a pistol and leveled it in a sweeping motion as he disembarked the elevator. This older man jogged toward the largest of the trucks and a couple of piercing chirps sounded from its alarm system. He was out of sight, but Andre heard as he opened the door on the rear of the vehicle.

Andre could not see the two other people that remained hidden in the elevator. He was aware of their presence as the smell of their fear-stained sweat drifted to his nostrils. There was something familiar about at least one of the scents. The stench from a pool of burnt motor oil, near him, hindered his ability to narrow its signature. His mind flashed hundreds of close comparisons, none of which were likely.

The older man bellowed the word, "COME!" loudly, and the female exited the elevator heading to the rear of the truck in obedience.

The command sounded again in the echoing garage. A second man, younger than the first, exited the metal doors and hurried to join his companions at the rear of the truck.

Andre's eyes fixed sharply upon him across the expanse of the garage and narrowed in recognition. White ethereal ribbons flowed from the man and undulated in some otherworldly breeze.

"Todd," Andre whispered to himself, as he marveled at the effect.

Andre thought momentarily of his exchanges with Todd, prior to and after his own change. He remembered how normal Todd had seemed. Then that day, after his change, he had seen the ribbons flowing from him. It had unnerved him, flat out scared him, truth be told. The sound of the door, as it slammed shut on the rear of truck, recaptured his attention.

An intricate chain around Andre's neck held a small crystal vial which brushed his arm when he moved. He picked up the vial and watched as a bubble rose through the thick ruby liquid.

His mind's eye replayed the memory in complete detail. The Cloaked Figure had pushed him through a portal to collect this sample of Todd's blood. It had been his first experience with the Cloaked Figure's ability to create dark portals to faraway places. Having been pushed through the portal, he had found Todd and that same woman, sprawled insensibly on the carpet of a room. Both of them had hemorrhaged blood from their noses. He remembered the strong scent of the blood, how it had called to him on some primal level. He would have sampled it, had it not been for the caution issued by his purple-cloaked companion. The Cloaked Figure had given him a small vial. Andre noticed a small ring attached to its ornate stopper.

"Catch a bit from under Todd's nose, but do not touch or taste it. I cannot tell you the unfathomable nightmares that would follow, if you were to ingest any of it," the painfully reverberating voice of the Cloaked Figure warned.

He had done as instructed and caught a few drops by placing the vial between Todd's nose and the carpet. He had risen carefully, replaced the stopper of the vial, and turned to hand it back to the Cloaked Figure. A hand had risen from the sleeve of the cloak and declined the vial's return. The other hand offered an intricate necklace. The necklace had a locking hook type clasp on it and looked very durable despite its intricacy. This locking clasp was separate from the one used to fasten it around the neck. He had taken the necklace to inspect it, as the Cloaked Figure watched wordlessly. His mind had seen the puzzle and solved it. He affixed the vial to the clasp at the end of the chain. He then dangled it before the Cloaked Figure as if to show his intelligence.

"Put it on, never lose it. There will come a time when you feel your strength diminish past a painful degree of measure. This, and only this, will be the time to drink it. If you ignore this warning and ingest it at any other time you will suffer untold levels of pain and despair," the Cloaked Figure had warned him, ominously.

He thought of the mysterious Cloaked Figure that had appeared to him for some time now. He was unsure if he should trust this being as he had never even seen its face. Given the foretold circumstances of utter doom, he supposed he had no choice. The Cloaked Figure had saved Marcus and Richard from death. It also had saved him from making a horrible mistake, though somehow it had managed to come between him and his brother. The Cloaked Figure had stolen, for lack of a better way to explain it, the woman that he loved. For this he would pay, Andre vowed.

The elevated heartbeat and increased respiration of the Mechanic brought Andre's attention back to the moment at hand.

"I should be with Richard. Why am I here?" Andre asked himself.

He was here at the sole direction of the Cloaked Figure, who had instructed him to watch and remain unseen.

"This has to be the greatest exercise in futility that I've ever been forced into. What'll it matter if I know how the world ends, if I'm dead?" he asked the air around him.

Andre shifted in his hiding spot and gasped as he tried to hold his breath. He was poised for action as he realized this to be a critical point of whatever the Cloaked Figure wanted him to see.

"They don't realize he is behind the dumpster," Andre said to himself, accidentally out loud.

As if she had heard, the woman who sat in the passenger seat of the black truck had directed her attention to the dumpster. She turned to the driver and had begun to have a heated exchange with him. This moment was a blur of confusion for him. The woman in the passenger seat seemed to disappear, that is to pass out of existence, in a flash of white light. He was sure that this effect would be imperceptible to eyes that were merely human. His mind had begun to work to analyze this. Simultaneously the world became a blast of orange and blue fire. The detonation ripped past Andre with concussive force. His blanket, his primary means of protection from the daylight, had been blown away. He sat and watched helplessly as it drifted through a large window in the cement wall. A small ember had landed on his shoulder and caused the sleeve of his shirt to smolder. He pinched the ember up and flicked it away as he peered around the column.

His eyes had barely fallen upon the burning hull of the truck, when a second explosion erupted from it. The vehicle ripped apart as it sent burning metal and plastic in every direction. To a human eye, the shrapnel from the truck would have appeared to fly out in an imperceptible spray. Andre, however, was no longer human and marveled as he watched the debris as it flew out in all directions, as if in slow motion. Burning metal and debris caromed off of the walls in a wailing orchestra of destruction. A burning plastic wheel cover rolled past Andre and proceeded to roll down the ramp to the next floor. The black bellows of smoke were pulled from the room by the vacuum of the hurricane force winds outside of the garage.

To Andre's sheer amazement, the man he knew as Todd crouched at the center of the blast point. He watched as Todd rose slowly. The last pieces of his burning clothes melted from him to fall to the concrete. Andre held fast to the concrete pillar and shook the effects of the blast's concussion from his jolted brain. Todd appeared to be in shock as he paced helplessly. He took a step and then another, turning back and forth as if lost. His lips began to tremble as the shock passed.

"Bree...Bree! Where are...?" Todd's voice croaked.

Andre was well aware of the burnt smell of flesh and hair.

Todd dropped to his knees and screamed "NO!!!" in a mournful bellowing wail.

The humanity left in Andre, cringed at this display and felt empathy for Todd's loss. Todd had risen again and turned to face the dumpster. The white ethereal ribbons were flowing; the effect was dizzying. Disoriented, he closed his eyes and steadied himself against the pillar. The sound of the dumpster's metal being bent, as though it were caught in the grip of a compactor, compelled him to look again.

As the dumpster was hurled sideways toward the concrete wall it collided and created a concussive thud. The Mechanic's heart thumped violently in his chest as he was exposed. He walked to the window, paused at its center, and stared at Todd. To Andre, the Mechanic had seemed to contemplate the thought of jumping out of the window to escape. Brilliant lightning tore through the sky behind the Mechanic. The flash blinded Andre, he strained to see the exchange through his blurry vision. Todd's eyes were locked upon the Mechanic where he stood, frozen in fear. The Mechanic's expression had melted into a mask of remorseful regret. Andre rubbed at his eyes as a woman began to materialize next to the Mechanic. This happening, perhaps so close to the other unexplainable events of the last few minutes, had sent his system into some sort of protective overload. His muscles had tightened and his senses grew to new levels of acuity. The woman grinned wickedly as she whispered into the Mechanics ear.

Andre's hand drifted to his mouth as he whispered in disbelief, "J.J.," in recognition of the woman.

He had been told that she was dead. A feeling of dread filled him as he watched her revel in the emotional anguish she induced with her whispered words. Andre had become accustomed to the way his eyes were able to perceive motion. At one point, in the recent past, he had watched a bullet fly from the end of a pistol. His eyes had been able to follow the projectile. It was no wonder that he gasped at the speed at which Todd's body flashed as light. Todd stood face to face with the Mechanic. J.J. had backed away and still radiated that malevolent self-amused grin.

There was no way to know what the Mechanic saw in Todd's eyes. Whatever vision he had been treated to had turned his neat coal-black hair, white.

Andre's eyes snapped to the woman, who had motioned to nothing he could see, in the distance behind Todd. He heard, what sounded like, bones being tapped on concrete. The sound traveled across the garage toward Todd and the Mechanic.

Andre's hands had become claws and he had instinctively settled into a defensive crouch. Whatever trekked its way across the concrete floor was invisible to him. The Mechanic's face was contorted into a mask of terror. He seemed to be struck in the chest and carried out of the window. Todd rushed forward to watch his descent.

"Where is he!?" Todd demanded looking over his shoulder at J.J.

"He has been taken to where he belongs," J.J. chided.

Andre's blood continued to issue warnings to him as it recognized the danger posed by his surroundings. His skin hardened and he felt his lip curling into a snarl. Todd had leaned forward with a murderous look. With clawed hands, he rounded on J.J. Andre's nails dug into the concrete pillar. This was a physical manifestation of the heightened readiness his body was undergoing. The crunching noise was masked by Todd's angry inquisition of the woman.

"Before I kill you, you will explain why you have done this to me!" Todd commanded.

359

True to Andre's memory of J.J., being an antagonistic bitch, she had placed her hands on her hips and was laughing at Todd mockingly. The thought of Todd tearing J.J. apart was not at all unpleasant to Andre. He hoped, if it came to that, Todd would be as unmerciful as he would be.

She was slammed sideways by some unseen force. Todd had flashed as light and was poised over her.

"I'm already dead. You can't hurt me," she stammered, her voice quavered with fear.

Andre adjusted himself, having realized he was edging away from the pillar, for a better view. J.J rose to her feet shakily and stared at Todd with fear.

"I want answers now!" Todd commanded.

Andre could hear the bones in J.J.'s arm crunch unevenly. She made an attempt to escape. The bones in her legs were simultaneously pulverized and she sprawled to the floor and turned up on one side.

"Help me! Help me, Master. Please!" she shrieked into the air around her.

Todd looked around mockingly for a moment and began to speak, "I don't think The Master can hear you," his voice was cold and dangerous.

"I...He...Master please? I have served you faithfully," she shrieked.

The bones, in the arm she supported herself on, crushed under the skin and she fell flatly onto her back, writhing in pain.

Todd appeared in a flash of light poised over her again.

"You will speak to me! I will destroy you slowly, unless you tell me what I want to know!" he growled as spit flew through his clenched teeth.

Andre felt a cold shiver shoot up his spine, something he had not experienced since his change. A cold malevolent presence crept into him and his blood sensed it keenly. As this coldness began to sweep through him, he felt his senses beginning to dull. His body felt sluggish and weak to the point of being lethargic. Some inner strength within him had begun to recede into obscurity and he felt despair.

He struggled to hide himself behind the pillar.

Andre's knees started to buckle and he let himself fall upon them. The last bit of strength left him and he crumpled involuntarily. He fell with a thud and was only partially aware of the feeling of the wet concrete against his cheek. His vision became blotchy, growing in severity until only darkness remained.

"Am I sleeping?" he asked himself with wonder.

He had not slept once since his change. Not counting being unconscious from sun exposure or having been bested by the Cloaked Figure. The full brightness of the day served to weaken him substantially. During these periods he could be found lying still usually covered in a blanket with his eyes closed. He would grow stronger as the light of the day waned, finally to rise as darkness fell.

He was aware of himself, whole, unharmed, but somehow diminished as he lay there. He could hear footsteps as they approached.

"Hard soled, probably dress shoes," he thought as he rose up onto his hands and knees to face the direction of the sound.

His memory, in its splendor, augmented a thousand fold since his change, worked to identify the owner. The sound that the shoes made in the darkness was familiar somehow. It seemed inconsequential to him and he tried to shake it from his mind. The precise rise and fall of each foot caused his mind to analyze thousands of similar memories. His mind continued to work, analyzing this as he grimaced at the distraction.

A bright light shone down from overhead. Andre cringed instinctively in self-defense. He realized the light to be harmless as he opened his eyes cautiously. He was alone in the circle of light on the floor. Standing to face the even noise of the footfalls, he waited and watched.

A man materialized from the darkness, stepped forward, and stopped. The man stood defenselessly with his arms behind his back and his head bowed.

"Hello?" Andre asked as he took a step back from this mysterious person.

The man did not answer; he had begun to shake his head as he muttered to himself.

"Who are you? Where are we? Are you the man in the purple cloak?" Andre asked as he tried to pierce the surrounding darkness in quick glances.

"By measure of your existence and continued survival, I am a friend. I have never clad myself in a purple cloak, but the idea has merit. It is my favorite color," the man said as he raised his head slowly to look at Andre.

A renewed sense of fear and despair ripped through Andre as he recognized this man from his past.

"Professor Bryce Hall?" Andre croaked and flinched at the weakness of his own voice.

"I have many names...You can use that one if it's comfortable for you. I have been called the Interloper, the Trespasser, even the Devil by minds who haven't the brilliance to grasp the depth of my greatness," Bryce explained.

"I don't believe in the Devil," Andre stated with a look of cold repose on his face.

At this Bryce threw his head back and laughed mirthlessly. The sound was horrible. It was as if death had been given a voice. The sound terrified him and caused weakness.

Bryce composed himself and said, "I get that a lot. I think people believe the mere utterance of the words have some power. Did you think that I might fall to my knees before you and disappear like a shadow fleeing from the birth of a dawn? Let me ask you this. Would your disbelief in a freight train that bore down upon you, save you? As the train turned you to liquid from asshole to elbow, would your disbelief cleanse the taste of your own bone, blood and shit from your mouth? You are where I have placed you. The location is of no consequence, as it could be anywhere...or nowhere at all," Bryce snapped in a superior tone.

"Why am I here?" Andre asked and was grateful that his tone had not failed in strength this time.

"I have brought you here to offer you an opportunity. As with most of my offers, it will be issued once. If you refuse my offer, I will visit upon you the shackles of an unending existence, richly steeped in anguish and torment," Bryce explained.

"It doesn't sound like I have much of a choice. I wonder though, if you could be so threatening without your head attached to your shoulders," Andre said and stumbled forward a few steps and stood stricken at his own awkwardness.

"Ah yes, your inhuman abilities are gone and wouldn't have saved you here. I like the fire and fight in you, however. I am your master in every way. Your acceptance of that station, as my servant, will afford you rewards of strength and power beyond your imagination. That is the opportunity on the table for your brief consideration," Bryce said warmly.

Andre glowered at Bryce now and spoke in a heated and angry tone, "I will not be your slave. You can forget...Urrk."

Andre's response was cut short. Bryce was upon him and had a single hand wrapped tightly around his neck. He sputtered and kicked with flailing arms, as his weight was lifted from the floor.

Bryce shook him as if he were weightless and drew Andre's face closer. His hands gripped tightly to Bryce's wrist and pulled pointlessly at the clutch around his neck. Bryce's face had become inhuman. The bones in his face undulated under the skin and his eyes were ablaze with a sickly yellow fire.

Bryce grinned at him wickedly and exposed rows of fangs.

His voice was unnatural and contained a hiss like that of a snake, "Would it please you to know that your brother's last thoughts were of you? He died screaming with no regard for his wife or children, a coward's death if there ever was one," Bryce chided.

Andre fell to the floor and worked to correct himself. He had managed to rise onto his hands and knees. His body was filled with pain, but he worked to raise his head to watch his attacker.

Bryce strode away from him thoughtfully and turned on the spot. His face was normal again and seemed to struggle to express levity.

"I get a little passionate about my work sometimes and forget my manners," Bryce said evenly and smiled.

Andre stared at him angrily as he worked to get to his feet.

"So would you like to accept now? You can take your place as my servant and transcend your brother's ineptitude in every way," Bryce explained.

Andre rose to his full height and walked deliberately forward with no concern for the threat Bryce posed. Bryce's mouth had pulled itself into a delighted smile and he raised his hand for Andre to kiss as a display of submissiveness.

Andre smiled and reached for Bryce's hand. As his own fingers were close to the hand, he reached forward and slapped Bryce across the face with all the force he could muster.

Bryce recoiled in surprise, rather, than out of necessity.

Andre pointed into Bryce's face as he spoke, "I accept that you're a liar. I don't believe anything you say. My brother would gladly dive in front of a bullet to save his family. He isn't capable of being a coward. You can take your offer and shove it up your...," Andre was slapped off of his feet before he could finish his sentence.

"Pathetic fool, you struck me! I have singly undone this entire world. I have taken it to the point of complete annihilation. Do you think there is any merit in your pathetic display of defiance?" Bryce asked angrily.

Andre had flown several feet before he landed and rolled to a stop in a crumpled pile. He growled gutturally and worked to rise to his feet. A smile parted his bloody lips. It was a defiant smile that leveled under his furrowed brow. Bryce had broken into a charge. One of his hands was drawn back. The fingers had become tipped in razor sharp talons. Bryce stopped at the center of the swipe, his talons inches from Andre's neck. He had noticed the vial of blood.

"What…have we here?" Bryce smiled and reached to touch the vial.

Andre recoiled and covered the vial with his hand defensively. Over Bryce's shoulder, he watched an ethereal hand, as tall as a man, approach them. White ethereal ribbons flowed from the giant hand as it opened and grasped Bryce. Andre looked on in amazement as Bryce shrieked while the hand drew him away into the darkness.

Upon blinking Andre realized himself to be on the floor of the parking garage again. He looked weakly around from where he lay. He had been freed from his mental prison, but his strength had not returned. He wondered if it ever would. The pillar, that had hid him previously, was out of reach. He looked up slowly to where Todd stood with his back to him. The white ethereal ribbons that flowed around Todd had increased dramatically in intensity. Andre winced and shielded his eyes for a moment. Despite his discomfort, he refocused his eyes, squinting and used one hand to partially shield him from the effect.

Todd's fist, which was held outstretched in a tight grip, shook angrily. Andre felt a mixture of panic and relief as he realized Todd to be the one who held Bryce. He imagined Bryce in Todd's grasp in that otherworldly plain. Having felt Bryce's considerable power first hand, Andre was awed as he tried to imagine and gauge Todd's strength.

Todd opened his hand and his eyes followed something, unseen to Andre, fall. Whatever malevolence that had taken his strength from him eroded and he felt strength coursing through him again. Todd turned his head to one side to address Andre, but never looked directly at him.

The voice that Andre heard was Todd's, but seemed to emanate from everywhere at once as he said, "You have looked into the darkness. I hope, for your sake, what you saw there was not to your liking."

Andre looked on with his jaw agape as Todd sprang upward into a white portal. He rubbed at his own eyes to abate the flash blindness from the white light that Todd had emitted.

Andre closed his mouth slowly, then muttered, "A leaf in the wind," as a recent memory occurred to him.

365

The sun, now mostly hidden behind the moon and storm clouds was losing its wearying effect over him. Andre felt his strength growing exponentially with each passing second. His muscles flexed in appreciation of the return to their full capability.

"The roof," Andre thought and looked through a nearby window.

The neighboring building was almost as tall as this one and would give him an adequate vantage point. He turned and sprinted for the large open window in the side of the parking garage. His eyes fixed upon the neighboring building, able to be seen at a distance, as he approached the garage window. As he reached the window's ledge, his muscles, that belied their strength in size, coiled and launched him between the two buildings. He looked down for a moment, as he glided toward his target, at the ground below.

The harsh wind at his back served to push him forward and augmented his velocity. He turned his attention to the oncoming face of the building. His fingers collided with the hardened bricks of the building and slid into them. The sensation was like that of his fingers sliding into firm mud. His lower body collided with the building hard, his bare toes clawed into the bricks. He pulled his right hand up in front of his face, looking at its unscathed condition. Tiny flakes of brick and mortar fell from around his fingers as he opened them. The thought to climb and continue to watch Todd occurred to him.

Andre replayed the events of the last few moments as he climbed up the face of the building toward its roof. As he reached the top, he turned on the spot, and saw walls of water that closed in from every direction at a distance.

Given the gauged acuity of his vision the water, that encroached rapidly could be no less than eight miles away. Having approximately four minutes until the waves reached him, time was a fleeting commodity and he felt his heart begin to race. The strength in him surged and quelled his fear. He watched, with an emotional detachment, as tornadoes and fires ripped through the remains of the city. He turned to face the other building and looked for Todd.

The neighboring roof had begun to disintegrate and he could see Todd rise to stand. He was able to hear Todd's heart, as it hammered in his chest, over the hurricane force winds. It sounded strained as it labored to push life giving blood through his body. The sound reverberated in Andre's ears, and then suddenly stopped. Todd collapsed. The thought to rush to him was abated when he saw a body of light that hovered above Todd's crumpled form. The ethereal presence had tendrils of light that flowed from it, as Todd's body had before he had fallen.

"God...," the word forced itself from his lips unconsciously.

The glowing white figure rose up through the darkened clouds and disappeared. A heavy and strong hand grasped his shoulder. He didn't even look back, knowing it to belong to the Cloaked Figure.

"That's an appropriate title. You will see him again, but you must go now. Go into the earth, dig deep, dig fast," the harsh, deep voice commanded.

At some level he wanted to ask questions as they welled up inside of him. But that strength was there again and his mind quickly grasped the severity of the Cloaked Figure's words. He nodded as he realized this to be his only salvation. He removed the vial of Todd's blood that had hung around his neck.

"God's blood," Andre muttered as he marveled at the realization of what he possessed.

He tore his shoulder away from the Cloaked Figure's hand, "Don't touch me...thing."

He placed the vial into the titanium case that his brother had given him and resealed it.

"Goodbye...Brother," he mournfully whispered as he stuffed the case into the waistband of his pants.

The walls of water that encroached on this point sounded like thunder and crashed in his ears. The Cloaked Figure was gone. He knew that he would be. Andre stood up and walked to the edge of the building. Closing his eyes, he recalled a memory that was not truly his own. The visage of the beautiful woman, Olivia, passed through his mind's eye. He had hoped against hope that he would find her somehow.

She was gone, changed by the Cloaked Figure's influence and out of his reach, possibly forever. Here at the end, he knew that there was no possibility of seeing her. A momentary wave of despair rushed through him. In response, his blood surged to counteract this emotion and replaced it with resolve.

Walking to the edge of the rooftop he looked down upon the sidewalk below. His toes coiled over the sharp edge of the bricks in preparation and dug in to the stone lip. Something within him calculated distance and velocity. He crouched with his muscles tightening and launched himself upward, arms outstretched. At the rising apex of his leap, he curled forward into a dive. His body streamlined as he fell. He delighted in the strange sensation that he felt as his body hardened, and increased in density.

There was no fear in him as he approached the sidewalk. The thunderous sound of titanic destructive waves reverberated in his ears. He realized the water to be in close proximity as he neared the ground.

His hands balled into fists and he thought to himself, "I'm harder than the concrete."

He crashed through the surface of the sidewalk as though it were made of delicate glass. Though he passed like a bullet through the stone, the aftermath was not so graceful. Above his body, as he descended into the earth, loud claps could be heard as the slabs of concrete imploded upon each other. At his point of impact, a hail of debris and rubble flew in every direction. The titanic walls of water collided on the spot. The enormous chunks of concrete whirled in a strong vortex. They were sucked into the vacuum of the hole, created by Andre's impact, sealing it.

His momentum carried him approximately seventy feet into the earth before he slid to a stop.

"Go into the earth, dig deep, dig fast," the words echoed in his mind.

His arms swung in wide arcs as he dug further into the rocky ground. Chunks of rock and hard earth provided footholds and were used to propel him downward. He marveled as his hands tore through the dirt. He kept his chin close to his chest, using his forehead as a barrier to keep dirt from being forced into his eyes. It felt as though he were swimming into the earth. The absence of oxygen was apparent and he wondered if he truly breathed anymore, or just went through the motions. He could feel the pressure of the surrounding earth, as it tried to crush him. His body would not allow it and reinforced itself further as he pressed forward.

Thank you for joining us.
We hope that you enjoyed the book.

Don't Forget... There's more to come!

For more information and updates on future releases please visit.
NocturnityBooks.com
and sign up for our email list.